THE POPPY FACTORY

Liz Trenow is a former journalist who spent fifteen years on regional and national newspapers, and on BBC radio and television news, before turning her hand to fiction. *The Poppy Factory* is her third novel. She lives in East Anglia, UK, with her artist husband, and they have two grown up daughters. Find out more at www.liztrenow.com and join her on Twitter @LizTrenow.

LIZ TRENOW

The Poppy Factory

AVON

This novel is entirely a work of fiction.
The names, characters and incidents portrayed in it are
the work of the author's imagination. Any resemblance to
actual persons, living or dead, events or localities is
entirely coincidental.

AVON

A division of HarperCollins*Publishers*
77–85 Fulham Palace Road,
London W6 8JB

www.harpercollins.co.uk

A Paperback Original 2014

1

Copyright © Liz Trenow 2014

Liz Trenow asserts the moral right to
be identified as the author of this work

A catalogue record for this book is
available from the British Library

ISBN-13: 978-0-00-751048-1

Set in Minion by Palimpsest Book Production Limited,
Falkirk, Stirlingshire

Printed and bound in Great Britain by
Clays Ltd, St Ives plc

Acknowledgements

This book would never have been written without the help and support of Melanie Waters, Kirsty Morgan, Tabitha Aldrich-Smith and others at The Poppy Factory in Richmond. For nearly a hundred years they have been employing disabled veterans to make the millions of poppies we buy every year to remember those who gave their lives in war. More recently they have been helping disabled veterans back into employment of all kinds, in their communities. My thanks, too, to several family members who contributed their memories of Major George Howson, the man who started it all in a former collar factory in the Old Kent Road. There's more information and history at www.poppyfactory.org.

The characters and events are of course entirely fictional, but they were inspired by real events and real people, who shared their time and their experiences with me so generously. For the contemporary storyline, I am indebted to four remarkable people: Lance Corporal Abbie Martin, Lance Corporal Jordan

Fern, Jenni Dudley and Annie Muir, HART Paramedics for the East of England Ambulance Service. Annie is also a reservist for the Royal Air Force. I can honestly say that meeting these extraordinary, brave and dedicated people has deeply affected me, and I hope that I have managed to capture some of the intensity of their experiences, and their quiet courage, in *The Poppy Factory*.

Finally, my thanks to my editor at HarperCollins Avon Lydia Vassar-Smith, my agent Caroline Hardman of Hardman & Swainson, and to my family and friends, all of whom have been unfailingly supportive throughout.

If you want to find out more about how I wrote *The Poppy Factory*, please go to www.liztrenow.com. You can also follow me on Twitter @liztrenow.

This book is dedicated to all those who have died in, or been disabled by, so many – too many – wars.

In Flanders fields the poppies blow
Between the crosses, row on row,
That mark our place; and in the sky
The larks, still bravely singing, fly
Scarce heard amid the guns below.

We are the Dead. Short days ago
We lived, felt dawn, saw sunset glow,
Loved and were loved, and now we lie
In Flanders fields.

Take up our quarrel with the foe:
To you from failing hands we throw
The torch; be yours to hold it high.
If ye break faith with us who die
We shall not sleep, though poppies grow
In Flanders fields.

John McCrea, 1915

Chapter One

An uneasy silence fell as the plane lurched bumpily around a spiral holding pattern above Heathrow. England was somewhere below, shrouded in slate grey clouds. Even the lads had finally stopped talking.

On reaching safe airspace half an hour out of Camp Bastion, six long months of constant fear and tension had been released like a spring-loaded jack-in-the-box into an eruption of shouting, singing and laughter. They'd bellowed loud boasts across the aisles detailing exactly what and how much they would drink on their first night of leave in six long dry months and bragged raucously about the sexual conquests they would make, forgetting that the two activities were usually incompatible. They'd embroidered ever more unlikely details about how they would spend their Long Overseas Allowance, the main bonus of the tour. And just a few of them, in quieter voices, had talked of family: parents and siblings, wives, girlfriends and children, the comfort of their own beds, and real, home-cooked food.

She'd come to tolerate and sometimes even enjoy the lads' banter, their insults and juvenile pranks, their lavatory humour. She knew now that it was just the way they got through; underneath they were thoughtful human beings with the same fears as anyone else. For all their piss-taking and petty squabbling, when everything kicked off, they'd gladly give their lives for each other. Some had even done so. She ran the names through her head: Jock, Baz and Millsie.

The girls, seated together in their small group, had spent the eight hour flight reading, plugged into headphones or, like Jess, wondering what this longed-for homecoming would really be like.

She listened to the changing notes of the engine and watched the wing flaps rise and fall as the pilot adjusted his position to the instructions of unseen masters. How unearthly it felt, suspended in this grey soup of cloud with heaven knows how many other aircraft above and below, giant metal birds flying terrifyingly close to each other at hundreds of miles an hour.

In Afghanistan, she had discovered that her fear of dying seemed to be inversely proportional to the level of danger they were in: thanks to the blessed pulse of adrenaline, the more life-threatening the situation, the less frightened she felt. It was only afterwards, once they were safely back in their compound, that she found herself trembling and nauseous, realising how close to death she had come.

Now that they were so nearly home and safe, just not quite, she found her stomach churning. But it wasn't the fear of a mid-air collision, or a crash landing. What she dreaded most, right now, was that in a few days' time this rowdy bunch of rough-carved individuals would be split up, probably never to live and work together as a group again. Over the past six months they had become more important to each other than anyone else in the world. They'd shared such highs and such lows, seen all life and all death, supported each other through moments more extreme and more intimate than she'd ever imagined. They had become closer than any family, but now they would be going their separate ways. It felt like a small bereavement.

Cut it, Jess. No time for soppy thoughts. She rubbed the skin behind her ear, just above the joint of her jaw. There used to be a little gingery curl there which, ever since she was a little girl, she would fiddle with, unconsciously trying to straighten. The curl had fallen victim to the military barbers but it would grow again soon enough. Joining the Army was only ever intended to be a short-term thing, something to get out of her system, to clear herself of guilt about James, she told herself. Now she could get back to real life, to her job as a paramedic, to her family, to Nate.

Nathaniel, Nathan, Naz, Nate: he had a different name for each part of his life. Nathaniel to his immigrant parents, proud to vaunt their Christian heritage in the freedom of their newly-adopted country;

Nathan to school friends who couldn't have cared less about his origins or the colour of his skin so long as he was on their side in any sports team, which was usually a guarantee of winning; Naz to his workmates and drinking pals – she loved the fact that he enjoyed being one of the boys.

Nate to Jess, the name she whispered when they were in bed together, as she marvelled at the length of his limbs, or stroked his skin, soft as a child's and deep chestnut brown except where it glowed almost blue-black from exposure to the sun. Nate, as she buried her fingers in the tough, twisted tendrils of his hair when he kissed her breasts. Nate, as they made love, and in that tumbling ecstasy of relief that sometimes left her crying with joy.

The first time she took him to Suffolk she'd glimpsed the two of them in a brief snapshot reflected in the window, as they waited on the doorstep of her parents' house. Perhaps it was just heightened aware-ness, a level of anxiety about this 'meet-the-folks' moment, but she realised for the first time what a dramatic contrast they made. Though at the peak of fitness and a good five foot six, she appeared positively petite beside him, almost ghostly pale and insubstan-tial, with her freckly skin and ginger elfin-cut. At six three he cut a powerful, imposing figure, lithe and athletic in his smartest skinny jeans, shoulder-length dreadlocks neatly restrained into a ponytail.

As they'd negotiated the sluggish traffic wending its way to the seaside that day, he had asked tentatively how she thought her parents might react, 'to . . .you know', he'd said, leaving the word unspoken. She hadn't told them in advance, she said, it seemed superfluous – the difference had barely entered her consciousness after the first few days of their relationship. So they'd probably be a bit surprised, she warned him, for the sole reason that there were very few non-Caucasians among their friends, if any.

As her mother, Susan, appeared at the other side of the glass ready to open the door, the smile seemed to freeze on her face for a fraction of a second. But within moments both parents had recovered; Jess was enfolded in her mother's arms, breathing in the reassuringly familiar smells of talcum powder and fabric conditioner, and her father was shaking Nate's hand – 'great to meet you. Call me Mike' – and steering him by the elbow through into the living room.

Of course Nate was the perfect gentleman and said all the right things: asking how long they'd lived here on the coast, enthusing about the pretty village, complimenting the house with its stunning views across the wide sweep of salt marsh and the silvery snake of the estuary in the distance. He greeted, without flinching, the flurry of furry delight which was Milly the mongrel, strolled into the garden with her father and submitted to a tour of the carefully tended garden and vegetable patch, his face intent with what looked like genuine interest.

She felt proud of him, even a slight stir of desire, as she watched them through the window, while fielding her mother's questions – yes, they'd been seeing each other for six months or so; yes, he was a sports teacher; no, she didn't think he'd ever been to Suffolk before; he was born and brought up in South London.

This had been her childhood home; she'd always thought the sixties-built mock Georgian house soulless, hated the isolation and having to be driven everywhere until she finally got her licence. As a teenager she could barely wait to get away. But now she began to see the place through Nate's eyes: she could see how the house had matured, blending into the architectural mix of the old village, the wild beauty of the marshland and the beach just ten minutes' walk away, the peace and the lack of traffic, not even a single streetlight.

Over coffee, she broke the news. Get all the difficult stuff over with at once, she'd decided. She'd graduated, with top marks, as a Combat Medical Technician, and would be going to Afghanistan in about three months' time. Of course she'd warned them it was a possibility but the confirmation was obviously a shock: they both blanched but then managed to stumble out their congratulations. Her mother had muttered a vague 'how lovely dear' before collecting the cups and scuttling out to the kitchen – probably to hide her tears.

At his end of the sofa, Nate stroked Milly and kept his head down, saying nothing. He hadn't been at all happy either, when she'd told him a few days before.

'How long?' He was cooking risotto in the kitchen of his tiny flat. She'd judged the moment carefully, knowing that he couldn't stop in the middle of the critical stirring process to have a proper row with her.

'Six months.'

'Bloody hell. *Six months.* That's an eternity.' He turned from the cooker to face her. 'Why the hell are you doing this, Jess?'

'You know why. It's for James. I told you.' She pulled at the curl behind her ear.

'But James is *dead*. He won't know you're doing it for him. Anyway, he wouldn't have wanted you to put yourself in the same danger.'

He turned back to the saucepan. 'Is there anything I can say to stop you?'

'I don't think so. I've committed myself to it now.'

In the silence that followed, she conjured up the image of beautiful, funny, sporty James, her brother Jonathan's best friend, who had spent many school holidays staying with the Merton family because his parents were usually posted abroad somewhere improbably exotic. She'd treated him like another big brother until, with adolescence, everything changed and she began to feel an almost irresistible affinity – he too had curly ginger hair and freckles – and to fantasise about him as a boyfriend. In her diary she secretly scribbled soppy love poems and drew pictures of the three red-haired children they would have (two girls and a boy). Yet, despite her desperate hints, he

7

remained oblivious to her growing attachment, and nothing happened.

James followed his father and older brother into the Army. When he came to say goodbye, even more heart-stoppingly handsome in his smartly pressed officer's uniform, Jess never imagined it would be for good. So when he went and died in a bomb explosion in Iraq, it broke her heart. 'Shrapnel injuries' was the phrase whispered in hushed corners but, later, Jonathan told her he'd learned that James had bled to death while waiting to be rescued. The image haunted her still. Why hadn't someone stopped the bleeding and saved him?

Throughout her volunteering days with St John Ambulance and her rookie period as an NHS paramedic, the idea had wormed its way into her head. As she learned the various techniques for stopping a bleed she'd found herself wondering whether she could have saved James, had she been there? She even dreamed about it: everyone else panicking at the sight of his blood leaching into the ground – weirdly, they were in a wood of pine trees rather than the sand of the desert – but her taking calm charge of the situation, applying a tourniquet, setting up a saline drip, watching the bleeding stop and the colour return to his face. She woke just as he stretched up to kiss her.

The dream transmuted itself into an idea which, over time, became an almost obsessive conviction: she couldn't bring James back but perhaps by saving the life of another soldier she could somehow give meaning to that terrible loss of such a vibrant life.

Three years ago, just qualified and about to accept a full time job with the ambulance service, she'd passed an Army Recruiting office and paused to read the posters in the window. A young soldier with a number one haircut and a sweet, shy smile had poked his head around the door and asked if he could help. Would she like more information? Almost blindly, as if in a dream, she'd followed him in and replied obediently to his questions, watching passively as he filled in a form. After signing it, she wandered out into the street in a daze and never mentioned it to anyone until the invitation to basic training arrived on her doormat.

'I can't explain it. Just has to be done, Nate. I've been through hell and high water for this, all that shit on the Brecon Beacons and the parade grounds. I can't give up now. I'll only be gone a few months.'

'So long as you really *do* come back,' he'd muttered.

They had talked about moving in together, in the way couples do, sounding out each other's aspirations. They even talked about what their children would look like: brown skinned, ginger and freckly or some curious mixture? At thirty-three – seven years older than Jess – he'd had his fill of racketing around the world, trying to make it as a musician. Now he was enjoying being a sports teacher in an inner city secondary school, genuinely believing that he could make a difference to the lives of very challenging kids. He earned a respectable salary and was ready to settle down.

'I want you to be part of my life,' he'd told Jess, even though they'd only known each other for six months, 'for good. Give up the Army. Please. For me?'

It felt like being torn between two lovers. She knew Nate loved her and she loved him, but wasn't entirely sure, not at that stage, that he would wait. But she couldn't give up on James and the thought of being able to make sense of his sacrifice, not now she was so close to being deployed.

The plane levelled out, the engine slowed and for a stomach-lurching moment seemed to stall in mid-air before starting to descend. Out of the window the clouds thinned, revealing fields and woods below in a dozen shades of green. She found herself smiling: the colour was so mild, so gentle on the eyes, such a relief after the blinding light of the desert.

Within minutes they were on the ground.

It was six o'clock and already dark by the time they got back to Eastminster. The arc lights on the parade ground shone through a twinkling veil of drizzle as the coaches pulled in. On the far side was a rainbow of umbrellas under which waiting families huddled against the autumn chill. They didn't feel the cold, of course, so buoyed were they with anticipation of this moment.

She'd spoken on the phone to her parents and they'd

agreed not to come, sensitive to the need for Jess and Nate to have their first evening together. He would travel up from London by train after work and had booked a hotel so they didn't have to stay in her barrack room. He'd even been given compassionate leave from school the following day. She was touched by the generous gesture, but almost dreaded the romantic expectations it implied. What she really wanted was a hot, deep bath and a very, very long sleep.

In one corner, Army press officers were attempting to marshal a small gaggle of newspaper reporters and television camera teams. They'd been warned about this, instructed that they must tolerate the intrusion, for the sake of Army PR. What the media wanted, they'd been told, was the 'aah' factor: beaming fathers sweeping up small children into strong arms, couples reunited in romantic embrace, proud parents wiping away tears of happiness.

Some of the younger lads were keen for their few seconds of fame, but Jess had already planned her avoidance strategy: she would keep Nate at arm's length until she could drag him into the shadows beside the old Cavalry Barrack buildings, away from the limelight. Only then would she allow him to kiss her. Through the coach window she scanned the waiting crowds – he was usually quite easy to spot – and felt her heart pummelling inside her chest when she couldn't immediately see him. At last, as she stood at the top of the steps ready to leave the coach, she saw him emerge into the light.

At dinner, barely caring that she had to report for duty at seven-thirty the following morning, she drank way too much wine. She could hear herself chattering brightly about nothing important, all the while acutely conscious of Nate's gaze. Was he scrutinising the 'desert lines' she'd acquired from squinting into the harsh sun, the roughened skin on her cheeks from the scouring of sand and dust? She'd lost weight, living on rations, and it gave her features a new sharpness, even severity. She was not the same Jess he'd waved goodbye to six months ago.

He, on the other hand, appeared to have barely changed at all. He was relaxed and affectionate, his face breaking into that easy smile at her touch, laughing appreciatively with his deep-chested chuckle at her stories of the lads' crazier antics. Already in her head she had categorised the experiences of the past six months: there were those too trivial to talk about, those she could happily share with him, with which he would be able to empathise. And there were those that she would never, ever, be able to put into words, to reveal, not with him, not with anyone.

Later, back in their room, she regretted that second bottle of wine. She crashed onto the bed and watched him take his clothes off, which was usually enough to send her crazy with desire. But after so many dry months the alcohol made her head spin and her stomach churn and, as he came to the bed and slowly undressed her, kissing each newly-exposed stretch of skin, she found her mind wandering. It was almost as if she were standing to one side, observing them both. But she went through the motions and it seemed to convince Nate. Next time, she promised herself, I won't drink so much and I will lose myself in our lovemaking, the way it always used to be.

Afterwards, when he headed off to the bathroom, dipping his head to avoid hitting the doorway, she observed his muscular back and shoulders, that balletic lope of his long limbs, the proud crown of dreadlocks, and knew that she still loved him. She just had to get her head sorted out and everything would soon be back to normal.

There followed a week in barracks, preparing for the service medals ceremony, and then she had seven weeks' POTL, the extended Post Operational Tour Leave. When Nate's school term finished in a month's time, they planned to go skiing. Neither had ever tried it before, and they agreed it would be a laugh learning together.

'I don't mind where we go so long as it's cold,' she'd stipulated on the phone from Camp Bastion, ignoring the eerie whispers and whines over the airwaves. She looked out of the cabin window: it was forty degrees in the shade and heatwaves rising from the sand made everything look swimmy and surreal.

'All I want is cold weather, no dust, hot baths, good food and lots to drink,' she'd added.

'All that,' he'd promised. 'You can roll in the snow every day.'

'Perfect.'

It was strange, going back to normal work. Living at the barracks, being among a larger group, having to be clean and orderly with your kit in pristine condition, sitting in classrooms for hours, taking orders, learning how to march in formation, being just a number again, rather than the individuals they had become on the front line. Off duty, they were strangely wary of each other. The more confident ones would brag about the things they'd seen and done in Afghanistan, but those who'd had the really tough experiences, like Jess, tended to keep themselves to themselves.

She went through the days in a haze, as if seeing everything through a gauze curtain. She steeled herself to make an appointment with her officer in command and told him she was applying for early release. She had promised Nate. They would live a civilian life – what he called a 'normal life' – together.

Her boss set up a further meeting with his boss, the commanding officer, and she filled in a dozen different forms to set everything in motion. The CO tried to persuade her to stay, of course, but could see that she was quite determined and simply ended the conversation with the usual pat phrases about how sorely she would be missed. Chances were, she'd only have to serve three further months after the POTL before starting her seven months 'resettlement leave'. She could be in her new job at the Ambulance Trust as early as April next year.

Four days later was Remembrance Sunday, where they were to represent the regiment at the annual service held at the town's War Memorial. For Jess, it was a welcome opportunity to honour James and now Jock, Baz and Millsie. She'd been every year since she'd turned fifteen, first as St John volunteer and later as a rookie soldier. The crowds of people gathered to remember the dead, the proud, stoical faces of the veterans with their medals weighing down fragile frames, the stirring sounds of military bands, the solemn hymns, the two minute silence and the pathos of the bugle sounding the Last Post never failed to move her.

It was miserable and overcast that day, with a spiteful wind and short vicious showers lashing them as they marched down the wide high street, with its handsome Victorian buildings disguised behind tacky shop fronts. This weather was almost enough to make you long for the heat of Kandahar, Jess thought, standing to attention in her combat uniform, perhaps for the last time. The day after tomorrow, she would make her way to Suffolk to see her parents for a few days by the sea before heading back to London for a long weekend with Nate. She found her mouth watering as she thought about the meal her mother had promised to prepare for dinner – roast lamb with all the trimmings.

On their last night at Camp Bastion she'd been sitting side by side on the ground outside her tent with her friend Siobhán, after a long day of packing and debriefings, having a final cigarette before turning in. 'Vorny' was a tough Catholic girl from Belfast so different from Jess in so many ways that they'd never have become friends in civilian life. But the two had worked alongside each other during some really horrific moments, and become so close that she felt like a sister.

Their conversation had turned idly to the meals they'd missed on tour. 'Gotta be an Ulster Fry,' Vorny said. 'With the proper soda bread and black pudding. What about you?'

'Roast lamb, roast potatoes, two veggies and gravy with red currant jelly.'

'Not even a proper fry-up is gonna make up for missing you lot, though,' Vorny said. 'And the lads.'

'Me too,' Jess had replied, keeping her eyes to the ground. If she looked at Siobhán she might start to cry. 'Tough one, that.'

They'd both gone quiet, then Jess lit up another cigarette. 'We've had some good times though, eh?'

'What are you most proud of?' Vorny asked.

'Finding that bleed under Gav's armour,' Jess said. 'I was so scared he was going to die.'

'But you saved his life, didn't you? Bloody good call that was.'

Gavin had been moaning about the minor foot injury he'd sustained, and they'd been busy attending to other more serious casualties when Jess noticed that the kid had stopped complaining and begun to go pale. She knew immediately that something else was wrong, something they'd missed. Checking him out, she discovered that a bullet had entered just beside his armpit, in the crack between the plates of Osprey body armour, and was probably causing all kinds of unseen havoc in his chest.

'Sucking chest wound, possible internal bleeding,' she'd yelled at once, applying a chest seal to the hole before checking his back for an exit wound. 'Cat A, he needs to be out of here urgently.'

Only later, when she heard that Gavin had emerged safely from surgery with no anticipated long-term effects, did she realise that she had saved her soldier and fulfilled her promise to James. It made her feel wobbly all over again, just thinking about it.

'What about you?' she asked.

'The time we nearly died in that field, that was probably my worst moment,' Vorny said.

'Christ, me too. That was a bad one.'

They'd been caught in ferocious cross-fire trying to get a couple of casualties to the helicopter and the pilot had pulled away at the last moment, realising that it was too dangerous to land. The lads carrying the stretchers had managed to get down into a ditch, but Vorny and she, lugging the men's heavy kit, had fallen behind. When the crackle of firing started, all they could do was drop to the ground, face down, below the level of the meagre, patchy crop, and pray they couldn't be seen.

'I thought we were going to die.'

The firing seemed to go on for hours, but was

probably only about ten minutes. They were completely pinned down with their faces in the dust, unable to make any move or noise for fear of attracting Taliban fire. All those gunmen had to do was tilt their barrels fractionally, raking the field with bullets, and it would have been all over.

At that moment, Jess felt quite sure she would never get out of that field alive and in her head began apologising to Nate, her mum and dad, and Jonathan for being so wilful as to insist on this insane venture. She remembered the letter she'd written, the one they would receive if she died: 'Forgive me. It's something I just have to do. . .' Her chest felt as though she was being sat on by an elephant. Then she realised she was hyperventilating, and knew that she had to concentrate on something to stop herself panicking and passing out.

And then . . . oh God, then . . . she'd lifted her eyes and seen the poppy.

Most of the crop was dried out and dull brown, but right in front of her nose was a late bloom, a green stem topped by a single red flower, and she fixed her eyes on it, like a totem. She noticed how the papery crimson petals were stained dark, like dried blood, where they joined the stem, how at its centre the delicate white stamens fluttered on their stalks. The seed head itself, the part of the plant that held the white liquid harvest which had so much to answer for, the drug that drove this war, was beguilingly beautiful, with an intricately symmetrical star pattern on the top and elegant vertical lines down its bowl-shaped sides.

The crackle of fire started again, interspersed with terrifying booms of exploding grenades. A volley whistled a few inches above them and she'd dropped her head to the ground, closing her eyes and praying fervently to a God she had never really believed in. When the firing stopped, she reopened her eyes and looked for the poppy.

It had gone.

For a moment she thought that she must have moved, but then her eyes caught the green stem, still in front of her, trembling from the assault. It was then she realised that the flower – just beside where her own head had been a few seconds before – had been blown off by a bullet and shattered into a thousand fragments.

She could hear a faint keening sound, and thought at first that Vorny must have been hit. It was only when the other girl reached across the dirt, shoving a hand into her face to shut her up, that Jess realised it was her own voice. Her mind had gone almost completely blank with fear and she seemed to be losing control of her body. She could feel her heart skittering under her ribs, her legs and arms trembling, her bowels churning dangerously. Christ, the last thing she needed was to shit herself out here.

Slowly, with desperate caution, to avoid disturbing any plant stems or rustling any dead leaves, she reached out her arm. They found each other's hands and squeezed tight, like clinging to a life raft, and this was enough to help her hold it together until the firing and explosions stopped, almost as suddenly as they had begun. The Taliban fighters could slip away like smoke, only to regroup and reappear again where they were least expected. These surprise tactics, along with their paradise-blinded perseverance and a constant resupply of willing martyrs, were surprisingly effective against even the heavy arms of the allied forces.

The rescue helicopter – the MERT – returned and landed this time, the casualties were airlifted away for treatment, and the rest of the troop dragged themselves back to the compound. At first everyone was silent in their own thoughts, taking drinks, lighting on cigarettes; and then the backchat began, as they tried to make sense of what had just happened and reassure each other about Scotty and the other casualties: 'The lengths some will go for a jammy ticket home, the bastards.' But beyond the banter, everyone knew it had been a very close call.

That evening Jess tried to eat and drink but had no appetite, she felt sick and shivery as if going down with the flu. Sleep was impossible – the video loop of those moments in the field replaying over and over in her head until the compound lightened into grey dawn. She told no-one about the poppy, not even Siobhán. She'd locked the memory away ever since.

And now . . . she glanced down at the bright red plastic flower on her lapel, glittering with raindrops.

Remembering the terror of that day, all over again, made her feel dangerously sick and lightheaded. Forcing herself to take deep breaths – just as she had in that field – she fixed her eyes ahead, towards the ranks of veterans, councillors, scout leaders, army reps, all waiting reverently in the rain, some holding wreaths ready to lay at the memorial. Those wreaths made of hundreds of red poppies with their black centres, just like the poppy in that field. The one that got the bullet instead of her.

Almost without warning, her stomach turned inside out and she was suddenly, violently sick onto the ground in front of her boots. No-one in the ranks around her turned a head or put out a comforting hand, all standing to attention with their eyes forward. These sorts of things – vomiting, passing out – happened on parade more often than anyone would admit: all in a normal day's work for the Army. They'd all been drilled how not to react, how to resist the normal human impulse to help someone in need.

Jess straightened her back, wiped her mouth with her hand and swallowed the disgusting taste of bile as best she could. She stood to attention, her face burning with humiliation, eyes swimming with tears, as the bugler flawlessly sounded the long, mournful notes of The Last Post.

Chapter Two

'It's good, this Pinot. Another bottle?'

They were the last customers left in their favourite Sicilian restaurant, just round the corner from Nate's flat. The chef had joined the waiters for a game of cards at a distant table in the corner. This was supposed to have been a romantic evening to celebrate Valentine's Day, although the date itself earlier in the week had already been marked with declarations of love on the phone, a card for Nate, a large bunch of roses for Jess.

'Not for me thanks, work tomorrow. Time we were getting back,' he said.

'You're such a wuss.' She checked her phone. 'It's not yet eleven. I've got work tomorrow too. All I want is one more drink, is that okay?'

He held her gaze, trying to make her back down.

'And don't say "don't you think you've had enough?", like you always do,' she taunted, waving the empty bottle in the direction of the waiters. Nate shook his head with disapproval and she pounced, feeling the familiar hot surge of anger rising up the back of her head.

'Can we just drop the morality police act? Let me be myself, for once. I've spent the past two years leaping to attention the moment anyone says jump, and I'm enjoying being irresponsible and silly. I'm only twenty-six, for God's sake.'

The waiter brought the bottle and she took it from him, defiantly pouring herself a glass and sloshing some on the tablecloth.

'Cheers,' she said, holding it up in front of Nate's stony face. He sat back in the chair and closed his eyes, clenching and unclenching his fists helplessly beneath the tablecloth. Whatever he said now would prompt a stand up row, and he hated conflict.

The 'self medication', as she liked to call it, had started around Christmas when the nightmares began to get out of control, so bad that she'd become afraid of sleeping. Curiously, the poppy field barely figured in her dreams. They were almost always a variation on the same scenario: being confronted with the raw flesh of a dismembered limb. Sometimes the limb was unattached and she found herself carrying it, trying to run on leaden legs as she searched desperately for its owner. Other times it was attached to a body and she might wake to find that she was holding her hands over her ears to block out the terrifying, visceral howls of a man in extreme agony. The worst times were when she knew the victim: it could be her brother, or Nate, or another male friend. Curiously, she never dreamed about James, or the real-life victims she had treated: Gav, Scotty, Dave . . . there had been so many.

Tourniquets usually featured, stretching and breaking like cooked spaghetti when tightened, the clips or Velcro refusing to stay fixed; also dressings, which might take flight and hover beyond her reach or, absurdly, turn out to be white bread instead.

But each variation had a constant theme: panic, the sort of extreme panic which freezes your brain and threatens to stop your heart. She would wake fighting for breath in a tangle of sheets damp with sweat, and sometimes weeping because she had failed to save the injured man.

She tried over-the-counter sleeping pills but, although they helped her get to sleep, they had little effect in preventing the nightmares. The only thing which seemed to work was booze – whisky or vodka seemed to work best, but almost any alcohol would do. She took to taking a couple of shots before cleaning her teeth each bedtime.

The anger thing started on the last day of their holiday.

They'd had such a joyful, exhilarating week. Both were absolute beginners but had, in their different ways, quickly mastered the art of skiing. Although never elegant, Nate's muscle-power helped him stay upright even on the toughest terrains. She, with her lower centre of gravity and fine-honed fitness, quickly mastered the art of carving a stylish turn. Her graceful stance regularly earned their otherwise dour instructor's weather-beaten smile, and his call of 'Ottimo, Jessica! Bellissimo!' had become a catch-phrase between them, even away from the slopes.

Elated by their success, the physical exertion, the breathtakingly beautiful mountains and the cold, bright air, they found themselves drinking a bottle of wine at lunchtime, meeting up with fellow chalet guests for several glasses of glühwein at teatime, imbibing more wine with dinner and at least one or two brandies as a nightcap. Jess slept better than she had in months – a whole week without a single nightmare.

Taking a midnight walk on the final evening, arm in arm, the snow crunching beneath their feet and clouds of warm breath mingling in the freezing air, Nate had stopped in his tracks and grabbed both of her hands.

'When you get out of the Army, shall we move in together?'

'Oh my God, Nate. Do you really mean it?'

'Of course I bloody mean it. Hurry up and say yes before we freeze to death.'

'Then of course I will, you idiot.' She jumped into his arms and knocked them both to the ground, finding herself flooded so powerfully with joy that she almost forgot to breathe. How lucky she was to be alive, so happy, with the man she loved and all their lives in front of her.

But even as they lay there, flat on their backs in

the soft snow at the side of the track, looking up at the stars, the memories intruded into her consciousness. She was reminded of the times she and Vorny would lie in the dust of the compound looking up at those same ribbons of brilliance in the blackness of the desert night sky, and how the lads used to tease them for it. Where were they all tonight, those boys, how were they adjusting to life at home? She hoped they were happy, too.

And then, out of the blue, she was hit by a wave of anger about James and the others, for the fact that she would never see them again, that they would never experience the joy of lying in the snow on a starry night with the person they loved. The anger quickly cooled into sorrow, and she began to weep silently, only this time the tears were from profound, irretrievable loss.

Where did these crazy, over-the-top emotions come from? She'd always prided herself on being level-headed, not prone to over-dramatics. These days her reactions seemed to be all over the place. It must just be the 'adjustment' they all talked about, she said to herself, it would pass, just as soon as she got back to work. She wiped away her tears, leaned over Nate and kissed him. 'I love you,' she whispered. 'More than you will ever know.'

The following day, for no reason she could fathom other than she had a hangover and their lovely holiday was over, she found herself becoming irritated by tiny, silly things: the way he insisted on tying a red ribbon on the handle of his suitcase so that he could recognise it on the luggage carousel, the way he opened every drawer and cupboard in their room to make sure nothing was left behind, the way he checked the hotel bill carefully, item by item.

Why should such small and perfectly reasonable acts annoy her so much? She simply couldn't understand it but, each time, she felt the anger prickling the back of her head, the nauseous churning of her stomach. She cursed herself for being so impatient – he was only taking care of her, after all.

'You okay? You're a bit quiet this morning,' he said, on the bus to the airport.

'Oh I don't know. I feel a bit rough, but it's probably more the thought of having to go back to work,' she said.

'I know what you mean. Year Nine first thing on Monday,' he said. 'At least you've only got three months to go, haven't you? Light duties and all?'

She grimaced. The prospect of 'light duties' made her feel even more irritable. She would be stuck in barracks, away from Nate all week staffing a daily clinic for malingering squaddies with sore throats and ingrowing toenails, being on the rota for out-of-hours emergency call-outs, serving time until her early release came up. Now they knew she was on the way out, there'd be no more advanced training courses, no going out on exercise, no requirement to keep fit.

She'd just have to grin and bear it. A job with the

London ambulance service was waiting for her after Easter, she would move in with Nate and they could start to plan their future together. It's all good, she told herself, firmly. Stop being such a misery.

But grinning and bearing it did not come easy.

The clinic sessions at the barracks were as dull and dispiriting as she'd feared. Time dragged more slowly than ever as she examined a succession of soldiers' smelly feet with their blisters, veruccas, and minor sprains or, for light relief perhaps, a touch of man flu, earache or tonsillitis. The highlight of her first week was being called out late one night to the Military Police cells for a soldier covered in blood and so drunk he could barely speak. He had a six centimetre gash from one ear to the back of his neck, obviously from falling backwards onto something hard.

The last time she'd seen this much blood was after a Taliban RPG had landed in the compound, knocking her out and sending shrapnel flying everywhere. She'd come round to a scene of carnage, lots of head wounds and blood everywhere because the soldiers had been at rest and not wearing helmets or body armour. Ignoring her own dizziness, she'd scrambled to her feet and set to work. When she and Vorny had finished checking everyone over they discovered that, by some miracle, most of the injuries were shallow cuts which needed only simple stitching. Only a couple of lads were more seriously hurt and needed evacuation, and they later heard back that both of them had survived and weren't likely to suffer any long term after-effects. 'Saved their bloody lives, those two lassies of yours,' the surgeon told her CO later.

She checked the drunken squaddie over, swabbed him down, shaved an unnecessarily wide strip of hair on either side of the wound, stitched him up and told them to wake him every half hour to check for concussion, with a bucket of cold water if necessary. That'll teach him, she thought to herself.

One day she diagnosed a case of 'housemaid's knee'. The spotty lad gazed at her in confusion: 'I ain't been doin' no housework.'

'It's an inflammation of the tissues in front of the kneecap. You just need to take it easy for a couple of weeks and it'll sort itself out.'

'Can't tell me sergeant I've got housemaid's knee,' he muttered. 'Never bloody live it down.'

She would normally have found this funny, but for some reason his pathetic embarrassment irritated the hell out of her. She took a deep breath, wrote 'Prepatellar Bursitis' on a note and passed it to him. 'Will that do?'

He tried to pronounce the Latin and gave up.

'Thank you, ma'am,' he said, with a brazen smile. 'Fancy a drink sometime?'

'Get lost, you cheeky bastard,' she said, showing him the door.

'I just can't cope with the pettiness of it all,' she shouted to her mother as they struggled along the shingle beach in the face of a bitter cold wind whistling off the North Sea. She'd been given a few mid-week days off and, to be honest, was pleased to have her parents to herself. 'Their stupid little complaints. I feel like slapping them, telling them to man up.'

Her mother had suggested the walk after she'd come downstairs at three in the morning to find Jess watching the shopping channel with a large glass of her father's whisky on the table in front of her.

'What's up, love?' she'd asked, rubbing the sleep out of her eyes. Jess noticed for the first time that her mother's hair, the gingery side of auburn like her own, was turning grey.

'Can't sleep. It's just too quiet here,' she replied, trying to make light of it. 'What are you doing up, anyway?'

'Saw the light on when I went for a pee.'

Jess had been looking forward to a few days by the seaside, where she could take long walks in the sea air and hopefully knock herself out with physical tiredness, but it hadn't worked like that. For the second night running she had lain awake for hours before giving up and going downstairs to raid her father's drinks cabinet.

'You shouldn't drink so much of that stuff,' Susan had said, looking pointedly at the glass.

'Don't worry,' Jess said. 'I'll buy Dad another bottle. Go back to bed. I'll be fine.'

Later that morning, out on the beach, she found

herself almost enjoying the distraction of physical discomfort as the wind slashed at their faces.

'Tell me about this drinking,' her mother had started.

'Oh, it's nothing,' Jess said. Admitting the nightmares to her mother would only make her more anxious – better to gloss over it. 'Just fed up with work. It's so boring. I can't wait to get out.'

'You haven't got long to go now, have you?'

'Four weeks, that's all. I can deal with it. Thanks for being so understanding, Mum.'

But that evening she lost it again. Her father had insisted on doing a barbecue in spite of the fact that it was still only February, and bitterly cold. The wind had dropped, he said, and besides the barbecue was under cover of the patio awning. He would be perfectly dry, and once everything was cooked they could eat inside. Except that it began to bucket with rain, and while Jess tried to persuade him to abandon the idea, Susan had been placatory.

'He does it all the time, don't worry,' she said. 'He enjoys it, and the food tastes so much better on the barbecue. You'll never dissuade him, so you might as well give up trying.'

'But it's pouring, Mum. He'll get soaked, and so will the food.' She felt her chest tightening, the telltale heat tingling at the back of her neck, and tried to take deep breaths, but it came out anyway. 'He could perfectly well come inside to cook, and we could have a lovely meal but he's just determined to spoil our evening with his pig-headed insistence. It's so fucking stupid,' she shouted.

'Watch your language, young woman,' Mike called through the patio door.

She exploded then, shouting, 'I can't bear to watch. I'm going out.'

She'd stomped off to the only pub in the village, hoping there would be no-one who recognised her or engaged her in conversation. Fortunately the place was deserted, so she sat by the fire and read a dog-eared red-top newspaper, sickened by the photos of semi-naked women on what seemed like every other page, while downing three double whiskies in quick succession. She paid the pub premium for a bottle to replace her father's Johnnie Walker and hid it inside her coat as she headed home.

Her parents were watching a nature documentary on television.

'We left you a plateful – it's on the side,' her mother said mildly, without a hint of reproach. How could they be so forgiving? It almost made her angry all over again.

'Not hungry,' she muttered. 'Going to bed.'

'Sleep well, sweetheart,' they chorused, to her departing back.

In the morning nothing was mentioned until she was alone in the car with her mother on the way to the train station.

'Forgive me, darling, but do you think you might

need some help?' her mother said, pulling out onto the main road.

'What do you mean, help?'

'Adjusting to life back home. I know it's hard.'

'Leave it, Mum. I'm fine.'

'Except you're barely sleeping, drinking way more than you ever used to and losing your temper at the drop of a hat. We're worried about you, love.'

They arrived at the station just in time and she kissed her mother on the cheek. 'See you soon,' she said, 'and don't you go worrying about me. I'm a big girl; I can take care of myself.'

The following Sunday evening was the Pinot incident.

As she drank her way purposefully through the bottle, Nate said barely a word and she was too angry to engage him in conversation. Next thing she knew, she was shocked awake by her phone. She peeled open her eyes and squinted at the numbers: 06.00. He must have set the alarm for her, knowing that she had to catch the train in time to get back for a nine o'clock clinic.

She slumped back onto the pillow with her head swimming and throbbing, realising that a) she was still fully clothed and b) she was still drunk. For a few minutes she contemplated calling in sick, but ingrained Army discipline got the better of her. She forced herself out of bed and took a cold shower to shock herself into consciousness. Nate was curled up asleep on the sofa and she crept out of the flat without waking him.

By the time she got back to the barracks she was feeling truly awful. 'Nothing for it,' she said to herself, opening the drawer where she stashed the whisky bottle. 'Hair of the dog.'

The clinic was full of the usual Monday morning complaints: sprained ankles and bruised knees from football games, black eyes and cut lips from knuckle fights. For once, she was grateful to have nothing too testing to deal with, feeling proud of herself for holding it together and making some reasonable diagnoses. Her boss didn't seem to notice a thing, even though she'd felt so nauseous that at times she'd had to rush to the toilet.

It was almost certainly the lad with the ear infection who gave her away, the little bastard. He must have smelled it when she'd leaned close to look down the otoscope. Not long after, the medic in charge had popped his head around the door.

'A word, Lance Corporal. My office. Now.' She stood to attention as he bent to bring his face within inches of her own and sniffed loudly, several times. She breathed as lightly as she could without passing out.

'You stink of booze. Are you drunk, Corporal Merton?'

'I don't believe so, sir. Not at eleven o'clock in the morning. Sir.'

'You certainly smell of alcohol, and I can't have

you on duty if there's any chance of it. You are dismissed for the day. Report to me here, eighteen hundred hours.'

'Yes, sir.'

She spent the day sleeping it off, and arrived at her boss's office fully sober but with her head pulsing with pain that even heavy doses of Co-codamol hadn't managed to shift.

'I can't have my medics drunk on duty, you understand?'

'Yes, sir.'

'I've had it reported to me that you are overdoing the booze in general, is that a fair observation?'

The anger started to swell as she wondered who could have grassed on her. 'I wouldn't say so, sir,' she muttered, through gritted teeth.

'How are things with you generally? Adjusting to life back home? Preparing for civvy street? Things okay with the boyfriend?'

How dare he bloody snoop into her private life? She could feel her cheeks flushing now, her breath stopping in her chest as she tried to control the fury. 'Well, Lance Corporal?'

Her jaw ached from clenching her teeth.

'It can be tricky, I know,' his voice droned on. 'If you need to talk to someone, of course we can lay it on.'

The nausea was rising again and she could feel her stomach turning over just as it had on Remembrance Sunday all those weeks back.

'Excuse me, sir,' was all she managed to say, before rushing into the corridor and puking all over the shiny linoleum.

'I'm sorry I was such a bitch last night,' she said to Nate on the phone later that evening.

He didn't reply, not at first. Then he said, 'Look, I can't deal with this right now. I've had a rough day at work and I just want to chill out and not have a row with you.'

'I haven't rung you to have a row,' she said, trying not to sound defensive. 'I've rung to apologise and tell you that I'm going to cut out the booze completely, for a while, just to get back on an even keel.'

'Sounds like a plan, Jess.'

'Look, can I come and stay with you this week? I could catch a train tonight.'

There was a surprised pause at the other end. Then, 'It's Monday night. What about work?'

'They've given me the rest of the week off – they're calling it sick leave, but I think they just want to keep me out of their hair. I've only got five weeks to go now and they don't want me causing any more trouble.'

'What trouble?'

She told him about the ticking off, but not about being sick in the corridor.

'The timing's not great, to be honest,' he said in a flat voice. 'I've got a heavy week. There are rumours that Ofsted might come calling, I've got two parents' evenings and a football trip on Thursday. Won't be back till pretty late most nights.'

'I'll shop and clean and cook you delicious meals,' she pleaded.

He went silent at the end of the phone and for a fleeting, frightening moment it occurred to her that he might be about to tell her it was over. Oh God, please no, she prayed. I love him, can't do it without him.

Then, at last: 'Okay. See you later. But Jess . . .'

'Yes?'

'What you said about quitting the booze? You're serious?'

'I promise.'

Each evening as she waited for Nate to return from work, she could feel her body shouting at her that it wanted alcohol, any alcohol, that nothing else would satisfy it. Several times, passing the off licence on the corner of his street, she sensed her feet pulling towards the door. *Just one little drink.* The feeling was almost irresistible but she marshalled her willpower and managed to hold it at bay, knowing that one would surely lead to another, and then several more. She drank cans of cola instead which made her burp unattractively and failed to satisfy the craving.

Without the sedative of alcohol she found it hard to sleep, sensing Nate's every movement, hearing each little snore, and blasted to open-eyed wakefulness by any police or ambulance siren within half a mile.

When she finally slept, the nightmares returned, but subtly altered. These were not of the breath-stopping panic, of torn flesh and limbs, nor the visceral howls of boys in pain, but of the aftermaths of those terrifying moments, of feeling so exhausted that her limbs would not move, of the heat which seemed to suffocate the air out of her lungs, and the dust storms that whipped her face as the rescue helicopter rose into the air taking the injured men to safety. And, always, the gut-wrenching anxiety that perhaps she could have done more to save a limb, or even a life.

One night she woke with her bladder aching and made it to the toilet just in time. She had been dreaming that she was back in the compound where the squats cabin was located twenty yards away. The men just pissed against the outside wall, the girls had to risk a scary dash in the dark across open ground. That, or pee discreetly into a yellow sharps container and hope the sound didn't wake anyone. Either way it was enough to make you go easy on your intake of liquids after sunset.

She also dreamt of the poppy, just the once: not of the flower with its silky red petals gently fluttering in the breeze, but of the headless green stem, trembling and twitching like a dying man.

After dinner on the second evening, Nate said, 'Tell me what's going on, Jess?'

'Going on?'

'Those nightmares of yours.'

'They come and go,' she said. 'It's getting better.'

'Doesn't feel like that to me. Last night you started shouting and then you sat up in bed and seemed to be fighting someone off. You nearly clocked me one.'

She laughed. 'I'm so sorry. I'll try and keep my arms to myself tonight.'

'Are you sure you don't need to get some help?'

'Quite sure. It'll be fine once I'm out of the Army. Only a week now.'

She rose exhausted each morning but found that she could not sit still for more than a few minutes. Trying to use up her restless energy, she went for long walks or jogged round the local park, observing the yummy mummies so distracted by their gossip that the babies crawled into flowerbeds to eat soil. Their pampered pedigree dogs ran out of control and, she hoped, were having unprotected sex with all the wrong species. Planning her life ahead with Nate, she visited a couple of letting agents and viewed four flats in the area; more spacious, two-bedroomed places that cost a fortune in rent.

On Friday evening he returned in high spirits, having been to the pub with his mates to celebrate the end of a tough week, and ate two helpings of her carefully-prepared lamb tagine with appreciative enthusiasm. Sitting beside him on the sofa, watching television with a mug of tea in her hand, she imagined that this was what their lives might be like forever. She felt more at peace than she'd known for months.

'I've invited a few friends from school round

tomorrow evening to meet you,' he said, out of the blue. 'Hope that's okay?'

'So they can approve me?' she said, feeling wary.

'No, you idiot, just to meet you. To celebrate.'

'Celebrate what?'

'Your safe return, the end of your contract? I dunno. Do we need a reason?'

'Can I invite a couple of my friends as well, to even the balance?'

She rang Vorny, who accepted eagerly, and her brother Jonny, who at first said he was busy and then, when she pressed him, admitted that he'd promised to spend the evening with his new girlfriend.

'Bring her too. What's her name?'

'Sarah,' he said. 'Oh, okay then. She's dying to meet the Afghanistan heroine, so I s'pose tomorrow's as good a time as any. Be gentle, won't you?'

'You know me.'

'Only too well.'

On Saturday morning she brought Nate toast, coffee and the newspaper in bed and headed off to the supermarket for party provisions. When she reached the checkout she discovered that, along with the crisps, nibbles and soft drinks, the boxes of wine and beer cans, she'd slipped a bottle of whisky into the trolley. She could barely remember doing it, but was too embarrassed to give it back to the cashier. At the flat, she hid it in the back of a drawer and tried to forget it was there.

I will not drink tonight, she promised herself.

But, getting ready that evening and finding herself unaccountably nervous at the prospect of meeting Nate's work colleagues, her resolve crumbled and, with trembling hands, she took a couple of slugs to steady her stomach. It worked a treat. Vorny arrived early – they'd planned it that way – and they had a couple more discreet glasses together.

Nate's friends were two couples, Matt and Louisa, Benjamin and Aleesha, and his head of PE, Mary, a tall, rangy woman of about forty. Jess submitted herself to their scrutiny: 'Good to meet Nate's mystery woman, after all this time', and, 'so you're the tough girl who went to the front line in Afghanistan?' She enlisted Vorny to help with the inevitable interrogation, which ranged from the benign: 'Did you actually volunteer to go out there? You must be so brave, I'd be terrified,' to the incredulous: 'Did you really have to carry guns? Even as medics?'

They were nice enough people, but conversations with civilians always made her feel like a stranger from another planet. It was impossible to explain, or for them to gain any understanding beyond the most superficial level, what being on tour in a country like Afghanistan is really like.

The arrival of Jonny and Sarah was the excuse she needed, and she left Vorny fielding questions while she opened more bottles of wine and took the opportunity to slosh a whisky top up into her innocent glass of coke.

41

Sarah was a tall, slim girl with a dark-eyed seriousness about her – quite a contrast to her sturdy blond
brother, whose open face was always ready with a
joker's smile. Jess could tell immediately that she was
different from her brother's previous girlfriends – less
glamorous and self-absorbed, more poised and alert
to the world around her. From their secret smiles
and his soft looks it was clear that this relationship
was the real thing, and she was glad for him.

In the past, to the anxious bewilderment of their
parents, he'd dropped out of two university courses
in consecutive years, and seemed to be settling for a
life of minimum-wage drudgery. Then, with the help
of a string-pulling uncle, he'd landed an IT post in
a law company. The boss had recognised his potential,
sent him on several training courses and promoted
him twice. It had been the making of him, as their
mother liked to say.

She'd never thought of her brother as much of a
looker, but his new sense of self-esteem had magically
given his features clearer definition, helped by the
fact that he seemed to have lost weight and revamped
his wardrobe. He's quite a catch, Jess found herself
thinking.

It turned out that Sarah was a teacher too, so it
became a party of two halves: the school gang having
a heated conversation about education, while Jess
joined Jonny and Vorny sneaking a clandestine smoke
in the tiny patio garden. Away from Nate's sharp eyes
she drank steadily and happily, sharing old jokes,

enjoying the way her brother and her best friend sparred with each other. Everything was going perfectly.

The rest of the evening passed in a flash, until everyone had made their excuses and left, except for Vorny, who was staying the night, and Matt, a short and slightly balding man with an incipient beer-belly whose girlfriend had fallen asleep in the bedroom. Jess and Vorny sat in a happily intoxicated blur on the sofa, half listening to the boys having a rambling, slightly drunken discussion about politics.

Without warning, Matt turned his unsteady gaze towards them. 'What do you Army girls think we should do about Syria then? Are we just going to let them go on killing each other till there's no-one left except crazy radicalised religious zealots?'

You Army girls. How could Nate be friends with such a plonker? Neither seemed willing to reply until Vorny piped up in a quiet, reasonable voice: 'There's no right answer of course. It's a tragic situation but it's really complex, and I don't think there's much we can do to resolve it without creating even more trouble for the future.'

That should shut him up, Jess thought gratefully.

It didn't. 'What, shouldn't we be riding in on white chargers this time, ready to implant the blessed gift of peaceful democracy? Like we've done in Iraq and Afghanistan?'

It was a deliberate challenge; Jess felt sure he'd been waiting all evening for the opportunity. She dug her fingernails painfully into her palm and tried to take a deep breath but her chest felt as though a large pair of hands was crushing her lungs. The anger flowed like a dangerous fire through her body, making her head ache, blurring her eyesight, cramping her stomach.

'Let's not go there, Matt,' she could hear Nate cautioning, but it was too late.

A voice in her head warned her to stop, but it was easily ignored. Her tongue loosened itself and the words spilled out, without consent from her brain. 'I suppose you've travelled widely in these countries, talked to many experts?'

'Jess, don't you think . . .?' she could hear Nate trying to intervene, but she talked over him. 'So, have you? *Have* you? And if not, then I'm just wondering what gives you the moral authority to prognosticate about the impact of military intervention in these countries?'

His piggy eyes stared back, widening with alarm. 'I was just asking your opinion. From two people who have been there.'

Nate was now sitting upright, on high alert. 'Enough, Jess. Lay off the dogs. This has been a nice evening. Don't ruin it.'

'I don't think for one minute you were asking for *our* opinion,' she heard her own voice, low and dangerous. 'You were giving *yours*. And you think you have the right to have an opinion, in your safe little job a million miles away from any conflict, having probably never even had a single conversation with an Afghan or an Iraqi, and certainly without an iota of understanding about what we have been trying to achieve for them out there. Or of the fact that good people, much better people than you will ever be, have given their lives to help free the people of those countries from oppression. And you have the nerve to take the piss.'

Matt rose unsteadily to his feet.

'I'm sorry to have offended. It's time we were going home.'

Jess stood too. Discovering that she was, in her heels, slightly taller than him made her feel invincible. She could have floored him with a single blow.

'Is that it? You run away, the moment anyone challenges you?' she snarled. 'What a great example you must be for your students. A pathetic, clever-dick, know-it-all little . . .'

'ENOUGH, Jess,' Nate bellowed, grabbing her by the arm and pulling her away, down the corridor into the bedroom, and throwing her roughly onto the bed. Shocked by his strength, she offered no resistance and she fell like a rag doll, arms and legs akimbo. The bed was still warm from Matt's girlfriend, who had disappeared. There were groaning noises coming from the bathroom. Nate slammed the door behind him but a moment later it reopened and Vorny was by her side.

'Christ, Jess, whatever happened there? You certainly know how to blow it, don't you?'

'He deserved it. The idiot.' Her anger was cooling now.

'You're not wrong, but you shouldn't call your boyfriend's boss a "pathetic, clever-dick know-it-all", however much he deserves it.'

'His *boss*? That was the other woman, the tall one, Mary.'

'No, Matt's his boss. Mary's the maths teacher.'

Icy fear replaced the vestiges of her fury. 'That little fat man's the head of sports? You're quite sure?'

''Fraid so.' Vorny shook her head. 'I was talking to him earlier. About how he rates Nate, what a great asset he is. How well the football team's been doing under his training.'

'Bloody hell. I've blown it, haven't I?'

'You've got some serious apologising to do, that's for sure.'

It would take a lot more than that, Jess knew.

She tried to apologise but Nate refused to discuss anything that evening, and when she offered to clear up he told her sharply that he didn't need any help, thank you, and she should go to bed before she caused any more damage. He'd sleep on the sofa. End of story.

In the morning she reached across the bed for him before remembering, with a wave of self-disgust, what had happened. She found him already at work on the dining table, marking school books.

'Nate, I am so, so sorry about last night.' She moved

behind him and stroked the back of his neck – his weak spot.

He swatted her hand away and swivelled round, his face fiercer than she'd ever seen before. No wonder he makes a good teacher, she found herself thinking, he must be utterly terrifying to the kids.

'I think you'd better sit down,' he said.

'I'm going to make a coffee.' Her mouth was dry, her stomach turning somersaults. 'Do you want one?'

He shook his head and turned back to his marking. She boiled the kettle and made a mug of strong black instant, then went to sit at the table, facing him.

'Okay. Let me say my piece first, please?'

He looked up and nodded, his face impassive, his eyes coal black.

'What I said last night was completely out of order,' she started. 'I don't know what got into me. It felt as though he was attacking everything I stand for, the reason why James and all those others have died. I just lost it, and the words came out without thinking. I am really, really sorry.' She looked back at his stony expression and felt tears burning the back of her eyes. 'Please forgive me, Nate. I can work through this and get better. I love you.'

He sighed wearily. 'I've been doing a lot of thinking. All night, as it happens. This is the conclusion I've come to: I can't deal with it any more, Jess. The drinking, the anger, all that. You've turned into someone I don't recognise.'

'I know. I'm sorry.'

'You keep saying you're sorry, but what have you done about it?'

'I didn't drink all last week.'

'And when you did, look what happened. What I'm sorry about, Jess, is that I've stopped believing that you want to change. When you've sorted yourself out, rediscovered the old Jess, then get in touch.'

She managed an aghast, 'Are you telling me it's over?'

He nodded, but could not meet her eyes. 'Till you get yourself sorted, yes.'

She just had time to say, 'You don't mean it? Just like that?' and hear his retort, 'I do, Jess. I really mean it, just like that,' before the nausea hit her. When she finally emerged from the bathroom, Nate didn't even raise his head. 'When you feel better, please pack and leave,' he said. 'I've got work to do today.'

'But . . .'

He held up a hand, like a policeman stopping traffic. 'Please, I don't want to talk about it. I've told you what I think and I'm not going to have another row. Don't make it more painful than it is already. Just go.'

Once she'd packed she tried again: pleading and trying to reason. But he was immovable. 'I've made up my mind,' was all he would say.

In the face of this resistance and his complete unwillingness to talk or compromise, Jess's anger returned in full flood; the red behind the eyes, the heat at the back of the neck. She wanted to hit him

48

but, as if sensing it, he stood and faced her at full height.

There was nothing else she could do.

'You bastard,' she shouted, before slamming the door.

Only when she got back to the safety and privacy of the barracks did she allow herself to weep, with burning, desperate rasps that seemed as though they would never stop. She texted Nate with abject apologies, but there was no response. She cursed herself over and over again: she had never loved anyone the way she loved this man, never trusted anyone so much, never fancied anyone in the way she fancied him, never met anyone else that she'd consider spending her life with. And now, for the sake of a few drinks, she had thrown it all away.

Without Nate, life felt bereft of all meaning, all anticipation, all joy.

Chapter Three

The next few weeks passed in an alcoholic haze. She averted her eyes from mirrors and hurried past shop windows to avoid seeing the dark rings shadowing the eyes in her haggard face, the hunched shoulders and gaunt frame, a woman looking old before her time. She persuaded a mate, a doctor, to prescribe tranquillisers and even, at Vorny's insistence, got herself referred for counselling, but bottled it at the last minute.

'I can't sit there like an idiot, whining about losing the love of my life,' she admitted, 'when I know perfectly well what I need to do.'

No-one except Vorny knew what had happened with Nate. When her mother inquired, she fobbed her off, saying they were both so busy it was hard to find enough time together. She would manage without drinking for a few days and then, buoyed by her own success, would call or text to tell him the good news. But when he failed to respond, yet again, her resolve weakened.

'What's the point in punishing myself even further, when he clearly doesn't want me, whatever I do?' she'd say to herself, pouring an extra large glass.

Nothing could cheer her. The days were lengthening, the sun gaining in warmth; the bare branches of the trees on the garrison had taken on a green tinge and would soon be in bud. Swathes of acid yellow daffodils cloaked the town's roundabouts, but the arrival of springtime made her feel even gloomier. She should have been looking forward to her new life. Instead here she was, single again, spending most evenings locked in her barrack room with a bottle, unable to face the world.

She dreaded her discharge from the Army. Without Nate, her life already felt empty and meaningless, and now she would be saying goodbye to the friends who had come to feel like family. She even, half-heartedly, considered asking to cancel the discharge, but was too proud to admit that it might have been a mistake, and the moment drew inexorably closer. Finally, the day of the dreaded leaving party arrived. Jess drank so heavily throughout the afternoon and early evening that she could remember nothing after about nine o'clock and, the following day, discovered scrapes and bruises all over her body including a blackening eye. She couldn't bear to ask Vorny what had happened. It took a full forty-eight hours to recover from the hangover, and she felt disgusted with herself.

Then, all in one week, three good things happened.

Firstly, she noticed that the tranquillisers had finally

kicked in; she felt calmer than she had in months, if a little light-headed and distanced from reality. She tried to cut down her drinking, restricting it to the evenings. The nightmares seemed to have become more sporadic, and less intense. Looking back, she realised that she hadn't experienced the red rush of anger for nearly a fortnight. Even Vorny noticed she seemed happier: 'You'd better watch out, I might catch you laughing,' she'd joked.

On Tuesday, it was confirmed that Vorny and another medic, Hatts, who were both staying in the Army, would be stationed in the town for at least the next six months. This meant that the three of them could move out of the barracks and rent a place together. By seven o'clock the following evening they'd found the perfect place – a small Victorian terraced house within walking distance of the garrison medical centre – and were celebrating in the pub just around the corner, a proper old-school bar with wooden floors and sticky tables, yellowing jars of pickled eggs and some dusty packets of pork scratchings the only food on offer. The décor of the house was old fashioned and rather worn, but the beds were comfortable, the kitchen clean and modern. They moved in the next day.

On Thursday she rang the local ambulance service to see whether they had any vacancies and they invited her to sit a pre-entry exam. She spent the weekend frantically boning up on current NHS techniques, and it seemed to work because they phoned to offer her a job the following day. She would start as an Emergency Care Assistant for the first three months before sitting her paramedic exams again, because they were concerned that her knowledge was three years out of date. It was less money, but in some ways a relief not to be given the full responsibilities on day one.

Her first few shifts went by in a daze of new faces and an encyclopaedia of things to remember, but her NHS colleagues were so friendly and welcoming she wondered why she'd ever felt nervous. They were intrigued to learn about her Afghanistan experiences, especially the technical aspects of managing major trauma, bleeds and limb injuries using only equipment that could be carried in back packs. She basked in the warmth of their interest and admiration and relished sharing her experience with people who genuinely understood and were keen to learn.

One evening she found herself on a shift with Janine, an air force reservist who'd spent three months on the helicopters bringing in casualties to Camp Bastion. In brief moments of respite they shared stories of life in the desert, gaining a perspective they'd never seen before. Jess had thought the MERT crews brave and dedicated, but superior in attitude and she'd felt an almost visceral envy of the fact that they were going back for a cold shower each evening.

From the other point of view, Janine said she'd been in awe of the front line medics and wondered how they survived the extreme conditions in which they lived and worked. Her only real contact had been in the turmoil and urgency of an emergency evacuation, when she'd found them brusque and pushy in their desperation to ensure that their injured mates were safely onto the chopper as fast as possible.

Most shifts were busy from beginning to end, so Jess found no time for drinking except for her bedtime 'medication'. And there was so much to learn that she fell into bed, exhausted, at the end of each day, usually managing to sleep through without nightmares.

It had been a month since she'd last tried to contact him, but now she felt strong enough to try again.

'Hello Nate,' she emailed. 'How are you? I'm fine, except that I miss you loads. Civvy street seems to suit me. I'm happier than I've been for weeks and really enjoying the work. I've stopped drinking, except socially, and am sleeping well which has made a massive difference. I have lots more patience and can't remember the last time I blew a fuse. I still love you, Nate. Can we meet? Jess x.'

They met, that first time, on neutral ground: a pub close to Liverpool Street Station.

As she waited, sipping her cola, she watched the loud braying City types and felt a certain sympathy. They were tanked up on the adrenaline of trading millions and having a couple of hours' 'decompression time' before catching the commuter trains back to their quiet suburban lives. It was how she sometimes felt at the end of a busy shift.

She hardly recognised Nate, at first. The dreadlocks were gone, replaced with a short mat of tight black curls. Was this a statement, symbolic of his new start without her? He spotted her and smiled, with that soft beam which lit up his face and made you feel as though someone had turned the lights on.

'Yup, all gone,' he said, rubbing his head. 'Got the job, too.'

'What job?'

'Head of Sports. Matt's leaving.'

Her heart lifted even further. 'Congratulations, Nate.' She touched his hand, and he didn't take it away.

The couple of hours they'd agreed on went by too fast. It felt curiously formal, air-kissing like strangers as they parted. But it was a start, Jess told herself, easy does it. They planned a meal together the following week, when she had a couple of days off. She began allowing herself to hope.

Although each ambulance call-out still got the adrenaline pumping and her heart racing, most of their busy shifts were filled with non-emergencies. Seven out of ten 'shouts' were for old people, many of them regulars. She loved the way their faces would light up when the crew arrived, the sheer relief showing in the colour of their cheeks, and admired their stoical bravery and humility. She couldn't count the times she heard the phrase, 'Sorry to be such a nuisance, dearie'.

She happily brewed cups of strong sugary tea, exchanged a few words of comfort or simple conversation, listened to their stories and gained satisfaction from having made a difference. Many did not need hospital treatment – it was just a matter of making sure the district nurse would call by or the carer could attend more often. They got to know some of the old folk so well that when something more serious happened and they had to be admitted to hospital, she found herself dwelling on them, wondering about their progress. If she learned that one of them hadn't made it, she experienced genuine sorrow.

At the end of most days she felt more like a social worker than a medical responder. It's bloody ridiculous, she said to herself, that no-one cares enough to put the system right and it's left to an expensive emergency service to pick up the pieces. Her colleagues never seemed to gripe about it – perhaps they'd accepted that nothing was likely to change – but it made her angry: why couldn't the state provide elderly and frail people with enough support to live with dignity in their own homes; why had society apparently washed its hands of them? They sometimes learned of a son or daughter who lived within easy driving distance yet hadn't visited for weeks. What were they thinking? Were they unaware that their elderly relative was desperately lonely but too proud to ask for help, or did they simply not care?

The time-wasters were far more difficult to cope with. She'd heard the stories, of course, the call-outs for broken nails or wasp stings, and the people who'd learned how to circumvent the categories of urgency and would describe every situation as 'life-threatening', even if it wasn't remotely so.

When faced with a fat, gobby middle-aged man demanding emergency treatment for a sprained ankle, or a woman who couldn't remember whether she'd taken her birth control pill, she felt the old anger rising again, the nausea starting to ferment in her stomach.

'How do you get through the day without giving them a slap?' she asked her crew mate Dave – an older man, steady and compassionate – after they left a call-out for a minor oven burn. The woman had fussed interminably about being scarred and demanded to see a cosmetic surgeon. Dave had been admirably firm.

'We all feel like that sometimes,' he said. 'Just give yourself a bit of distance. Say you need to take a couple of minutes, go outside and take a few deep breaths. I find it works a treat.'

The worst shifts were Friday and Saturday evenings, when gangs of otherwise sensible, intelligent young people who probably lived decent, law abiding lives the rest of the time seemed to abandon their collective sanity by taking party drugs, drinking themselves senseless and getting into fights in every town centre.

At first, Jess managed to summon reserves of compassion by trying to see herself in each of them. This was more or less me, just a few months ago, she'd say to herself when, for example, attending to a drunken young woman who'd been in a cat fight and had minor abrasions to her face. She'd eventually been persuaded to call it a night and get into a taxi. When a young man took a swipe at her as she tried to examine the hand he'd just punched through a window, she recalled the blinding effects of her own alcohol-fuelled anger and how she felt like lashing out at anything or anyone around her.

But mostly she failed to find any sympathy. Did they have any idea how much time and taxpayers' money they were wasting? What if they were made to pay for the medical treatment they received – would that make any difference? The only people benefiting from these nightly binges were the alcohol companies and bar owners, she thought bitterly. Perhaps they should be made to pay up too?

It was August, and a stifling heatwave had brought crowds out of the bars onto the streets when, one Saturday night, she lost it. They'd been asked by the police to help a semi-naked young woman found unconscious in the gutter, and the others were briefly called away to help a more serious casualty, leaving Jess to look after the girl. As she knelt down to examine her, a large, burly man with a beer belly protruding beneath his shirt began to stagger unsteadily across the street towards them, shouting obscenities.

'Leave her be, you stupid bitch,' he shouted, lurching closer.

'Just stand back, sir, please,' Jess said, pleased with herself for refusing to rise to the insult.

'Fuck you,' the man said, taking a few steps nearer. For a moment he seemed to stop in his tracks and went quiet, so Jess turned her attention back to the casualty. Then, out of the corner of her eye, she saw that he was fiddling with his flies and, before she knew what was happening, both she and the young woman were drenched in foul-smelling urine.

'What the hell?' she shouted, powerless to resist the heat of her fury. A dense red mist descended in front of her eyes and all common sense deserted her. Instead of leaving the scene and calling for help as she had been trained to do, her only thought was to stop him pissing onto the poor woman. She leapt at him, trying to spin him round by pushing his shoulder. For all his inebriation he managed to stand his ground, the urine now running down his trousers and splashing her feet.

'Try that again, bitch,' he said, laughing in her face with a blast of beery breath.

'You bastard.' She was about to push him again when she heard Dave's shout.

'Back off, Jess.'

'He's pissing all over us.'

'Just. Back. Off. *Now*. Go to the van and get yourself cleaned up. Stay there till I get back.'

She slunk away and, as the anger dissipated, she was left feeling sick and ashamed, waiting in the ambulance and stinking of urine.

'I'm sorry, Dave,' she said when he returned. 'It was so disgusting. I just lost it. How's the girl?'

'Come round now, and we got her into a taxi. The police have arrested him for abuse and assault.' He laughed. 'Can't wait to read the police report: "detail of assault weapon: stream of stinking piss". It's gotta be a first.'

'Thanks for the sympathy,' she said, managing a smile.

Dave started up the engine and pulled off. 'We'd better get you back to the station for a change – you don't half smell.' And then, after driving for a few moments, 'In theory I ought to write this up, you know?'

She held herself still, heart in mouth.

He gave a deep sigh. 'But it's been a bloody awful night and you were under severe provocation, so I'll keep it under my hat this time.'

She spent her days off cramming for the exams which were now just a couple of weeks away: anatomy, physiology, cardiology, pharmacology. Study had always come easy in the past but these days she found herself struggling to remember facts, vital information like drug dosages per weight for children; the exact position to insert the needle to reinflate a lung with needle chest compressions; the APGAR score calculation for newborns.

One morning as she went to take her tranquilliser pill, it dawned on her. Perhaps the drug was affecting her ability to retain facts? She felt fine now; surely she didn't need them any more? She put the packet back into her bedside drawer. I'll see how it feels for a few days, she thought to herself.

It seemed to work: she passed the exams with flying colours. Nate took her out to dinner to celebrate, and they ended up back at his flat for the first time since the party. They were tentative at first, circling each other warily as he made coffee and she wandered around, checking to see what had changed, looking for clues about the life he had spent without her, these past months.

But it was still the same old bachelor pad, with the broken blinds, the brimming waste bins, DVDs and Xbox paraphernalia scattered around the giant television. In the bathroom cabinet were shaving cream, deodorant, his familiar brand of cologne and a packet of paracetamol but, to her relief, no sign of any female occupation.

The wariness lasted only as long as it took them to finish their coffee and have their first proper kiss, and after that the weekend passed in making up for lost time. They left the bedroom only to eat and watch a bit of tv, and Nate dragged on a tracksuit once in a while to go out for takeaways and bottles of wine. He poured her drinks without a single enquiring glance, and she made sure that two glasses were her top limit – this weekend was too precious to spoil.

She knew she had to wait for him to say it, but she longed for him to reassure her, to talk about their future together once more. It wasn't until Sunday evening was drawing on and she was preparing to leave, that he finally said, 'I think we're okay again, J. Don't you?'

'God, I love it when you get all romantic,' she laughed, hugging him. 'But "okay" will do me, for now.'

It started as a normal shift: 6am to 6pm, on the van with Dave and a new Emergency Care Assistant, a sweet kid called Emma. It was a blustery day with towering cumulus clouds like fantasy castles in the sky. Emma remarked how lucky they were, driving around the countryside amid the beauty of the autumn colours, and the two others agreed.

By coffee time they'd dealt with four shouts including one of their regulars, an old boy called Bert who kept a garrulous and foul-mouthed parrot. He'd fallen on the way to the toilet, so they just checked him out, cleaned him up and waited for the district nurse to arrive while the parrot hurled abuse from its cage: 'ge' me out of here, you 'uckers,' it squawked, interspersed with a repetitive refrain of 'stupid old git, stupid old git'. Emma giggled and blushed but Jess and Dave took it in their stride. They'd heard the parrot say much worse things in their time.

'Let's hope we get a decent break,' Dave said, more in hope than expectation, as they pulled into the ambulance station. As usual, they'd just sat down when the next call came in: 'Emergency RTC High Street. Two life-threatening, two walking wounded. Police on scene.'

Jess felt the welcome surge of adrenaline, more powerful than any caffeine rush, as they clambered back on board and the siren started its familiar wail. The incident was only ten minutes away but a sudden heavy downpour made the traffic even more of a nightmare than usual, with dopey drivers taking an age to move aside and let them past. When they reached the lights at the top of the High Street, it was jammed and at a standstill. Dave whooped the siren a couple of times but it made little difference – nothing was moving. In the distance, they could see the flashing blue lights of a police car.

'Take the packs and run for it,' Dave shouted. 'I'll get there soon as.'

It was still raining heavily as they panted down the slick pavement. I must be losing fitness, Jess thought to herself; she'd run much further with a heavy Army Bergen on her back with no problem at all in the past. They pushed their way through a crowd of gawpers with umbrellas to a scene of carnage: a car had obviously driven onto the narrow pavement at some speed and hit two people, both of them now on the ground. The driver was still in his seat, a very old man, his face ashen, and a baby buggy lay on its side near the front wheels. She looked around frantically to see where the child could be before spying it in the arms of a policewoman, apparently unhurt.

Over to her right, a policeman was doing CPR on a girl whose face already had that grey, hollowed-out look of a dying person. As she approached he shook his head grimly and gestured with a nod in the other direction, towards a shattered shop window behind the car. 'There's a guy over there who needs your help.'

'I'll get that one if you take over here,' she told Emma.

Lying amid the shards of glass was a young man, moaning slightly, his legs in a pool of shocking red that was being washed across the pavement by the rain. Her stomach turned over as she approached, smelling that terrifying metallic stench of blood and fear. At first she thought the man's leg was twisted beneath him but her stomach lurched again, even more violently, when she saw that the lower leg was completely missing.

Stop thinking. Get on with it, no time to waste. The checklist ran over and over in her head, like a mantra: C.A.B.C, C.A.B.C. Catastrophic haemorrhage, airway, breathing, circulation.

Barely noticing the blood and glass, she kneeled down, tore open her medipack and grabbed a tourniquet. 'My name's Jess and I'm a paramedic,' she said. 'This is going to hurt a bit. Just hang in there, we're going to get you to hospital as soon as we can.' She secured the band swiftly and efficiently just above the knee and observed with satisfaction as the pumping gush of brilliant red arterial blood slowed to a dribble.

Lifting her head for a moment, desperate for Dave to arrive, she caught sight of the ankle and foot a couple of metres away near a litter bin. It looked just like part of a discarded shop dummy, still wearing a sock and trainer, the canvas type in show-off scarlet, just like Nate sometimes wore. She thrust a dressing towards a middle-aged woman standing nearby. 'This is really important,' she said, urgently. 'Get that limb, wrap it up and get it somewhere cold. Find a shop with a drinks cooler or ice cream freezer, soon as you can.'

The injured man's eyes were a maelstrom of panic and fear. Even through the pallor she could see his well-made features: a handsome young man, perhaps in his twenties, with all his life before him. Like James. Like Scott. Come to think of it, he had a look of Scotty, with that mouse-blond hair and freckles all over his nose. He was breathing, fast and shallow: his airway was clear. She quickly took his pulse. It was faint, but at least it was there.

Airway okay, breathing okay-ish, circulation okay-ish. Where the hell is Dave?

It was only when she went to cover the end of the severed leg that she faltered. The shattered ends of the tibia and fibula bones glowed shocking pearly pink-white against a bloody mess of skin and flesh, like a leg of meat hacked by a crazed butcher.

It wasn't as though she'd never seen this kind of injury before – in fact she'd seen it too many times in the heat and sand of the desert. She grabbed a pack of dressings, but when she went to lift the stump the man whimpered again and then uttered another long, loud, terrifying howl. Her head began to spin. That sound, that gut-wrenching primeval animal sound of a man in agony, the sound that Scotty was making as she worked so desperately to save him that day.

Get a grip, Jess. Don't think. Get the leg wrapped and get up a morphine drip. Put the guy out of his agony.

But however much she tried to push it away, Scott's face swam in front of her eyes. The young man's groans were Scotty's groans.

It was her first ever foot patrol in the desert, her heart pummelling inside her chest with terror and the effort of carrying the medical back-pack, at twenty-five kilos the weight of an average eight year old, as well as her own heavy body armour. Her head felt as though it was boiling inside her helmet as the group cautiously circled the edge of the village in the ferocious heat. No-one spoke a word as the searcher moved ahead, sweeping the dust with his long-handled detector to check for improvised explosive devices while the man behind him marked the borders of the cleared area with spray paint. Everyone else scanned the landscape for markers, piles of stones, wire or a piece of broken glass which might have been left as a secret signal to mark the position of a bomb or anything designed to divert their path towards a mined area.

They could tell the Taliban were close by, watching and waiting, because the place was deserted. The villagers were hiding in their homes and even the dogs had taken cover. The enemy would never show themselves, and knew quite well that the allied troops couldn't fire a single shot unless they were fired at first. The tension was almost unbearable.

And then: an ear-splitting crack. Jess twisted round to see a geyser of earth erupting to the side of the patrol, just where they had passed. Someone must have stepped unwarily just a few centimetres outside the cleared zone – that was all it took. The screams of pain started instantly and, as she turned back, trying to run but encumbered by her heavy pack and body armour, the screech of yelled orders in her earpiece was almost deafening. 'Medic! Medic! Men down, *three* men down.' It was just like those training exercises, except this was for real. Everything seemed to be moving in slow motion.

She heard Vorny puffing beside her and, as the clouds of soil and dust settled, the scene ahead appeared in almost surreal clarity. Captain Jones was lying beside the blast crater cursing loudly, clutching his right hand and covered in dirt. At least if he's swearing he's alive, she thought. Another man was seated, holding his face in his hands. Vorny paused to see if he was okay, and Jess lumbered on towards the Captain.

'I'm fine, just get over there,' he shouted, gesturing impatiently into the crater. 'It's Scott.'

The figure was almost completely obscured by the dust and rocks that had settled on it after the blast, but just then the soldier lifted his head and emitted a long and terrifying howl which seemed to echo off the mud walls of the compound behind her, reverberating through her very being.

She fell, rather than ran, down the sloping side of the crater and, when she picked herself up, the true horror of the boy's injuries became apparent. The blood-curdling screams and streams of profanity meant he was certainly still alive, but both his lower legs were missing, vaporised by the blast. The village dogs would come scavenging later, she knew.

The earth around his lower body was already stained red with the blood gushing from the mess of mangled flesh and bone where his legs used to be. There were only moments to save his life. She ripped two tourniquets from her own upper arm, stored there for instant access and, with hands trembling so much she could scarcely grip the webbing, managed to secure one on each leg, above the knees. She glanced towards his face, pale as the sand dusting it. Even through his goggles she could see the panic in his eyes, darting from side to side, trying to focus.

'Hang in there, Scotty,' she said. 'We'll get you sorted.'

'Jess. Thank Christ, it's you,' he whimpered, through gritted teeth. 'Just save me feckin' life, will ya? Get me home for Chrissake. Please.'

'Don't you worry, you're going to make it,' she said, trying to convince herself as much as him.

Vorny slithered down the slope to join her and they worked together, wrapping the shattered stumps with white dressings, all the while talking to the lad, trying to calm him.

'Nearly there. MERT's on its way. We're going to get you out of here. Hang in there. You're going to make it.'

Vorny set up a drip into one arm and held the bag high, squeezing it to push the life-saving liquid into Scott's system, while Jess pulled out a morphine autojet and punched a hefty dose directly into the muscle of the upper arm on the other side. 'That's it, Scotty. When you wake up you'll be in Bastion,' she said, as the howls tailed off into moans.

By now Captain Jones was on his feet but very pale and holding his hand gingerly, with the other lad, McVeigh, who was shocked and deafened, but otherwise unharmed. They'd identified a landing site just beyond the brown poppy field at the edge of the village. The helicopter was circling, just about to land, and she was heading across the field behind the stretcher team, carrying Scotty's pack, when the shooting started. There was no cover, and it seemed to be coming from both sides.

She dropped to the ground, cursing the fact that any delay could cost Scotty's life after all the work they'd done to save him. But as the helicopter turned away without landing, and the firing continued without any apparent response from their own side, she realised it was not only Scott's life in danger. Bullets could slice through the brittle brown stems of the crop at any moment. The adrenaline rush that had kept her going throughout the time they'd been working on Scotty was dissipating, and she began to panic. It was then that she saw the red poppy.

'Christ, Jess, what the fuck are you playing at?'

Dave's shout, close to her ear, brought her instantly back to the High Street in the pouring rain, a scene painted in grey and red, the smell of blood, the young man's groans, his shattered limb in her arms. She had absolutely no idea how long she'd been kneeling there.

'Let me take over,' Dave barked, taking hold of the leg and shoving her aside brusquely. 'Just give the poor sod some morphine. Get a drip going and pump in some fluids, for Christ's sake.'

Dragging herself back to the present, she stood and picked up her pack. Through the shattered glass of the shop window she could see an array of meat, liver, sausages, lamb chops, trussed chickens, all glistening with broken glass. The centrepiece was a large whole leg of lamb, the severed end pointing towards her, a neatly trimmed version of this young man's leg. Like Scotty's legs after that blast.

She forced her eyes away, searching the pack for a morphine syringe.

'I'm just going to give you something for the pain,' she said, squatting down by his head. But when she looked into his face she could see that he had gone, his eyes rolled back, his skin a deadly grey.

She shook his shoulder. 'Stay with us,' she shouted, shaking him harder. She pressed her finger to his neck.

'No pulse, Dave. Christ, he's got no pulse.' She ripped open his jacket and shirt, and pressed the pads onto his chest. 'Flatline.'

'I'll secure his airway,' Dave shouted. 'Start CPR, now. '

No, no, no, no, she muttered to herself, in rhythm with the pumps on his chest, like a mantra. Not again, not again. It can't be, can't be. Now, the rest of the world disappeared and the only thing that mattered was counting out loud the chest compression pumps: one – two – three – four – five – six – seven – eight – nine. Eighty to a hundred pumps a minute for two minutes, a quick check of the pulse and then start again. Dave was squeezing air into his lungs from the bag now, twelve breaths a minute. If we keep doing this he will come back, she said to herself, I've seen it happen, just so long as we can keep it up.

Just as the muscles in her arms felt as though they would crumple with exhaustion Emma returned and took over for a while, and they alternated for what seemed like hours, all through loading him onto the ambulance and the crazy race back to the hospital; even as they were wheeling him into A&E.

The doctors declared both casualties dead on arrival. They were the young parents of the baby. The old man who'd lost control of his car and driven onto the pavement at forty miles an hour was completely unharmed.

When they got back to the ambulance station Dave said, 'Want a coffee?'

She nodded numbly and followed him into the kitchen, barely aware of her surroundings, finding it strange that she could even breathe or put one foot in front of another when she felt so completely shell-shocked. He placed a mug of hot sweet tea onto the table in front of her but when she went to pick it up her hands shook so badly that she slopped it all over her uniform.

He put a gentle hand on her shoulder. 'It happens to all of us, you know,' he said, kindly.

She shook her head vehemently. 'No, it doesn't happen to all of us, not like that. You saw me, Dave. I lost it again. Some kind of flashback thing. God knows how long it was before you arrived and took over.'

'Only a few moments, I'm sure. Besides, you'd already controlled his bleeding.'

'But the delay could have meant the difference . . .' The thought was simply too enormous and too terrible to contemplate. She felt overwhelmed and exhausted; barely able to think straight.

After a long pause Dave said: 'I think you need to take a few days off. Why don't you ask Frank?'

'Oh God, I couldn't face Frank, right now.'

'Do you want me to ask him for you?'

She nodded.

'Okay. I think you need to talk to someone, but perhaps not today. The best thing for you now is to go straight home, have something to eat and a couple of glasses of wine. Try to think about something else. I'll text to let you know what Frank says.'

It was this simple act of kindness and understanding which finally broke the dam, opening the door to all the horror, the guilt and the shame. She began to weep, with long, agonising gasps that seemed to wrench all the air out of her lungs. Dave moved his arm around her and she rested her head on his warm, broad shoulder till the sobs abated.

Chapter Four

She was relieved to see her father in the station car park because he wouldn't ask too many questions; after a heavy date with a whisky bottle, she was feeling particularly fragile.

When she'd got back to the flat the previous day she'd found it deserted and remembered that Vorny and Hatts were away on exercise for two weeks. She slumped down on the sofa and wept, desolate and desperate for someone to talk to. Why weren't they here, when she'd needed them most? She considered calling Nate but decided she couldn't dump her problems on him, not just yet. After a while she dried her eyes and stomped around the flat wondering what to do with herself. Then, reluctantly, she dialled her parents' number.

'I've got a few days unexpected leave, Mum. Can I come and stay?'

'Of course, dear. Are you all right?'

'Ish. Talk tomorrow, okay? I'll be there on the five o'clock train. Can someone pick me up?'

As they drew up to the house her mother was on the doorstep, with Milly the dog, both regarding her with inquiring eyes. Why the unexpected leave? Why wasn't she spending it with Nathan? Of course her mother was far too wise to ask directly. Jess would share any problems, in her own time. She always did.

'How's things?'

'Fine, thanks. Glad to be here.'

'You look pale, love. Are you feeling okay?'

'Just a bit weary. Heavy week.'

The truth was that she didn't really feel anything much right now, except numb and confused. All her adult life had been spent working towards, training and then becoming a medic. She'd wanted to make a difference, to save lives and she'd loved it, mostly. Until yesterday she had been determined to spend the rest of her life doing it, couldn't imagine any other form of career.

But somehow all that certainty had now disappeared, washed away like the poor young man's blood on that dismal pavement. She had broken her promise to James, her vow to prevent anyone dying through any delay in stemming their loss of blood.

The future felt like a quicksand, untrustworthy and perilous. Last night, during her long commune with the bottle, she'd argued with herself, sometimes out loud, as the logical, calm voice of reason struggled to be heard over what her instincts seemed to be shouting:

You're a good medic, well-trained, highly experienced. You've made a difference, even saved lives.

I've failed to save lives. I failed that young man. I punched that idiot in the street.

Just a couple of blips, you'll get over it.

It's not that. I can't trust myself any more: the flashbacks, the anger. I failed my promise to James.

Just two events in four months, Jess.

I'm a danger to patients. My confidence is gone. The thought of going back to work makes me feel panicky and sick.

You could get help, counselling perhaps? That'll sort it.

Do I want to put myself through all that self-examination crap? Anyway, I don't know if I really want to go on putting myself on the line every day.

Okay, so give up being a medic. But you need to earn a living somehow. What would you do instead?

Oh Christ, that's it. What else could I do? There is nothing else.

The argument raged in her head until, finally, she'd passed out, fully dressed, on the sofa.

Jess had envisaged walking with her mother on the beach, perhaps sitting on the dunes, a neutral, impersonal place to talk because you naturally sat looking outwards, your eyes drawn to the sea and the horizon, rather than facing your companion. Quite why this made it so much easier to be honest with yourself she never completely understood, but it always seemed to work.

She recalled days and nights of teenage angst when she would rush to the sea, weeping her eyes out over some spotty, undeserving youth, or spending hours with her best friend in the dunes dissecting every nuance of their latest romances, imagined or real. Alone or in company, self-pity never survived for long out on the beach. The soothing, rhythmical shush of the waves, the wide open skies and grey sea stretching to infinity always helped her to find a sense of proportion, reminding her of how small and insignificant we are in this vast universe, how unimportant our problems in the wider scheme of things.

But this time it didn't turn out like that.

After breakfast, she'd just made another pot of coffee and was sitting at the kitchen table while her mother fussed around, washing up, putting away. Her father had drifted off to his greenhouse.

'Look what I got for supper,' Susan said, pulling something out of the fridge. 'I went to that lovely butcher's yesterday. I know it's your favourite.' She placed the parcel on the table and unwrapped it, revealing a large leg of lamb, its severed flesh oozing dark red blood onto the worktop.

Jess had time to blurt out, 'Lovely . . .' before the nausea hit her, like an unstoppable wave. She made it to the cloakroom just before she vomited, violently and uncontrollably, into the toilet, groaning with pain as her guts turned themselves inside out. She gagged, again and again, her throat burning with the vicious acid residue of last night's whisky.

She heard her mother at the door and then by her side, and a soothing hand stroking her shuddering back. When it was all over she allowed herself to be led back to the living room, on trembling legs, gratefully accepting the glass of cool, clear water she was offered.

Her mother sat down on the chair opposite. 'Are you feeling better now?'

Jess nodded.

'What was it? Something you ate, do you think?'

Jess took a sip of water, trying to delay answering until she'd put her jumbled emotions into some expressible order. She was about to brush it off with a jokey remark about a dodgy take-away but then, as if the phrase had formed itself independently of any conscious thought, the words came out of her mouth: 'I'm giving it up, Mum.'

'Giving what up, love?'

'Being a paramedic. I'm going to quit. I can't do it any more.' Just as soon as she heard herself admit it, an almost overwhelming wave of relief sluiced through her body.

Her mother's eyes widened, but she managed to keep her voice calm. 'This is sudden, Jess. I thought you loved the job? Has something bad happened?'

The tears began to flow freely as she found herself describing the events of yesterday. The way she'd lost control, found her mind flashing back to the desert, the shocking outcome.

The discussion that followed went much along the same lines as the internal debate she'd had on the sofa with the whisky bottle last night. Her mother made all the reasonable responses: *take your time, seek some help, you're a great medic, it would be a loss to the service, it's what you've been working for all your life.* But the more the conversation continued, the more Jess became convinced that what her inner voice had been telling her head was right. She couldn't carry the responsibility of saving people's lives, not any longer.

Eventually her mother stopped offering suggestions. 'It's your life, my love. Whatever you decide will be for the best.' She leaned over and stroked Jess's hand. 'But shouldn't you also get yourself checked over by a doctor to find out what caused you to be so violently sick?'

Jess hesitated, unwilling to inflict another disappointment, but she would have to admit it in the end. 'I'm sorry, Mum, but it was the leg of lamb. It brought everything back. It's what that terrible stump yesterday reminded me of, and when I stood up afterwards there was a butcher's just beside us and the meat was just like that poor young man's flesh.' She shuddered involuntarily, remembering the red of the meat and the silvery slivers of shattered glass.

They had fish and chips for supper instead and, much later that evening, after her father had gone to bed, they sat on the patio together watching the stars come out. It was September now, the evenings were drawing in and there was a dampness in the air with that autumnal countryside smell. She always found this time of year melancholy: the swallows gathering for their long migrations, the changing sounds of bird-song, dew on the grass in the morning, the yellowing of the leaves. They all felt like endings. Only this year she was facing a very personal ending, a big, terrifyingly full stop to what had been driving her, her reason for living, her passion for the past ten years.

After a while it grew cold and they went inside. 'Whatever am I going to do with myself now, Mum?' Jess said, cuddling up on the sofa with Milly, who wasn't usually allowed to sit there.

'Have you got any ideas?'

'Not a clue,' she admitted.

'What about something to do with animals?' Susan said. 'You've always loved them, and when you were a very little girl – before you joined the St John Ambulance – you used to say you wanted to be a vet.'

'It's a six year training. Anyway you have to be super-bright. I'd never have got in with my two Bs and a C.'

They chatted for a while and then, out of the blue, her mother said, 'You know what you told me about the leg of lamb today?'

'Uh huh.'

'It reminded me of something I'd read somewhere and it was really annoying me because I couldn't remember where.'

'And have you remembered now?'

'I have. Something rather like that happened to your great-grandfather Alfred, too.'

'Like what?'

'He was in the First World War and came back injured – lost a leg. Afterwards he tried working as a butcher, but he couldn't take it because the raw flesh reminded him of something he'd experienced in the war.'

'That's strange. How do you know all this, anyway?'

Her mother disappeared upstairs and returned a few minutes later with a small cardboard box. 'It's all in here,' she said. 'Your great-grandmother's diaries.'

As Jess opened the box, a comforting, musty smell of old paper wafted out into the room. Inside were stacked six dog-eared notebooks, the old-fashioned kind once issued by schools, yellowing pages of cheap lined paper stapled between soft buff-coloured covers. On the front of each one was written, in a neat rounded hand in fading blue ink, 'Rose Barker. PRIVATE'.

'Oh my goodness, look at this. They were written by your grandmother? My great-grandmother?'

Susan nodded. 'Everyone knew her as Rose but her full name was Jessica Rose. You are named after her. She died when I was only five so I barely knew her, but she was a tough cookie by all accounts.'

'This is amazing. Why haven't I seen these before?'

'We only discovered them after granny died last year.' Jess had been given leave to return home for the funeral but had to fly back immediately afterwards. She'd been sad not to be able to stay longer, to help her mother with the gloomy task of sorting out her grandmother's belongings.

'Have you read them yet?' Jess said, starting to rifle through the notebooks.

'Not completely. I got up to the bit about poor old Alfie but then I got too busy to carry on.'

'Did you know about them before?'

'Mum never mentioned them, but then her memory was pretty dodgy and I suspect she just forgot they were there, locked way in the attic all those years.'

'Shall we look at them together, now?' Jess asked

Susan looked at her watch and yawned. 'Not tonight, love, it's gone midnight,' she said, stroking Jess's hair. 'Are you coming up?'

'In a while,' Jess said. 'I'm not sleepy yet. I'm going to have a bit of a read, if you don't mind. I'm really curious to find out about Alfie.'

'Are you feeling better?'

Jess nodded. 'Thanks for being so understanding, Mum.'

'No drinking now?' She gave her daughter a stern look.

'I'll do my best,' Jess said. 'See you in the morning.'

After her mother had gone, Jess made herself a cup of coffee with a whisky chaser, and placed the cardboard box beside her on the sofa. Milly came to join her, snuggling her furry face onto Jess's knee.

She lifted out the top notebook and flicked through the pages filled with the same careful handwriting, interspersed with stuck-in cuttings and letters. Then she checked the dates on the other notebooks to make sure they were in the right order, and began to read.

BOOK ONE

Rose Barker – PRIVATE

Monday 11 November 1918.

RED LETTER DAY!

Even now I have to pinch myself!

I have sorely neglected my writing since starting at the munitions factory, having felt so exhausted and dispirited each evening, and my entries so dull. I found these notebooks on a charity stall a few weeks ago and they are begging to be filled. And now there is so much to tell I barely know where to begin.

Today started out as another gloomy winter Monday with us all bent over our benches carefully filling shells with 'devil's porridge' and then, at 11 o'clock this morning, the siren wailed. We jumped out of our skins, of course, we always do. Explosion warning? An air raid? Everyone stood stock still, looking at each other over our respirators like yellow-faced frogs. And then we twigged. We'd heard rumours and read plenty of reports in the newspapers, but no-one really believed them. There've been so many false promises. Could it really happen this time?

Then the boss came over the tannoy and told us it was official: fighting had been suspended on the Western Front. A moment later all the church bells of East London started clanging with a deafening din – such a surprising sound that we hadn't heard for four years – and we were cheering and laughing so loud that we couldn't hear the rest of what he said. But the word got round soon enough: not that we'd have gone on working, in any case, but they were closing the factory for the day.

We threw off our overalls, grabbed our coats and tumbled out into the street like a pack of puppies, where there was already such a great crush of excited people singing and cheering, running and dancing, hugging and kissing, that we could barely make our way through the streets. Being so short, Freda was virtually carried along, and I had to hold her tight so as we wouldn't get separated. A group of young lads adopted us: 'Come on canaries,' they yelled, 'we'll look after you, show you a good time.'

On a normal day we wouldn't have given them a second glance, but the world had suddenly been painted in bright colours and even spotty boys looked handsome. It may have been grey and a bit drizzly, but it felt as though the sun had come out, beaming down on us lot all lit up with happiness.

We had a notion to get ourselves to the West End and somewhere near Buckingham Palace cos word was that the King and Queen were going to come out and wave to us but there wasn't a cat's chance of that. The buses were crammed to the nines with people piled high on the top decks and hanging off the rear doorways, but they weren't going anywhere due to the crowds. It was almost impossible to push your way through even on foot, so we just let ourselves be carried wherever the crowd took us.

We passed by Smithfield where a surge of greasy, blood-stained lads had poured out of the meat market, and on to the edges of the City where a great black wave of clerks and business types had pushed out onto the street. They were throwing their bowlers in the air, hanging out of windows and balconies and climbing lampposts, without a thought for their smart city clothes. No-one cared a jot.

The pubs were opening by now, and tankards being handed out around the crowd, and buntings being hung from upstairs windows so the city looked like a fairground. At one junction they'd set a wind-up gramophone going in an open window, and we started dancing to it. After a while, as we moved slowly forwards, the bands came out: the Sally Army, musicians from the clubs and just about anyone who had an instrument seemed to gather on every street corner and they played together, all the old favourites: Pack up Your Troubles and It's a Long Way to Tipperary. If they stopped, someone would hand them each a pint and we'd shout for more till they tuned up again.

Freda and me both got horribly drunk and kissed a dozen unsuitable types, which as a married woman I really shouldn't have, but we were so happy we just didn't care.

Then there was a great roar from the crowd and

people shouted 'God Save The King' again and again, and the musicians struck up with the national anthem. We were still in Cheapside and nowhere near The Mall, but word had spread through the crowd that King George and Queen Mary had come out onto the balcony of Buckingham Palace and waved to all those lucky beggars who managed to get within sight of them.

After He's a Jolly Good Fellow, the crowd started on other songs and I was joining in happily until they struck up with the hymn All People That on Earth Do Dwell, and a sudden wave of sadness hit me. I don't suppose the beer we'd drunk on empty stomachs helped, but my legs went wobbly and I felt as though I might fall over if I didn't find somewhere to sit. I pushed my way through the crowd to the side of the road and found an empty doorstep.

Then the tears came, coursing down my face like a waterfall, as I remembered all those poor boys. Those thousands and thousands of boys, even millions, who were never coming back, who would never be able to celebrate the victory they lost their lives for. Not just Ray and Johnnie, but my uncles Fred and Ken and the three Garner brothers, Billy and Stan, Tony and Ernest, Joe, William and Tom Parsons. And those were just the ones in our neighbourhood we knew well.

After a while, Freda came and sat down beside me and put her arm around my shoulders.

'What was it all for?' I wailed. 'They'll never come home, never get married, have children or grow old.'

'But my brother's alive, Rose,' she said, putting her arm around me. 'That's a blessing, isn't it? It won't be long before he's home.'

We sat there for a while, both of us lost in our thoughts despite the great noise going on around us, until we realised that we were both ravenously hungry. Freda managed to grab the last two baked potatoes from a street vendor, and a cup of tea, which made us feel a little better.

The afternoon was drawing in and it was starting to rain. 'Let's get home,' I said. 'Our folks will be wanting to see us.' I couldn't imagine what Ma might be doing – she's spent so long in mourning for my brothers I wasn't sure she'd have the heart to celebrate.

The best sight of all was as we crossed London Bridge and it seemed every craft on the Thames had taken to the water: ferries and tugs and steamboats and skiffs, all decorated with flags and full of happy cheering people.

My hand is so tired I can write no more, except for these words:

THE WAR IS OVER!

Yes, my dearest Alfie, perhaps it won't be long until we are together again. I must stay strong for you and prepare for the start of our married lives together.

Tuesday 12 November 1918

Thick head and early shift, ugh.

When I woke this morning I thought at first I must have dreamt it, but it must be true because it's all over the newspaper billboards. You wouldn't have thought they'd still need us to carry on making shells, now the war is over, but the manager says there is still a job for us for the moment and we will continue until they tell us to stop. I don't care. We're earning good wages and heaven knows what we'll do when they lay us off.

At tea break we had such a laugh, telling tales of yesterday and what we'd all got up to. When Freda and I finally made it back to the Old Kent Road we'd found her mum and my ma and pa well stuck in at The Nelson, singing old wartime songs along with the rest of them except those who were past it, slumped in their chairs and on the floor.

Ma was weeping even while she sang, not even bothering to stop and wipe the tears flowing down her cheeks, so I managed to squeeze in and tried to comfort her. But what can ever make up for the loss of two sons? Nothing, I suppose, except perhaps grandchildren. When Alfie comes home we will do our best to oblige.

At teatime today Pa told me I had to be patient. It would be weeks before we were likely to hear anything and I shouldn't expect 'young Alfred', as he calls him, to be demobbed any time soon. There was all kinds of clearing up to be done after a war, he said, and it takes time to get all those thousands of troops back to the coast and then ferry them home. We haven't heard anything from him for weeks, but there's been no knock at the door, no telegram, so surely that means he is safe? And that is enough for me.

Freda says her brother's got the luck of the innocent, though I haven't a clue what that means and nor do I believe it, either. Were Ray and Johnnie not innocent enough to be saved? May they rest in peace, wherever they lie.

Monday 18 November 1918

ALL over the world, on November 11, 1918, people were celebrating, dancing in the streets, drinking champagne, hailing the armistice that meant the end of the war. But at the front there was no celebration. Many soldiers believed the Armistice only a temporary measure and that the war would soon go on.

As night came, the quietness, unearthly in its penetration, began to eat into their souls. The men sat around log fires, the first they had ever had at the front. They were trying to reassure themselves that there were no enemy batteries spying on them from the next hill and no German bombing planes approaching to blast them out of existence. They talked in low tones. They were nervous.

After the long months of intense strain, of

keying themselves up to the daily mortal danger, of thinking always in terms of war and the enemy, the abrupt release from it all was physical and psychological agony. Some suffered a total nervous collapse. Some, of a steadier temperament, began to hope they would someday return to home and the embrace of loved ones. Some could think only of the crude little crosses that marked the graves of their comrades. Some fell into an exhausted sleep. All were bewildered by the sudden meaninglessness of their existence as soldiers. What was to come next? They did not know, and hardly cared. Their minds were numbed by the shock of peace. The past consumed their whole consciousness. The present did not exist, and the future was inconceivable.

This is a cutting from a feature in the *Daily Sketch*. It makes me so sad to think about the 'crude little crosses' which might be the only thing that marks my brothers' graves, and I pray that we might one day see them laid to rest in a proper place, where we can visit and spend some time with them, that time we've been denied.

It set me to wondering about the living, and whether Alfie is one of those with a 'steadier temperament', or one of the other types? Does he find the future inconceivable? I have been so wrapped up with planning his homecoming (in my mind I've been imagining a party with banners and barrels of beer, a feast of meat pies and mash and then, of course, some quiet time just for ourselves), that I haven't for one moment considered that he might actually be worried about returning to 'normal life'.

Saturday 14th December 1918

Nearly a month has passed since my last entry but it is so difficult to keep up this diary when I am still working hard and so little seems to be happening.

Rationing is getting worse and there seems no end in sight. Meat, butter and sugar are all very short, though surely the blockades must have stopped by now and supplies will start up shortly. Pa hoped to recruit a new boy to help him in the butcher's shop but with hardly any meat to sell he's opening just a couple of days a week and barely making enough to pay the rent. It's only from my earnings and the little that Ma makes taking in mending that we manage to cover the other bills.

So I don't know what we'll do for money, now my job is finishing. At the end of our shift today the boss called us all together and told us that the factory will close early for Christmas – i.e. at the end of this week – and would not be re-opening. Of course we'd been expecting it, but that didn't stop it being a real shock. Some of the girls were in tears.

'Merry Christmas, maties, thanks for working your fingers to the bone and ruining your complexions for the past few years. Now you can go back to being obedient little housewives,' Freda whispered as we watched the boss's departing back.

When we clocked off this afternoon someone started to sing, softly at first: 'Good-bye-ee, good-bye-ee, wipe the tears, baby dear, from your eye-ee', till all the rest of us picked it up and there was a great chorus of us going down the street.

It's not just the pay I'll miss. It's a terrible job, dangerous and all (none of us can forget the explosion at Silvertown), but we've had such a good time with the other girls and made so many good friends here, it will be a wrench to leave them.

Some of the men are starting to come home now and most seem to be in good heart. The Nelson is doing great trade and the dance halls are busy. But yesterday a young stranger came into the corner shop when I was buying needles and thread for Ma. He looked like a ghost, so pale and thin. When he came to the counter and spoke, he could only manage a hoarse kind of whisper and struggled to get his breath, but I recognised the voice from somewhere. It was only later I realised that it was Percy Gittins, who used to be a great lardy lump at my old school and terrorised the smaller boys. Now he was reduced to a wraith who walked in a shuffle and could barely speak.

'Must have been gassed,' Ma said, when I told her about it later. 'Destroys their lungs.'

The lost generation, they're calling it. All the

sacrifices they've made. Was it really worth it? That's the main topic of conversation in the pub these days.

Still no word from Alfie.

Sunday 15th December

Ma helped me cook a meat pie for Sunday dinner, the first I've ever made.

She'd decided it was time to cheer us all up and invited the Barkers over, too. Before the war they used to be always in and out of each other's houses, Freda's parents and mine but, after Ray and Johnnie died, Ma said she felt so angry with anyone whose sons were still alive that she could barely stand to be in the same room as them.

Of course when Alfie and me got married she had to be nice to them, and the Barkers are now part of our extended family, being my in-laws and all. So I really appreciated that Ma was 'extending the hand of friendship' as she says, and offered to help with the cooking.

Pa came home on Friday with some scraps of meat, mostly beef, pork and rabbit that he'd been collecting over the week, he said, that were too small to sell, and some streaky rashers, a lump of dripping and a bag of bones for the jelly stock. We started boiling and skimming the stock on Friday evening and yesterday morning we chopped up the meat together with potato, a few carrots and spices, and made the pastry by boiling the dripping with water and mixing the flour into it – what a lovely sticky mixture!

When we were ready to build the pie we rolled out the pastry and pressed it up the sides of the ring with our fingers till it reached the top, lined the inside with bacon and then laid the layers of meat inside until we were ready to give it a lid. We pinched the edges to make a pretty crust and Ma cut out some leaves to decorate the top but we couldn't afford a precious egg for the glaze like she said you're supposed to.

Once it had cooked we let it cool for a bit then poured the stock in through a hole in the top and let it all cool properly in the larder. Ma says the jelly seals the air out of the meat so it would last several weeks if needed, a bit like how a tin can works, she said. But that pie smelled so good and was such a pretty sight that my mouth watered just to look at it, so it was never going to last long around here. I was so curious to see whether the jelly had set properly, I could hardly wait for today to cut it open.

It had taken an age to make, but the end result was delicious and the dinner was a great success. Everyone loved the pie and said we should go into business making them. The Barkers were in great spirits and brought two jugs of ale with them which made us all very merry. First of all we toasted to peace, and to the memory of Ray and Johnnie, my two brave brothers, and to all those others who weren't coming home.

Then they made me blush all over when they toasted the newly-weds who would soon be reunited, and Pa let slip that he'd been thinking that when he gets home we might have a proper wedding reception for me and Alfie to make up for what we missed at the time. Perhaps in the parish hall, he said, and I got so excited that I nearly hugged him. Freda said this time I should have a proper wedding dress ('but she can't wear white, not now,' some joker said) and she could have a proper bridesmaid's dress.

The talk got round to politics and the fact the Kaiser has now actually, formally, abdicated but an armistice was one thing, what we needed was a proper peace treaty. Mr Barker said he'd heard there were going to be discussions in the New Year so that all those countries who had been fighting, and been fought over, could get back to normal life again. Everyone agreed that Germany should be properly punished for starting such a terrible war.

Friday 20th December
Last day at the factory. We got paid up to the end of the month which is a bonus, because I have no idea what I'll do after Christmas. I'll have to find work somewhere but the newspapers are all reporting that jobs should be reserved for returning servicemen. I agree with that, it's only fair, but what about us women who have worked hard all this time? Are we to be sent back to the kitchen?

Here's a cutting I kept from the *Daily Mail*:

THE world is fresh and new for womenhood. It is not possible for us to go back to what we were before the flame of war tried us as in a fire. And why should we?'

Still no word from Alfie and I have given up hoping he'll be home for Christmas.

Sunday 22nd December

Freda has a new beau called Claude which sounded like a made-up name to me till he explained that his mother was French. Anyway he uses too much hair oil, flashes his money around and has all kinds of airs and graces, even using a cigarette holder! She is all doe-eyed about him, not the usual feisty Freda I'm used to.

When I asked him what he did during the war he mumbled something vague so I suspect it wasn't anything very valiant, and he's not wearing uniform nor an injury band. I am trying to reserve judgement but first impressions are not good, which is a worry. I so want her boyfriend/husband to be a straight sort of chap like Alfie, so that we can all be friends together.

Monday 23rd December

It's our first wedding anniversary, and I can't summon up the slightest spark of excitement about Christmas because Alfie is not here to celebrate with me.

Ma got out the photos and they reminded me what a rushed affair our wedding was – no special outfits and just down the Town Hall followed by drinks at

The Nelson – but he was being posted on Boxing Day and we were determined to tie the knot before he went. We've known each other forever, ever since our first day at school and he came dashing round the playground to meet Freda and his ma at coming out time. I liked him more than the other boys, even then, because he was the only one who didn't pull my pigtails.

Though I pleaded with him not to, he was dead set on signing up as soon as he became of an age. And when he was about to turn nineteen and got back on Christmas leave before they were all shipped out to France, he asked me to marry him. Neither of us said it, but we both knew it was 'just in case'.

I'm struck by how young we look, even though it was only a year ago. He's in uniform, of course, and all his lovely curls shorn off into that horrible army haircut. His face is already leaner with all the exercise he'd been doing on training, his chubby cheeks disappearing and, although it's hard to see under the bulk of his jacket, his chest and arms were already shaping up nicely. I thought him the handsomest boy in the world.

All I had to wear at short notice was the navy blue wool serge dress that matches the colour of my eyes. It looks unfashionably long, now that hemlines are rising, and not helped by the low heels I always have to wear, since Alfie's only an inch or so taller than me. I put my hair up under a black narrow-brimmed hat borrowed from his mum that Ma trimmed with some netting that matched the dress.

My face is split with a grin like a monkey, partly from the happiness of the moment but also to stop my teeth chattering with the cold, it being a bitter day and me being too vain to wear my ugly old topcoat.

There were no fresh flowers to be had at that time of year of course, but a neighbour lent me a posy of artificial roses, which I'm gripping with white knuckles as we pose on the Town Hall steps, me with the grin and him with his strangely shorn hair and a faraway look, as if his mind is already on his big adventure.

The second photo is with the families posed in the lounge bar of The Nelson after the ceremony: Alfie and me, Ma and Pa, Freda and my new in-laws, Mr and Mrs Barker. Pa is on the edge of the group and I noticed for the first time tonight that there's a space next to him at the edge of the photograph: as if we've left a space for Johnnie and Ray. Johnnie was already dead by then, of course, and Ray was out in France. It's tempting to draw their faces onto the gap, because if it is possible to conjure up the presence of the dead by the power of thoughts from the living, they were definitely there in spirit that day.

He promised me a weekend in Brighton when he gets home. I wish! A letter would do me, right now.

Tuesday 24th December
I had a miserable Christmas Eve. The Nelson was packed with newly-home soldiers and their families

celebrating together. Everyone was in high spirits and why not, it's our first Christmas of peace, after all?

But I had no Alfie, and I had to put up with Freda and her new beau Claude canoodling all the time without a thought for anyone else. I can't bring myself to like him and I wish he would just tell the truth about what he did during the war. He seems to have too many sophisticated ways and too much money, and I can't help wondering whether he's one of those black marketeers who Pa says should be shot at dawn.

Ma couldn't take it, and went home early. It was bad enough when all mothers seemed to be in the same boat, but the pain is even harder to bear now the war is over, and everyone else's sons and brothers are returning. I worry about her: she is pale and listless and although we tell her that getting on with something will make her feel better – even just taking Bessie for a walk up the park – she prefers to sit in the house by the fire. Which is all very well but coal is getting so short and pricey we can ill afford to keep the fire banked up all the time. This time of year there are no vegetables growing in our little plot at the back, which she would normally tend, and there's been no laundry or mending coming in of late, either. Everyone's pulling in their horns at the moment.

Most of the time she won't allow us to mention them. But sometimes she says: 'If only we could bury my boys, so's we'd have a grave to lay flowers on.'

For the lack of a grave, she's turned their bedroom into a shrine, with nothing touched since Ray's last leave home. She sneaks in there when no-one else is around and, on their birthdays she places cards in the room, same as at Christmas, addressed to them as if they were alive.

I like to go in there too, from time to time, and think about my brothers, and what they might have become had they been allowed to grow into men, with wives and families and homes of their own.

A niggling worry eats at me: when Alfie comes back we won't be able to afford a house of our own until we both get some work. He's got a room at his parents' place, of course, but it's tiny. So we'd have to stay here, and my room is only big enough for a single bed. The most obvious thing would be for us to have the boys' room, but I can't see Ma ever accepting that.

What seems to upset Pa most is the fact that the boys won't be around for him to train up as butchers, and there'll be no-one to take over the family business my grandfather started back in the last century. Perhaps he could take on Alfie, now that he's family?

All this thinking about my brothers has made me sad. It's a bitter coincidence that they both died at the very same age, one I haven't even reached myself, yet:

RIP: Johnnie Appleby: b. 17th January 1897 d. 1st July 1916, on the first day of the Battle of The Somme, aged 19 years and 6 months.

RIP: Ray Appleby: b. 7th April 1898 d. 13th October 1917 at Passchendaele, aged 19 years and 6 months.

Friday 27th December

ANOTHER RED LETTER DAY!

This time it's a real letter! The best Christmas present of all, even if it was a couple of days late. It has taken over two weeks to arrive.

> *12th December 1918*
> *My darling Rose,*
> *At last I can write with good news. We are being demobbed! They say it should be next week or the week after so there's a chance I might be home for Christmas or at least soon after. It's been chaos over here since the Armistice and they say it will take a while to get us all back to the coast and across the Channel. I am so impatient to see you again. Please send my best regards to your parents.*
> *Your loving husband, Alfie.*

I'm sure I shall not sleep tonight with the excitement, so I'll keep on writing until I feel tired.

Christmas was a very quiet affair and Pa had sold the few turkeys and chickens he'd managed to lay his hands on, so he brought home more scraps, bones and dripping and we made two more large pies – one for the Barkers and one for us. Mrs B was so grateful when we took it round and said again that they were so delicious we should start selling them. It certainly set me thinking. Pies are ideal for making a little meat go a long way, so there would surely be a good demand while rationing is still on?

'What about you and me going into business, Pa?' I said, only half joking, and although he looked a little shocked because he thinks a woman's place is in the home, I could see him thinking. I've been a working girl for over two years now, so I've proved that I can do it. Of course he'd hoped my brothers would follow him into the shop, but all he's got left is a daughter.

My presents were a new scarf and a lovely bar of Pears, and Freda gave me some Elizabeth Arden talcum powder which smells delicious. The yellow munitions tinge is almost gone from my skin and I'm seriously considering getting my hair cut into a bob. It would be so much easier to manage. Freda said that Alfie wouldn't like it. Well, he might be her brother but he's *my* husband, so I should know what he likes and doesn't like, shouldn't I?

Tuesday 31st December. New Year's Eve.
Writing this at one o'clock in the morning but I am so excited I cannot sleep. At last this year is over, and we can start to celebrate peace properly.

All the talk in The Nelson this evening was about plans for a public celebration next summer and they're going to set up a Peace Committee to organise it, though some people are already saying they shouldn't waste money on official occasions but should give the money to the returning servicemen. I agree with this. We should just have an enormous street party (lots more pie customers for me!) and then provide proper houses and good jobs for everyone who fought in the war.

Heaven knows where Alfie and me will get to live, otherwise. And I must get a job or I'll go crazy hanging around the house, getting under Ma's feet, as she says. I can see her point: I've taken over her kitchen completely for the past three days, making pies – twenty in all! We've only got two pie rings but I managed to borrow two more from Mrs Barker. To make the smaller ones Ma asked Pa to make me what she called a 'dolly', which is a simple piece of wood like a very fat rolling pin which you just press the pastry around with your hands, pulling up the sides to make the casing. You fill it with meat and cover and crimp it as usual before baking. It's a bit of a trick, and some of the pies collapsed at first, but we soon got the hang of it.

Then I took them down to The Nelson this afternoon and sold every single one. Plus one or two said 'keep the change, love'. I came back with nine shillings – which would buy me a single shoe (!) so if I can do it again I'll have nearly enough to buy a pair. Not bad for a few hours' work, and Pa hasn't exactly said whether he wants any cash back for the meat etc. Bert says to make it official we ought to ask for people's coupons, but he's not telling if I'm not. Besides, the amount of meat in each of them is hardly worth the effort of accounting for.

1919

Thursday 2nd January

> Dearest Rose,
> I've hurt my leg so am in a base hospital at
> Boulogne. Nothing too much to worry about.
> They are sending me back to a hospital in
> London soon to get it sorted out. I will try to
> send a telegram when I know.
> Your ever-loving Alfie.

Ma and I looked up Boulogne on a map in the library
and it is on the coast of France, just over the water
from England. Almost within touching distance. Of
course it is worrying that he is injured but it doesn't
sound too serious. They always try to stop you fretting by telling you only half the story, if that, but this
time I believe him. Now the war is over, what would
he need to conceal from me?

But I can't sit around at home waiting and
wondering. On Monday I am going to look for

another job. Freda and Claude are still thick as thieves so I don't see much of her at the moment. I think she's given up the idea of going back to work. She probably hopes Claude will have enough money for both of them. I've still no idea what he does for a living.

Tuesday 7th January
Depressing day, bitter cold and trying to snow. My feet are blistered and my legs feel like lead weights. I must have covered miles. This morning I put on my best skirt and coat and walked and walked, going into every factory and workshop I could find, showing them my letter of reference from the munitions factory, but they just looked at me as if I was mad.

'Sorry, dear,' they'd say – or something like it – sucking their teeth and gazing past me. 'Can't help you. We've got no vacancies, and a list as long as your arm of returning soldiers wanting work.' The kinder ones tried to be helpful by suggesting other places I might try, but most of them just turned me away without so much as a by-your-leave.

Besides being exhausted, my head is weary and confused. It's right that the boys should have jobs to come home to, so that they can start to build their lives again. But we girls have worked hard, too, and in some dangerous occupations. Surely we should be given some opportunities as well? But who should get priority? The boys, I suppose, but I still feel the smart of all those sneery looks.

I talked about it with Ma at teatime. She says her generation never expected to get jobs and nor did they want to. 'Too much to do at home,' she said. 'Besides, if you girls all go out to work, who'll stay at home to look after the babies?' I told her I didn't have any babies just yet, just in case she hadn't noticed and she barked back at me to watch my cheek. 'Any roads, even without babies, someone needs to do the washing and ironing and cooking and cleaning.'

When I said that Alfie and me would share it when we got home from work, she nearly choked on her bread and jam. 'Catch your father cooking dinner or washing the dishes? When he's been on his feet in the shop all day? Not a cat-in-hell's chance. And I've no doubt your young Alfred will feel the same.' It was good to see Ma getting some of her spirit back, even though it was only because she was annoyed at me giving her the lip.

Tonight I got to thinking about politics. In the election before Christmas, women were allowed to vote for the first time, but I couldn't because we have to wait until we are thirty! It's a stupid rule because when I am twenty-one, in two years' time, I can become a Member of Parliament. Perhaps I'll find out how I can get elected, so that I can campaign for equal rights for women in work and get us the vote at twenty-one, like the men.

I read in the newspaper that 18,000 soldiers marched to Brighton Town Hall yesterday demonstrating about the slowness of demobilisation. There was a photograph of some of the demobbed lads who had dressed up in crinolines and bonnets to complain about the lack of jobs and being treated 'little better than women'.

It would be funny if things weren't so serious.

Monday 13th January
　　AT SOUTHAMPTON STOP WILL PHONE
　　YOU NELSON 6PM STOP ALFIE

HURRAY! Alfie is safe on home soil at last!

It had nearly turned seven and I'd pretty much given up hope when Bert shouted that there was a 'call for Miss Rose'. My heart nearly jumped out of my chest, and I almost flew across the bar and through into their office.

Our conversation went a bit like this:

'Alfie?' (though who else I thought it could be, I don't know).

'Yes. It's me.' For an awkward moment, neither of us knew what to say. 'Listen, I've only got tuppence for the phone. And I had to borrow a pair of crutches to get here. There are never enough to go round. I can't talk long.'

'What's the matter with your leg? When are they letting you home?'

'Don't worry it's nothing too serious, but they say it'll take a few weeks yet. They're going to move me to a hospital in London, though.'

'So I can come and see you?'

'With a bit of luck. Will you let my folks know, and Freda?'

'Course I will. I'll pop round right away. It's so wonderful to hear your voice. I love you, Alfie.'

'I'll let you know when I'm being transferred.' I could hear him sigh and felt sure he was about to say something important, but all he managed was: 'Oh, Rose, it's . . .' when the pips started and I couldn't hear the rest of the sentence, then the line cut off.

Freda's first question was: what did he sound like?

Just like the usual Alfie, I said. Not soppy, that was never his style, but perfectly matter-of-fact. He told me nothing about his injury except that it was going to take a while to heal, and he would probably be transferred to a hospital in London fairly soon.

'Well that's a blessing,' his ma said. 'At least we'll be able to see him for ourselves. I never trust the telephone.'

In the newspapers today was a report about how Lloyd George had talked to 3,000 soldiers who marched on Downing Street complaining about the slow demob process. I'd rather Alfie hadn't been injured, but at least he's home, unlike so many thousands of others still waiting.

Sunday 19th January

I have been scanning the newspapers for vacancies but absolutely NOTHING is coming up. Bert at The Nelson has asked me to make him more pies – he'd like twenty each weekend. But I had to turn him down – it is impossible to get hold of enough meat or flour, even though it's not rationed.

Sunday 26th January 1919

It's been such a day I barely know where to start.

On Friday we received this telegram:

PLEASED TO INFORM PTE A BARKER TO BE TRANSFERRED
KING GEORGE MILITARY HOSP LONDON
SAT 25 JAN STOP

I nearly whooped out loud with joy. Waterloo is only a couple of miles walk away, or two buses: up the Old Kent Road and then change at the Bricklayers' for Elephant and Castle. So close I could almost reach out and touch him.

Oh, we were so excited, all of us, and went to The Nelson to celebrate. Even Ma put on a brave face. Out of three boys in our two families, at least one of them has come back safely, so that's something. There are families along our street where every single male, fathers and sons included, will never return home.

Freda and me went to the public baths for a good old soak and hairwash yesterday evening, but I could barely sleep for excitement and the thoughts of what I was going to say and do when I saw my darling Alfie at last, after twelve long months.

This morning when I woke up, my heart sank: it

111

was snowing! What typical bloody luck. I rose early to tog up in my old blue serge and spent a great deal longer than usual on my hair (by the way, I have postponed having it cut off into a bob until I've asked Alfie's opinion. It seems only fair). Then me, Ma and Pa met Mr and Mrs Barker and Freda at the corner as arranged and although the side streets and pavements were all white, the Old Kent was still clear enough. We decided that walking would be difficult but, judging by the tracks, the buses were still running and one would come along soon. Ha!

So we waited, and waited, and waited. I was so impatient to see my lovely boy that I could barely keep still, thinking we could have been there by now if we'd walked, but I was wearing my Sunday best shoes that would have been ruined in the snow. By the time the bus finally arrived half an hour later, my feet were like blocks of ice.

When we got to the hospital around midday it was mayhem, with Red Cross ambulances and other military vehicles all queuing to unload stretchers and walking wounded. The place is enormous – five storeys high and taking up the whole of Stamford Street, corner to corner.

We went inside a great echoing foyer full of people taking no notice of us, and tried to find someone in charge. Pa got talking to a porter who told him the building had never been intended as a hospital, hence comings and goings were always chaotic. It was built as a government office but got taken over as a military hospital just after the war started and has been ever since. I'd been scanning the faces of every patient arriving just in case Alfie's transfer had been postponed until today, but the man explained that some patients are brought in through the tunnels which reach all the way to Waterloo station.

It was all so overwhelming that we began to despair of ever finding him today, after our cold and difficult journey. I even started to wonder whether his transfer might have been cancelled because of the snow. There were no seats, we were perishing and famished, and Mrs Barker started sniffling, though she was doing her best to conceal it, bless her soul. Pa and Mr B were busy approaching anyone who might be able to direct us to the right ward.

Eventually they asked a fierce-looking nurse wearing a white starched headdress like a nun, who said there were over sixty wards and nearly two thousand patients so how could she know the name of every single one? In any case, it wasn't visiting hours yet. We should come back at four o'clock.

This time I nearly started crying too, I was that disappointed. We had more than two hours to wait but how could we possibly afford to sit in a café all that time? But Pa and Mr Barker went into a confab and said they would stand us all a cuppa and a teacake if we could find somewhere nearby.

When we got back at four, feeling a lot better, the place was a good deal calmer and we joined the queue of anxious families waiting at the front desk. The nurse in charge looked on her list and directed us to 'Ward 42, fourth floor'. As we set off she shouted at us to come back.

'Excuse me, how many are there of you in this party?'

'Six,' Pa said.

'Next of kin?'

'His parents, sister and wife, and parents-in-law.'

'Don't you know that it's only two at a time by each bedside?' My, she was a right battleaxe. 'You'll have to go in by turns. Visiting hours end at six o'clock prompt.'

I checked the huge clock on the wall and did a quick calculation: it was already half past four – we would have, at most, half an hour for each pair. Only thirty short minutes, after what had seemed like a lifetime.

My hand is cramped from writing so much. I'll have to carry on tomorrow.

They've started the Peace Conference, in Paris. Let's hope it works.

Monday 27th January
As we peeped through the door we could see a long room with iron bedsteads in a row down each side like – well, my first thought was that they looked like gravestones, because they were all white and neat and the people in them all in uniform pale blue hospital pyjamas, lying or sitting stock still so you barely saw them at first. Ma and Pa found a bench seat in the foyer at the top of the stairs, and told the rest of us to try our luck.

114

It didn't work.

'Only two persons by a bedside,' the nurse barked, but one of the patients, sitting up in bed half way down on the left, by a window, was waving and calling to us: 'Rose, Rose. Over here.' He could see us hesitating and he bellowed even louder: 'For Christ's sake, woman, let them in. She's my wife!'

Well, I wasn't waiting any longer, not for anyone, so I sprinted down the ward before anyone could stop me and threw my arms around him and held him tight and kissed him until he whispered, 'Ma's behind you, better give her a turn.' As he was hugging her, I stood back and took a proper gander at him. He was my Alfie, all right, but thin faced and ghostly pale which made his eyes look even deeper set and his eyelashes even longer, but his hair was growing back curly as ever, and his grin was just the same, cheeky and confidential, the kind of smile that feels like it's just for you, and you alone.

But under the bedcovers was some kind of box. What had happened to his legs? Mrs Barker took the chair and held his hand, and I sat on the bed till the nurse came and told me that was forbidden, so I stood and took his other hand.

She asked him how he was feeling and he grimaced. 'Been better. But at least I'm back in Blighty, and in good hands.'

I told him we couldn't wait to get him home and then, as casually as possible, asked what was up with his leg.

'Copped an unexploded bomb,' he said. 'One of ours and all, would you believe it, on Boxing Day when we was checking through the streets of this town for snipers. Our footsteps must have set it off. Couple of my mates took the full blast and died instantly, so I was the lucky one. They've tried to set it but the bones don't seem to want to heal on their own. They're going to operate tomorrow.'

Mrs Barker was shocked into silence, and her face had gone almost as pale as Alfie's, so I wittered on about what wonderful things surgeons can do these days and how he'd be out of here in no time. He just looked at me with those beautiful dark eyes and whispered, 'I love you, Rose Barker'. Of course that set me off, weeping tears of happiness and hugging him all over again.

After a bit, we realised that we ought to give the others time to see him too. I could hardly bear to be parted after such a few brief, precious moments; wanting to have him all to myself and not share it with anyone else.

As we walked back down the long length of the ward I started to look around and take in more of the surroundings – those thirty or so poor shadows of men with terrible injuries: arms missing, legs encased in plaster suspended by loops and pulleys, both eyes bandaged and even whole faces obscured by dressings. Heaven knows what lies beneath the bandages.

How lucky we are to have Alfie home with only an injured leg which will surely mend soon.

I went to the hospital again today with one of my home-made pies, a book and a new toothbrush, as he'd requested, as well as some warm clothes in case he is allowed out in a wheelchair, but they said he'd had the operation and was still recovering from the anaesthetic, so I should give it a couple of days before coming back again.

Sunday 2nd February 1919
It's been a difficult week. The operation to mend Alfie's leg went well, they told us, but then he started going downhill. It was his twenty-first birthday today, and when I went to visit with Freda and Mrs B, all bearing cards and little gifts, he was really out of it, delirious and muttering to himself and barely recognising us. It's an infection in the bone, the nurse said, but he's young and strong, he'll pull through. Looking at his dear face, white as the pillow, and the way his body shakes, I'm beginning to wonder.

I don't believe in God and never prayed once while he was away fighting because it seemed two-faced to do so. But tonight I am so afraid for my beautiful husband, and feeling so powerless to help him, that I actually kneeled beside my bed and whispered: 'Dear God, you have brought him home safely. Don't take him from me now.'

Wednesday 5th February
I barely know how to write this, it is too awful. I went to the hospital again today with Mrs Barker.

Alfie's bed was empty and I daren't even repeat the dreadful thought that entered my head. Then Matron called us over and said he was having another operation.

'It was gas gangrene, I'm afraid. Removing the injured limb is the only way to save his life,' she said.

At first the words didn't make any sense. Removing the injured limb? And then it hit me, like being knocked down by a steamroller. 'They're cutting his leg off?' Even though it was my voice the words seemed detached, as if they were coming from someone else's mouth.

'I'm afraid so, my dear,' she said. 'We had to act fast. The infection was spreading and if it reached the top of the leg it would almost certainly have killed him. I am so sorry.'

I felt suddenly, shockingly sick and made a dash for the basin by the side of the nurse's station, my head so giddy that I had to grip the cold white porcelain to stop myself falling. Surely this couldn't be happening? We'd read about men dying in the trenches with gangrene but in a clean English hospital like this one surely they could have stopped it, somehow? After a bit I went to sit down beside Mrs B and put my arm around her shoulders. Her whole body was shaking, and tears pouring down her cheeks.

'My poor darling boy,' she wailed. 'Went through a whole year in the trenches with hardly a scratch, and now . . .'

'They're saving his life,' I whispered. 'We're lucky to have him back at all.'

She squeezed my hand. 'You're right, dearie. Your poor dear brothers. At least my boy is alive.'

Monday 17th February

Can this week get any worse? My brother Johnnie would have been twenty-two today. Over tea we all sat and said hardly a word, then we each of us disappeared – Pa went back to work, Ma went up to the boys' room and I took Bessie for a walk and then over to see Freda.

She was miserable too, worried about Claude who hasn't been in touch for a couple of weeks. I could barely stop myself from shouting at her: you're concerned about that creepy man when my brothers are dead and your brother's had his leg cut off? But I didn't of course.

I feel too upset to write any more.

Wednesday 19th February

It's been a long haul, but Alfie seems to be pulling through, at last.

I've been to the hospital every day, sometimes with Mrs B and sometimes with Freda. Two days ago was the first time he recognised us, and today he was actually sitting up in bed. Matron says he's been eating and drinking. 'We'll have him out of here in no time,' she said, in her jolly way.

He is even thinner and paler than ever and says

very little. We bring him newspapers and pies, and the occasional bit of chocolate if we can get hold of it, and chatter away about things going on in the outside world: how Billy Brotherstone got drunk in The Nelson the night he got demobbed, climbed a drainpipe trying to reach his girlfriend's bedroom window, fell off and broke both his arms; how spraying the buses with disinfectant seems to be working because the cases of Spanish flu seem at last to be reducing; about the death of little Prince John, the Queen's son who had the fits; the miners' strikes and the worry about whether we'll have enough coal, and how everyone loves my pies.

The only thing we don't mention is his leg, or rather the lack of it, and I don't even know how much of it they've left him. Is there a knee, or did they have to cut that off too? It seems indelicate to ask.

Odd how a tragedy like this turns people back into strangers.

Sunday 9th March

Spring is here, the daffodils are out in the parks, and Alfie is finally recovering properly. At least, his body seems to be mending, though it's much harder to find out what's going on in his head.

They're getting him out of bed and he's learning to walk on crutches, which means at least that he can get to the toilet on his own. Matron told us he would probably be moved to a new hospital very soon, for fitting with an artificial leg. It'll be difficult, she said, because he's only got about eight inches of thighbone left after they cut out all the gangrene. He makes sure he's always in bed and covered up when we visit, but there's a very obvious dip in the sheet where his leg ends.

He still won't discuss it, and it's hard to get him to talk about anything, much. But he seems to enjoy it when I read to him from the newspapers, and he's eating the pies I bring him. Heaven knows what the future holds for us. I just try not to worry and persuade myself to take it day by day.

Gloomy news in the papers: another war has started, between Russia and Poland. When will it all end?

Sunday 16th March
Yesterday, Alfie was moved to Queen Mary's Hospital in Roehampton which is miles away, so I won't be able to visit him very often. We've agreed to write every day. I am trying to believe there will be a silver lining: perhaps it will be easier to communicate in writing. It's been impossible to talk to him in that big ward at King George's, especially since there's always been Freda, or Mrs B with me, and the other boys in the nearby beds listening, too.

Friday 21st March
I have written at least four letters to Alfie this week so when an envelope finally arrived for me this

morning my heart nearly leapt out of my chest and I rushed up to my room to read it in private.

Why was I ever foolish enough to imagine that we would be able to communicate more easily by letter? Here it is:

> Dearest Rose,
> Thank you for your letters. Am settling in fine.
> It's quieter here. Missing your pies.
> Love Alfie.

It's no good. I am going to have to find a way of visiting him.

BOOK 2

Rose Barker – PRIVATE

Wednesday 26th March

I went to visit Alfie yesterday; Pa stumped up the fare which was very generous of him. It took two buses and a train ride to get to Queen Mary's Hospital in Roehampton.

It's an enormous place like the grandest of stately homes in beautiful parkland with huge trees: cedars and oaks with the daffodils in bloom beneath them. As I walked up the driveway there were catcalls from the men sitting on seats and in wheelchairs around the gardens, and I didn't mind a bit. It made me smile to see them enjoying themselves in the first of the spring sunshine, after the troubles they'd surely been through. If it wasn't for the reason they're all here, I'd be a tiny bit envious of them.

So I was in high spirits when I finally found Alfie, not in a long dreary hospital ward like the King George, but in a posh drawing room with beautiful carpets, chintz three piece suites and standard lamps with fringed lampshades all around. The other men were playing dominoes or cards, or reading the papers for all the world like well-bred gentlemen in a country club. But Alfie was sat apart from the rest in a wheelchair, in the new pyjamas and dressing gown we'd bought for him by pooling our rations.

He was just staring out of the window with his hands in his lap.

When I said hello and kissed his cheek he didn't really respond, not a smile nor anything. 'You're looking a bit better,' I said, 'they must be looking after you well.' It was true: even though he was still painfully thin, his cheeks were a healthier colour.

'It's taken me ages to get here,' I carried on, by way of conversation, 'but I didn't mind a bit because it's a lovely day and I was coming to see you. Will they let us go outside together, d'you think, like the others?'

I took off my coat and went to hang it on the rack by the door, and when I got back to him it was all I could do not to gasp. His face was screwed up with the veins standing out on his temple and the side of his neck as if he might be having some kind of fit. I sat down, stroked his hand and just said, 'Alfie, Alfie, it's all right, Alfie, I'm here now.'

And then, to my horror, he let out his breath with a great sighing groan which caught into a sob, and tears started running down both cheeks. It was such a shock to see him out of control like this. He's the strong one and I'd never seen him cry before, not even when he was fourteen and broke his arm playing football.

I gave him a handkerchief, but he made no effort to wipe his eyes or reply to my questions, but just sat there weeping and gasping for breath as if the end of the world had come. So I went for a glass of water and finally managed to make him take a few gulps which stopped the sobbing but not the tears, which by now I was wiping away myself, since he seemed incapable of lifting his hands.

He muttered something under his breath which I couldn't hear, and I pressed him to repeat it. 'For Christ's sake go home, Rose,' he said. 'I don't want to see all that ****ing pity in your ****ing eyes.'

I've never heard him swear like that before, and it made me cross that he was being so crude, so I got all school-marmy on him (as he might have said, before all this).

'Look, I've spent two whole hours travelling to see my husband and if you think I'm going all that way back without having a proper conversation with him you've got another think coming,' I said, sharply and a bit too loudly because some of the men nearby turned their heads, taking a quick glance before turning away with embarrassment.

Getting angry seemed to work. He wiped his own face and looked at me for the first time, his eyes all bloodshot from the weeping. 'Oh Christ,' he sighed. 'I'm such a ****ing mess, Rose, can't stop breaking down like this. Seeing you just makes it worse; you're too beautiful to waste your time with a cripple like me. Go away and find yourself a proper husband.'

I'm not sure why I found this funny, but it made me laugh. 'All right then, Alfred Barker,' I said. 'Just wait here a moment till I go and make myself ugly. Perhaps I'll hack off my hair and daub my face with spots. Will you have me then?'

For a moment he looked horrified that I should be joking about his misery, but then his face cracked and he started to laugh too, and I was soon hugging him and we were giggling together like naughty schoolchildren.

Not long after that a nurse came round with a tea trolley and I took out the home-made cheesy scones that I'd brought, and we had a nice snack before I got permission from the Matron to take Alfie out into the sunshine. We had a happy time trundling along and laughing because I couldn't push his wheelchair in a straight line, and kept getting it stuck in flowerbeds, before we found a bench free and sat in the sunshine, chatting away as if none of those hysterics had ever happened.

Least said, soonest mended, has always been my motto, but when he began to tell me what he'd been going through with the artificial leg fittings and the pain of his stump, not to mention the agonising 'phantom pains' in the leg that isn't even there any more, it helped me understand why he might be feeling so low.

It is going to take some time to get my own beloved Alfie back, but we will do it, together. I am determined.

Friday 28th March
Bert's been on at me again about the pies, says he wants thirty for Easter. Suggested I might decorate them with bunnies or some such nonsense. When I

told him it was impossible to get the flour, not to mention the eggs you're supposed to use to glaze the pies, he asked me how much I would need and then said, 'If I can get hold of supplies, would you make them pies?' and I had to say I would. To be honest I am so absorbed in thinking about Alfie and preparing for him to come home that I'd rather not be thinking about pies.

But we could certainly do with the money, if we are going to set up our own home.

Saturday 5th April

ALFIE IS COMING HOME!

I went with Ma and Mrs Barker for a visit today and they told us that he will be home in time for Easter, which is just a fortnight away. At first he was quite cheerful, almost like the Alfie I once knew, talking about how, as soon as he is demobbed, he'll go back to the warehouse because apparently employers have been told they must keep soldiers' jobs for them. I can't imagine how he will ever again be strong enough to hump sacks about the place, but I suppose they might have some lighter work he could do. Desk work is probably off: he never was much of a one for reading and writing.

I've learned from reading the newspapers that he will have to be assessed for a disability pension. Because he has lost most of his leg he should get 70%, but since he was only in service for under two years it won't amount to much. He's got his army payments in the Post Office of course but I don't suppose that will last long. He will definitely need a job of some kind, to get back to 'normal', whatever that turns out to be.

The sun was shining again and the Matron suggested we should go out into the garden to give him some practice with his artificial leg. When I asked if I could see it, he scowled and asked did I have to? But then I said, 'It's going to be as much a part of my life as it is of yours', so he gave in and pointed to something hidden under a towel beside the cabinet next to his bed. Like an idiot I immediately went over and pulled off the sheet without a second thought, quite unprepared for what I was going to see.

It really is a ferocious-looking contraption made of wood (from willow trees, he said, and later we had a laugh about how he could carve it into a cricket bat if he got fed up with wearing it) with metal hinges at the knee and uncomfortable-looking straps that hold it onto his waist and around his shoulder. At the top is a leather socket where his stump fits, which was hard to look at. But the worst thing was the foot, still with a sock and shoe on it, which made the whole thing look like a real leg that had just got separated from its owner.

I was so shocked it was all I could do to keep my voice level and ask him if he'd like any help getting dressed.

He said a bit sharply that it'd be best if I let him be for twenty minutes, so I went out into the garden where Ma and Mrs B were waiting. When I got back he was completely dressed in civvy clothes, standing by his bed on his two legs, looking so pale and proud that I nearly cried, seeing him upright for the first time in over a year, looking almost like the man I married before he went away to war. I tried to hug him but it was difficult with the two walking sticks in the way, so I just took his arm and said, 'Tell me how to help you.'

He shrugged me off and said he could manage on his own thank you very much, and we set off down the ward on a slow, painful journey, one step at a time. The stairs were even trickier but he gritted his teeth and managed them all on his own, and then, as we emerged into the sunshine, Mrs Barker and Ma rushed forward and wanted to hug him too.

My brave darling Alfie was so determined to prove that he could walk all the way but after a short distance I could see he was starting to wobble and his artificial leg was dragging on the gravel, so I said I was feeling a bit tired and could we have a rest on the next bench, which he accepted, even though we all knew it was a lie.

I am going to have to learn new ways of helping without undermining his dignity. That'll be my biggest challenge, when he gets home.

Sunday 6th April
On the way back, Mrs Barker started on about where Alfie and me would live once he comes home. Of

course she doesn't know what Ma feels about the boys' room so I can't really blame her for jumping in with her size nines.

'You are both very welcome with us,' she said, and I thanked her quickly, hoping that she wouldn't go on about it. But she went on anyway, saying that of course Freda's room was the larger of the two, so perhaps she could persuade her to swap with us.

Honestly I cannot think of anything worse than starting my married life with just a thin wall between us and where my best friend is sleeping, especially since Freda would certainly be furious about having to move into a tiny box room instead. The only sensible option is for Alfie and me to have the room my brothers used to share, but would Ma ever get used to the idea? I'm certainly not going to be the first to suggest it, for fear of setting her off.

Tonight when I was getting ready for bed I heard raised voices downstairs. Ma and Pa were arguing about something. Afterwards I heard her coming upstairs and though she was tiptoeing I could tell by the squeak of the floorboards that she was going into the boys' room. A bit later I heard her sobbing.

If only we could have their bodies back, she might be able to accept it and move on.

Monday 7th April
It is Ray's birthday. He would have turned twenty-one today. Everyone is very sombre.

Tuesday 8th April

I've been in a strange mood all day, probably not helped by the events of the weekend and the realisation that, at last, my darling Alfie will be coming home. Instead of feeling excited, as a wife should be, I find myself apprehensive, even a bit tearful, about it all.

It's not so much the practical things, such as the business of where we are going to live or what we will live on. We can go together to see the housing people and the pension office and that will all get resolved, one way or another, before long. And with our two families with their own houses and living so close by, we will never be actually homeless, as some poor folk are these days.

It's not even anything to do with his leg, or rather lack of one. Seeing his wooden leg for the first time certainly gave me a shock, but I am sure I'll get used to it. And when Freda asked whether the idea of his stump was a bit off-putting I replied, quite honestly, that I am not the least bit squeamish about it and while it might be strange at first, and a bit embarrassing for both him and me, after a while I would probably just come to see it as a normal part of Alfie, my beautiful boy.

No, I think my mood is to do with something deeper. After mulling it over this evening I've come to the conclusion that it's because, since Alfie and I got engaged and married, I've changed. After the worry of the past couple of years it's hardly surprising:

losing two brothers, becoming an only child, working at the factory, doing a good job and earning my own money, gaining respect from the boss and enjoying the company of the other girls. I was always of an independent mind – too much so, Ma would say – but now I've grown up, become more self-reliant, tougher and less sentimental. I was just a girl, and now I feel much more like a woman, capable of making my own decisions, determining my own future.

Not that I think it will trouble Alfie, in fact he might even like the new version of me. And it doesn't make me love him any less, not in the slightest.

Perhaps what's worrying me most is that he will have changed, too. He's lost a limb, for start, and has to get used to using an artificial leg, with all the difficulties that will bring. But what of the effect the past two years will have had on him? He was eighteen and just a fresh-faced boy when he joined up. Okay, he'd been in work at the warehouse for a while but he was still carefree and a bit crazy. Then, as soon as he turned nineteen, he was out on the front line and although he's never said anything about it, I'm sure he's seen things that no man should have to experience, endured conditions that would be cruel for animals, been utterly terrified for his life much of the time, and suffered the excruciating pain of his injury not to mention seeing his friends blown to bits. That sort of thing is bound to change a man. Will he be the Alfie I fell in love with, I wonder?

Oh, it's no good worrying like this. We are married now, and will have to make a new life for ourselves, come what may.

Monday 14th April
Spent all weekend making pies! Pork pies and game pies, large and small ones! I decorated the game pies with pastry rabbits, just as Bert asked, and then took them to The Nelson where he's going to store them ready for Easter.

He was pleased as punch, and gave me 24/- less 3/- for the flour and eggs he'd got hold of for me. A whole guinea profit, so long as Pa doesn't ask me to pay for the meat and Ma doesn't ask for a contribution to the coal! It's set me wondering all over again whether I should go into business with Pa. When rationing is lifted and he can afford to take Alfie on as an apprentice, we could have a husband-and-wife partnership. But I'm letting my imagination run away with me!

Easter Sunday 20 April
Alfie's homecoming has been such a disaster, I barely know where to begin.

It is well past midnight and I have been sitting here on the sofa crying for the past half hour. I think my marriage might be over.

Although he was set against it, I insisted on going to collect him on Maundy Thursday, and the journey home was very tough. Not that he complained at all, but I could see in his face that he was gritting his teeth with pain much of the time. Just getting onto the platform at the back of the bus was hard enough let alone the walking at either end, and he wouldn't accept any help at all, of course. People could see he was disabled and a few came up to shake his hand and say 'Good on yer, laddie,' and that sort of thing, but he just kept his face down and didn't want to talk.

When we finally arrived home it was nearly teatime and everyone was there: Ma and Pa, the Barker parents, Freda and creepy Claude, all in the street and cheering, which brought the neighbours out too, and they all applauded and came up to clap him on the shoulder. Poor boy, he was nearly dead with the effort but he managed to smile and act friendly until we got inside and then he collapsed into a chair and looked around in a kind of daze at everyone crammed into our little parlour, as if he was seeing it for the first time. Of course they were all talking at once and asking him questions about the journey and the hospital, and what it had been like over there, till I had to jump in and tell them to give him a break because he was exhausted.

He scowled at me when I said this, but I knew that deep down he was grateful because after that people started chatting about other things and he was able just to listen and ease back into our lives slowly. Ma served tea and cake and then the beer began to flow and everyone started to get quite merry but after just a single pint, Alfie's eyes began to close and his head slumped to one side. We began to whisper for fear of waking him and, when he didn't stir, Ma shepherded everyone into the back room saying we should let the poor boy sleep. She fetched a rug and wrapped it around him, tucking it in so carefully and tenderly I could see she was cherishing him like her own son, which made me feel weepy and happy all at the same time.

Around seven o'clock, when the Barkers had gone, he woke and ate a sandwich and when I asked him if he wanted anything more, he said he just wanted to sleep. Well, I'd turned down Mrs Barker's offer of Freda's room, and the business of the boys' room in our house hasn't been sorted out yet, so I'd resigned myself to the fact that we would have to share my single bed. We did it before, so I reckoned we could probably put up with it for a few nights longer.

We went upstairs and I brought water for him to wash but when I offered to help he muttered rather grumpily that he was perfectly capable of doing it himself, thank you, and would I leave him be for the moment? By the time I went back up again, he was already asleep taking up the whole bed, and didn't stir even when I kissed his forehead, so I decided that it was probably best to leave him be, and spent the night on the sofa.

Yesterday, Easter Saturday, we went to the Barkers' for lunch and tea, then at six o'clock some of Alfie's mates came round and took us off to The Nelson where everyone stood him a pint till the glasses were lined up all along the bar. It was wonderful to see him relaxing at last, laughing and joking almost like his old self, but it began to get a bit out of hand and Bert told them firmly to quieten down or take themselves off home.

One of the lads suggested they went elsewhere and Alfie seemed happy to go along but I was weary by now and thought it might be best to let him have some freedom from my watchful eyes, so said I would go home and wait for him.

About midnight I was snoozing on the sofa when there was such a racket outside I nearly jumped out of my skin. There was Alfie on the doorstep, pickled as a newt and completely unable to stand, being supported by two of his mates. 'Sorry, Mrs Rose,' one of them slurred, as the others sniggered. 'Can we bring him in?'

So this time he slept on the sofa and I went to my own bed, tossing and turning and thinking bitterly what a poor start this had been to our new life as man and wife.

Tonight was supposed to be different. He apologised for his behaviour yesterday and has been the perfect gentleman all day, making polite conversation when his parents came round to ours for Easter Sunday lunch of roast spring lamb, roast potatoes, greens, gravy and mint sauce followed by apple pie and custard. He ate like a horse and even had second and third helpings!

Come this evening, though, we went up to bed together and I tried to kiss him but he turned away and told me to wait downstairs while he got into bed. It's understandable, I told myself, that he doesn't want me to see him wearing his artificial leg, not just yet, so I agreed, but when I went up again it felt uncomfortable and embarrassing getting undressed and into my nightdress, as he watched. On the only other nights we've had together, after our wedding before he went away, we'd been so passionate that we'd just torn our clothes off as we stood, and fallen into bed together. This time felt so cold and clinical, I felt like crying.

Still, I climbed in and we kissed and started to warm up, so to speak, but then I noticed that he winced every time I came too close, as if it hurt him. Any interest he'd been showing seemed to disappear, and he pulled himself away from me, turning his head to the wall.

'Did I touch something painful?' I asked him. 'Or was it something I said?'

He muttered something under his breath and I asked him to repeat it.

'It's no ****ing good,' he swore, starting to get out of bed. 'I'll never be any good for you. I'm going home.'

'No you're not,' I said, pushing him back and getting angry now. 'You're my husband and I love you and it's up to me to decide whether you're good enough. Now, you stay here and get some sleep.'

He started to answer back but I just leapt up, grabbed my dressing gown and this notebook and came downstairs, holding my breath for fear that I would hear his footsteps clomping above and that he would stick to his threat. Him going home seemed to be admitting defeat, a sign that our marriage was over. Thankfully he seems to be staying put.

So here I am, two hours later, still writing. In my better moments I tell myself that we can sort it out, but right now I'm starting to wonder.

Tuesday 22nd April
Things are looking up!

When Ma came downstairs yesterday morning and found me sleeping on the sofa she asked what was wrong and I burst into tears and told her it was impossible for Alfie and me to share a single bed any more, what with his injury and the pain it causes him. She looked a bit surprised and said surely we'd be getting our own place soon and couldn't we put up with it for a little while? But I said it could take weeks or even months before Alfie got his pension sorted out and found a job so we could afford to rent our own flat, and in the meantime were we supposed to sleep apart every night?

I stomped out to the privy then and later I heard her and Pa talking. Today while Alfie went with another Tommy to see the pensions people, me and Ma have been in the boys' room, packing up their stuff into some boxes and cases Pa fetched down from the attic.

It was the small things that hurt the most, the cricket bat, the school cap, a broken toy car, and even a dirty sock that had rolled under the bed and been missed. We cried a lot and made endless cups of tea and I had to grit my teeth to keep going and keep her going too. She refused to throw a single thing away, even the dirty sock, so by the end we had three huge boxes and two suitcases of clothes and toys ready for Pa to hoist up into the loft somehow.

After that it got a bit easier. When we took the carpets out into the yard to beat them, I imagined that every thwack was hitting a German soldier over the head for killing my brothers, and it made me feel better to get angry. Ma took down the curtains, washed them and hung them on the line; we pushed the beds together and tied the legs with string, then put an extra blanket over the two mattresses to smooth out the join. We sat and sewed the single blankets and sheets together, and then made up the bed as a double.

Ma cleaned the mirror and the windows and I found the little lace runner that I'd been given by one of Alfie's aunties on our wedding day and laid it out along the top of the chest of drawers. With a bunch of primroses as a finishing touch, it looked so pretty.

Alfie came back in good spirits, having been told that he would probably get 70% of the disability pension which is not enough to live on but a great help to supplement his wages (and mine) if we can both find jobs. He now has to wait for the Board to assess how disabled he is. They also went to the housing office but he was told there's such a shortage of housing we don't stand a chance, not unless we had children.

So I said, 'We can work on it.' And he smiled in his suggestive way and said, 'I like the sound of that,' and then I said, 'We'll just have to find somewhere that doesn't cost an arm and a leg.' The words were out of my mouth before I could stop them. What a stupid thing to say to a man with only one leg. But he just laughed and said, 'I can't afford to lose another one!' We were both in hysterics when Ma came in and offered us tea.

When I showed him our new room he took me in his arms and kissed me then and there, and promised things would be better come that evening. He was right: we had a lovely, loving night, almost like old times and although he is still very embarrassed about it, I am even getting quite used to his poor stump and his missing leg.

That's not to say it didn't feel a bit sad and strange, at first, sleeping in the room where both of my brothers had spent their first twenty years or so. They were so close and such good friends, they spent hours holed up in here, playing games or just reading and talking together. I was only allowed into their sanctuary on very special occasions, and if I dared to creep in when they were safely out of the house it always felt like trespassing.

Oh God, I hope you are keeping them safe in heaven. I miss them so much.

Friday 2nd May
Today was my birthday and everyone made a big fuss of me. Ma baked a cake and Freda bought me a beautiful bead necklace. How ever could she afford it, I thought, but said nothing. I suspect Claude may have had something to do with it, so it's better not to ask. Alfie gave me some white socks. Dear man, he'd heard me saying I needed some, but has absolutely no idea that it's not the sort of thing a girl wants for a birthday present! Nylons would have been much more welcome.

Pa came home with pork chops for our tea, all excited because they've announced that from now on children will get a full meat ration instead of half as it's been up till now. He reckons he can open three days a week instead of two, and his profits will nearly double, on account of there being so many littl'uns around here.

Saturday 24th May
Nearly a month has passed since my last entry, but with Alfie around I never seem to get enough time on my own to write. Reading back, I seemed so optimistic that with him safely home, everything would fall into place. Sadly, the past few weeks have proved otherwise.

In the first instance, I am constantly tired because of Alfie's nightmares. He shouts in his sleep and sometimes swears quite horribly, imagining himself back in the trenches or going over the top. I have to put my arms around him and whisper in his ear until it stops and he falls asleep again. Sometimes he sits up in bed suddenly, and seems to be fighting off the person he's dreaming about, flailing his arms around quite dangerously, so all I can do is talk to him, trying to wake him from the dream. The other night he rolled right out onto the floor and cowered on the bedside rug, quivering and moaning at some imagined terror, so I had to climb out too, and help him back into bed.

I've tried talking to him, but he just clams up. I've also suggested he might go back to see the doctor but he just pooh poohs the idea and says they can't do anything and it will go away before long, just as soon as he can get back to some kind of normal life. But it pains me dreadfully to see him suffering in this way – and it brings home the horrors that he and his fellows have endured. It's not only the visible injuries, but the invisible scars in their brains that they are having to cope with, even months after the war has ended.

When he's not having nightmares he gets what the doctor in the hospital called 'phantom pains', which is what he feels in the leg that isn't there any more. He won't talk about it much but I can see his face clenching with the agony, and apparently there's nothing they can do for it. The strange thing is that he can go for days without a problem and then it'll hit him again, there doesn't seem to be any rhyme or reason.

Secondly, although he's tried his very best, he's still unemployed, and jobs seem to be scarce as hens' teeth. We read in the newspapers almost every day about soldiers having to sell matches in the street, or even take up begging to get by, but we just assumed these were the weaker kind of man, not prepared to put in the kind of hard work needed to find a proper job.

The government has told companies to offer returning soldiers their old positions wherever possible, so I helped Alfie write a letter to the boss at the warehouse where he worked before he signed up. They invited him for an interview and he made the difficult journey (lots of walking) only to be told that all the light work jobs were filled and because of his leg he wouldn't be strong enough to do the heavy lifting.

He's never been a shirker, and not one to give up without a fight. He spent the rest of the week walking the streets and offering himself for work at every factory and warehouse he could find, but all he ended up with was a vicious blister on his stump which has turned into a sore and means that now he can hardly bear to wear his leg any more.

Yesterday was the date for his appearance at the Disability Board and he was determined not to miss it. I persuaded him to let me wrap the stump with soft bandages and antiseptic cream so that he could at least get to the bus. It broke my heart to see the way he had to grit his teeth with every step, trying not to show the pain though it was clear from his face all the same. By the time we reached the bus stop his cheeks were quite grey with the effort, and although he seemed to recover himself on the journey, the walk from the bus stop to the office in the West End was even longer and more exhausting.

I bought a cup of sweet tea from a street vendor and forced him to drink it before he went in, and then I sat in the park waiting for him. Heaven knows what they did in there, because it seemed to take hours. But it's good news: they have confirmed that he will get 70% of a full disability pension and should be able to collect it from the Post Office in a couple of weeks' time.

We have to give thanks for small mercies, I suppose.

Monday 2 June

Today I'd had enough and managed to persuade Alfie to allow a doctor to visit. Pa kindly offered to pay for it. The ulcer on his stump is now a full two inches round, and looks disgusting but strangely doesn't seem to be causing him as much pain as before, so he insists on wearing the leg and it just gets worse and worse.

The doctor just gave us some cream and told Alfie he would have to rest and not use his artificial leg until the abscess has fully healed. He said the wound was now so deep that it had destroyed the nerve endings in his skin, which is why he doesn't feel so much pain. When I asked how long the healing would take, he sucked his teeth and said at least a couple of months, and if Alfie went on using the artificial leg before his wound had properly healed, it could make it much worse and take even longer. He must use crutches instead, he said, or rent a wheelchair.

As I showed the doctor to the door he whispered, 'Make sure your husband takes care, won't you, Mrs Barker? He's already had a close shave, so don't let him risk his health for the sake of a few weeks taking it easy.' If only it was that simple.

After all that Alfie went into one of his black moods again, cursing the fact that he would be stuck indoors now that summer is here, and when I tried to suggest we should get hold of a wheelchair he refused to speak to me. I know how he detests the things, hates being at other people's waist height, loathes the idea that people might pity him for being a cripple, but it's only for a few weeks, and then he can get back on his feet again.

Tonight he was still sulky and turned away from me, and I was so upset that I came downstairs to write this. It feels like we are back at square one.

Wednesday 25 June
PEACE IS OFFICIAL. The Versailles Treaty will be signed in the next few days. Today was showery

and at teatime Pa was full of a story about the rainbow which appeared in the sky just as the news broke.

'I was just serving Mrs Gittins, and was asking about her son, you know, the one who got gassed, and we was talking about the peace announcement when we looked out of the shop window and there it was, right across the sky.'

I imagined them peering between the carcasses of meat, and the hares hung up by their hind legs, wondering at the rainbow. 'It's a sign,' Ma said. 'A symbol of hope, like the one that came to Noah at the end of the flood.' Pa pooh-poohed it but I could tell he was a bit moved by the whole affair too.

Well, it might be peace in the world, but it doesn't make life any easier here at 25 Trafalgar Road. Alfie hobbles along to the pub on his crutches every lunch-time and evening, for the company, he says, and I can hardly blame him. It's no fun being stuck here with his in-laws without a place of his own. He can't afford to buy more than a pint for himself but there is usually someone who's happy to stand a few drinks to a disabled serviceman, so he often comes home a bit worse for wear.

They are talking about a peace celebration next month, with parades and parties and the rest, but at teatime Alfie had a moan about how the whole thing will be a waste of money and they ought to spend it on getting soldiers back to work or building homes for them. 'A land fit for heroes, is that what Lloyd

George calls it?' he grumbled. 'Fit for ruddy nothing, if you ask me.'

Pa wisely held his counsel but Ma weighed in, muttering something about, 'All the victory marches in the world can't bring my boys back.' It doesn't help that it's the 3rd anniversary of Johnnie's death next week, even though no-one is mentioning it.

I'm not sure what I think. It would be good for our morale to have a little celebration, but I can see what Alfie means about expensive parades and the rest.

The nightmares seem to have quietened down, recently, but maybe this is because he's been drinking so much.

Monday 30 June
It's been decided. There's to be a street party in Trafalgar Road on Peace Day, Saturday 19th July.

After all the fireworks and maroons and the rest being set off all over London yesterday to celebrate the news of the signing, Bert held a meeting with the regulars at the pub and announced that he would support it with a free half pint for every adult and lemonade for the children.

We had a right row at teatime though. Ma has completely set her heart against any kind of celebration and Alfie said he would rather go to Whitehall to see the march past at the new Cenotaph that's been built to honour the dead, even though it's a struggle for him to get down the road, let alone to central London. The last thing he wanted was a stupid party, he said, because it was an insult to those who lost their lives and whose lives have been destroyed by the war. 'And all for what? For the men who fought in those bloody trenches to spend their days begging for bread and their nights on the streets.' He thumped the table, making the cutlery rattle.

Pa argued that it would look a bit strange if the Applebys and the Barkers – the two families in the street who have suffered most – refused to take part. 'It'd make us look like we're snubbing everyone,' he said. 'And I can't afford to lose local custom, when trade's bad enough already.'

Alfie clomped upstairs in a grump but came down again a little later and said he was sorry, especially when Ma and Pa had been so generous towards him. And Ma agreed that she would take part so long as she wasn't expected to look happy about it. I suggested we put Ray and Johnnie's photographs in the front room window with a sign asking folk to remember those who were lost, and she thought that was a good idea.

Friday 18 July
Alfie and me have spent all day making pies for the party. He didn't want to handle the meat but offered to peel potatoes and chop vegetables, and then I showed him how to make the pastry and raise a pie case. To start with, he couldn't make it work and cursed so much I thought he'd give up, but I persuaded him that everyone finds it difficult at first, and that he just needed to practise. So he carried on and after a

while he got it perfect, and quickly made thirty more. That's one of the things I love about Alfie, he's a sticker, never gives up. It was such a joy to see him smiling and taking pleasure in achieving something, something he could take pride in, after so long.

When we'd stoked up the oven and put the pies in, we sat and had a cup of tea together and I caught him looking at me and said, 'What is it? Have I got flour on my nose or something?' But he just laughed and said, 'I've been watching you cooking. You're really good at it, aren't you?'

Well, I blushed to the roots because he's not a great one for compliments, and told him about my idea of setting up a pie business, as a sideline in Pa's shop, once rationing was over. After a moment he said, 'That's a point, where did you get all that flour, and those eggs?' and I told him Bert had got them for me, from a wholesaler I assumed, and that seemed to satisfy him. Anyway, soon afterwards Ma came back and said the pies smelled wonderful and could we have one for our tea tonight?

She was flushed in the face and that excited she didn't even complain about the mess we'd made of the kitchen and, when we asked where she'd been, she said she'd been helping the children at the school to make decorations for the party tomorrow: bunting and streamers, table mats and hats.

Out of the blue, one of the little boys she'd been working with told her that his big brother had died in the war, and asked Ma if she knew anyone who had died. The teacher shushed him, and Ma was grateful for that, because she was afraid she'd burst into tears in front of the children. But then she thought about it and after a little while she got the urge to tell them what war had really meant.

'I just started talking about my two wonderful boys and how proud they had been at first, going out to fight against the Kaiser, how brave, never questioning their own safety, and just following orders because that was the only way to win a war,' she told us.

'How they never knew the horrors till they got out there, and how many thousands and thousands of young men like them would die. I told the children that their generation must make sure there is never, ever, another war like this one.'

'You were very brave, doing that, Ma.'

'When I was talking, a little girl put her hand in mine,' she went on. 'And afterwards she came up and whispered that I was a lovely lady and she wished I could be her nanna because her own granny had died from a Zeppelin bomb.'

'That must have made you feel proud,' I said.

'It did. And you know, walking home I realised that for the first time in years I was feeling happy. I never thought it would help, talking about the boys, but it seems to have done.'

Saturday 19 July
It's midnight on Peace Day and Alfie is snoring peacefully by my side. He looks so innocent when he's

asleep, like a small boy again, but I can't sleep for thinking what a strange day it's been.

It was a wonderful afternoon, in many ways. The sun came out, the street was decorated with bunting and streamers and everyone brought out their dining tables and chairs and set them up into one long stretch all the way down the middle of the street. Then the food started to appear: from each house came plate-fuls of cheese sandwiches and egg rolls, cakes with union jack designs and biscuits iced in red white and blue, and each table had one of my pies, sliced thin so that everyone could have at least a sliver to taste.

There was home-made barley water for the children, and Bert was good as his word, bringing out a half pint of beer for every single adult in the street, which must have cost him a penny or two. We were togged up in our Sunday best for the occasion, but we all put on the coloured paper hats the children had made and everyone was so happy we forgot to worry about looking stupid.

Except for Freda, that is, cos she was already wearing a fashionable little number with feathers in it. She said she'd spent hours pinning it to the side of her head and she was damned if she was going to ruin the effect, not after all that effort. The hat must have cost at least a guinea, but when I asked her where she'd got it she just sniggered and pointed at Claude, who seems to have become part of the family these days, more's the pity.

I understand that it's flattering to have presents

showered on you but otherwise, in all honesty, I can't think what she sees in him. He's tall and quite good looking, I suppose, but so slick and smarmy with it, making up to Mr and Mrs Barker like they were royalty. The only time I tried to have a proper conversation with him, his eyes darted around every which way except at me, as if he was expecting someone else to arrive at any moment. I wouldn't trust him further than I could throw him, which isn't very far.

All the food was eaten in a matter of minutes and after that Bert made a speech about how grateful we all were to those who fought and won this terrible war, and especially to those who made what everyone calls 'the ultimate sacrifice' which is a phrase I specially hate. Of course at that point everyone turned to look at the photographs of Ray and Johnnie pinned up in our front window, and raised their hats to Ma and Pa out of respect for their losses. I felt pretty weepy and I could see Ma biting her lip, and Pa reaching out to hold her hand, but we all managed to hold off the tears. Call it progress, of a sort.

Then Bert proposed three cheers and we all raised our glasses to 'our brave boys' and especially to Alfie and Percy Gittins who are the only two to return home alive. The littl'uns were allowed down from the tables to run around, playing hopscotch and games of tag much as they do every day after school, the women cleared the plates away and the men got into the serious business of drinking.

A little later the newsagent from the corner store

brought out copies of the evening papers, so we passed them round, reading news of the crowds that had gathered in Whitehall to watch a Victory Parade of fifteen thousand servicemen, and how they stopped and saluted the huge pillar they've built, called a 'Cenotaph', in honour of the dead.

> TO these, the sick and wounded who cannot take part in the festival of victory, I send out greetings and bid them good cheer, assuring them that the wounds and scars so honourable in themselves, inspire in the hearts of their fellow countrymen the warmest feelings of gratitude and respect.
>
> HRH King George V

When Alfie read this cutting from the *Daily Express* he snorted and muttered that if the King *really* respected wounded servicemen he'd make sure there were jobs and homes for them to return to. But even his sour mood couldn't dampen the general atmosphere of celebration.

Until the evening, that is.

By the time Ma and me had finished cleaning up and dropped in for another cuppa with Freda and Mrs Barker it was well past nine o'clock, so we decided to join the men in the pub. Of course they were very merry by now, singing all the old songs and having a high old time. Alfie offered to get in the round and I went to help him bring it back to the table because his walking's a bit unsteady even when he's sober, which he wasn't, and I feared for the safety of our hard-earned drinks.

When we came up to the bar Bert complimented me on the pies and, when I told him that Alfie had done half the work this time, and was becoming a dab hand at raising pastry cases, he said, 'Good on yer, laddie. You could make a bob or two if you really put your minds to it, set up in business, the two of you.'

'Not till they lift meat rationing, we can't,' Alfie said. 'Anyway we'd never get enough flour or eggs.' But Bert just winked and tapped the side of his nose and said that wasn't a problem, because he'd got a good contact. 'Know what I mean?'

Before we sat down Alfie pulled me aside and whispered furiously, 'Why didn't you tell me the flour and eggs we used were knocked off?'

'What do you mean, knocked off?' I said.

'These contacts of Bert's, it's the black market, can't you see? You could go to gaol for that.' To be honest it had never crossed my mind.

'You're not going to make any more pies for him, that's for certain,' Alfie said, and for a moment I thought he might make a real scene but he just let it go, and we went back to the table and joined in the singing.

Come ten to eleven when they rang last orders, Claude went to the bar to buy the final round and I watched him chatting with Bert, who handed him a wad of notes. It took me a few seconds to realise what was wrong: Claude should have been paying Bert for the drinks, not the other way round. I wasn't the only one watching. When Claude returned to the table with the drinks, Alfie struggled to his feet and gestured to him that they should go outside.

'Whatever it is, you can say it here, Alf,' Claude said, smooth as oil. Why would he feel threatened by a one-legged man a head shorter than him, in any case?

Alfie flushed redder than before. He hates being called Alf. 'Then perhaps you can tell me and everyone else where you got those eggs, and that flour from, what Bert sold us for making the pies,' he barked.

Claude started to look a bit shifty then, and muttered something like, 'I don't know what you are talking about.'

'I think you do,' Alfie said in a menacing voice I've never heard before. 'How come you have so much cash to splash around, when you never went near the war?'

'I played my part.' Claude was cool as a cucumber.

'Played at ripping people off, you mean, while the rest of us were out there getting killed or having our limbs smashed up.'

Claude lost his silver tongue at that and snarled something like, 'I think you'd better take that back, Alf, or you might regret it.'

By now, Freda was beside him, holding his arm and trying to pull him away but it was Alfie she should have been holding back because he just launched out with his right fist and landed a great punch on Claude's nose, which instantly began bleeding all down the front of his white shirt. Claude must have punched Alfie back, because a second later he collapsed onto the ground, white as a sheet.

Pa and Mr Barker leapt up from their seats and dragged Claude out of the door, while I held Alfie's head in my lap until he came round and dragged himself up onto a chair. I felt sorry for Freda: standing there torn two ways, it was her brother who started the fight but Claude had hit a disabled serviceman, which was far worse. In the end, she went outside to find Claude, and they never came back.

Finally we helped Alfie home and into bed and even though Pa pressed him on what the fight was about, he flatly refused to say anything more, for which I was grateful, because this business of the eggs and flour implicated me and Bert as well. But it got me wondering whether Freda knew about Claude's underhand business dealings and whether she had just tried to ignore them because she enjoyed the little luxuries he bought her. Only time will tell, I suspect.

One thing's for sure, we won't be making any more pies until rationing is lifted.

Sunday 20th July
Freda is furious with Alfie for punching her boyfriend, and with me for defending him. When I pointed out

that Claude had punched back, Freda claims he never did. Alfie is tight-lipped about the whole affair except for saying he's disappointed in me for not realising we were using knocked off flour and eggs. What a mess.

Tuesday 26th August

The past few weeks have been the happiest in my life:

1. Alfie's stump has finally healed and he can wear his artificial leg again. Not that it's ever very comfortable, mind, but at least it's now bearable. We've both been out looking for jobs but many of the factories and warehouses are closed for their summer break, or told us to come back in September. Though there was nothing for me, a couple of places asked for his details and address, which has cheered him up a great deal.

2. Alfie's pension has come through, backdated to the date of his discharge, and so he's decided he can afford to spend some of the wages that have been paid into the Post Office for the whole eighteen months that he was in the Army.

3. We finally had our HONEYMOON IN BRIGHTON! There's so much to tell but I can only do a brief summary here.

We caught the train from Victoria Station and a bus to our little guesthouse, just a few minutes' walk from the seafront. As we were signing in, the landlady asked, 'Where was you serving, son?' and when he told her she said her own son had been killed not far from there, just two years back. We gave her our condolences and as she took us upstairs she said, 'I keep my best rooms for our brave boys. I hope you like this one.'

Well, as soon as she closed the door, we fell about laughing. It was the most enormous bedroom either of us had ever seen, with a big bay window looking out onto the street. The bed was a full five feet wide, ever so comfy with a fat silky eiderdown, there was a dressing table with a three-way mirror, and we even had our own basin for washing in! Down the hallway was a bathroom with a proper water closet – no struggling out to the privy on our honeymoon.

On Saturday it was warm enough but a bit overcast so we went on the funfair at the end of the Promenade and in the afternoon to the music hall on the pier, before getting fish and chips and a couple of pints and then falling into bed worn out from having so much fun.

Next day turned out sunny and very hot, and I really wanted to go in the sea but Alfie wouldn't get undressed in public so I went paddling instead and we hired deckchairs on the pier and read the newspapers and I had my first-ever ice cream (delicious). We even watched a Punch and Judy show, feeling like big kids again. There was a gentle breeze and the sun sparkling on the sea made the whole world seem so bright and cheerful, as if the fear and sadness of the past few years had never happened, the dark days and bombings, the grafting in the munitions factory and the grim hospital visits.

Ray and Johnnie are never far from my mind of course, and I wish they had lived to see that peace – what they gave their lives for – could make a world as beautiful as this.

Sunday teatime we went to a little café down the road that our landlady recommended. She must have warned them in advance, because we were treated like royalty. Nothing was too much trouble, and we ate so much steak and kidney pudding and apple crumble that I thought I might actually burst.

It was hard, come Monday, to leave such a magical place. But it's helped us find ourselves again. I felt silly and carefree for the first time in years, he told me he loved me a dozen times, and whispered that he wants us to have our own children, now that the world has a chance of peace. Even though we have a hard road ahead of us in getting jobs and finding our own flat, I know that Alfie and me will definitely pull through.

BOOK 3

Rose Barker - PRIVATE

Sunday 21st September

It's been the hottest week of the year: 89 degrees on Thursday. People are fainting in the streets. But I'm not complaining because on Saturday, at last, Alfie and me moved into our own place.

It's hardly The Ritz – just two rooms on the ground floor of a small terraced house just around the corner from Trafalgar Road – but we have our own 'front door', which is really the back door, leading out into the garden and down the alleyway out to the street.

Ma, Pa, and the Barkers all came round to inspect and were very envious of our 'facilities'. The alcove under the stairs in the back room – which will be our parlour – has been converted into a kitchen area with a butler's sink and a paraffin stove for cooking, and linoleum on the floor. Pa has offered to put up shelves and build a cupboard for food. Best of all, we have a proper water closet in its own brick shed just outside the back door, that's been converted from the coal hole.

At the moment we are sitting on boxes and sleeping on our old single mattresses on the floor, but Mr Barker, who's a bit of a jack of all trades, knows someone who deals in second-hand furnishings and says he can get a good deal for us.

Sitting here, in our own little parlour, with Alfie outside in the yard having a cigarette, I have to pinch myself to believe that my dream has come true. This is our first home.

How can we afford it? Well, Alfie's finally got a job!

When we got back from Brighton there was a letter waiting for him from his old employer, the warehouse on Cumberland Wharf, offering him a job in the packing room, and asking him to report for work the following Monday. Of course Alfie was made up, and set off extra early to make sure he was there on time – it's only a few miles away but it's a difficult journey with two buses and quite a walk at the other end.

He returned completely exhausted and fell into bed without any tea the first day, but gradually he is getting stronger and more used to the work, which seems to involve packing boxes and wrapping parcels, and making sure they are shipped off to the right places. He says most of the lads there are demobbed Tommies, and a couple have war wounds like himself, so they have a few laughs and he reckons he'll fit in pretty well.

It's only been three weeks but Alfie is like a new man, cheerful and cheeky, making plans and playing jokes on people. He only goes to the pub every now and again instead of every day, and is talking about going back to watch his old football team. His face is filling out, his cheeks are still rosy from our weekend by the seaside, his curls have grown back

161

and his chest and arms are strong as a weightlifter's because he has to use them so much to compensate for his leg.

I have never loved him more.

The only thing missing from my life now is my best friend. Freda's been quite distant ever since the incident with Claude on Peace Day. He's still very much around, more's the pity, but they don't come down The Nelson any more (hardly surprising, I suppose) and she's got herself a job, something Claude fixed up for her. When I asked what it is she put on a posh voice and said she was doing 'office work' which sounds very grand but for all we know it could just be stuffing envelopes.

Sunday 5th October

Freda's finally been to visit our new home! She just blew in this afternoon wafting perfume and the first thing I noticed was the great gaudy stone on her engagement finger.

'Me and Claude are getting married,' she announced, 'next year probably.'

What could we say? Alfie and me just looked at each other, not knowing how to react, but finally I managed to crack a smile and give her a big hug to congratulate her and Alfie shook her hand and offered to make tea.

She babbled on about how excited she was and how she was already planning her wedding dress – like the one she'd seen Mary Pickford wearing in a magazine – and would I be her maid of honour? Of course I said yes, although Alfie was scowling (he told me afterwards he was afraid she was going to insist on him being Claude's best man, though thankfully she didn't).

When we'd shown her around the flat – it doesn't take long – and she'd made all the right noises about how envious she was, we sat down on our new (second-hand, thanks to Mr Barker) chairs around the kitchen table for tea, and shared out the scones I'd made with our coupons, and I asked her how the job was going. She brushed it off – 'Oh, they're a very dull lot after the canaries,' she said – and then rabbited on for about half an hour, barely taking a single breath, about how she and Claude went to the new Palais de Danse in Hammersmith last night.

It went something like this:

'You wouldn't believe the size of the place. I thought I'd died and gone to heaven. It's all decorated in Chinese style, with a pagoda on columns and in the middle of the dance floor – honestly, I hardly believed my eyes – they've built a miniature mountain! Yes, a real mountain, out of rocks, and waterfalls with real water cascading out of it. I know it sounds crazy, you *must* come and see for yourselves.

'They haven't got a boring old orchestra, it's a jazz band and they play this American ragtime music, and when they start up you literally cannot keep your feet still, you just *have* to get up and dance! I'm lucky I've got Claude who knows all the latest dances anyway, so I just copy him, but you don't have to come with a partner because you can hire one for just sixpence! You can even have lessons there, too, and there's a special area of the floor for people who're learning.

'It's so fast and exhausting, that kind of dancing, but when you're worn out you can sit at one of the little tables around the edge and have tea or lemonade, and watching the other dancers is like going to the movies because some of them are just as good as any of the Hollywood stars. No, it's even better than that because you're actually *in* the movie itself.

'Oh my goodness, it's so much fun, you simply *must* come.'

When she'd gone, Alfie and me had an argument, the first we've had in our new home. He said Freda was a silly little girl and nothing good would come of it with a wide boy like Claude. I said he could be right, but she was my friend after all, and it didn't stop me wanting to see the Palais de Dance for myself, and have a go at these new dances, and we could learn together, perhaps.

He told me not to be an idiot, how would he ever be able to dance properly with his leg? And I said he could stand and walk perfectly well so he could at least try, and he shouted back that he wasn't going to make a fool of himself in front of all those thousands of people and why didn't I just go on my own and rent myself a dancing partner like Freda said, and I said I might just ruddy well do that, and walked out and slammed the door.

I went home to Trafalgar Road and had a bit of a weep till Ma told me I had to make allowances and perhaps dancing was something me and Alfie wouldn't be able to do together, but didn't we have so many other things going for us? She's right, of course, but it doesn't stop me wanting to try out the new dances, all the same.

Sunday 19th October

I finally persuaded Alfie to go dancing with me, and we went to the Palais de Danse in Hammersmith last night. It was even more fun than Freda had described.

Alfie only agreed because he knew Claude was not going to be there. Freda came round in the week to ask a favour: Claude had invited her to go away with him for the weekend and she'd told her parents that she was going to stay with one of the girls from work. So, in case they made enquiries, she wanted me to cover her back (or lie for her, as Alfie put it later).

She's a fool to sleep with Claude before they're married (actually, she's a fool to sleep with Claude at all) but I can't claim Alfie and me were pure as driven snow, so who are we to judge? On her way out I told her, 'if you can't be good, be careful', and she winked at me cheekily.

Anyway, I saw this as an opportunity to get Alfie

dancing, so spent the rest of the week dropping heavy hints until, finally, he caved in. Ma ran up a dress for me from some cotton she'd bought at the market, in the modern straight style with a hemline just below the knees like the newspapers say is absolutely vital if you are to do the new dances. It felt so fashionable, and so free, not having fabric tangling around your ankles. I really wanted a pair of sheer silk stockings like Freda's, but I'll have to save up for them. When he saw me togged up and wearing my new red lipstick, Alfie's eyes nearly fell out of his head!

I loved every bit of the Palais, the pagoda and the lights and the huge dance floor with the mountain and its cascades in the centre. We took one of the little tables and drank lemonade (they don't serve alcohol) until the music started up and everyone else took to the dance floor, but Alfie refused to budge. He wanted to watch the dancers before having a go, he said, which was fair enough.

Freda was not exaggerating: it is simply *impossible* to sit still with that music playing. My feet were jiggling under the table, and I could see Alfie's foot tapping, so I knew he was enjoying it too so after a couple of numbers I couldn't bear it any longer, and dragged him onto the floor with me.

'All you have to do is wriggle your bottom and wave your arms about,' I shouted. 'You don't need any fancy footwork.'

The wonderful thing about these new dances is that because you are not dancing in each other's arms, you really don't have to know what you're doing. Of course some do, and make a great show of it, kicking up their heels and swinging each other around, but many simply jiggle about, and that is what we did. We managed just fine. I had to pinch myself once or twice – here I was, dancing with Alfie! There have been many times when I've wondered whether we would ever go dancing again.

The band took a break and we had a pleasant conversation with two lads and a girl who joined us at the table. When the band started up again, the girl and one of the lads went onto the floor, leaving the three of us still sitting. Alfie said his leg was too painful to dance any more so the boy politely asked whether he could invite me to partner him. Alfie seemed agreeable enough and said it was up to me to decide, so I took him at his word and accepted the offer.

I knew it wasn't fair to leave Alfie on his own for long, and that I should go back after a couple of dances, but it was such fun I stayed on the floor far longer than I'd intended. When I got back, he was in quite a strop and said he was ready to leave, with me or without me.

On the bus home I apologised for dancing so long and after a bit he thawed out and forgave me. We agreed it had definitely been great fun and good value for the shilling entrance fee and, when I asked whether he might go another time, he said, 'Perhaps. We'll just have to wait and see.'

Which is a whole lot better than a definite no.

Tuesday 11th November – The Great Silence

Today the most extraordinary thing happened – and we were actually there to witness it.

A few days ago there was an announcement in the newspaper that the King had asked for today to be a special Remembrance Day, and that at eleven o'clock in the morning, everyone and everything should go silent, to mark the very moment that the war ended, a year ago. He has decreed that, 'All loco-motion should cease, so that, in perfect stillness, the thoughts of everyone may be concentrated on reverent remembrance of the glorious dead.'

Much as we respect the King, none of us believed that daily life would really stop on a working day.

'What about the traffic and the trams?' Alfie said. 'Are they going to stop in the middle of the street? And the trains, are they going to screech to a halt in the middle of nowhere? Anyway, I can't see my boss letting us stop work – he's such a slave driver.'

Ma suddenly got it into her head that she would like to go to the new Cenotaph for the event, so's she could remember Ray and Johnnie in what she called 'proper reverent company', meaning other people who had come especially for the purpose. Anyway, since Pa said he couldn't shut up shop all day just because of a two minute silence, I said I'd go with her.

We set off early, well wrapped up since it was bitter cold and foggy, with snow still on the ground in places from the falls we'd had earlier in the week. The buses were slowed by all the traffic, so when we finally got there around ten o'clock Whitehall was already knee-deep with crowds and I felt sure we'd never be able to see anything at all.

In the event, it wasn't the seeing that mattered.

At about five minutes to the hour it seemed like every bell in London began to peal: Big Ben and Westminster Abbey, and Southwark Cathedral over the river, and lots of smaller churches besides. Then, just before eleven, the maroons went up, and the drivers of every car, bus and tram seemed to lean on their klaxons, with the booming horns of the river-boats seemed almost to vibrate through the ground. It was such a thunderous noise that Ma and me, and plenty of others in the crowd, clapped our hands over our ears.

Big Ben tolled eleven slow chimes, and then everything stopped. The traffic halted and men took off their caps and the crowd around us stood stock still for what seemed like forever, certainly far longer than two minutes. The silence was like being in the countryside at the dead of night, or down a deep tunnel lined with velvet. You could almost touch it. And the effect of being among those thousands of muted people, some of them weeping noiselessly, made the hairs stand up on the back of my neck. A woman nearby gave a single sob, unable to stifle her grief.

A blackbird started up in a tree and my thoughts turned to my brothers. It seemed as though one of them, probably Ray, who was the lippy one, was calling to us through the bird's beautiful song, comforting us and telling us all was well. I put my arm around Ma and felt her warmth running through me. It was reassuring to think that, after those terrible years, we were still here and the world would eventually heal itself.

When the single maroon went off to mark the end of the two minutes, we nearly jumped out of our skins, and still no-one moved or spoke at first, as though people felt reluctant to let go of the silence and their memories. But slowly a gentle murmur began, and people stretched themselves and turned to each other. Ma and I hugged for a long minute more and then, without saying anything, held hands and looked around.

'Thank you for coming with me,' she said. 'The boys might be gone, but I'm so lucky to have you.' It's the first time she's ever said that. The way she's mourned Ray and Johnnie has sometimes made me feel that she doesn't love me as much as she loved them. Silly really, but that's the way a human mind works.

'I felt they were there, didn't you?'

'They were definitely with us,' was all she said back, as we started towards the bus stop.

This evening, Pa said all the traffic on the Old Kent Road had pulled to a halt and everyone stopped in the street and in the shops and bent their heads. In the warehouse, Alfie told us, all machines were turned off and a hundred men stood stock still by their workbenches, and when the two minutes ended they gave three cheers to 'lost comrades'.

We all agreed it was a very fitting tribute. I hope they do this every year, for ever and ever.

Sunday 30th November

All the talk in the pub at lunchtime today was about the fact that women are taking over the world (according to the men) and no good will come of it! It's all because the first woman Member of Parliament will take up her seat in the House of Commons tomorrow. She's a toff, of course, and taking over the seat from her husband because he's become a peer and will toddle off to the House of Lords.

Still, she was voted in properly and mostly by men because women still can't vote until they turn thirty, so I take my hat off to her. Will there ever be a woman Prime Minister, that's what I wonder? That'd shake them up.

Monday 8th December

Meat rationing has been lifted!

We had a right old celebration in The Nelson last night, with Pa getting in most of the rounds, so this morning Alfie and me were suffering. Now, even though his phantom pains were terrible in the night, he's gone off to work and I've been doing the washing, as usual. I hate housework, it's boring and repetitive and I want some money of my own instead of scrimping and saving all the time, and never being able to afford anything new.

Alfie says he likes me being home, keeping house and cooking him hot dinners. That would be fine, I suppose, if we had children to look after. But as yet we don't, so I'm bored. After Christmas and New Year, I am going to look for a job.

Pa says it will take a week or two for supplies to come through and it might be slow at first because people have less cash than they did before rationing began. But he expects to be busy in time for Christmas and dropped hints that he might need help in the shop. Of course I'd be happy to serve customers for a week or two but I'd be no good at the butchery side of things, sawing up carcasses and the like. And I've given up the idea of making pies because I'd be working alone. I miss the company of the 'canaries' and would prefer to find another factory job.

I'm sure that when business picks up Pa would like to have Alfie working with him, give him a proper training, so he can take over the business when he retires, just as the boys would have done had they been spared. The journey to the warehouse is getting Alfie down, and he's always complaining about his pay. Just like me, though, he enjoys the company of the other lads at the warehouse.

I wonder if Pa will talk to him? It's so hard to tell what's going on in men's heads.

Sunday 21st December
I've been helping out Pa in the shop for a few days, and with my wages we've been able to afford a few little extras for the festive season ahead. This weekend Alfie and me went to the market and bought our very first Christmas tree, and today I used some of our precious flour and sugar rations making iced gingerbread men to decorate it. The tree looks so pretty and it's got me into a really festive mood.

I am determined that our first Christmas together in our own home will be a memorable one, and hope the New Year brings more good things to us – perhaps even a little addition to our family.

Thursday 1st January 1920
On his first day back at work after the Christmas break, the boss called Alfie and ten of his workmates into the office and told them the warehouse had lost a major contract and they were being laid off, as of today, with just a week's wages for goodwill. Last in, first out, no special circumstances. That was it.

He came home late afternoon, already drunk, having spent lunchtime in the pub with his laid off workmates, still cursing and muttering dark threats about joining the communist party, whatever that is. I don't care what party he joins so long as he can find another job, otherwise we are sunk.

Thank heavens I put a bit by from my shifts in the shop, because although I spent a fair bit on presents, buying a beautiful wool scarf for Ma and a bottle of whisky for Pa, we should have enough to keep the rent paid for a couple of weeks. But then what? I couldn't bear to go back to living with the parents, not now we've had a taste of having our own home. And what of our plans for starting our own family?

I am at my wits' end.

Sunday 4th January
Pa has offered Alfie an apprenticeship in the shop. As we sat down to Sunday dinner Ma nudged him and said, 'Go on then, John.' Pa cleared his throat and said he'd got something important to say, and then looked across the table at Alfie and said something like:

'I'd planned on waiting to see how trade picked up after Christmas before raising your hopes but what with you getting laid off and all, I'd like to make you a proper formal offer of an apprenticeship at Appleby & Sons. We'd like you to join the family business, lad.'

It felt like a long pause but was probably only half a minute. Ma was beaming expectantly, holding a serving spoon in mid air, and Pa took a sip from his tankard, put it down and said, 'Well, what d'you think?'

I was that excited, I couldn't help gabbling about what a generous offer it was, but Alfie's face told another story: he seemed unable to meet my gaze. At last he muttered his thanks, and said he'd give it careful consideration.

'Consideration?' I almost shouted. 'We've only got enough to pay the rent for a couple of weeks, and you're going to give Pa's offer "careful consideration"? Are you mad?'

Ma told me to give the lad some space, because it was a big decision, changing jobs like that. 'He hasn't got a job to *change*,' I answered back. 'And in case you haven't noticed, dearest husband, there are more than a million people unemployed. Jobs aren't two a penny, you know.'

Alfie's face flushed, he pushed back his chair mumbling some excuse and limped out of the room. I went to follow him but Ma put her hand on my arm and told me to leave him be, for the moment. He'd had a shock this week losing his job, she said, and that he'd soon come round, bless him.

Pa served himself a pile of potatoes and greens and tucked into his plate as if nothing had happened, but my appetite had vanished. I picked at my food for a while and then said I should really go and find out what Alfie was getting up to, apologising for upsetting their lovely meal. I found Alfie in The Nelson, of course, ordering his second pint. He greeted me with a face like thunder.

'What do you mean, shouting at me like that in front of your Ma and Pa?' he said, under his breath so Bert couldn't hear.

'What do *you* mean, turning down the offer of a job with a decent wage, for the rest of your life?' I came right back, not caring who heard me. 'Have you any idea how close we are to being unable to pay our rent or buy food, let alone *that*?' I gestured to the pint he was just about to raise to his mouth.

He took a long draught anyway. 'I haven't turned it down,' he said, 'I just want a bit of time to think.'

'Think about what, exactly? About all those other wonderful jobs out there, paying great wages, what with millions of people unemployed?' He shrugged his shoulders as if to say 'why not', which infuriated me even further. But I knew I was on a hiding to nothing, so I stomped out and came home and now here I am, writing away, and waiting for him to roll in, stinking of beer and cigarettes, like so many nights before.

Is this what married life is supposed to be like? What happened to all those dreams we had, before this bloody war destroyed everything? Sorry to swear, dear diary, but that's how angry I feel at the moment.

Sunday 18th January
It's been a fortnight since Pa's offer and Alfie is still flatly refusing to discuss it with him, which is down-right rude, in my book. If I try to raise the subject he clams up, and he seems to be trying to avoid me, heading out every morning looking for work at the factories and warehouses he's already tried a dozen times. You can't fault him for perseverance.

I've been doing the same, knocking on doors, feeling like a beggar, and they look at me as though I've got a screw loose. 'A million men out of work and she thinks there might be a vacancy for a lassie?' I can hear them saying to themselves. It is clearly hopeless.

To make matters worse, Alfie's nightmares seem to have returned, just when I'd been hoping they had disappeared for good. Last night he tossed and moaned words I couldn't understand at first, but after a while I could make out what he was saying, in a desperate, pleading whisper that sounded like: 'Don't let him die, don't let him die'. Then he started up with heart-wrenching sobs that shook his whole body, whimpering, 'Oh no, oh no, oh no,' repeating it time and time again.

I woke him and held him in my arms, whispering that it was only a dream, and he was safe here at home, with me.

In the morning I asked if he wanted to talk about it but he shook his head and clammed up. I can only assume that whatever happened is just too horrible for him to recall.

Sunday 1st February
Yesterday the landlord came for the rent and when I went to the jar on the mantelpiece where I'd been saving it, I found there wasn't nearly enough. He's given us a week's grace, but is not noted for his patience with late payers.

When Alfie got back I challenged him, and he admitted taking 'a couple of half-crowns' out of the pot. 'For beer, I suppose?' I shouted, and he looked so shamefaced that I knew it was true. Even though it's bitterly cold I suggested we went for a short walk in Burgess Park. Somehow it's usually easier to get him to talk if we're not facing each other. So, as we walked, our conversation went a bit like this:

Me: We have to do something, Alfie. We'll lose the flat unless we can find the money by next week.

(Long silence)

Me: Alfie?

(An even longer silence)

Me: For goodness' sake, what *is* the problem? Butchery's not that bad, is it? Pa's been happy doing it all these years, and his father before him. It's a skilled trade, a good step up from factory work and makes a good living, when there isn't any rationing.

Him: It's nothing to do with that, Rose. I just can't . . .

Me: You can't what? Is it that you don't think you'll be up to it, managing the money and all? Pa'll teach you everything, he's very patient like that.

Him (after another great pause): No, it's not that. I can't explain why . . .

Me (trying not to lose my temper, but failing): Well, instead perhaps you'd like to explain to me how we're going to pay the rent and what we're going to eat, if you turn this down. He'll have to take on someone else, and then where would we be?

Him (resigned sigh): All right, all right. I'll talk to your pa this evening.

Me (relieved sigh): Thank you. And for goodness' sake, tell him you're sorry for taking so long about it, will you?

Him: Let's go home and light the fire. It's cold as buggery out here.

Monday 9th February

Hurrah! Alfie's gone into the shop with Pa today. To see if it works out, he says. Quite why he didn't agree weeks ago I'll never know, but I held my tongue and said I was sure he'd enjoy it, learning a craft and how to manage the business side of things. Suggested we went out for a drink to celebrate this evening. At least now we can afford it.

Sunday 15th February

It's the strangest thing. Pa asked me to come round to the house, on my own, as there was 'something he wanted to discuss'. Oh, and I was not to tell Alfie. Perhaps I could go when he was having his usual Sunday lunchtime pint?

Ma disappeared into the kitchen to make tea, and when I asked what this was all about there was Pa looking shifty. Eventually, he said, 'This is difficult for me, my dear.'

Whatever he was about to tell me was definitely not going to be good news. And then it all came pouring out: what he'd been trying to figure out all week. He got Alfie on the light work, to begin with, serving customers and the rest, and at first he seemed to get on well. He's a friendly chap, good with people, Pa said, and the punters seem to take to him. When the shop was quiet Pa started introducing him to accounts and the rest – and though he's not very confident with numbers, he's a quick learner. In fact, he said, he seems to be most at home when he is in the office, adding up columns and making them square.'

'Go on,' I said, dreading what was still to come.

'He seems okay with minced beef, sausages and bacon, and cold cuts like ham and cooked poultry, but he flat refuses to handle other meat, especially the large joints. He won't help me carry out the carcasses in the morning to hang out on the display hooks, or bring them back in the evening. I could understand that, it's heavy work and takes two hands, which means he can't use his stick. But he won't even go into the cold store, or handle a saw or a hatchet. I even caught him using a fork to lift the liver onto the scale. When I questioned him, he said he's just getting used to it, wants to take it one step at a time.'

I said perhaps it was just something he needed to get used to, but then Pa said there was something else. When I pressed him, he said, 'I set him to cleaning the trays of an evening after we'd closed, and even that seems to be a problem. I caught him carrying them to the sink with his eyes closed.'

'What? Walking across the shop with his eyes closed?'

'When I asked him about it, he denied it. Said I must have caught him blinking. D'you think the poor lad's experiences over there have made him afraid of blood?'

'Have you asked him, directly?'

'No, I was hoping you'd do it. Might be easier for him to open up to his wife.'

I doubted it. What I didn't tell Pa is that Alfie's nightmares have been terrible this week: every night struggling with the sheets as if he's trying to fight someone off, crying out in his sleep or waking up in a pool of sweat, shaking and crying. But he still refuses to talk about it.

So here I am, waiting for my husband to come home. I don't expect the conversation to go well.

Monday 16th February

Alfie has gone off to work this morning, with a weak smile.

'Weak', because he knows that I know what's really going on in his head, after yesterday.

When he got back from The Nelson we had 'the conversation'. I told him what Pa had said, and asked him the questions I'd been composing in my mind. At first he did the usual Alfie thing, refusing to speak, but then I got cross and started to shout about the need for him to face up to whatever was going on, or it would get worse and worse and he would never be able to face Pa again or even make a proper life for himself.

He started shouting back at me, then, about why didn't I stop criticising him all the time, that he was doing his best and if it wasn't good enough then why had I married him in the first place? And hadn't he told me, in the hospital, that I should go off and find a 'proper' man, someone who could take me dancing and have enough money to buy me decent clothes and not have to live in this hovel?

That made me even more angry because, although it is small, I like our little flat and have worked hard to make it homely and comfortable, and I said just that, and if he didn't like it he could always go back to his parents' house.

I regretted it immediately because he went paler still, his face crumpled and his head slumped on his shoulders. Then the sobs came deep from inside his chest, like an animal in pain. It started me off too, and there was little else I could do except keep my arms round him.

Eventually he found his voice and said he was sorry, and I apologised back, we had a big hug, and I made tea. Then I told him that unless he could talk about it, Pa would never be able to understand or give him any leeway, he'd lose the job and we'd be penniless again. What harm was there in trying to tell me? Even if it was something terrible he'd done in the war, I would never think the worse of him for it.

After another long silence, he took a deep breath

and cleared his throat. It wasn't easy, that much was clear from the way his hands wrestled with each other in his lap, as if they were locked in some kind of fight to the death. But once he'd started talking, it was as if nothing would stop him. The words just poured out like water from a tap, although never once did he catch my eye.

I'll do my best to record what he said:

'It was Thomas, my mate Tommy, who I was out on patrol with that day. We'd been together all through – met on day one, when we were first mustered for France, and got on right away. After a week or so we'd got like brothers, looking out for each other, covering each other's backs, you know the kind of thing. We went through some rough times, I tell you, it's impossible for anyone who wasn't there to understand what it was like, all the mud and the lice and the chaos, with no-one knowing what the hell's going on, and the shells coming over day and night, and the snipers ready to get you if you make the smallest slip. People were dying every day, even when we weren't on a big push. It's like being in hell. Bloody weird how we got quite used to it. After a while it felt almost like normal.

When Tommy's brother bought it, and they wouldn't give him leave to see his folks, he was so angry he was on the point of deserting. But I talked him out of it – they always get caught and some even got shot for it. It was selfish, really, cos the truth was,

I wasn't sure I'd be able to cope on my own, without him.

One time when we were going over the top, a shell landed that close I got knocked out by a clod of something – not injured but out cold. I came round lying in a shell hole with Tommy, who was unhurt, and a couple of others who were moaning like hell because they'd had bits blown off. We tried so hard, but we couldn't save them, and afterwards we just lay and cried in each other's arms till it got dark and we could crawl back to our line.

It wasn't till later one of the other lads told me they thought I'd been a goner that day. Where I'd been knocked out was right in the open, the most dangerous place to be, and Tommy had crawled through the wire with bullets whistling past him, to drag me to safety in that shell hole. I owed my life to that man, Rose, and he risked his own life to save me.'

(He went quiet for a long time after that but I held my tongue, and eventually he gathered himself and started again.)

'How we survived, I'll never know. Half of our unit dead, and we'd seen three officers come and go but Tommy and me were still alive, heaven knows why. The other lads used to touch us, for good luck.

When Armistice Day finally arrived it was almost a let-down. They'd told us the previous evening but we didn't believe it, and that morning the Germans were shelling us just as fierce as ever. We even had a direct hit in the trench that killed three men at around half nine – could you believe it? Then, at eleven on the dot, everything stopped. Complete silence, except for the ringing in our ears. Some of the lads said even the birds stopped singing, though there were precious few trees or bushes left for them to sing in.

A few people cheered but most of us just moved along the trenches shaking hands and not saying much. I think we were too exhausted to celebrate, and some people just sat down and cried. Got a bit sad myself, thinking of your brothers.

All Tommy and me wanted to do was have a bath and a good meal, and we got our wish soon enough. By the evening we were back in the village and the French women couldn't do enough for us: we had baths and delicious meals and they unearthed bottles of wine and beer that they'd hidden underground.

Next day we were nursing sore heads and looking forward to a bit of relaxation, so it was a real shock when our commanding officer came by and said that although the fighting had stopped we still had work to do, so we wouldn't be going home for several weeks. Weeks! We were so shocked – stupid really, I suppose we'd just expected to get on the next boat home. We'd be helping the Frenchies clear up, restoring homes, shell clearance, that sort of thing. He promised not to work us too hard and we'd have proper days rest, too, and good rations, so we reckoned we could live with it for a while.

We got pretty excited when they said we might be demobbed in time for Christmas but that passed with no news and Tommy and me was pretty fed up when they told us we had to go out again with our unit the day after Boxing Day. It was a new town where we hadn't been before, about twenty miles away where there was still buildings to be searched and much work to be done to help get the place back on its feet again. We sang our hearts out marching there, trying to cheer ourselves up. We were split up into units of four to spread across the town, with an order to report back at the Otell Dervee – that's what they call the Town Hall – at midday. We was on our way back there when it happened.'

(His face had turned the colour of a plucked chicken, with beads of sweat breaking out on his upper lip. I suggested he should take a breather while I made more tea, but he just carried on.)

'I've got to tell it, Rose, now I've come this far, need to tell you what it's like, when I go to the shop . . . that meat . . . the blood, and those bones. I get visions . . .'

(Go on then, I said, if you are sure.)

'So that's when it happened, when the unexploded shell went off. We were picking our way through an empty building, must have been a factory or something, and Tommy and the two others were ahead of me when 'whoomph'. I felt myself being blown backwards against the wall, and the crack of my leg and then, silence. Well, I knew immediately what had happened and started shouting for help. I couldn't stand on the leg but for some reason I didn't feel any pain, that didn't come until later, so I crawled over towards where they'd been. Christ, I wish I hadn't made it.'

(He stopped again, his jaw clenching and unclenching, trying to stop himself breaking down. I could sense what was coming and felt like crying myself but knew I had to hold it together for him.)

'One of them had most of his face blown away, and he was moaning, calling for his mother. The other one was silent, dead already, his guts spilling out onto the concrete in a pool of his own blood. Tommy was a few yards away from them, lying on his front and calling out for me: get me out of here, mate, get me home, please, Alfie, get me home. Please, Alfie, please, Alfie, he kept saying, over and over again.

I was talking to him, telling him to hang on in there, that help was on the way and we'd get him home in no time, which seemed to settle him. Jesus, I'd have given my own life to save him, but there was no way any of them could have survived. Didn't stop me praying, all the same.

He asked for water and went to turn him over so's I could give him a sip, and then I saw what that shell had done to him. It had just ripped his leg right off him, and the skin, so the whole right hand side of his body, his leg and arm, his crotch, his chest, was just bare, like raw. . . raw . . .'

(The tears were pouring down Alfie's face by now, and he wasn't even trying to wipe them away any more. He didn't need to finish, the picture was so clear in my head: the young man's body flayed by the blast, the missing leg and the mess of raw muscle and bone, like one of those carcasses hanging in Pa's shop.)

'He died in my arms, Rose, right then. He looked up at me and whispered again, take me home, mate. Then he closed his eyes and sighed and I was willing him to breathe in again, but when he didn't I just started screaming for help because I still believed he could be saved. Then I must have passed out myself, because by the time they got to us I was nearly dead too from all the blood I'd lost.'

'You did your best,' I said, putting my arm around him while he sobbed. 'You could never have saved him, not with those injuries.'

We were too exhausted to talk much more, that evening, just had a quiet tea and went to bed early. I woke in the night with my own visions of what that shell had caused, of the young soldier with his face blown off, the other in a pool of his own blood. And of Tommy's leg torn away and his poor flesh, mangled and stripped of its skin like the carcass of an animal in the butcher's shop.

But Alfie slept on peacefully by my side and, for the first time in a fortnight, he went through the whole night without a nightmare. Perhaps talking about it is the start of purging those terrible memories.

PS: I almost forgot. Tomorrow is Johnnie's birthday. My big handsome brother would have been turning twenty-three, probably married with a couple of children, and working with Pa in the shop. At least Alfie is alive, even if I hate what that bloody war has done to him.

Sunday 14th March
After opening up to me, Alfie's nightmares really did seem to get better, at least for a while.

He's been going to work every day as usual, and if I pass by the shop he gives me a cheery wave. When I ask Pa, all he'll say is that Alfie's doing his best, though there are some tasks he still feels he won't do. Gently does it, he said.

But he's struggling, I know it. Not that he's said anything, I can just tell. A dozen times I have been about to ask him, but have bitten my tongue. For a week or so I thought I was just imagining things, exaggerating the little signs in my head. Leave it to Pa and Alfie to sort it out, I tell myself, it's not your business to interfere.

But I can't ignore what I see with my own eyes:

a) The nightmares have returned, and we are both short of sleep.

b) He's exhausted at the end of day, not only because of the nightmares. The work isn't physically that hard, even bearing in mind his disability, but I think the effort of holding himself together is draining every ounce of energy.

c) He's drinking again, every evening, sometimes to the point of coming home incoherent. When I tackled him about it the other day, he got all prickly, telling me to stop criticising him, and wasn't it perfectly natural to want to relax at the end of a hard day, like most men? Most men don't drink to get drunk, I wanted to say back, only the unhappy ones who're trying to forget.

d) Sum total of the above, he seems to have lost his sense of fun. Worse than that, although he's still affectionate with me, he has little interest in the intimate side of our marriage. How will we ever have a family, if this carries on?

Tuesday 16th March
Alfie has lost the battle against his nightmares – they've invaded his days as well.

Today, Pa had to close up shop in the middle of the morning because Alfie properly lost his wits and started cursing customers in the shop.

At first Pa asked him politely to leave, but Alfie got even more angry and had to be manhandled into the back room, which is where the butchery proper happens, where they cut up the large slabs of meat. Pa said it was at that point Alfie reached for a knife, so he had to hold him down on the floor and call for help. Apparently he was flailing about, yelling for someone to save his dying friend – I can imagine all too clearly what must have been going on in his mind.

By the time they got him home, Alfie had stopped fighting and shouting, but his whole body was wracked with those terrible animal sobs once more. We sat him in a chair and he just slumped over, weeping and gibbering nonsense. Pa was worried about leaving me alone with him, so he went to ask Ma to come and help. We made strong sugary tea and built up the fire, hoping that the warmth and comfort would ease his pain, but an hour later he was still weeping. There was nothing for it: we had to call out the doctor.

We got him into bed and the doctor made him drink a dose of what he called knock-out juice, and now he is sleeping like a baby. Heaven knows what tomorrow will bring, but I am almost certain that he won't be going back to the shop again.

It's such a bitter irony. There we were, worrying about how he would cope with his physical injury but it's the effect on his mind that is disabling him now. I think it might be what the newspapers are talking about as 'shell shock'. I barely like to admit it to myself, but I'm terrified that he might never be normal again.

Chapter Five

Jess woke with a start and found herself still on the sofa, shivering with cold.

She stretched and yawned, pushed Milly off her knee, carefully placed Rose's notebook back into the box with the others and dragged herself upstairs to bed. Around the time dawn broke she woke again, gasping for breath, with cries of terror stuck in her throat: she'd been dreaming of a curly-haired man trying to slash her with a blood-stained knife, surrounded by corpses hanging by their feet from the ceiling of a white, echoing cell.

Once she'd realised that it was just a nightmare, the horrific vision seemed grimly comic, somehow. 'Christ, the last thing I need is a murderous great grandfather haunting my dreams,' she said to herself, trying to snuggle back to sleep.

But her mind wandered back to Rose's words, and her struggle to help Alfie fight his disability and get back to civilian life, to find a proper job, to remind him that life was for having fun, too. The voice in the writing was so strong that Jess could almost hear the shrill exclamation of frustration: 'I am at my wits' ends', or, the calmer, more reflective tone: 'At least Alfie is alive, even if I hate what that bloody war has done to him.' I wish I could have been able to talk to her in person, she thought. Rose hadn't even turned twenty but, for all her youth, she sounded like someone with a very mature head on her shoulders.

The next thing she knew was hearing two male voices booming in the hallway downstairs. Someone – the postman perhaps – talking to her father? Then she remembered her mother saying that her brother was coming home this weekend, with Sarah. 'They've been together nearly a year,' Susan had said. 'Do you think it might be serious?' Jess blinked at her phone with disbelief: it was 11.30 a.m.

'Rough night?' her brother asked, as she appeared downstairs in her dressing gown.

'It's a pleasure to see you too, Jon.' Jess raked her hair with her fingers. 'Hello, Sarah. Welcome to Suffolk. Coffee anyone?'

Later that afternoon, when she offered to pick up some items for her mother from the village shop, Jonathan leapt to his feet. 'I'll keep you company, shall I? Could do with stretching my legs. C'mon, Milly.'

'Okay, so what's up?' he said, as they walked down the lane.

193

'Nothing. Why?' The dog darted ahead of them, in and out of the high pillows of bramble on either side, trying unsuccessfully to chase rabbits.

'You won't talk about work or Nate, you refused a glass of wine at lunchtime and, forgive me, you look like hell.'

'Charming of you to say so.'

They turned onto the footpath across the heath, the shortcut to the village centre. It was a still, golden day. An Indian summer, the weather forecasters were calling it.

'Seriously, though. Is something wrong?'

'How long have you got?'

'In a nutshell?'

'Okay. In a nutshell: I've been having a really crap time since I got back, and the job's just not working out, so I've decided to quit.'

'Quit being a paramedic? Shit, it's *that* bad?' He sounded truly shocked. 'Why?'

She sighed. 'A young man died, you see, after he was hit by a car. I didn't manage to save him and I'm not entirely certain that it wasn't my fault. I hesitated, just for a few moments, but the delay could have cost his life.'

'Phew, scary stuff. But surely that sort of thing could happen to anyone, couldn't it? You can't save every casualty.'

'It's more about not being able to trust myself. I can't risk it again.'

'Can't they put you onto some kind of course, or

something, help you get over it? You've spent your whole adult life working towards being a paramedic – it's been your thing ever since James died, hasn't it? You mustn't quit now.'

'I've lost confidence. And anyway I've felt such a sense of relief since making the decision, I can't help thinking it must be the right thing to do.'

They'd reached the end of the path where it met the village street, and stopped to put the dog on a lead. Automatically, they both turned to look at the estuary. However familiar, the sight was always somehow uplifting: that great expanse of slate grey water or, at low tide, the purple-brown mud flats, bordered by reed beds and pine trees, and the wide open spaces of sky.

'Whatever would you do instead?'

Milly was waiting impatiently, looking up with her sad enquiring eyes. The words came out in a rush: 'Maybe something to do with animals?'

'A vet, you mean? Doesn't that take years of training?'

'To be honest, I haven't really thought it through.'

'A veterinary nurse, maybe?'

'Perhaps.' The idea was surprising, but not entirely alien. They started walking again.

'But if you can't face the idea of humans dying, how would you feel about animals?'

'Don't mince your words, will you?'

'If your brother can't ask the question, then who can?'

She leaned down and scratched Milly behind the ears. 'I'd hate seeing an animal die, but it's not quite the same as losing a person, is it?' However much she might love her dog, nothing could ever replace James, not to mention Jock, Baz and Millsy.

'Wouldn't you miss the adrenaline?'

'I might, long term. But right now, no adrenaline would be good.'

They walked on in silence. Jonathan seemed to sense it best to leave the subject, Jess felt too exhausted to talk about it any more. They reached the shop, exchanged pleasantries with an elderly couple who remembered them both from their schooldays, and paid for their items. On the way home they passed the bench by the playing field.

'Let's stop for a few minutes,' he said.

'Shouldn't you get back to Sarah? Isn't it a bit unfair to abandon her at the mercy of the parents?'

'We won't be long,' he said, patting the seat beside him. This had been the site of many an adolescent experiment involving illicit substances, bottles of cider and furtive gropings. She'd mooned over James here, longing for him to notice her, and then she'd wept her heart out here, when she heard he'd died.

Even now, she wished he could be with them, enjoying the sunshine that warmed their faces and enveloped the heath in a dazzling golden haze. She missed Nate, too, and made a mental note to ring him when she got home. They'd been texting but she'd felt too stressed to speak on the phone, worried about admitting what had happened to her and whether it might shake his faith in the delicate balance of their relationship.

'I can't believe you really want to give up being a medic, Jess. Are you sure?'

'I think so,' she said. 'I told you. After that accident, I can't trust myself any more.'

'Tell me about this young man who died,' he said.

She summarised the scene on the pavement, the rain and the blood, the splinters of glass in the butcher's shop window, and her flashback.

'The problem is I can't guarantee that won't happen again. I'm afraid of myself, afraid that I'll lose it, somehow. And it's not only that: I get this uncontrollable anger and lash out at people, and I have terrible nightmares which only go away if I drink, so that's obviously making things difficult between me and Nate. Sometimes I think I'm going mad.'

'You seem perfectly sane to me.'

They sat without speaking for a few seconds, listening to a bird singing in the bush behind them. A robin, perhaps, or was it a blackbird? She thought of Rose and her mother at the very first Remembrance Day, how only the birdsong broke the silence among all those thousands gathered around the wooden cenotaph in Whitehall, how the ceremony seemed to help give them solace.

'It's the strangest thing, Jon.'

'What's that?'

'Something very similar happened to our great-great grandfather after the First World War,' she said.

'The one who had a wooden leg?' As children they'd always been fascinated by the idea – imagining him to look like Long John Silver in the cartoon. It had become the stuff of family mythology.

She nodded. 'That's right: Alfie. Married to Rose. She wrote these amazing diaries. Mum discovered them at Granny's. I was up reading them till late last night.'

'What do you mean, something similar happened to him?'

She tried to summarise what Rose had described of Alfie's homecoming, how his leg had to be amputated because of gangrene, and how he struggled to accept the disability. The job hunting and then getting laid off, then the nightmares and anger, his drinking, how he reluctantly agreed to try working for Rose's father at the butcher's shop but couldn't face the blood and raw flesh because of what had happened to his best mate.

'He had a breakdown, Jon. They called it shell shock in those days but he got through the shelling in the trenches okay and made it to the end of the war almost without a scratch. But it was his friend dying that he couldn't cope with.' She gave an involuntary shiver, remembering how Alfie hadn't even bothered to wipe away his tears as he described what Tommy had whispered: *Take me home, mate.*

'Are you okay, Jess?'

She took a deep breath. 'Rose said she was afraid Alfie might never be normal again.'

'And?'

'It's got me worried that perhaps it's going to be the same for me.'

She caught the glance of concern in his eyes as he swivelled on the seat to face her. 'You mean *you've* had a breakdown?'

'Not as such. But I feel terrible much of the time. I tried taking tranquillisers and the nightmares went away for a while but they made my head all fuzzy, and when I stopped them everything came back, the anger and nightmares and the rest.'

'Does Mum know about this?'

'Some of it.'

'Have you seen a doctor?'

She shook her head.

'You ought to. It's very common, this sort of thing. Post-traumatic stress and all that. You of all people should know about it.'

'Do you really think that's what it is?'

The alarm in her voice made him backtrack. 'Could be. Mild version or something. Have you thought of counselling?'

'I'm sure it's not as serious as all that.'

'You said yourself it's affecting your work, your relationship with Nate. I really think you could do with some help, Jess.'

'It's just that . . .' he waited as she struggled to find the words. 'The thought of spilling out all my personal problems to a stranger just makes me feel rather queasy,' she said, finally. 'Besides, it's expensive, counselling.'

'You served your country, for God's sake, the Army ought to support you. Promise me you'll go and get help?'

'I'll give it some thought,' she said. 'Come on, Sarah will think I've abducted you.'

By the end of the weekend they'd ganged up on her. Jonathan talked to their mother, who talked to Jess and offered to pay for five sessions of counselling, 'just to get you back on your feet again, love'. There wasn't any point in resisting.

She also managed to persuade Susan to let her borrow the rest of Rose's notebooks, so that she could finish reading them at home. 'Take great care of them, won't you? Don't get them wet, or lose them? Remember I haven't read all of them myself yet.'

'I'll guard them with my life, promise.'

The counsellor's room had to be the blandest, most featureless space she'd ever entered: beige walls, oatmeal carpet and curtains, straw-coloured furnishings. It smelled neutral, too, somewhere between dust and emulsion paint, and there was nothing to see out of the window except the off-white wall of the building opposite. Today, even Alison the counsellor – a pleasant woman in her middle years with grey eyes and greying hair in a sensible cut – was wearing shades of cream and taupe.

Jess could hardly bear to drag herself back to this room again, to face the kindly half-smile that seemed to be Alison's default expression, but she felt a sense of obligation to her mother and brother to see it through. *To prove it wouldn't make any difference*, is what she secretly thought.

At the first session, the previous week, she'd found herself instantly irritated by Alison's ordinariness and the anodyne questions she asked. How could this middle-aged, middle-class do-gooder ever understand in a million years what she had been through? For a while they sat in silence as Jess grappled to find the right words.

What she wanted to say was that she didn't really need any help, it was something she'd be able to work out in her own time, she was only here to please her family, she honestly couldn't be bothered to go over it all again and anyway she was bored with her own voice. But somehow, haltingly, she had begun, and before she'd even said a few words she'd found herself weeping uncontrollably, using up almost a whole box of tissues. Alison made no move towards her, continuing to sit upright in the chair opposite and regard her with those sympathetic eyes, but saying not a single word as the seconds ticked loudly by on the wall clock above the door, and the session drew to an end.

Afterwards Jess had felt raw and exhausted, and even more certain that dragging everything up again was not going to do any good. Yet here she was for a second time, obediently making her way up the stairs to this dull, unremarkable room and taking her seat on the pale leather chair, determined that she would make a more sensible, reasoned attempt to describe her problems this time.

'As I said last week, I've been struggling at work, you see? I get angry and have nightmares and flash-backs. But you get on with it, you know, everyone does. It's what you do, in the Army.'

She paused and looked up. Alison nodded encour-agingly, her expression ripe with the confident assumption that her client would continue to unburden herself and make everything all right.

'To be honest I don't think it's anything I can't deal with myself, given a bit of time and space. Anyway, I've decided to leave this job and do some-thing different. Have a complete change of scene.'

Another long pause, another kindly smile from the other chair.

'What matters most to me at the moment is the relationship with my boyfriend – it's been under a lot of strain. I did some fairly horrible things and he broke up with me. We're back together now, thank heavens, but it's early days and I don't want to risk . . .'

Oh God, the tears were prickling the back of her eyes again. She hadn't seen Nate for a couple of weeks and, although they'd texted almost daily and talked on the phone several times, she had bottled out from telling the truth when he'd asked her about work:

'It's fine, thanks,' she'd said. 'Going really well.' Not a word of the accident, her conversation with her boss, the 'gardening leave' that he'd gently but firmly proposed. She'd have to confess soon enough, but the thought of the disappointed look that would come across his face when he learned that she'd been lying to him, the lowering of his eyes, the small frown that would flicker across his forehead, made her feel sick inside.

She reached for a tissue and blew her nose. Alison was waiting, and something about her nondescript features and compassionate smile were somehow so infuriating that Jess pulled up short, hardly able to believe that she was confiding her own, very personal thoughts about her relationship to this perfect stranger. The half-empty bottle of whisky, hidden in a drawer in her bedroom, was calling to her.

'Do you mind if I stop now?' she said, glancing up at the clock. Only a quarter of an hour had passed.

'You may do as you wish, Jess,' Alison said in her quiet, well-modulated voice. 'These sessions are for you to use as you want. I am absolutely confident that we can make progress but you are going to have to stick with it a little longer if you want to get to the bottom of what's troubling you . . .'

As she spoke, Jess could feel her heart contracting as irritation fomented into anger. She'd gone along with this through a sense of duty to her mother but found herself hating every minute. It wouldn't do any good anyway. How could anyone who hadn't been there ever understand? She tried to bite her tongue but the words burst out of her mouth all the same, cutting off Alison in mid flow.

'I'll tell you what's troubling me, if you want,' she heard herself saying in a threatening whisper. 'I've lost friends, beautiful, talented young men with their whole lives ahead of them, who bled to death in the desert fighting for some spurious made-up bollocks about weapons of mass destruction which never existed. I've seen young men maimed for life by IEDs, trying to save them while the fucking Taliban went on firing. And I've been that close to death myself – there were definitely times when I thought I'd never make it home.'

The energy of anger brought her to her feet, and she began to pace the room.

'So is it any bloody wonder it's taking me a bit of time to readjust to dealing with drunken idiots on Saturday nights and trying to help poor vulnerable old people who can't get any ruddy support from the state after working hard and paying taxes their whole lives? Is it? *Is it?* Go on tell me, is it any *bloody* wonder?'

Alison's stick-on smile had disappeared but her voice was still calm. 'No, it isn't any wonder. But we can help you with your anger . . .'

Jess stopped pacing and glared down at her. 'Help me with my anger? Oh *please*, spare me the clichés.' She hated herself for being so unpleasant to this inoffensive, well-meaning woman, and needed to get out, fast, before it got any worse. 'D'you know, I really don't care anymore,' she said, grabbing her coat and bag and heading for the door, pausing in the doorway to add, 'It's not your fault, Alison, but this simply isn't going to work.'

Vorny and Hatts were still away on exercise, so Jess had the flat to herself. Even as she sucked the last drops from the whisky bottle in her bedroom and later, as she prowled the drinks aisle of the supermarket, purchasing six more, plus two cases of wine and a carton of cigarettes, she promised herself that it would be just a temporary refuge.

'Just giving myself a little break,' she'd reasoned, pouring the first glass. 'Enough of trying to save people's lives, being all dutiful and responsible. I need to forget things for a while, to do what I want without anyone getting all holier than thou about it.'

To stop Nate worrying, she texted him: Last-minute place came up on HART training course. No signal. Will phone when I get back. XX

The drink eased the pain of remorse and helped her postpone, for the moment, having to think about what to do with the rest of her life. She recalled the overwhelming wave of relief when she'd admitted to her mother that she couldn't cope with the responsibility for saving lives any more, and felt sure that giving up being a paramedic was the right, indeed the only, thing to do. But in her more sober moments she experienced all over again the reciprocal swell of panic at the thought of giving up her life's career. It felt like standing at the edge of a chasm so deep you couldn't see the bottom, yet knowing that you would have to jump.

Vorny and Hatts returned late one evening, filthy and exhausted from two weeks of bivouacking and fighting mock battles in torrential rain on some remote stretch of bleak moorland in the west country.

'Bloody hell, what's going on here?' Hatts said. 'Looks like dossers have moved in.'

The air was thick with the stench of stale alcohol and cigarette smoke, and every surface of the living room, the coffee table, mantelpiece, sideboard and part of the carpet, was covered with empty bottles and glasses, take-away cartons and overflowing ashtrays. On the sofa was a tangled pile of blankets, cushions and a sleeping bag from under which they could hear gentle snores. Vorny pulled back the blanket and shook Jess's shoulder, gently at first and then more firmly.

'Wake up, Jess, we're back.'

Jess groaned quietly before falling back into sleep.

'She's out of it. However did she get herself into this state? I thought she'd sworn off the booze, and she quit smoking when I did, when we got back off tour.'

'Not any more, she didn't,' Hatts said, grimacing at a saucer brimming with cigarette butts. 'Come on.

Let's just clear up a bit and leave her tonight, let her sleep it off.'

Waking at dawn, Jess had a vague memory of hearing their voices but thought it must have been a dream until, in the dimly rising light, she saw their backpacks and waterproofs piled high in the corner. The room seemed to have been cleared of the bottles and take-away cartons she had so defiantly strewn around her.

She slumped back onto the sofa and pulled the sleeping bag over her face but the alcohol was dissipating from her body, leaving her edgy and fidgety. She sat up, looked around and cursed her friends for hiding the bottles before recalling that the wine had gone a few days ago and she'd finished the last of the whisky yesterday evening. The shops wouldn't be open yet – she'd have to wait.

Vorny found her in the kitchen making coffee.

'What have you done to yourself?' she said, watching Jess's hands shaking as she spooned the grounds into the cafetiére, the yellow pallor of her skin and dark lines under her eyes.

'Long story.'

Hatts arrived in her dressing gown, tousled and sleepy, they took their mugs into the living room and Vorny opened windows to let out the fug. It was a chill, bright October morning and the smells of autumn, falling leaves, newly-turned earth, floated into the room along with the rumble of morning traffic and the faraway wail of an ambulance siren that made Jess's guts clench.

'You haven't answered me,' Vorny said. 'What's happened? Why aren't you at work? Why all the booze and fags?'

'How long have you got?'

'We've got three days' leave. Take all the time you like.'

Explaining to her friends what had happened that day in the high street, and why she felt that she could not carry on as a paramedic, was relatively easy – they could understand exactly what she was going through. In their own separate ways, both girls had experienced flashbacks to their time in Afghanistan. No-one could do what they had done or see what they had seen without suffering some long term impact.

To her relief, they did not insist that she should return to counselling, but accepted her own analysis: the anger and panic attacks were caused by the fear of making mistakes which might cost someone's life. However hard she tried to persuade herself that she was perfectly competent and at least as skilled as any of her colleagues, the anxiety could not be quelled. The best solution, they agreed, would be to remove herself from situations which made her anxious, for a while. Taking a break from working as a paramedic seemed the best plan.

They helped her write a letter of resignation and, when she wavered, talked everything through again and again with her, for hours on end, until she felt certain enough to post it. As the letter dropped into the box, she felt the weight lifting from her shoulders and knew that she had done the right thing.

What they couldn't help with was the harder part: facing the future.

'First things first,' Vorny said, that first morning. 'You've got to sort yourself out, not drink any more, not even a sip. Do you promise?'

Jess nodded.

'Say it.'

'I promise not to drink any more, not even a sip.'

'We'll be watching you,' Vorny said.

Later that evening she rang Nate, apologising for not returning his calls. She'd been poorly with the flu, she lied, off sick from work. To her great relief he sounded genuinely sympathetic and pleased to hear from her, saying he hoped she'd feel better in time to come to the wedding of his old friend Barnie, for whom he'd been invited to be best man, and then chattering on about how they would get there and where they would stay.

'It sounds great. I'm really looking forward to it,' she said as brightly as possible, trying to persuade herself that, by then, she would feel strong enough to admit to him what had been happening.

'Me too, Jess. It's been ages.'

'I'm sorry. It's been so manic here.' *Stop now, no more lies.*

'I love you,' he added quietly, almost as a throwaway.

Her heart felt ready to burst. 'Me too, Nate. See you soon.'

Brimming with new resolution, she went shopping for a new outfit for the wedding only to discover that she seemed to have gained a whole dress size from lack of exercise, too much booze and unhealthy eating. In the dressing room mirror she saw a short, pallid, slightly pudgy person, who seemed to have gained not only several kilos but also about ten years in age. The face that was once smooth and bright-eyed was now hollow-looking with dark rings under the eyes and lines on her forehead even when she stopped frowning. How could Nate ever love me again, she asked herself, sighing with silent despair. She thought of his beautiful long brown limbs, his wide surprising smile, the soft look in his eyes, the way he towered over her and made her feel both vulnerable and safe at the same time.

Whatever else was happening in her life, however unsure she felt about her future she knew, more than anything in the world, that she wanted to be worthy of his love, and she would do her damnedest to make sure that she didn't ever disappoint him again.

BOOK Four

Rose Barker - PRIVATE

Saturday 20th March 1920

Alfie is recovering, slowly. He's starting to eat properly again and today, when we went to the park to feed the ducks, I even caught him smiling at the sight of the little troupes of fluffy ducklings. Tomorrow we are invited to Sunday dinner with his parents – the first time he's agreed to socialise since what we are calling 'the incident'.

Saturday 27th March

At Alfie's insistence I've told no-one about what we now know was some kind of breakdown, although I am certain the stories had been circulating the neighbourhood. For the moment it is unspoken, even between me and Freda, and even though I am certain she knows all about it she is respecting our need to pretend that nothing has happened.

I think she was being kind when she invited me to go with her to the Ideal Home Exhibition at Olympia to get ideas for furnishing the house she says Claude is going to buy for them. She even suggested Alfie might like to come too, because they're offering free tickets for returning soldiers as part of the so-called 'Homes for Heroes' plan, but we both know he hasn't the slightest interest in that sort of thing, so in the end it was decided that just me and Freda would go.

We were looking forward to having a bit of fun, which, in a way, it was. The exhibition hall itself is as tall as a cathedral, with a beautiful arched glass roof. Seeing that alone would have been worth the journey. But when, after an hour of queuing, we finally made it to the turnstiles and walked inside, the sight that greeted us was quite simply jaw-dropping.

In a space the size of several football pitches, rows of stalls were set out like real rooms in a house, only unlike any house I've ever been into. There were living rooms with matching carpets and upholstery, carpets of every pattern and colour combination under the sun, tiled white bathrooms with enamel baths, basins and water closets of every description, and bedrooms with beds, blankets and pillows so soft and luxurious it was tempting to snuggle down on them, right then and there.

But it was the kitchens that attracted the biggest crowds. After half an hour's gawping at all the wonderful inventions at a stand called 'A vision of the future,' Freda and me agreed that we didn't want to wait till then. Imagine, a machine to cook toast, a flat iron heated by electricity, a washtub which does everything including the scrubbing, and another which does all the wringing? The cooking ranges were so clean and compact, and could run on gas or coal, or even both. And in future people won't need pantries – they'll have huge steel ice-boxes which will keep the food fresh for days.

There's a new kind of furniture for these kitchens, too, called 'cabinets', which come in cream or white and have special drawers for different kitchen utensils, and marble or enamel worktops that are 'super hygienic', or 'ideal for pastry'.

On the bus back Freda babbled on about how she was going to furnish her new home, about colour schemes and floor coverings and, of course, how she was going to have all the latest kitchen cabinets and labour-saving devices. I listened with half an ear, watching out of the window and wondering how ordinary people will ever earn enough to buy these wonderful new things, or whether they would only be for the wealthiest, like Freda and Claude? Even if Alfie and me were both working, we'd never save enough for even one of those gadgets let alone a whole kitchen full, as Freda seems to be planning for.

Back home, I snapped at Alfie and after tea he headed down to the pub even sooner than usual. I promised to join him later after clearing up, but in truth I haven't the stomach for it tonight. Now that I've seen 'A vision of the future', my own life seems flat and dull, our cosy little flat dowdy and old-fashioned.

I wish I'd never agreed to go to that bloody exhibition. From thinking myself the luckiest wife in the world to have my Alfie home, I'm turning into a grumpy, dissatisfied old grouch.

Saturday 17th April

Freda came round on Monday and told me she and Claude were planning to go dancing at the Palais to celebrate her birthday, and would we like to go with them? Alfie flatly refused, as I expected, mainly because of Claude. You don't have to talk to the man, I told him after she'd left, it would just be merrier to go with another couple. Don't we need to enjoy ourselves, once in a while? We've had so little fun together recently.

He set his face against the idea and it pains me to admit that I got so angry with him that I threatened to go on my own if he wouldn't come with me. He stomped out of the house, down to The Nelson as usual, and came back a few hours later in his cups, again. But the following day he came in from work and just said, 'You win. We're going dancing. But don't expect me to talk to that man.'

Of course, I threw my arms around him and immediately began to fret about what I was going to wear, until Freda said she would lend me one of her dresses. She came around later with a couple to choose from, both in the new 'flapper' style, with no waist and a six-inch fringe all around the hem. I loved the really colourful one with pink flowers and, with a pair of borrowed silk stockings and a splash of 'cerise' lipstick, I felt so modern that I barely knew myself.

'You'll have to do something about that hair,' Freda proclaimed, bursting my bubble. But she was right, the wavy shoulder length I thought so stylish just a year ago suddenly looked old fashioned. She offered to lend me the cash, and I emerged from the salon with a bob, all straight and swingy and just below my ears!

Even Alfie was impressed – I could tell because he kept sneaking glances at me – and the evening began with a swing. We went to a little bar beforehand and Claude paid for delicious cocktails that came with little paper parasols which Freda and me stuck behind our ears (Alfie drank beer, of course). After two of those, I began to feel quite light headed, and Claude was in very high spirits, telling slightly risqué stories which had Freda shrieking with laughter and made me giggle in spite of myself. Alfie stayed quiet and I was just grateful he'd agreed to tolerate Claude for the sake of my friendship with Freda, and what was supposed to be our romantic evening out together.

Unfortunately it didn't turn out like that.

We'd had a few numbers on the dance floor, doing our simple jigging and arm waving to the music and trying to ignore all the clever dancers like Claude and Freda who knew all the proper steps, when they swirled up to us and Claude shouted over the music to Alfie, 'May I have the pleasure of dancing with your beautiful wife?'

Now, I know it is considered quite normal, even polite, to ask your friend's partner for a dance, but Alfie obviously wasn't aware of it because his face was like a thundercloud, not so much out of jealousy of Claude, I suspected, but more about him being worried about keeping up with Freda. But in the circumstances he could hardly refuse, so he nodded and Claude whisked me away in a ballroom hold, spinning me around at such a pace that I got quite giddy. Then he started on another dance style, kicking out his heels and swinging my hands from side to side so that I nearly fell over, but after a while I got the hang of it and began to enjoy myself and, when the music ended, I agreed to another one.

Alfie stood up for me when we got back to the table, and I thought he was being unusually courteous until I realised that he wasn't going to sit down again. He hissed in my ear, 'I'm going to get my coat now, whether you want to leave or not. You can stay, or come if you like, I don't care.'

When we got home we had the most terrible, vicious row, and said things to each other that I am sure we will regret. But for now, he has gone to bed and I am sitting up writing, because I know I will not sleep for all the thoughts scrambling my mind.

I want the old Alfie back.

I don't care a jot about his missing leg – it's become quite normal for me now – but I don't like what he has become: angry, jealous, bitter and miserable much of the time. I am trying my best to make it work, but sometimes it feels as though nothing will help.

Sunday 2 May

Today I turned twenty! Alfie bought me my very own pair of sheer silk stockings and Ma made a beautiful cake, so I felt very spoiled.

I think we might be turning a corner. I've written this many times before, I know, but this time there are several good reasons for hoping it might be true.

Reason 1: Alfie is so much happier now he's not fighting his fear of blood and raw meat every day. It took him three weeks to recover fully from his collapse (and a fortune in doctor's bills which Ma and Pa kindly stumped up), but that gave us time to think. He was all for going back to the shop – 'got to beat the bloody thing' he kept saying – but after a while he agreed it wasn't worth making himself miserable over, and Pa said he'd given it his best shot so shouldn't feel bad about admitting defeat. He is now unemployed again, but so much happier.

Reason 2: I start next week as a trainee machinist at Mitchell's collar factory. It's only a ten minute walk from home, just the other side of the Old Kent Road, and I'd been there several times before asking for work, but they never had any vacancies. This time a friend of Ma's put in a good word and they asked me to go in for a test. I'd never used a sewing machine before but it seemed pretty straightforward, so long as you're careful not to put your finger in the way of the needle. I must have done okay because they wrote the next day and offered me the job. Apparently they only employ women for this work because it requires delicate fingers and an eye for detail, so I don't feel as though I am stealing the job from Alfie or any other demobbed soldier. The pay's no great shakes but it will help eke out his pension until he can find himself work.

Reason 3: Alfie and me are getting on so much better in every way. He's affectionate and loving again, and sometimes we can't wait to get to bed! We're trying to be careful, though. Don't want to get pregnant just as I've started my new job – and while Alfie is still unemployed.

Monday 31st May
Terrible weather. It's been raining cats and dogs for three days, but here in London we've had it lucky. The newspapers are reporting that in Lincolnshire more than twenty people drowned in floods over the weekend.

Sunday 6th June
All the talk in the pub today was how Pa's favourite singer in the world, Nellie Melba, sang a song in Chelmsford yesterday which could be heard all over the country through something they're calling an 'electric wireless'. Apparently with one of these contraptions you can listen to your favourite music in your own living room just by turning a button! But even if we had the electric in our house I'm sure we'll never be able to afford such a wireless, let alone the licence, which costs ten shillings a year.

I've been at the collar factory a full month, and I'm loving it: the sewing is tricky and keeps you on your toes, we work hard but have a great laugh in the tea and lunch breaks. Today, the boss said I was making excellent progress. If I carry on like this I will be fully trained in just two months' time and my pay will go up by two shillings.

It's good to be in the company of other women my age again – hadn't realised how much I missed it. Getting that cash at the end of the week is really satisfying, not only because it's keeping a roof over our heads, but because it makes me feel worthwhile, that I'm not just living off the back of my husband.

Which is just as well because, despite trudging the streets every day, Alfie has found nothing, yet. Mr Barker has given him the odd little job in the second hand furniture trade, which keeps him in beer money and he seems to be keeping reasonably cheerful, even in the face of all the knockbacks he's had.

PS Butter rationing is over. Hurrah!

Monday 14th June
Percy Gittins has started as Pa's butcher's apprentice. It was a tough moment for us all, seeing someone who isn't even part of the family working alongside Pa where my brothers ought to be, or Alfie, if only he'd been able to cope with it.

But Pa says the business has got so busy now that he has no choice but to take on someone else to help him, and why not support another lad who's had his fair share of suffering after doing his bit for the war?

Percy is still breathless as a consequence of the gassing, and his mum told Ma that the doctors don't reckon his lungs will ever fully recover. But he looks so much better than when he first returned, and he was always a strong lad if not the brightest at schoolwork.

Pa says he may never manage the business side but he's becoming quite skilled at the butchery.

Saturday 3rd July

Ma called round for tea this afternoon, looking flushed and feverish, but when I asked if she was unwell, she said it was precisely the opposite.

'Never felt better, dearest,' she babbled. 'It's so exciting, I barely know where to start.'

It seems she'd read in the newspaper about a man called Alfred Newsom, who claimed to be able to talk to people's lost loved ones. When she mentioned it to Pa, he told her, 'don't touch it with a bargepole, it'll only lead to trouble'. But the idea preyed on her mind, she said, and then she saw a poster in the corner shop about 'psychic sessions' and noticed that the man would be appearing at the community hall in the Old Kent Road just a few minutes' walk away.

'You know I would never do anything to go against your Pa,' she said. 'But when I saw the date, I knew right deep in my heart that I'd never live with myself if I didn't try it, just the once. I'd do anything to ease the pain.' Turns out the session in our neighbourhood was on none other than July 1st, the very day my brother Johnnie died, at the Somme, three years ago.

Ma reckoned that, being a Thursday evening, Pa would be at his regular darts match either at The Nelson or at an away event, so she would be able to get to the session and back without him ever knowing a thing.

So she paid her sixpence and went into a hall packed to the brim with women, the mothers and wives of lost soldiers. 'There was a comfort in just being there, I suppose,' Ma said, 'all of us suffering in the same way.'

After about forty minutes of summoning up other people's fathers, sons and husbands, Mr Newsom asked if there was anyone in the room who knew John? Ma swears he looked in her direction but she wasn't going to own up at first because it's such a common name. Then he said that this John was also known as Johnnie, and he knew that his family would be especially sad today, because this was the very date of his death and there was no grave to visit.

Well, that was too much for Ma. 'It must have been him. How else would he know that Johnnie died today and had no grave?' In her excitement she completely forgot to be shy or careful, shouting out that this must be her son Johnnie and pleading to speak to him.

I bit my tongue to stop myself saying that twenty thousand British boys died on the first day of the Battle of the Somme, many of them were never properly buried, and a fair few of them could have been named John. But I could also imagine how easy it would have been to be swept away by the moment, especially being surrounded by so many other women desperate for reassurance.

She went all wide eyed as she described what happened. Apparently Mr Newsom was quite calm, 'like it was something you do every day'. He said Johnnie wanted to tell her that he was quite well and in no pain and, even though we had no grave to visit, he would always be with us in our hearts so all we had to do was find ourselves a quiet place and think of him, and he would hear us. Ma said she found herself 'coming over all faint', and had to be helped out of her seat to the back of the hall where a couple of kindly ladies gave her a cup of sweet tea and looked after her till she felt better.

'It was *him*, Rose, I know it,' she said. 'Just the little turns of phrase he used, and the way he called me Ma. Oh, it's such a relief to hear that he is not suffering any more.'

She went home so excited that she found herself blurting it all out to Pa, who lost his temper and shouted a lot, saying it was a load of old cobblers and that Arthur Newsom was just some charlatan out to take her money. But she says it's already brought her peace of mind and that's worth more than a dozen sixpences, any time.

Like Pa, I have a more sceptical nature, but reckoned that no harm was done if it had left Ma reassured rather than upset. But then, just as she was leaving, she let slip that she was planning to attend another of Mr Newsom's sessions, being held in a hall near Waterloo Station, in six weeks' time.

'Now I've heard from Johnnie I want to know that

Ray is all right,' she said. 'You'd've thought Johnnie might have mentioned his brother, but he didn't. What if Ray's spirit is still unsettled and wandering? What if he is still suffering? I have to know, Rose, whatever your father says.'

On the spur of the moment, perhaps because I was concerned that the next time might not have such a happy result, I found myself offering to go with her. I am already regretting it.

Sunday 22nd August
This diary has been very neglected, what with work and holidays. I've finished my training at Mitchell's and am officially now a fully qualified machinist, with a nice pay rise to go with it. Alfie is now working almost full time for his father, delivering second-hand furniture and suchlike in his cart. Rather to his surprise he's enjoying working with the pony, in spite of its stubborn ways, and is earning quite well. Business seems to be booming now that more of the damaged homes have been repaired, and new ones being built. It's all cash in hand and unofficial, which has always been Mr Barker's way.

With two wages coming in, we've finally been able to indulge in a few luxuries. Last week we went to Brighton again and the lovely guest house we discovered last time. The landlady immediately recognised us and welcomed us with open arms. It's been a miserable cold summer and trade had been slow, she said, but we managed a couple of days warm enough to sit on the Promenade, and went to the funfair again.

Alfie may not been keen on dancing but he loves the flicks, so every other Saturday we treat ourselves to an evening out at the Electric Cinema. Last night it was *Way Down East*, where Lilian Gish played an innocent young girl seduced by a sophisticated rich man and ends up pregnant and destitute. The blizzard scene was so realistic and the pianist accompanied it so cleverly that I found myself actually shivering in sympathy with poor Lilian.

On the way home Alfie joked that he reckoned the lead actor had Claude in mind when he played the man-about-town character, and he's right: he has precisely the same arrogance, the smooth chat-up lines, the way he splashes the cash around. We laughed, but it's a worrying reminder. Freda seems to have lost her way with this man, blinded by his flashy ways. I only hope she's sensible enough to avoid the same fate.

Sunday 12th September
On Tuesday I went with Ma to see Arthur Newsom, the psychic. Pa and Alfie were out with the darts team for an away match, so we could slip out without either of them knowing.

I was certain it would just be a room full of gullible people prepared to believe anything and that nothing would happen but, as we arrived, the butterflies began in my stomach. What if it were really possible to 'channel' the voices of the dead, as his advertisements claimed? And how would I react if there was a 'message' from Ray? The very thought made me a little wobbly.

Inside, the hall was packed, but if you closed your eyes you would never have known it; there was such a sombre hush over the place with just the occasional whispers of people moving into their seats. No chatter, no excited greetings, people just sitting and waiting in silence, with their hands folded and heads bowed.

At last Arthur Newsom arrived on stage, an impressive figure of a man – at least six feet and broad with it, a full head of wiry black hair, a finely tailored grey flannel suit and the shiniest shoes I've ever seen. But his voice failed to match: high and hoarse, quite quiet, which made you strain your ears to hear him. The hall was silent as a tomb, the audience hanging on his every word. You could have cut the atmosphere with a knife.

In his quiet, calm way he told us that although he understood we had all come with hope in our hearts, he was not going to be able to help everyone, but that at least ten people in the hall would hear news of their lost loved ones tonight. At this there was a collective intake of breath – and I couldn't decide which I feared most: a 'message' from Ray, or no message, which would leave Ma desolate all over again.

Then he closed his eyes and there was a moment's

silence before he started to whisper, tentatively at first, something like: 'I've got someone named Frederick with me, a young man killed in battle. He's coming over loud and clear. Hello, Frederick. Do you have a message for someone with us in the hall tonight? Perhaps they know you as Fred, or Freddie?'

There was an anguished yelp from a few rows behind us, and a woman shouted, 'It's me, Freddie. Your ma, Elsie. Can you hear me?' Mr Newsom quickly established that Freddie was her son, killed in action nearly three years ago. The message for his mother was reassuring, very similar to that he'd given Ma about Johnnie. 'He is well and not in any pain, Elsie, and wants you to know that he is with you every day, with love in his heart.' When it ended, the woman began to weep loudly, falling into the arms of her companion, shouting 'My darling Freddie, dearest boy, thank you my son. May God bless you and keep you safe.'

Mr Newsom closed his eyes again and one or two began to urge him, crying out: 'Sam, can you hear me', and suchlike, sending shivers down my spine, and he was soon talking to Albert, then Jimmy and David, always with a similar pattern: the question, establishing the links, giving the message. My butterflies had gone, and by now I was feeling very uneasy about the whole affair, the way he seemed able to manipulate these grieving women. I could feel Ma beside me, straining every muscle in her body, desperate for him to mention the name Ray or Raymond. But the evening drew to a close, and it never came. As we walked home I tried to comfort her, but what could I say? She'd been drawn into the spell, and was so convinced that because she'd actually had a message from Johnnie the previous time, Ray's 'silence' meant he was unhappy or in pain. I didn't tell her what I think, which is that Mr Newsom bases his success rate on sticking to the more common names, which is why he would not risk a more unusual one like Raymond.

Monday 11 October
This evening Alfie came home all made up because his pa has bought a second-hand motorised van, and they'd been out for a spin.

'By God, you should have seen us flying along, it was the best fun I've had in ages. The speed of the thing: it gets up to a full forty miles an hour! You're supposed to stick to twenty, but no-one takes any notice. Why would you, when you can reach double that on a straight road?'

I love to see his eyes sparkling once more – it's been so long.

The idea is that Alfie will drive the van for deliveries, and this means saying farewell to the pony, which saddens him because he'd grown fond of the old thing, but nothing can dampen his joy at the idea of learning to drive a motorised van.

I know nothing about driving but from watching bus drivers using both feet to press down the pedals in the floor, I wondered how Alfie would manage with his one leg. It seems Mr B has already thought of this. He'd seen another man using what he calls a 'hand-throttle' which Alfie explained is a lever on the gearstick that you push to make the car go faster or slower, while your foot is busy braking or pushing down the clutch to change gear. Even though he explained it to me twice, it's still gobbledegook. But he's happy as Larry and that's all that matters.

Ma went to another of what she calls her 'meetings' last week, but still no sign of Ray. 'Even if I can't have a message, if I only had a place where I could go and talk to him,' she said, when she came round afterwards, 'at least that would allow me some peace.' It's getting quite the thing these days for people to travel to France to visit the places where their loved ones died, I told her, perhaps we could save up? But she says that would probably make her feel even worse and I tend to agree. Imagining Ray's broken body lost somewhere beneath those muddy trenches and shell-pocked fields we've seen so much of in the *London Illustrated* certainly fills me with horror.

It's little comfort, but we are not alone – hundreds of thousands of bodies have never been recovered, and their families will never have a grave to visit. The war may be over but the pain doesn't seem to get any easier with the passing months.

Friday 8th October
Alfie received a letter today from his old regiment, inviting him to take part in this year's events to mark

Armistice Day. Apparently there are places for four thousand injured veterans to witness the ceremony at the Cenotaph, and his name is among those who have been chosen. At first he said he couldn't afford to lose a day's money, but Mr B obviously prevailed.

Ma and me are going anyway, like we said we would last year. This time they will unveil a permanent stone version of the old wooden Cenotaph, which will be quite an event to see.

Monday 25th October
Terrible accident in the Old Kent Road today, and nearly on our doorstep. It was such a foggy morning you could barely see your hand in front of your face, and two trams crashed into each other just as they were going into New Cross. Dozens of people were hurt, some of them not likely to live.

Pa saw the ambulances going past the shop and then a customer came in who'd been there just a few minutes after the accident happened – he tried to help but was moved away by the police. He said the screams of the wounded were something terrible.

When Alfie came home he said they'd only been using the pony cart today. 'Too foggy for the van,' he said, which reassured me a little.

Monday 1st November
I simply have to write about this, it is such a wonderful, bold idea: to create a 'tomb of the unknown soldier', as the newspapers are putting it.

They say it was suggested by an army chaplain who saw a rough wooden cross in a Frenchman's garden with the words 'An Unknown British Soldier' pencilled onto it. The Prime Minister has agreed: so they are going to bring the remains of just one anonymous body back to England and give it a proper burial ceremony and a permanent gravestone in Westminster Abbey. And because no-one will ever know who the soldier was, we can all live with the thought that it represents our own lost ones.

Alfie is going to be with fellow soldiers who will line the route of the coffin and salute as it goes past. What an honour.

I have asked Mr Mitchell if I can have the day off so's I can go with Ma to the Cenotaph. He knows my two brothers were killed so I'm hoping he'll look kindly on my request.

Wednesday 10th November
Today the talk at the factory was about nothing else: the 'unknown soldier' is on his way, and everyone is very stirred up about it – that's the only phrase I can find to describe the mixture of emotion and excitement we all seem to feel.

Apparently four bodies were dug up and one was chosen at random by an army bigwig so no-one will ever be able to trace the real identity. When it arrived at Dover this morning on a destroyer, they gave a nineteen-gun salute (which Alfie tells me is the highest possible army honour) from Dover Castle high up on the white cliffs, before it was put onto a train to Victoria Station.

The newspapers reported that every station it passed, even the smallest village, was thronged with people in black, paying their respects. How dramatic that must have been, the train thundering through the night, past crowds of silent mourning people?

Alfie went off to Westminster this afternoon with a pack of sandwiches. They are being given tea and will sleep in tents in St James's Park so they're ready to move into position early tomorrow morning. Ma and me discussed whether we might go tonight too, so's to secure a good spot for seeing the coffin, but we wouldn't get a tent to sleep in and she didn't feel up to a night on the pavement, so we've decided to set off very early in the morning, instead.

It's an odd thing: even when we should be sad, I find myself almost elated. As if my brothers are actually coming home, at last. Which is stupid, because of course it is not them at all. The two-minute silence last year was something special, but this year is going to be even more of an occasion to remember.

Friday 12th November
Well, it certainly was a day I'll never forget, nor Alfie neither. When we finally got home around eleven o'clock last night we both agreed we were so pleased to have 'been there', even though it was completely

exhausting, and he has a new sore on his stump from walking and standing so much. But we were both too excited to sleep, and talked in bed until the small hours about our different experiences of the day.

Ma and me managed to get there earlier this time and found a spot where we could see the Cenotaph monument, still draped with the largest Union Jack flags I've ever seen. It looked so tall and impressive, reaching up to the third floor of the office buildings on either side of the road, we could hardly wait for it to be unveiled.

There were even more people in Whitehall than last year, but there was no jostling or pushing, everyone was polite and mostly silent, as we moved into our places and waited for eleven o'clock to arrive. There was a buzz among the crowd as the procession approached, and by standing on tiptoe we could just about get a glimpse.

It wasn't so much the pomp and ceremony, the fancy gun carriage with its six black horses, nor the men marching in perfect unison with their eyes turned to the coffin, nor even the King, whose head we could just catch sight of through the crowds as he saluted the coffin and laid a wreath on the top of it. What really brought it home was the steel helmet, just a soldier's old 'tin hat' they had placed on top of the Union Jack draped over the coffin. It made me realise that, in spite of all the grandness of the occasion, whoever was inside (and his identity didn't matter any more), was just an ordinary soldier, like

Johnnie, or Ray, or countless others, who'd died in the mud and blood of the trenches.

Our handkerchiefs were already soaked with tears by the last chime of Big Ben. All the men took off their caps and we bowed our heads for the two minute silence, which seemed longer and more profound even than last year. From where we stood, it wasn't entirely clear what happened next (someone said the King pressed a button), but after that the flags fell down from the Cenotaph and we could see the enormous stone column reaching up into the sky. Once the coffin and the procession had moved off, Ma and me joined the queue waiting to lay their wreaths at the foot of the monument. We only had two modest bunches of flowers, with ordinary brown labels tied to them on which Ma had written Johnnie and Ray's names and dates, and it took us nearly three hours, but she was that determined to get there I reckon we probably would've queued all night if that's what it took.

Alfie didn't see any of this. He was part of the guard of honour on both sides of the streets all the way to Westminster Abbey. After the burial service proper inside the Abbey, he said, another enormous queue formed outside, of people come from all over England to see the actual grave. It's curious to think that most of them will hardly even notice the tombs of the kings and queens and other famous people buried nearby.

As they were preparing to leave, Alfie exchanged

a few words with an old woman in the queue who'd spent two days travelling from the far north of Scotland and was preparing to wait all night if necessary. She was holding a bunch of withered flowers she'd picked from a garden her son had planted when he was only six. Now the boy was lost somewhere in the mud of France.

I told him how much the day had meant to Ma. Although she'd wept a fair bit during the day, it was when we were sitting down with a cuppa in her little parlour that the tears really started to fall.

'Don't mind me,' she'd said. 'It's relief, more than sadness. I know it's peculiar, but it doesn't matter who that soldier was, he represents all of them. So now I know my boys are safe. I can sleep in peace.'

That pretty much says it all.

Tuesday 7th December
I was right. For a couple of weeks now I've been feeling strange: dog-tired and a bit queasy. At first I put it down to a touch of the flu but it didn't get any better or worse, and now my monthlies have failed to appear. I must be expecting!

Alfie is over the moon of course, and was ready to go down The Nelson to 'wet the baby's head' that very moment, but I persuaded him to hold his tongue for a couple more weeks – to Christmas, say – till we announce it, just in case of mishaps. I'm not even going to tell Ma and Pa, not just yet.

I just find myself humming all the time, any old

tune that pops into my head, whatever fits the rhythm of the machine I'm working on, imagining the day when our little one will arrive and complete our family. Although I know that bringing up a baby is no bed of clover, I feel so sure that this little scrap of new life will help to put all the trials and problems of the past few years behind us.

Freda will be so excited when I tell her, but I'll have to bite my tongue for a few weeks longer.

Monday 13th December
What a weekend! All day Saturday and Sunday it blew a terrible blizzard. About a foot of snow fell and it turned the world into a kind of wonderland. Of course the roads and pavements are very slippery and it's difficult to walk, especially for Alfie. He even resorted to using a stick today, which he normally hates, being too proud to admit to his false leg. The papers say it will probably go on snowing for the rest of the week.

Sunday 26th December
It's been a wonderful Christmas. My goodness, what a long way we've come since last year. Alfie was still stuck in France and we had no idea of the ordeal he was about to endure, Pa could open the shop only two days a week because of rationing, Mr Barker's business was on its knees, Ma was withered into a shadow, grieving so terribly for the boys.

Now, Alfie is home and back at work, earning good

money and loving the freedom of driving Mr B's van. Appleby's Fine Butchers has had a bumper Christmas – they sold nearly a hundred turkeys this year. People seem to have decided that it was time to celebrate, making up for what they've been missing the past five years.

Mr Barker seems to have more work than he and Alfie can cope with, mostly in the second-hand furniture line. 'When the rich start buying new, you get a better quality of used,' he told us over Christmas dinner. 'Now even the common folk are taking more pride in their homes. It's the perfect equation of supply and demand.' He's even invested in a proper warehouse now, rather than the old lock-up he'd been using to store goods during the war.

Ma is a new person, and seems at last to have found peace with herself. No more shrine in the boys' old bedroom, no languishing in bed half the day complaining of headaches, and no more visits to Mr Newsom, thank heavens. On the boys' birthdays and the anniversaries of their deaths she places a vase of flowers by their photographs in the parlour, and these small acts seem to ease her sadness. She is cooking proper meals, and eating healthily, and has even signed up as a volunteer street collector for a charity that looks after war handicapped. It's given her a new sense of purpose, helping the living instead of grieving for the dead, she says.

And me? Well, I could not be happier. Alfie and me are making good money and can buy ourselves the little luxuries we could only have dreamed of in the past. We are talking about moving to a bigger flat with a second bedroom, and planning a week in Brighton in June or July, before the baby arrives. He's even hoping to save up enough for a small motor – more likely a motorcycle with a sidecar – so that we can go touring with the baby. I told him not to get too many big ideas because we need to put a bit away for when I have to give up work.

Everyone in the Appleby and Barker families is cock-a-hoop about the baby, especially Ma, who said she'd have to start knitting right away. Pa was a bit gruff, as usual, but Alfie says he was proudly buying rounds in the pub at lunchtime today and enjoying the joshing he got about becoming a grandpa with pipe and slippers etc. So I reckon he's pretty pleased too.

Freda said she was over the moon for me, although her face told a different story. She and Claude have been engaged for more than a year now, and there's still no date for a wedding. To make it worse, he keeps disappearing for weeks at a time, on business in Europe, he says, and I'm really starting to wonder if he has another woman somewhere.

She would be heartbroken if it all fell apart, and I long to warn her that he's never looked like a very safe bet in my eyes, but she won't hear a single word against him and sounds off at me if I so much as utter a word of doubt, so I hold my tongue.

BOOK FIVE

Rose Barker - PRIVATE

Saturday 1st January 1921

Spent New Year's Eve in The Nelson again, with me in a strop because Alfie flat refused to go dancing at the Palais with Freda and Claude.

I had so wanted to wear the new dress with the fringe around the hem that Ma had made me for Christmas. Alfie said I could wear it down the pub, couldn't I, and I got even more angry because the whole point of the fringe is that it jiggles around when you dance, and would just look plain stupid in a boring old pub. So the evening didn't start off well and got worse, as he got more drunk and I got more grumpy. I didn't feel like drinking but stuck it out till midnight, because I didn't want tongues wagging, and came home straight after the Auld Lang Syne.

Also, a bit of a dampener: in the pub was a woman I know slightly from Mitchell's – she works in the office. When she heard everyone raising their glasses to our 'new arrival' she came over to congratulate me.

'When's it due?' she asked and when I told her August she said, 'Take my advice, dearie, keep it quiet at the factory till you start to show.'

When I asked what she meant, she told me that Mr Mitchell didn't like pregnant girls working there because he said they got clumsy and it was dangerous on the machines. There'd been an incident a few years ago when someone put a needle through her finger and they'd discovered later she was three months gone. Ever since then, the boss had given women their cards just as soon as he learned of their condition.

'Is that legal, to sack you just because you're expecting?' I asked her and she said there was absolutely no law against it, so I thanked her for the advice and said I'd keep quiet and hope for the best.

Wednesday 16th February

The papers are reporting that unemployment in Britain has topped a million, and it's not just the men out of work, it's their families who're affected too, so at least four million must be on the breadline. It doesn't bear thinking about. The government's going to increase dole money but that's scant consolation for men who are keen and willing to work.

Alfie and I were talking about the news this evening and I said, 'At least your pa and mine are self-employed so they don't have to worry about being laid off.' He looked at me as though I was stupid and pointed out that of course it affects them too: the more people out of work, the less they are likely to spend in Pa's shop and on the sort of things Mr Barker sells. How naïve I am about such things – I wish I could have spent more time learning about today's world in school, instead of ox-bow lakes and the Wars of the Roses. Still, they did teach me to read and write for which I am very grateful – if I couldn't write this diary I'd go mad, bottling up my thoughts and not being able to express them.

I've stopped feeling sick and tired and I'm really starting to enjoy being pregnant. But when my belly starts to swell – as it will soon – I'll have to be careful when putting on my overalls in the factory changing room. Gossip flies around that place like a swarm of ants in June.

Easter Saturday 26th March

It was only last week Freda and me were having a giggle about the first ever 'family planning' service that's just opened in north London and how it ought to be available for all women, not just the married ones. Finding you're pregnant when you're married might be a problem if you already have too many children, though not the end of the world. Getting knocked up when you're *not* married – now that's a real disaster, we both agreed.

But now the disaster's happened: Freda has missed her period, and is feeling the same as I was, with tender titties and feeling sick in the mornings. My heart sank, because my first thought was: 'Now she'll *have* to marry that creep Claude.' But she doesn't seem to be distressed about it at all. In fact she's positively over the moon and just says they'll have to get married sooner and make their wedding a simpler affair than she'd imagined.

I asked all the right questions, trying to sound excited for her: 'when's it due?', and 'do you want a boy or a girl?' and she twittered on about how being pregnant has made her feel 'fulfilled'. Filled she certainly will be, in a few months' time.

'You're the first person I've told,' she whispered, even though we were alone in the flat.

'You haven't told Claude yet?' I tried to keep the astonishment out of my voice. 'Don't you think he should be the first to know?'

She just said he was away on business and she'll tell him when he comes back next weekend. She's sure he will be 'thrilled to bits' (her words), but I'm not convinced. One thing is for certain, her parents are going to be *furious,* and if I were in her shoes I'd be quaking: her pa has a ferocious temper. Alfie's going to be hopping mad, too. She made me swear not to tell him and I promised to leave that pleasure to her.

When I asked where they were going to live she said Claude had his eye on a house off Dulwich Park and I nearly choked on my tea.

'Dulwich Park? That's where the toffs live. However can you afford it?'

She said Claude's businesses were doing really well, and he wanted to live in a 'nice area'. The words slipped out before I could stop them. 'Meaning he thinks this isn't a *nice* area?'

She got a bit flustered and said of course it was, but surely I had to agree it would be nice to have electric lights and a water closet inside the house, and a bit more than just a back-to-back yard for their kiddie to play in? I was about to retort that we'd been happy enough, playing out in the streets with the other children, hadn't we? But I held my tongue because the truth is that my irritation is really more to do with envy. Alfie and me do have a water closet, at least, but electricity would be nice, and of course I would like a proper garden for my children to play in.

Friday 1st April
The coal miners in the north have called a 'strike' for a fortnight's time and the government's called a 'state of emergency' which would allow them to take over the mines if the miners downed tools. Everyone's very worried because there would be no fuel to make electricity or run the railways, the country would grind to a standstill, and I'm afraid we might be laid off from the factory.

Saturday 16th April
Panic over. The miners couldn't get support from other workers so they called off their strike. But the rumblings are still rolling around: people are very unhappy about unemployment and low wages. Thank heavens Alfie and me both have jobs.

Monday 2nd May
My twenty-first birthday – it should have been a day for celebration but it didn't exactly turn out that way.

I decided not to tell anyone until afterwards, so as not to spoil the party. Ma had cooked a delicious fruit cake and invited us both round for tea after work. When we arrived, she and Pa presented their gifts – a lovely box of Pears soap and a new rug for our hallway – and Alfie produced the best surprise of all: a letter confirming our booking at the guest house in Brighton for a week in June.

Although I did my best to put on a cheerful face and pretend that all was well, he soon spotted that something was wrong and whispered, 'What's up?' I muttered that I'd tell him later but Ma overheard and said, 'You're not yourself, Rose, I can tell. What is it?'

There wasn't any point in pretending any more. I told them that Mr Mitchell had given me notice.

They were all very shocked and began asking What? Why? and When? all at once. I pointed to my belly, which is now unmistakably tubby. One of the girls had noticed and, though I denied it, word got round and he'd called me into the office this afternoon and asked me straight. There wasn't any point in lying – he'd have found out sooner or later. He said I'd have to leave at the end of the week because he never allows pregnant women to operate the machines for fear of accidents. I pleaded with him, saying I still had over three months to go and felt perfectly healthy, and he knew my work was good. But he said it was company policy and I'd have to come off the machines but I could work in the packing room for another couple of months if that's what I really wanted.

'That'd be better than nothing, you'd have to leave when the baby comes anyway,' Alfie said. I was feeling close to tears now, but angry too. I told him that wasn't the point. Having a baby's a normal thing, not an illness. I'll only get unskilled wages in the packing room. It's just not fair to treat us like that just because we are women.

I asked Pa if he'd sack a girl who worked for him because she got pregnant, but he said that would depend. When I asked him what it would depend on he thought for a bit, then said he'd never employed a girl so it had never come up, but he supposed he'd have to be sure she was still capable of doing the job, in her condition. It wasn't any help.

When we got home Alfie tried to reassure me by saying he was earning good money and what with his war pension we'd always be able to muddle through, as he put it. But it's so unfair. I'm still *perfectly* capable, but there's no law against being treated like this, so there's nothing I can do to stop it. And I don't want to have to 'muddle through'. I want to give our baby a lovely home with holidays by the seaside and enough for a few luxuries. Otherwise, what's it all been for, fighting this war and all those hardships we've endured?

He gave me a cuddle and said we should go to bed, but I feel so churned up I need to sit here and calm my thoughts for a while. Writing it down helps, but

I still can't get over the unfairness of it all, and how powerless we are to change anything.

Saturday 28th May
Three weeks in the packing room and I am bored out of my mind and so resentful I can hardly bring myself to socialise with the other girls. And we used to be such a friendly bunch. The lads I work with in the packing room are nice enough, but dull as ditch water. Still I suppose I ought to be grateful for a job of any kind at the moment.

All hell is breaking loose in Ireland; a bunch of Irish men attacked the British Army and tried to burn down the government building. I really don't understand the ins and outs but people are killing each other again, which makes my stomach turn – how could we start another war so soon after the horrors of the last one? When will we ever learn?

Saturday 11th June
More than two million people are unemployed, and I'm soon going to be one of them. Mr Mitchell says I'm getting too big to work in the packing room and have to leave at the end of the month.

We talked about cancelling our holiday to Brighton but Alfie says he's going to spend some of his war savings to make sure we have a bit of fun, as he puts it, before the baby arrives. So we have just postponed it until after I finish.

Haven't told him yet, but 'fun' is the last thing on

my mind. I'm so exhausted that I'll probably spend most of the time sleeping.

Freda told her parents about the baby yesterday and Alfie says his pa was all for throwing her out into the street, but his ma prevailed and said she could stay with them until she gets married or it starts to show, whichever is the sooner.

Sunday 17th July

Alfie and I are both brown as chestnuts and I'm round as one, too. The sun shone on Brighton every day and we didn't have a drop of rain, so we spent much of our time in deckchairs under an umbrella on the beach. Every now and again I would heave myself up with Alfie's help and waddle down to the water's edge to ease my swollen ankles in the cool sea. Bliss.

Trust me to be eight months pregnant in the hottest July for years. Back in London there's no air and even walking leaves me sweating and breathless, so I've spent the past week skulking indoors. And there's still no sign of the weather breaking.

Freda is worried about Claude. He went away on 'business' at the start of the month and was supposed to return last week. They were meant to be married by now and even though she's taken to wearing baggy blouses her condition is pretty obvious.

Plus, she's been given notice at work for the end of September, so will have no income of her own after that.

Bank holiday Monday 1st August

Claude has disappeared and Freda is beside herself.

Five weeks ago he said he was off to Paris 'on business' and would be back in a fortnight. Since then, no-one seems to have seen neither hide nor hair of the man. She's been round to his lodgings three or four times and his landlady is going up the wall because his July rent was due.

Alfie is ready to murder Claude if he ever re-appears. He's wretched with worry for his sister and furious with his pa for not telling him that some of the 'fetching and carrying' work he's been doing is actually part of a job that Claude had commissioned. And now he's disappeared, owing Mr Barker a fair amount of cash, so that he can't pay Alfie. He said it wasn't even so much about the money but the fact that the work was for that creep and probably wasn't even legit. 'Whatever was Pa thinking about?' he said.

This morning Freda arrived at the flat in tears, convinced that the blessed Claude, of whom she will hear no wrong, has come to some mortal harm – an accident on the roads, perhaps, or on the ferry crossing. She talks to her belly as if the child can hear her: 'Whatever has happened to your dear papa,' she says, and, another time, 'What are we going to do without daddy Claude, my little darling?' I tried my best to console her by saying that he'd probably been held up on business.

If that was the case, why hadn't he written to her by now, she asked, and I had no answer for that except to try to reassure her that if anything bad had happened, the authorities would surely notify her, or his family, before long.

'But that's the thing,' she said, starting to sob all over again. 'He hasn't been in touch with them for years. His father died and his mother went back to her family in France, but he hasn't seen her since before the war.'

'No brothers or sisters?'

It seems not, at least none that Claude is admitting to. He's always been such a mystery, that man – and I don't believe half of what he's told her. Later, Alfie put into words the thoughts I'd been trying not to admit. 'He's probably done a bunk,' he said. 'I expect the authorities have caught up with him at last, and he needs to lie low for a while.'

'Surely he wouldn't just desert her with the baby?'

'What do *you* think?' was all he'd say, and I'm afraid he's right – Claude looks after number one and would cheerfully sacrifice the lot of us to save his own skin.

Poor Freda. Six months gone and no husband in sight.

Today is my due date, but there's no sign of any activity.

Sunday 7th August
A week overdue and I keep dreaming that the baby is trying to climb out of my belly button! I'm so huge

that I can barely think, let alone move around in this heat.

Alfie's keeping it from me so as not to alarm me, but I can tell he's worried as hell about Claude and the money he owes. If he doesn't come back soon and repay his debts, Mr B won't be able to keep up the never-never on the van, let alone pay Alfie's wages.

Wednesday 24th August

Johnnie Raymond Barker was born at six o'clock in the morning on Friday 12th August, weighing a whopping nine pounds twelve ounces. Little wonder it took forever and was sheer agony, but just to look into his beautiful blue eyes, rub my face into the little blonde curls already forming at the back of his head (like Alfie's) and breathe in his sweet baby smell makes it all worthwhile.

I was in labour so long they sent for an ambulance to take me into the hospital. Everything happened fairly fast after that, but I was in quite a bad state afterwards, so they kept me in for a week to allow my insides to heal a bit. The hospital bill might be waived, they said, on account of Alfie being an unemployed, disabled Tommy. Heaven knows how we will pay it, if not.

Coming home was truly the best moment of my life. Just to have our little chap in our own little flat, with Alfie tucking us both up into bed and then going to make cocoa. The sound of the bolts in the door as he locked up for the night made me feel so safe and secure – I was quite weepy with the happiness of it all. Johnnie is a darling and sleeps much of the time so what with Alfie around to help with the shopping and washing, I am gradually starting to recover my strength.

That's not to say everything is rosy, quite the opposite. Claude is still missing, as is the money he owes Mr Barker, Freda is devastated, Mr B's creditors are chasing him and there's no work or wages for Alfie. Mrs B is beside herself with the shame of Freda's now very obvious bump, but is still refusing to bow to Mr B's demands that she should be sent away. Where would she go, anyway?

For the moment, Alfie and me are trying to live on his pension but we're also having to nibble into our savings, and they won't last forever.

Thursday 1st September
What a black day.

Alfie went to the pub at lunchtime with Pa to talk with Mr Barker about their predicament. The landlord visited the Barkers last week in person, and threatened to send in the bailiffs unless they pay the rent by the end of this week. Of course since Claude disappeared there's been little trade and no money coming in, plus his creditors know that Mr B was working for him so they're turning up and demanding to be paid or given back their goods that are now long gone.

Alfie offered some of his war savings to tide them over, but they refused because they know we're both unemployed and will need it till he gets new work. So then Pa said he would lend them fifty quid, which is a huge sum, but he knows Mr B is honest as the day is long and a hard worker to boot, so he will get it back some time, somehow.

Alfie came back home rather the worse for wear, and fell snoring in the armchair while I fed and settled Johnnie, who seems to have a sudden great hunger on him and has been waking frequently for the past couple of nights.

I was just catching forty winks myself when there was a loud hammering on the door and Freda's voice shouting, 'Alfie, Alf? Come quick!' He jumped up like a rocket and dashed off leaving me stranded with the baby asleep in the crib and worried sick that she might have gone into premature labour. She's not due until November and, much as I disapprove of Claude, I wouldn't wish any further unhappiness on my dearest friend.

I considered waking Johnnie and walking round with him to the Barkers, but the little lad needs his sleep and by the time he began to stir Alfie was back, looking paler and more upset than I've seen for a long time. I made him a good strong cup of tea while he told me the story.

The long and short of it is that this afternoon two coppers turned up at the Barkers' house asking whether they knew of Claude's whereabouts. They proceeded to inform them that the lying b****** was wanted for theft and fraud, and that Mr B could be charged with 'handling stolen goods' for which he could be sent to gaol. By the time Alfie got there, his Pa was busily protesting his innocence and looking to him to confirm that neither of them had the first clue that the second-hand household goods they'd been selling were anything other than legitimate. Alfie was furious. If he'd known they were doing business for Claude he would have refused right out, long ago.

Of course this alerted the police to the fact that Alfie had also been working for his pa, albeit cash in hand, and at that point it was all looking so serious he daren't lie. 'Anyone would confirm it,' he said, 'and then where would I be?' What he didn't expect was they then turned to him and said that he too could be charged for the same crime, along with his pa.

'It's a bloody disaster. The business is in ruins and both of us could end up in prison. And all for that effing crooked b*****.' He used a great deal more colourful language, but it's not pleasant to repeat in writing.

Then the coppers asked to visit the warehouse but after firing a million questions seemed to be satisfied that the Barkers had no further information about Claude's whereabouts, and said they would be back once they'd tracked him down.

But what about Freda, I wanted to know? She's supposed to be his fiancée, after all, and is having his child? But she sensibly kept out of the way, he said, and no-one mentioned it so they thought it best to say nothing and pray the policemen didn't make the connection.

I wish now with all my heart that I'd been more open with Freda about what I thought of Claude, right from the start. You could tell from a hundred paces that he was up to no good, but she was blinded by love and it would have caused a rift between us. Besides, you can't really go round accusing people on the basis of a 'sixth sense', unless you have proper evidence.

Well, we've got that now, in spades. Apparently his way of operating was to travel around the country visiting large country houses which looked a bit down at heel, offering to help the owners raise the money to cover their repair bills. He'd wheedle his way into their trust at first by selling a few pieces of ordinary furniture (through Mr B) and coming back with the cash, usually. Then he'd turn his attention to the more valuable antiques and works of art, saying he needed a second opinion on something and persuading them to let him take it away, and then of course he'd never return. Mr B suspects that some of the items were sold on the continent – hence his frequent 'business trips' to France and elsewhere – so that they couldn't be traced so easily.

So there we are: my husband and father-in-law both unemployed and facing a possible criminal charge and prison sentence, my best friend up the duff, engaged to a crook and her whole family deep in debt and threatened with homelessness, all on account of a man who duped them with his slick suits and silver cigarette case into believing he was a legitimate businessman.

And this is the world that all those boys fought and died for?

Friday 30th September
Little Johnnie is seven weeks old and yesterday I caught him smiling! Of course it might have been wind, but it looked like a smile to me.

Alfie missed it, of course, being at the pub as usual. This Claude business, plus having no work, has hit him really hard and he is taking solace in the beer, which is no help at all. He's done a bit of job hunting, but with more than two million unemployed it's looking even bleaker than before.

Still no news from the police. Freda is understandably miserable, and barely ventures out of the house. The news is all over the neighbourhood and she says she can't bear the critical looks of people who grew used to seeing her and Claude together in happier times. Her ma has taught her how to knit, which is how she passes her days, mostly. The baby is due in less than two months.

Friday 14th October
I read about this in *The Daily Sketch* and found it so inspirational, a little glimmer of hope in what feels like such a gloomy time for our family, that I had to write it down in my own words.

They showed a photograph of women selling artificial flowers on the streets of London – red poppies – in memory of those who died in the war. The flowers were made by French soldiers who have been disabled in the fighting, and all the money they raise from selling them goes to restore places ruined in the war and also for orphaned children.

What a brilliant idea – providing work for injured soldiers and helping others at the same time. It was dreamed up by someone called Anna Guerin, and what a woman she must be! She's even been to visit Field Marshal Earl Douglas Haig, in person, and persuaded him to adopt the poppy as an emblem for the British Legion.

Apparently she took her lead from another extraordinary woman, an American teacher called Moina Michaels, who was inspired by a poem written by a Canadian soldier to buy some artificial poppies and start selling them herself in America, in memory of all who died in Flanders Fields. She must be a determined soul too, because she's already managed to get the powers that be over there to adopt the poppy as their official symbol.

Imagine, two such clever and influential women: one chose the poppy as an emblem so we won't ever forget, the other used it as a way to help injured soldiers get back to work. And now we've got it in Britain too, in time for Remembrance Day. I wonder if they will start making the poppies here, like they do in France? Anyway, I plan to buy one just as soon as I can and will persuade everyone I know to do the same.

I took the newspaper over to Ma, who is going to show it to the charity she sometimes helps with, to see if they can drum up support for it at their end. We read the poem together and of course we both cried buckets, thinking of my brothers and all those other young men. They are building graveyards in France, and Ma and me promised ourselves that one day we will go to visit their graves.

The Sketch printed the poem by John McCrae that started it all off :

> *In Flanders fields the poppies blow*
> *Between the crosses, row on row,*
> *That mark our place; and in the sky*
> *The larks, still bravely singing, fly*
> *Scarce heard amid the guns below.*
>
> *We are the Dead. Short days ago*
> *We lived, felt dawn, saw sunset glow,*
> *Loved and were loved, and now we lie*
> *In Flanders fields.*
>
> *Take up our quarrel with the foe:*
> *To you from failing hands we throw*
> *The torch; be yours to hold it high.*
> *If ye break faith with us who die*
> *We shall not sleep, though poppies grow*
> *In Flanders fields.*

Friday 11th November

We didn't go to the Cenotaph again this year because Ma has a heavy cold and wasn't feeling up to it. But we got hold of some poppies and persuaded Bert to sell them in The Nelson. He raised nearly £5 from donations – a tremendous success.

It's only two weeks until Freda's baby is due, and there is still no news from Claude. I have persuaded her to help me walk Bessie each morning in the park because Johnnie sleeps so well when he's being pushed in the pram and that leaves me free for chatting. I think it's finally coming home to her that his 'business' was actually illegal, and he's run away to France to avoid the police and his debts. But she still believes that he truly loved her and was only doing it to raise money for their lives together. I haven't the heart to tell her I think he's doing a runner from her and the baby, too.

She's very low and a bit tearful – not really surprising I suppose, when I consider how I felt in the last few weeks of my own pregnancy, and all the other worries she has on top of that. Life in the Barker household is grim at the moment, Mr B working all hours desperately trying to drum up more business so he can repay his debts, Mrs B has been reduced to taking in washing and ironing to make a few extra pennies, and Freda locks herself up in her bedroom, hiding from what she calls the prying eyes and tittle tattle of the neighbours. I'm sure the neighbours have moved on to other scandal by now, since her condition has been plainly obvious for months, but of course I didn't say that.

We are all on tenterhooks waiting for the police to come knocking at the door again.

Monday 21st November
Freda's baby girl was born yesterday – Annie Louise. She is beautiful and so tiny (not quite 6lbs) that Johnnie seems a lump of a boy beside her. I am envious of the fact that her labour was so straightforward. In the last few weeks Freda's been talking about giving her up for adoption but seeing them together now I don't think there's any chance of that. They'll muddle through, somehow. Heaven knows what kind of life is in store for little Annie, but in spite of the difficult circumstances and the shame of being born out of wedlock, just for the moment it is wonderful to see the joy that a baby brings to the family.

It's been a strange, gloomy weekend with thick fog blanketing the whole of the south of England for three whole days. Lorries, trains and ships have all been out of action because it was too dangerous to travel, and this is having a knock-on effect on trade. Half of Pa's meat deliveries failed to arrive this morning and when I went to the corner shop for bread the shelves were empty. So I bought flour instead and took Johnnie round to Ma's and we made bread together, which was a lot of hard work but quite fun, and certainly the most delicious bread I've tasted for a long year.

Thankfully the fog is lighter today and seems to be lifting.

Thursday 1st December
Claude has been arrested! The first we heard of it was a letter Freda received yesterday.

> *My dearest, most beautiful one* (he's such a creep),
>
> *You will gather from this letter that I am in gaol, in Dover. I was on my way back to see you, my darling, because you are the love of my life and I cannot live without you, when the police arrested me. I have tried to persuade them that it has all been a terrible mistake, but to no avail.*
>
> *It is imperative that I am freed, so that I can visit the people who will vouch for me and clear my name so that we can start our lives together again. But the police have set bail at £200 which is currently beyond my means. Could you ask your father and the Barkers if perhaps they can help? I have also written to Bert at The Nelson.*
>
> *Please don't worry yourself as I am sure that all will get sorted out and we will be in each other's arms again soon. But only if you can act quickly, my dearest, to ensure my freedom.*
>
> *Your ever-loving fiancé*
> *Claude*

The gall of the man! He doesn't even ask about the baby even though he knew she would have been born by now. Of course Freda was in a great fret, wittering on about how she could raise the money to get him freed. Alfie came back unexpectedly and she had to tell him what was going on. When he read the letter he nearly blew a gasket, and shouted a lot until I managed to calm him down. Between us we finally managed to talk some sense into her.

Then, today, the coppers came knocking at the Barkers' door, putting everyone into a spin. They told them Claude had been trying to get back into the country using a stolen French passport which he'd doctored – not too well it seems, because the customs men immediately smelled a rat and held him while they alerted their colleagues in the police. So now he's been charged with fraud and evading arrest, on top of the theft he was already being sought for.

It turns out that the police are now inclined to believe Mr B's claim that he sold the furniture for Claude in good faith, and gave him the money for it less a small commission, even though there's no paperwork to prove it, and that he genuinely had no idea that on several occasions rather large sums of cash failed to find their way back to the clients.

So they're not pressing any charges against him or Alfie (phew) on condition that they appear as witnesses to give evidence against Claude when his trial comes to court. They were both so relieved not to be facing charges that they readily agreed. 'Anything to see that b***** locked way', is what Alfie says.

The trial is set for early in January.

Monday 12th December

Johnnie is four months old today. I can hardly believe that he's growing so fast. He is so solid now, twice the size of little Annie, can hold up his head and is starting to make noises that sound like words. Alfie claims his first word was Dada although I know it's only baby babble really. He lies happily in his pram, gurgling and cooing to himself, and it makes my heart burst with love just to listen to him.

Being more alert to the world has drawbacks though. He's not sleeping so well these days, and sometimes cries when I put him to bed. Ma suggested that we sing to him, which Alfie refuses to do (says he's got a voice like a crow), but she reminded me of all those nursery rhymes she used to sing to us, like *Rock-a-bye Baby*, and *Twinkle, Twinkle Little Star*. I find that the singing calms me down, too. There's so much anxiety in our lives at the moment, what with no money coming in and the trial looming next month.

In the corner shop today I met a girl I used to know from the collar factory. I asked how she and the other girls were getting on and was shocked when she told me the place has closed down. But there's talk of it reopening in new premises, so they're all keeping their fingers crossed.

Sunday 1st January 1922

My New Year wishes:
- Get the trial over with and see Claude safely behind bars.
- Alfie finds a job and can get some of his self-respect back instead of spending all his time down the pub.
- Mr B's business starts to take off again and he can repay his debts to Pa.
- Freda meets a nice, ordinary young man who falls so much in love with her that he is happy to accept Annie as his own.

I'd be so happy if all this could come true, but life is never quite as straightforward as that.

Monday 16th January

Claude's trial was scheduled to start today, but there was a heavy blizzard all over the weekend. Alfie and Mr B set off early this morning to struggle through the snow to reach the court, only to be told that the judge was stuck in the country and the trial was postponed until the following day.

They weren't very happy, and Alfie spent the rest of the afternoon in the pub and came home tonight drunk as a newt. I am trying to be patient because I know he is under great strain at the moment, but his drinking is getting out of hand again. What worries me most is where he's getting the money from. Although he denies it when I confront him, I'm really afraid that he is running through his army savings without telling me.

Tuesday 17th January

They went to the court again today, and sat all day in a little back room not being allowed to talk to anyone else, and then were never called to give evidence. Alfie went to the pub afterwards and didn't come home till gone ten o'clock looking white as a sheet but beyond telling me they'd been stuck in that little room all day he refused to talk to me and went straight to bed.

Wednesday 18th January

I had a thought that I might go with Alfie today to keep him company, and now I so wish that I had, but Johnnie has been so fretful these last few days (could he be teething, already?), and I can't take a crying baby into a courtroom. I'd have left him with Ma but she's still a bit poorly with another cold.

Alfie and his pa set off early this morning and didn't mention a word and it was only when Freda came round with little Annie this morning that I learned about the horrible things that happened yesterday. Now, both of us are sitting here in such a state of anxiety that we barely know what to do with ourselves.

Apparently Alfie and his pa were followed as they

left Southwark Crown Court by two heavies, who cornered them and threatened to beat them up if they gave evidence against Claude. They refused to say who was paying them but they must be working for Claude. Heaven knows where he's getting the cash from when he is stuck in gaol. Is there no end to this man's evil?

Mr B was cussing away, saying he wouldn't let a couple of thugs stop him making sure that b***** goes to prison for a good long time, but Mrs B made him promise that they would tell the police, when they got to the court this morning. Of course I knew nothing about all of this. Alfie just stumbled out of bed, threw on his clothes and left without any breakfast, in a great hurry to meet his pa at the time they'd agreed.

They are supposed to give evidence today – and surely the police can't protect them every moment of their lives. What if the heavies carry out their threat? The two of them would be no match in a fist fight; Alfie certainly wouldn't be able to run away and Mr B neither, cos he's a heavy smoker and always out of breath. I'm sitting here with visions of the two of them in hospital with broken faces or even – the thought makes me shiver – more serious injuries.

Johnnie seems to sense my anxiety and he's refusing to settle even though Freda and I walked out to the park with both babies. They looked so pretty, top to tail in the pram. It's still bitter cold so even though they were well wrapped up we couldn't stay out long, so we came home and made more tea and have been trying to keep ourselves busy. Right now we're drinking our third cup of tea by the fire, Freda's knitting and I'm writing this, ears pinned for Alfie's footstep on the path.

It's gone five. Surely they should be home by now?

LATER

It's after midnight and I am exhausted, but so wound up that I cannot sleep. Perhaps writing it down will help.

Eventually Freda and I gave up sitting by the fire and took the babies in the pram to The Nelson where, sure enough, Mr B and Alfie were 'soothing their nerves' with a pint or two. When Mr B told us what happened, I could scarcely believe my ears.

Apparently they waited for ages and then, finally, Mr B was called into the courtroom. He gave his evidence, as he had so carefully rehearsed with the lawyers, and felt he was doing fine until the 'counsel for the defence' started (he bandied these titles around but we could only guess at what they meant).

Anyway, this man began to dig up all kinds of unpleasant things about Mr B's business, about how he never makes any returns to the tax man, and how he was completely unable to show what money was coming in and going out and suggesting that, because of this, Mr B wasn't exactly the best judge of another man's character, and nor could he prove one way or another that Claude had actually stolen anything. Poor old Mick, he admitted that at this point he 'fell 'apart' and couldn't find the words to defend himself, so he started swearing at the lawyer and got told by the judge to hold his tongue or he would be arrested for 'contempt of court'.

Then it was Alfie's turn in the witness box. He wasn't allowed to talk to Mr B beforehand as they were kept apart in separate rooms, so had no idea what had gone on in the courtroom and was completely unprepared for when the defence man started his tricks. Claude must have told them about Alfie's breakdown and apparently he homed in on this. Poor Alfie – he didn't stand a chance.

Mr B imitated the man's voice, full of marbles, as he spoke to the judge and jury at the end: 'Your Honour, none of us can appreciate the horrors endured in the trenches by our brave soldiers. We owe them an enormous debt. But for some unfortunate individuals those horrors have not only damaged bodies and limbs, they have damaged minds too – and Mr Barker Junior is one of these, as shown by the medical records of his recent nervous breakdown.' He went on to say that the court should not find Claude – 'an upstanding businessman of impeccable character' is what he called him – guilty on the basis of evidence of a father and son, both of whom were what he called 'unreliable witnesses'.

But what about the people Claude ripped off, I wanted to know? The people whose furniture he stole? Why weren't *they* there giving evidence against him?

Apparently there *were* supposed to be three other

witnesses – one an old boy who had suffered a heart attack just a few days ago and was not well enough to attend, and a couple who'd had several valuable paintings stolen simply did not turn up. When Mr B asked the police where they were, he was told they had decided to 'withdraw their evidence'.

He said he expected they got nobbled too and were too frightened to go ahead. And all the time there was that b***** sitting in the dock with a smug grin on his face, watching the trial collapse, just as he planned. Freda asked why they didn't warn the police, surely they should have been on alert? But he said that of course they'd warned them, and the police actually brought them home in a car, just in case. He thought perhaps the others were just too scared to tell them.

It seems that what happens next is the judge's summing up and then the jury adjourns to decide whether Claude is guilty. Mr B said he thought it would probably all be over by tomorrow afternoon.

Throughout this whole conversation – an hour at least, Alfie sat slumped in the corner seat, his eyes down, not saying a word. When Johnnie started crying I said that the little lad wanted his tea and we should go home and have a bite to eat together. But he refused to budge or even meet my eyes.

Mr B said it had been a lot to take in and they both needed time to mull it over and Alfie muttered that he'd be home in a couple of hours. He finally rolled in at half past eleven, aided by Bert and another regular – apparently he'd refused to come back with his father and went on drinking, eventually falling asleep in his corner. We put him to bed and now he's snoring.

I am terrified about what the strain of this trial is doing to Alfie, with the story of his breakdown talked about in public like that, and maybe even reported in the newspapers. His confidence is already at a low ebb, with no work and his savings dwindling fast, as far as I can tell.

What if Claude is found innocent, and allowed to go free? What would he do next? Would he come smarming back to Freda, or try to wheedle his way back into our family again? Alfie is so angry about the whole affair, I could not vouch for what he might do should Claude come within a mile of our neighbourhood again.

Friday 20th January
It's the most dreadful thing – I can barely bring myself to write it down.

The jury found Claude 'not guilty' and he was allowed to leave the court a free man. The police were furious, but it's the decision of the twelve 'good men and true' in the Jury, and there's absolutely nothing anyone can do about it.

It seems so awfully unfair, after all the terrible things he has put our families through: the ignominy for Mr B and Alfie having to go to court and admit all kinds of minor wrongdoings (the tax etc) when Claude, the thief, gets away with blue murder. The Barkers are almost bankrupt, owing money left right and centre, and in danger of losing their home. I don't suppose Pa will get back the fifty pounds he lent them any time soon. And poor Freda is still suffering the shame of being an unmarried mother. When we are out with the babies in the pram together I can't help noticing the neighbours casting snide glances and muttering behind their hands, but she holds her head up high and claims she doesn't care – says she's just happy to have her beautiful baby Annie, who is a delight (much easier than Johnnie, who's been a little terror of late).

Alfie is beside himself with fury and refuses to talk about it. He muttered something about wanting to 'tear the b******'s ****'s off' if he's ever seen in the neighbourhood again. My guess is that Claude will make himself scarce, if he knows what's good for him. I wish he would just go back to France and stay out of our lives forever.

Thursday 2nd February

It was Alfie's birthday today. I was determined to celebrate it properly – we deserve a bit of fun after all the horrible things that have happened lately.

So I made a special game pie with all the trimmings and, for afters, a Victoria sponge birthday cake with butter icing, and invited the whole family around for tea: Ma and Pa, Mr and Mrs B and Freda. We managed to get the babies to sleep early so that we could enjoy ourselves properly. Of course we only have four chairs so Alfie, Freda and me sat on boxes and we all managed to squeeze around our kitchen table. Pa brought a couple of jugs of beer from the pub and after a few glasses everyone seemed to be having a good time.

When we'd finished the pie I brought out the cake, with twenty-four special small candles on it that I'd found in a fancy shop along the Old Kent Road a few weeks ago. It was a silly little luxury given how short we are at the moment, but I wanted to make it special for Alfie and they looked so jolly, flickering their light all over the room as we called for him to make a wish.

He played along all right, blew them out with a single puff, and cut the cake with his eyes shut. When everyone had gone I asked him what he'd wished, and his reply made my heart weep. What he said was: 'I wished that just for one day I could be a whole man again.' Most of the time he manages so well that sometimes it is almost possible to forget that he has only one leg. But of course I know that every day is a struggle, that walking any distance is uncomfortable at best but sometimes excruciating, and that the 'phantom pains' sometimes arrive out of nowhere and shoot through his stump like burning needles. Nothing seems to work – not even a double dose of aspirin touches the pain.

When I replied that I loved him just as much as I

ever had, even with the one leg, he muttered that he couldn't understand why: he wasn't much of a man, a cripple without a proper job and no prospects. Well, that's for me to decide, isn't it? I replied. You're just having a run of bad luck at the moment but things will get better soon, you'll see.

He looked so downhearted that I wanted to rock him in my arms to soothe the misery, like I can with the baby. He said everything felt so hopeless at the moment, even though he knew there were millions in the same boat.

I have to admit that there wasn't much I could offer to reassure him on that one. Heaven knows what will happen and where we will end up living, unless one of us can get a job before too long.

Saturday 4th March
Oh Freda, what have you gone and done?

We were woken at seven o'clock this morning by a great commotion: someone banging on our front door and another voice shouting at the window. Alfie had a skin full last night so he was dead to the world, and I'd been up with Johnnie in the small hours, so it took a few minutes to drag myself out of bed and get to the door.

It was Mr and Mrs B, both of them pale-faced and anxious, standing in the rain and getting drenched but apparently not even noticing. Mick asked if Freda and Annie were with us and I shook my head. I hadn't seen her since yesterday.

271

At this point, Alfie appeared in the doorway in his pyjamas and on his crutches, struggling to hold Johnnie who was bawling his head off with a sopping wet nappy falling down his legs. Mrs B wailed that Freda had gone, taken her clothes and everything and Mr B waved a piece of paper saying she's gone with that b******* Claude.

I couldn't believe it! After all he did to her. Alfie leaned on the doorjamb, whacking a crutch against the wall with each word. 'The stupid, stupid, stupid girl. By god, if I ever lay my hands on that man . . .'

Mrs B looked like she might collapse so I found her a chair, took Johnnie from Alfie's arms and told him to put the kettle on. By the time I'd got the baby changed and made him a bottle, they were sitting around the table reading the note that Freda had left on the Barkers' mantelpiece, in a hurried scrawl on the back of an old laundry slip.

Dearest Ma and Pa,

Please do not be angry with me. I know what you think of Claude, but he is the father of my baby and I still love him. He is deeply sorry that our family got caught up in problems the police caused by jumping to conclusions about his business affairs, and hopes that you will find it in your hearts to forgive him one day.

He wants us to get married and go to France for a new life, and it seems the right thing to do.

Annie will grow up with her father, and you will be relieved of the shame I have brought on our family, as well as the financial burden of two extra mouths to feed.

Please do not try to stop me – I have been thinking carefully about it for a couple of weeks and I know it is the right thing to do. Tell Alfie and Rose that I will miss them loads and loads and will write as soon as we are settled.

Your ever-loving daughter and granddaughter,

Freda and Annie.

I said we had to stop her. Had they been to the police? But Mr B said there was nothing they could do because she's an adult now and it wasn't illegal to go off with her so-called fiancé. Freda is deluding herself. What possibility of happiness can she expect from a man who is so unreliable, selfish, immoral and without a speck of common decency? The gall of the man to suggest it was all about the police 'jumping to conclusions'! How could she be so naïve as to believe him?

Alfie suggested they could go to Dover, to catch them before they get on the ferry, but his pa said that by the time they caught the train down there, they'd be long gone. I was so proud of him, he just said that it was worth a try and if they set out now they stood a chance. I blurted out something about the cost of the fares and immediately regretted it

– what's money when you're faced with the loss of a daughter? And Alfie said they could worry about that later, so while he went to get dressed, his ma and me made a couple of sandwiches for them to take on the train, and then waved the two of them off into the pouring rain.

Now, I am sitting by the fire with Mrs B and I have tried my best to persuade her that it is not her fault Freda has chosen to run off with that slimy creep, and nothing she has said or done, or not said or done, could have prevented it. But it is a mother's lot to feel guilty and there's little more I can say. All we can do now is pray that Alfie and his pa get there in time to stop her, and make her see sense before she disappears into France.

Sunday 5th March
Alfie and his pa returned early this morning looking thoroughly dejected.

At Dover they discovered that they had missed the departure of the last ferry but by then they'd also missed the last train back to London, so had to spend a freezing night sleeping on the station without any bedding or even a spare ha'penny for a cup of tea. Poor boy, he looked chilled to the bone, so I sent him straight to bed.

I feel utterly miserable: my best friend Freda, who I shared all my secrets with, has gone, probably for ever. I can't see her showing her face around here again – she'd be too ashamed. I can only hope that my worst fears are not realised and that she and Claude can find a happy life together.

Sunday 12th March
Johnnie is seven months old today – I can scarcely believe how the time has flown by. He's such an active little chap now: he can roll onto his back and back again, and even sit up with cushions wedged behind him. His legs are getting stronger too and he loves to bounce on Pa's knee. Ma says it won't be long before he's walking.

What a joy he is, when everything else seems so grim these days.

Alfie is still poorly with the flu he got from sleeping on Dover Station.

Friday 14th April
It's Good Friday and although I'm no church-goer, when I passed St Mark's on my way back from the shop I heard singing and found myself walking up the steps. Without really thinking I popped my head around the door and, to my embarrassment, a lady stood up to welcome me and showed me to a pew in the back row. I could hardly refuse when she was so kindly.

I listened to the service with only half an ear because my eyes were so busy looking at the church: enormous, brilliantly coloured painted glass windows showing bible scenes I could not recognise, the tall pillars reaching up into the gloom of the roof with carved stone faces all around the tops, and a vaulted ceiling with painted angels and stars. There was so much to look at that I could have sat there for hours. And I suppose the gawping stopped me thinking about all my worries and helped clear my mind. Either way I came out of there feeling a lot better than when I went in.

Alfie once told me that any faith he might once have felt got buried in the mud of the trenches, and it's certainly hard to believe in a god who allows such terrible things to happen in the world he supposedly created. All the same, I found myself sending up a few prayers, just in case someone was listening.

Alfie's flu got worse and worse but he refused to see the doctor until one day I took matters into my own hands and called him. He whipped out his stethoscope, listened to Alfie's chest and said, 'It's pneumonia – he's got to go to hospital, at once.'

A week later, Alfie was home but still feeling very sorry for himself, and he hasn't really picked up since. He mopes around the house in his pyjamas most days, sometimes not even bothering to get dressed and put on his leg. He's still smoking, which is crazy after all the breathing problems he's had, and still seems to have the energy to go down the pub with his mates at weekends, spending money we can ill afford. There's no work for his pa and he's given up all talk of trying to find another job. Our savings are almost gone.

This is what I prayed last night: 'Dear God, please

bring Alfie back to good health, look kindly on our little family and find a way of helping us get through our difficulties. Also, dear God, please keep Freda and Annie safe. Let them be happy and bring them back to us one day.'

Tuesday 2nd May

My twenty-second birthday, and at last there's something to celebrate. Yesterday I started work at the collar factory again.

Two weeks ago I met one of my former work-mates in the shop and she told me that Mitchell's has opened a new factory just opposite the old one. One of our other friends, Marian, had just been given notice because she was expecting, just like I'd been.

Nothing changes, does it? I still feel bitter about Mr Mitchell's refusal to accept that pregnant women are just as capable as anyone else, but she pointed out it might mean there could be a vacancy for me, if I wanted it. My first reaction was that I couldn't possibly. Who'd look after Johnnie? As soon as I'd said it, the question answered itself. Of course I could do it, I'd be an idiot to turn it down. Ma would love to have her grandchild a couple of days a week and the rest of the time – well, Alfie was sitting at home doing nothing much. He wouldn't be very pleased about the idea, that was for sure, but we are in such dire straits I reasoned that he wouldn't have a leg . . . (oh dear, I nearly wrote 'to stand on', how silly of me.)

The following day I left Johnnie with Ma, and went

to the factory. Mr Mitchell said he was very pleased to see me, because I was one of their best seamstresses, which made me blush. And then he astonished me by saying that as it happened, they had a vacancy coming up and how would I like to start next week?

Just as I feared, Alfie refused to consider the idea. 'You can't take it,' was his first reaction. 'It's not right for a married woman to go out to work.'

I chose my words carefully, trying not to rub salt in the wound, saying I was sure he'd find a job soon, but in the meantime we couldn't afford to turn this down. If we didn't get some money coming in from somewhere we'd soon get turned out of the flat and was that what he really wanted? So then he got even more annoyed, and started going on about who was going to do the cooking and cleaning, the washing and ironing, and look after the boy, while I was out at work?

I suggested that Ma would have Johnnie for a day or two each week, and he'd enjoy being with his daddy the rest of the time. We could do the chores together, when I got back from work. Alfie didn't say much after that, but got his coat and left, saying he needed a pint. I know it is hard to accept that I have to be the breadwinner for a while, and I would far rather it was the other way round. A job would make him feel so much better about himself, give him a reason for getting out of bed every morning. But this is the situation we are in right now, and he has to recognise that it won't be for ever.

When we were courting and planning our lives together, we used to talk for hours about how we would share everything, be equal partners, have the same rights when making decisions. But it irks me that this never seems to work in practice. Do all men revert to their fathers' ways? Will they always assume that the chores and boring stuff are women's work, while they swan around making decisions and doing what they please?

He still hasn't really accepted it, but Ma's been looking after Johnnie for the past couple of days since I started back at the factory. Although I have to pretend to Alfie that I'm only doing it because of the money, I absolutely love being back at work. The new factory is airy and light, and Mr Mitchell's invested in more modern machines, too. But what I love most is the feeling of satisfaction from doing a good, careful piece of sewing to make a collar that sits perfectly, the chatter and fun with the other girls, and freedom from the drudgery of cooking, cleaning, laundering and ironing filling my days.

For my birthday, Alfie got me some talcum powder that he knows I love, and Ma had made a delicious walnut cake for tea. Johnnie helped me blow out the candles.

Saturday 27th May
Ma has been a Trojan these past few weeks, looking after Johnnie almost all day every day. Alfie does a few stints, but usually seems to find some excuse for not

looking after him for more than an hour at a time. He claims that he's busy going out looking for a job but surely he can't be doing that eight hours a day?

He still hasn't forgiven me for going back to work. He's surly and miserable much of the time and spends most evenings with his mates in the pub. Yet if I come home with something nice for tea he'll grumble about the cost of it – he really seems to resent the fact that I am bringing some money back into our household. I can understand his pride is injured, but I try to tell him it's just tiding us over a tough patch, till he can find a job.

But what if he *does* find a job? He seems to assume that as soon as he's back at work I will stop work and stay at home with Johnnie, but I'd be really sorry to give it up.

Sunday 4th June

We went to Sunday dinner at the Barkers' house today. Mr B has just landed a couple of new contracts to supply second-hand furniture, and they'd splashed out on a leg of lamb to celebrate, with all the trimmings. The meat was delicious – Pa had selected a top quality joint for the occasion. They told him they'd soon be able to repay his £50 loan, too, which I know has been weighing on their conscience for the past six months, but for the moment there's no chance of enough work to employ Alfie again.

There's still no news from Freda, and Alfie warned

me not to mention her name because his ma is still very fragile. It's a bit like being bereaved, I suppose, and we know all about that. Just when you've got so you think you can cope with the idea, it jumps up and bites you again and there's absolutely nothing you can do to stop yourself from crying.

Mr B started talking about the new contracts he'd got. One is for a landlord who he's worried might be another shyster like Claude, but this time he's being extra careful about keeping the paperwork squeaky clean, and making sure he knows where the goods have come from. The other is much more interesting, and really made me prick up my ears: he has been asked to supply some 'cheap but sturdy' chairs, tables and workbenches for a new venture being set up in the old Mitchell's collar factory premises opposite the new place where I work.

He's obviously impressed with the man. 'Grand chap, very posh,' he said, 'but very pleasant and not stuck up. He's dead keen to make sure he gets what he calls "value for money" because it's something to do with a charity – the British Legion, I think he said, though heaven knows what kind of business it'd be.'

I vaguely remember that it was the British Legion who organised the poppies we sold last year to raise money for disabled soldiers. I'm going to keep my ears to the ground when I go back to work tomorrow.

Wednesday 7th June

I didn't have to wait long: today a big sign went up on the wall of the old factory opposite:

DISABLED SOCIETY
POPPY FACTORY

I was so excited that I could barely concentrate on my work and, in the tea break, couldn't help telling the girls about the American teacher who came up with the idea of a poppy symbol to remember the fallen, and the French lady who'd set up workshops and paid disabled soldiers to make them. 'Looks like the same thing's happening here, isn't that wonderful?'

But they just sucked on their ciggies and nodded, looking bored. I suppose it means so much more to me, having lost two brothers and being married to a disabled soldier.

Then, as I was going out of the door at the end of my shift this afternoon, I happened to meet Mr Mitchell who was just coming back in.

'Hope you don't mind me asking, Mr Mitchell.' I pointed to the new sign. 'Do you know anything about that?'

'Ah yes, as it happens, I do,' he said. 'Because I've leased the premises to a chap called Howson, Major George Howson MC, no less.' (I didn't know what MC stood for, but it sounded impressive, and Alfie would soon tell me.) 'He set up the society with the idea of making poppies, you know, like were sold last

November for remembrance. And he's got some cash out of the British Legion now, so it's all systems go.'

'Is he going to employ disabled soldiers, like that French woman?'

Mr M looked puzzled. 'Don't know about any French woman, but that seems to be the general idea, far as I can tell. Got some extraordinary bits of kit in there – tells me he's designed it 'specially so it can be used by chaps with no arms or legs, that sort of thing.'

I can't wait for Alfie to get home, so I can tell him about it. Just imagine? He might even be able to get a job there.

Saturday 1st July

I've found out lots more about the new Poppy Factory. I was on my way home from work last week when I saw six men arranging chairs on the pavement, preparing to have their photograph taken in front of the sign. It was a beautiful sunny afternoon and they looked so pleased with themselves that I couldn't help giving them a wave and one of them, a lad with one arm and a thick bush of wiry, almost yellow-blond hair waved back with a cheeky smile as I went by.

I thought nothing of it until I was walking to work the following Monday morning and my path coincided with that same lad, at the corner of the road. He tipped his hat with that chirpy grin and wished me good morning. So I saw an opportunity to quiz him and asked if he worked at the Poppy Factory.

'As of two weeks. Best thing that's happened to me since this.' He waved his stump cheerfully. 'Been out of work four years, and when they gave me my first pay packet last Friday I thought I'd died and gone to heaven. Been celebrating all weekend! D'you like dancing, Miss?'

I ignored his question and asked if anyone could apply and he told me it was especially for disabled servicemen. He'd just read about it in the newspaper and went along and the Major took him on right away. 'He's a good egg and all,' he said.

Was that Major Howson, I asked?

'That's the one: tall chap, dark hair and big moustache,' he said. 'Set the whole place up on a shoestring with some grant or other from the Legion. He's ever so clever at inventing machines, you know, what people who're missing bits, like me, can operate. We're turning out poppies by the hundreds now. The design of 'em is so simple, you can make them with only one hand, which suits me to a T.'

When I asked if he knew whether there were any vacancies he said I'd have to ask the Major. By this time we'd reached the door of the factory. 'Tell him Walter sent you – that's me, by the way. Can I ask your name?'

I thought this a bit forward, but I told him all the same, he was that charming.

'"A rose by any other name would smell as sweet . . ."' he quoted, winking at me. 'William Shakespeare, learned it at school. See you again Miss Rose.'

I was about to correct him, to tell him I was a Mrs, actually, but he'd disappeared.

Anyway, of course I rushed home that day to tell Alfie, but he just got cross again.

'Don't you ever give up, Rose?' he growled. 'I'm not a bloody basket case you know. I'm perfectly capable of doing a normal job and I don't need f****** charity from some do-gooding Major whass'name. Just leave me be, will you?'

I felt a hot fury coming over me and was about to shout back that if he's no basket case he ought to get off his backside and go out looking for a job, for once, and not sit around moping all day and drinking all night. About how he could at least pull his weight and help around the house, or look after Johnnie more often. But just then Ma arrived back with the little lad, who was so happy and smiley it was impossible to stay angry any more.

So now my proud Alfie has gone to drown his sorrows at the pub as usual, spending what little money is left over after the rent and food. I know he's miserable, and the only thing that will cheer him up is to get a job – any job – that would give his dignity back. But he seems to have given up.

We can't go on living the rest of our lives like this. Before long, Johnnie will need to have his own bedroom but there's no chance, just now, of us being able to afford a two-bedroom flat. The little lad's growing out of all his clothes and I would dearly love to be able to buy him something new, for once, instead of the second-hand jumble-sale stuff he wears at the moment. And I'm desperate for a pair of new nylons.

My husband is so surly and miserable these days, and he doesn't even seem to be interested in bedroom business any more. Not that I fancy it much, either, when he comes home smelling of beer and fags most nights. I can't remember when we last had any fun together, we never go dancing or to the flicks. This is the time of year when we might be thinking of going to Brighton – even though it's cold and rainy right now, hardly seaside weather – but that's about as likely as flying to the moon, right now. If it wasn't for my job we'd be on the streets.

I suppose I should be grateful. Six years ago, to the day, my big brother Johnnie died on the first day of the Somme. His namesake, Johnnie Barker, will be one year old in just over a month's time.

Chapter Six

They hadn't seen each other for more than a month and Jess's stomach churned with nerves as she waited for Nate at Paddington Station.

She'd overslept and almost missed the train after staying up late again, reading the diaries that she'd neglected since returning from Suffolk. Rose's plaintive words: 'I want the old Alfie back', played over and over in her head, chiming with something similar she remembered Nate saying, once: 'Where's the Jess I used to know?' This weekend would prove whether she had done enough to rediscover her old confident self, the woman he'd fallen in love with.

Supported by her friends' constant vigilance and by great effort of willpower she'd managed to stay sober for a week. She dug heavily into her savings for two new outfits, some gloriously impractical shoes, a new hairstyle and colouring to enhance her natural auburn, a facial and manicure.

The smile on his face was worth every penny.

'Seems like we haven't seen each other forever,' he

said, giving her a long hug and then stepping back. 'You're looking great, Jess. Love the new hair.' He picked up her case. 'Come on, let's get coffee, then we can have a proper catch-up.' As they walked down the platform together her head fizzled with optimism. It was going to be a brilliant weekend.

She could barely take her eyes off him – how had she forgotten that he was so very, very fit? His skin glowed and the previously shorn haircut had grown into a halo of tight black ringlets that she longed to pull through her fingers. When he reached up to put their luggage on the rack, and help an old lady with hers, she noticed the new black jeans that hugged his bum and felt a ripple of desire as the shirt pulled away to expose his tummy button and the small sworl of soft hair which, she knew, led like a pathway downwards.

When the train began to pull out of the station, he leaned back in his seat. 'It's wonderful to see you looking so well. How *are* you? How's it going on the NHS front line?'

'Oh fine, fine,' she blurted. She'd been so mesmerised that she'd entirely forgotten she had some serious owning-up to do.

He gave her a quizzical look. 'Just fine?'

Jess took a sip of her coffee. It tasted soapy and sour – what it really needed was a double shot of whisky. She glanced around the carriage. Fortunately it was relatively empty, because her next words would, she knew, lead to a long, uncomfortable conversation.

She took a deep breath, bracing herself. If she could only handle it properly, avoiding any more lies but avoiding the worst of the truth, then perhaps he would not think too badly of her, and they could move on. But she had a feeling it might not be quite so simple.

'Well, perhaps not entirely fine,' she started, noting the look of concern that instantly replaced his smile. 'I've been having a few problems . . .'

By the time the guard announced over the tannoy that they would shortly be arriving in Swindon she had said her prepared piece, told him about the accident, the flashbacks and her relief at having made the decision to quit the NHS.

Nate had expressed surprise, just as she had anticipated, asked the difficult questions she had expected, and she had managed to avoid telling too many lies. He seemed to accept why she had wanted to wait before telling him about 'the incident', till she could speak to him face-to-face, which was why she'd glossed over the truth on the phone. She omitted the bit about the drinking and, when he asked how the training course had gone, she told him she'd pulled out because she'd got sick. Better that he didn't know the gruesome truth. She told him about the counselling and the long conversations she'd had with Vorny and Hatts, and how she'd decided that, for the moment, taking a break from being a paramedic was the best thing to do.

The train slowed and pulled into the station. The old lady stood up, so Nate went to help with her luggage, and then a large group of over-excited schoolchildren flooded into the carriage, settling into their seats like a flock of garrulous birds.

'Anyway, that's enough about me,' she said. 'What about you? And what are we in for this weekend?'

The wedding would be a traditional church affair, Nate said, with a reception at the bride's family home, a Cotswold manor dating back to the seventeenth century.

Nate and the groom – Barnaby, aka Big Barnie – had known each other for most of their lives, having been best friends at their south London comprehensive and then formed their first band together at college. When the band split up, discouraged by lack of progress in getting a recording deal and having exhausted their parents' funds, they had gone travelling together. On their return Nate turned to teaching as a safer option, but Barnie had persevered with the music, working as a session drummer and then, to everyone's astonishment and Nate's extreme envy, getting booked as a last-minute sub with a group touring the UK and Europe as the support for a big name band.

It was on this tour he'd met and fallen in love with the astonishingly beautiful Anna – Vogue model and only daughter of a family of minor aristocrats. When he wasn't sitting in the House of Lords, her father did something important in the city.

'Proper old money,' Barnie had told Nate.

'He's punching above his weight with this one,' Nate had whispered when they were first introduced, while Jess had tried not to gasp at this vision of English rose elegance. Anna stood at least six feet tall, her blonde hair was improbably thick and shiny like a shampoo advertisement, her cut-glass accent terrifying and yet, wonderfully, she turned out to be perfectly normal, down to earth, funny and completely smitten with Barnie.

Nate confessed to being terrified at the prospect of making the best man's speech, of saying something wrong and embarrassing his old friend.

'Come on, you're a teacher. You do this public speaking thing every day,' she said. 'You'll be great.'

They would be sitting at the 'top table' he said, giving her a serious look, and they would both have to be on their very best behaviour.

'Don't you trust me?'

'Of course I do,' he said, with a smile that was obviously intended to reassure. But she knew that even now, three months later, the reverberations of her *faux pas* with Matt still hung in the air between them.

As the train drew into Oxford, she asked about the other guests. It had the potential to be an incendiary mix, Nate said, laughing: crusty landed gentry like something out of Downton Abbey, a gaggle of Anna's boarding school girlfriends, Barnie's gang of south London mates and a ragbag of random musicians.

There would be a few starry names too: Barnie had mentioned celebrity photographers and fashionistas, as well as the lead singer from the band his group had supported on tour, a man famous not only for his pop career but also for his very vocal opposition to the wars in Iraq and Afghanistan.

'Let's hope he doesn't get on his soap box,' Jess said. 'I might have to gun him down in defence of Queen and country.' She caught Nate's nervous glance. 'Only joking, you dope. Haven't I promised to be on my best behaviour?'

As special guests, Nate and Jess were invited to stay at Anna's parents' house. The building that came into view as their cab crunched up the gravel driveway wasn't quite the sprawling mansion that Jess had imagined, more the size of an overgrown farmhouse; ancient, homely, asymmetrical and infinitely desirable. Its weathered, honey-coloured stone glowed in the late afternoon sunlight, partly covered by an ancient Virginia creeper gently turning autumnal shades of red and gold. The house reeked of history, of generations being born, growing, marrying, ageing and dying. It rested confidently at ease in its landscape, nestled between gently rolling hills behind and a wide stretch of parkland in front, dotted with fine old oak trees.

Anna's mother met them at the top of the steps; it was clear where her daughter's good looks had come from. She greeted them with only the slightest lift of an elegantly shaped eyebrow.

'Nate, isn't it? Barnaby's best man? The sports teacher? We've heard so much about you. And you must be Jess? Back from Afghanistan safe and sound, thank heavens, we worried so much about you when he told us. Goodness, what a striking couple you make. Come in, come in. I'm afraid tea's over but you've got time for a wash and brush up before cocktails at seven thirty in the drawing room. Dinner's at eight.'

'Please take them up to the yellow room,' she said, turning to the man who had taken custody of their luggage.

'Was he for real? You didn't tell me they had a butler!' Jess giggled, after he'd gone.

'Should I have tipped him?'

'No, don't be silly. They don't tip servants in Downton Abbey.'

'No, I suppose not.' Nate looked around the room uncomfortably. 'It's certainly yellow.' The king sized bed, curtains and bedroom chairs were covered in flowery lemon chintz, the deep pile carpet was pale apricot, the walls and ceiling in cream.

'It's yellow in here, too,' she called from the *en suite*. 'The tub's enormous – have we got time for a bath?'

Jess kept having to remind herself that she was not playing a role in some classy period drama. The drinks flowed freely but, with Vorny's words ringing in her ears, she asked for sparkling water. *Don't blow it, Jess,*

293

stay off it completely. Just one drink will weaken your willpower.

They were both relieved when Barnie and his parents arrived, and talk of schooldays in London and their exploits with the band helped them feel more at ease. After dinner, when the groom was banished to a nearby pub to avoid seeing his bride before her arrival at the church, they gratefully took this as an excuse for an early night.

Next day dawned breezy and cool, certainly too chilly for the figure-hugging sleeveless dress she'd chosen. Nate kissed her and said she looked beautiful, but she knew that even with a pashmina around her shoulders she'd spend most of the day trying not to shiver. As he struggled into his penguin suit, moaning about the tight starched collar and waistcoat affair, she told him not to complain: at least he'd be warm.

The church service went like clockwork: Anna was a vision of loveliness, her three tiny bridesmaids and pageboy perfectly behaved. Bride and groom said their vows fluently, Nate didn't drop the ring, the organist played the most exuberant of voluntaries and the sun shone as the happy couple emerged into a shower of real rose petals.

Because Nate was required to be part of the reception line they were ushered into one of the first cars returning to the house. 'Can you imagine the torture,' he grumbled under his breath, 'having to smile and say hello to a hundred strangers?' She patted his knee. 'Just be your usual charming self. They'll all love you.'

For a while she had the marquee almost all to herself and found herself swarmed by over-eager waiters with trays of freshly-poured drinks. She took a glass of what she thought was orange juice and discovered, too late, that it was Buck's Fizz. Then, as she wandered around inspecting the table decorations, the flower arrangements in cream, pink and gold, the luxuriant frills and swags, and the stylishly looped lace and ribbons, she realised that she'd managed to drink two more glasses of the stuff, without thinking.

Her stomach was rumbling and she knew that she ought to eat something but, by the look of the queue of guests still waiting to be 'received', food would be some time coming. She would have gone for a look around the garden only it was too chilly out there and the heels of her impractical shoes would sink into the grass, making any progress tricky and inelegant.

After a while, other guests joined her, making polite but tedious conversation as they drank champagne and nibbled at tiny canapés. She spent a few moments eavesdropping at the edge of a group clustered around the famous pop star but decided to slip away just as he started on his anti-war rant. After listening to a large man with an overfed stomach sounding off about the credit crunch she found her attention wandering, and glanced towards the entrance of the marquee to see how Nate was getting on.

The queue had dwindled to just a few but, just at

that moment, a new figure appeared at the back of the line: a tall, beautiful black woman in a flowing cerise dress, her hair tied back with a flourish of feathers, her long elegant neck bent in greeting to the bride, kissing her on both cheeks.

Jess was not the only one whose attention had been hooked. She could see that Nate, even as he was shaking hands with the guests in front of him, could barely take his eyes off the new arrival. As she watched, the woman moved with feline grace along the line towards him. Their smiles and body language made it plain that they already knew each other, possibly intimately. Instead of the usual formal hand-shake, Nate took the woman's hands in his and they stood, wordlessly beaming at each other for a painfully-long moment: these two tall, elegant dark-skinned people, conspicuous in a sea of pale, pasty faces and the pink and cream confection of the marquee decor. Who *was* this woman, how did Nate know her, and what did she mean to him? Why hadn't he mentioned before that she was coming? Jess found herself winded with jealousy, smashing like a boulder straight into her stomach.

The two of them laughed, apparently at some unspoken joke, then kissed each other on both cheeks in the usual way. She could hardly bear to look, but sensed that the kisses were especially tender and lingering. The woman was the last guest in the queue, so the reception line broke up and the pair of them walked together into the main part of the marquee.

They seemed perfectly paired – both slim and long limbed, with the same skin tone and similarly fine facial features, high cheekbones and full lips. Hers were painted bright crimson.

Jess froze as he caught her eye and led his new friend towards her. 'Jess, this is Nerissa. Nerissa, my girlfriend Jess,' he shouted over the well-lubricated hubbub. She took the proffered hand and tried to smile. It was a limp, long-fingered handshake, as though its owner couldn't really be bothered to make an impression.

'Ahm soo pleased to meet you,' Nerissa drawled – an American, or perhaps Canadian accent? 'Nathan and I go way back, don't we?' She put a hand up to his cheek in a shockingly intimate gesture which, to his credit, he seemed to find embarrassing. Or was it a flush of excitement that glowed beneath his skin?

'And did you know Nate was going to be here?' Jess could hear the sharp edge in her voice, and hoped he would notice it too, to understand how painful this meeting was for her.

'Nope, no idea,' Nerissa said. 'It's just a wunnerful surprise, isn't it, Nathan?'

'We met in Australia when I was travelling,' he said, apparently completely unaware of Jess's discomfort. 'We were at a gig together – Nerissa's a great singer.'

'Drinks anyone?' Jess hailed a passing waiter, helped herself to a glass of champagne and took a slug that half emptied it.

'Melbourne, wasn't it? That awful dive in Brunswick Street? That terrible band?' They giggled conspiratorially at the mutual memories. 'Who'd have thought I'd meet you here, Nathan, all dressed up in your penguin suit?'

'And how do you know Barnie and Anna?' Jess asked, finishing off her drink, replacing the empty glass and taking a full one. Nate would be glaring at her, she knew, but she chose not to look at him.

'Oh, I've known Anna for years.' Nerissa waved her elegant hand airily. 'We've worked on dozens of shoots together in New York. She's such a pro.'

'And you had no idea Anna was marrying Nate's best friend?' Jess asked. 'That Nate was going to be best man at her wedding?'

'Nope. Like I said, it's a complete coincidence.'

Coincidence? She meets Nate in Australia, and Anna in New York? Then she turns up here and Nate knows nothing about it. I don't think so, Jess thought.

'You're a *model* now?' Nate asked. 'Is there no end to your talents?' The look of naked admiration on his face was almost too much to bear.

'Yeah. Got scouted when I got back to New York. Been doing it ever since. It's a boring existence, but you get to travel, and if one wants to live in Manhattan one has to pay the rent somehow, if you know what I mean?'

'But you have such a great voice.' He turned to Jess. 'You should hear Nissa singing the blues. It's enough to send shivers down your spine.'

Nissa indeed. Pet names now. This was purgatory. How long would it be before they served the wedding breakfast, so they could get away from this woman?

A few moments later the bell sounded, and she and Nate were ushered to the long top table on a raised daïs at one end of the marquee. The settings were laid only along one side, with Jess at the very end, next to Nate. On his other side was Barnie's mother, and he spent what seemed like ages talking to her, leaving Jess feeling like a lemon, or was it a gooseberry? Some sour kind of fruit anyway – that was certainly how she felt. She accepted the wine poured by the waiter and stared out across the guests taking their seats at the round tables below, wishing she could be among them. No, what she actually wished was that she could run away from this whole terrible affair, taking Nate with her, back to the safety of his flat.

She downed her glass and felt the alcohol doing its work, easing the edges of her anxiety. In the distance she could see the crimson feathers in Nerissa's hair fluttering like a flag, noticed the curious and admiring glances of her table companions, watched them turn to engage her in conversation and saw how she instantly became their centre of attention.

At last Nate turned to her. 'Are you okay?' She nodded, unable to find the right words. Was he blind? Could he not see how miserable she was? 'Watch the booze, Jess. Please?'

'Oh for Christ's sake, it's a wedding,' she said, allowing the waiter to refill her glass.

'Why do you always do this?' The staccato whisper sounded like distant machine-gun fire.

'Do what?' She felt the anger rising and was about to snap back but, with great force of will, managed to stop herself. The last thing she wanted was a row, there on the top table, in view of the assembled guests.

'You know perfectly well what I mean. Just stop drinking, please? And try not to embarrass me. I've got to concentrate on my speech.'

Just then, a waiter arrived at her elbow, offering a plate of food. It looked delicious but, to Jess, tasted like cardboard. She drank steadily throughout the meal and tried to avoid looking in Nerissa's direction, but bitter jealousy tainted every mouthful. Her head was spinning now, and she was desperate for fresh air.

She rose to her feet, just a little unsteadily. 'Going to the loo,' she whispered to Nate.

'The speeches are about to start. Can't you wait till afterwards?'

'Won't be long. Promise.'

Negotiating the steps down from the daïs was tricky with no handrail; she tripped and nearly knocked over an elaborate flower arrangement but managed to get down without further mishap and threaded her way between the tables, stepping carefully over the lumpy sisal floor covering. She'd almost reached the safety of the marquee entrance when a particularly uneven spot caught her heel and, failing to steady herself on the shoulder of a nearby guest, she fell headlong into an ungainly heap.

At that very moment there was a tinkling of cutlery on glasses, and the marquee hushed. Anna's father was on his feet, about to speak, but his eye was caught by the kerfuffle near the doorway, and everyone else turned to watch as people tried to help Jess to her feet. She seemed to have knocked her head on the way down, her knees were grazed and her tights shredded. 'Sorry, so sorry, I'm fine, really, please don't worry,' she heard her own voice loudly in the silence. A hundred stares felt like darts piercing her skin.

'Need to go to the toilet,' she whispered, shaking off a woman's attempts to make her sit down and take a glass of water. All she could think about was getting away, to avoid drawing even more attention to herself, just before Nate's big moment.

Finally she managed to make it outside and, taking gulps of fresh air, slipped off her heels and set a meandering course across the lawn to the house. There were portaloos behind the marquee, but she didn't really need the toilet. What she really wanted was to sit down for a few minutes, alone, to regain her composure, change her tights and sober up. Then she would return to the reception and perhaps be able to pretend that nothing had happened. She made her way up the stairs in the deserted house, and along the corridor to the very yellow room.

'What the fuck, Jess? I looked everywhere for you. What the hell are you doing?'

Nate's shout startled her from the depths of sleep,

and for a second or two she wondered where she was. As she opened her eyes and saw his furious face peering down at her, she caught sight of the white tie and penguin suit. It all flooded horribly back: the wedding reception, that bloody Nerissa woman, that ungainly fall.

'Fell and knocked my head,' she mumbled. 'Needed to lie down.'

'You got drunk and made a spectacle of yourself,' he said, coldly. 'You promised me you wouldn't, and then you go and drink like a bloody fish, even after I warned you. Why, Jess, why?' His face was flushed, his body like a coiled spring, and he emphasised every word with the shake of a clenched fist.

Shocked by his aggressiveness, Jess decided that attack was the best form of defence. She swung her legs around and sat up, ignoring the throbbing head and a throat like sandpaper. 'Why'd you lie about that woman, Nate?' Her tongue felt too big for her mouth and the words came out garbled.

'What woman?'

'Your long lost friend, Nerissa. Sorry, "Nissa". 'Mazing blues singer turned model who juss *happened* to be here. What an *amazing* coincidence.'

'What the hell are you getting at, Jess?' The anger was burning in his face.

'What the hell're *you* playing at, Nate? Beautiful woman walks in . . . turns out to be your long lost friend . . .'scuse me, long lost *girlfriend* . . . and iss all a big surprise.'

302

He slumped into an armchair by the window and gave a resigned sigh. 'She's *not* a girlfriend, for heaven's sake. We only met a few times, just as I said, and neither of us knew we'd both be here today. It was a complete surprise.'

''Spect me to believe that? You met in Australia 'n she turns up here,' Jess slurred. 'Thass a mighty big coincidence. You obviously fancy her like hell, anyone can see that juss by looking at you. What d'you 'spect me to do? Smile and simper and be on my best behaviour?'

His expression hardened. 'I expect you to act like an *adult*, not a stupid jealous teenager. I expect you *not* to get drunk at every party, *not* to go blundering around putting your foot in it, falling over and making an idiot of yourself. I know you've had your issues after the tour, and I've tried my very best to be helpful and sympathetic. It's over a year now since you got back and you don't seem to be making any effort to sort them. I'm getting to the end of the road, Jess.'

'So thass what you think of me, then? Stupid jealous teenager?'

'That's how you're acting, right now. And to be honest, I don't think I can take it any more.'

The blood seemed to congeal in her veins. This was, suddenly, very serious.

'I thought we were all right, Nate?' she pleaded. 'Been having a really rough time, I tole you. It'll get better soon.'

'We tried that before and it didn't work.' He stood up, pulled his wallet from a pocket and took out a twenty pound note and her train ticket. 'Look, I suggest you sober up, call a taxi and get yourself to the station.'

She heard his words with painful clarity. 'You're telling me to *leave*? Go back to London. Now? What about the wedding?' Her heart was pounding in her ears as she willed herself not to cry.

He nodded and turned to the door. 'Yup. Right now. I've had enough.'

'Please, Nate . . .' She tried to stand but lost her footing and lurched forward, catching herself on the chair. 'Don't go. We can sort it out. I love you . . .'

He opened the door and walked away. 'Goodbye, Jess.'

In London, she jumped onto the last connecting train with seconds to spare, slumped into a seat and texted her mother: Can I come home this evening? I'll catch a taxi. Leave out the key, please? Like an injured animal needing to hide away and lick its wounds, Suffolk was the only place she could bear to be.

It was past midnight when she arrived but Susan was there, in her dressing gown, to let her in. 'Thanks so much for waiting up,' she said, trying to avoid meeting her anxious eyes. 'Talk tomorrow? I just need some time to myself right now.'

Sleep was impossible. She poured herself a glass of her father's whisky but on top of her wedding hangover it tasted like acid. The enforced jollity of late-night chat shows on television made her feel even more desolate. There was nothing for it – she went upstairs to bed and began to unpack the small weekend case.

Then she found, still tucked in the side pocket, Rose's last notebook.

BOOK SIX

Rose Barker - PRIVATE

Monday 10 July 1922

The Major came to our factory today for a pow-wow with Mr Mitchell and the upshot of it seems to be that we've offered to let the poppy lads use our canteen for their lunch and tea breaks, because there isn't enough room on their side. Mr M gave us girls a lecture about how they will take their breaks at different times from ours and that we are *not* to fraternise. He's afraid we may get distracted from our work.

The truth is that I am already distracted.

The blond-haired lad, Walter, seems to arrive at the same corner each morning, and insists on walking the last few hundred yards with me before we get to work. Not that I'm complaining, he always seems to cheer me up with some crazy story in the few minutes we spend together.

This morning he handed me a curious-looking cardboard cylinder with a lid on it. I really shouldn't be seen accepting gifts from strange men but when he told me to pull the string for a 'nice surprise' I couldn't resist the temptation.

Instantly, the cover flipped back like a jack-in-the-box, and up popped a green stem with a bright red poppy on top, and leaves sprouting out from the sides. Of course I shrieked with astonishment and then laughed out loud, and he chuckled along with me.

I asked him wherever did he get it, thinking how Johnnie would absolutely love the surprise, too. He looked down modestly and said he'd made it himself. 'It's just a bit of fun. The Major let me have some of the poppy fabrics and I thought you needed a bit of cheering up.'

It's such a clever thing, I said, he could go into business making them. And I thanked him for making me smile. How did he know I was feeling a bit glum these days? Was it really showing on my face?

We'd reached the factory door by now and I didn't want to be seen lingering outside with him so I went to give the poppy back, but he refused. 'It's for you, Rose,' he said, 'to remember me by.' And he disappeared inside with that naughty smile on his face. I showed it to the girls at tea break and they all loved it.

Maisie said I ought to watch out for 'that one' because he was such a flirt, always asking girls to the Palais. Not that he'd ever ask me – he must have seen my ring and know that I'm a married woman – but there's a little bit of me that can't help wishing he would, and that I was free to go dancing with him. In August the factory will close for the annual fortnight's holidays, and all I can think of is that I'll miss seeing him every morning. I really shouldn't, but he makes me laugh and I can't resist him.

Monday 31st July

Is it only three weeks since I wrote the last entry in my diary? So much has happened, I can hardly think where to start.

Johnnie is coming up to his first birthday and he's been a little terror of late, refusing to eat the things we put in front of him and throwing tantrums at the slightest thing. Alfie says it's impossible to manage him, so Ma has been doing most of the looking after while I've been at work. But two weeks ago she went down with a terrible cold and so Alfie had him for four days in a row and, my goodness, did he make a fuss. At the end of each day he'd almost throw Johnnie into my arms, saying he'd had enough, and I should give up my job and stay home, and that men weren't designed for looking after whinging snotty toddlers. Then he'd grabbed his coat and rushed off down the pub, again, not returning till the early hours.

By the end of the week I'd had enough, and that Saturday morning we had a blazing row in which we traded all kinds of insults, with me saying that unless we took care, our marriage would end up on the rocks. It ended with him agreeing to go to the flicks with me that evening, and asking his ma to look after Johnnie so we could have a good evening out together.

It didn't work out like that: we argued about which show to see, the detective story with John Barrymore, or a vampire movie which, strangely, given his fear of blood, Alfie wanted to see but which didn't appeal to me the tiniest bit. In the end, we missed the start of *Nosferatu* and got to see my choice after all. Alfie sighed and tutted all the way through, muttering about how Sherlock had missed obvious clues while pretending to be even cleverer than Dr Watson. All the while I was thinking about how it used to be, when he would insist on us having back row seats and we'd be so busy kissing that we hardly saw anything of the movie.

Of course, on our way home, Alfie insisted on going to The Nelson for 'a quick half' which turned into several pints and we ended up continuing the row when we got back to the flat, with me going to bed alone and him falling asleep on the sofa, where I found him the next morning, still wearing his artificial leg. And he knows that he has to take it off at night, to give the skin on his stump time to breathe and prevent it getting ulcerated. If it does, I'll have no sympathy.

Things went downhill from there. On Monday when I got home exhausted from a really busy day at the machines trying to meet the deadline for delivery to an important customer, I found Alfie asleep in a drunken stupor, and Johnnie toddling around on his own with a sopping wet nappy round his ankles.

I hit the roof, threw a glass of water over Alfie and shouted at him to get up and sort himself out. He hadn't even remembered to get milk and bread so I changed the baby's nappy and stomped out with him to the corner shop. On the way back I met old Elsie, the neighbourhood busybody, who cooed at the baby and said, 'He do love his pram, the little darlin', don't he?' When I asked what she meant, she told me she'd seen him in it outside the pub that lunchtime. 'There well over an hour, dearie, and not a whimper,' she said.

Well, that was it. I'd always told Alfie not to take Johnnie to the pub. It wasn't fair, and the way he drinks it certainly wasn't safe. I was so angry I barely knew where to put myself, and spent the next two hours walking the streets, trying to calm down, trying to figure out what to do next.

I'd worked so hard to help Alfie get back to normal life after the war, but he seems to be on a downward slide, refusing all my offers to help and determined to drown his sorrows at every opportunity. I can understand that he is angry about the lot he's been dealt, but it almost feels as though he wants to prove that because he'd lost a leg, he is worthless. I'm at my wits' end and really need someone to talk to. How I miss Freda.

Everything came to a head two days ago. I had to work overtime, and didn't get home till seven o'clock in the evening. As I approached our flat I could hear Johnnie crying, with that shrill, panicky scream that means he is really angry or really frightened. I rushed down the passageway fearing the worst and, as I passed the kitchen window, was stopped dead in my tracks by the sight of Alfie, his face screwed up in a horrible scowl, holding his son out at arm's length and shaking him so furiously that the little lad's head and limbs were flopping like a rag doll.

Alfie didn't even stop when I came in. He'd completely lost control, bellowing at the boy to 'stop that f******* noise, for Christ's sake'. He was clearly drunk. I tried to grab Johnnie out of his arms but he held onto him tightly, staggering to stay on his feet without his walking stick. I shouted so loudly that the baby was shocked into silence and this caught Alfie off guard long enough for me to make another grab and pull the child away from him. He staggered, tried to hold onto the side of the table, then fell on the floor with a thump.

I was that furious, I wasn't the slightest concerned whether he'd hurt himself and just yelled at him to get out of the flat and never come back. Which he did, hobbling as fast as he could down the street in the direction of the pub.

Johnnie recovered quite quickly after I made him a bottle of warm milk with a teaspoon of honey stirred into it, which he loves, and I had half a cup, too, to calm my nerves. When he finally fell asleep in my arms I buried my face in his hair and sobbed. Even breathing his sweet baby smell could not console me.

Alfie went back to his parents' house late that night, and has been there ever since. He hasn't been round to apologise – and in a way I'm relieved because I am certainly not ready to forgive him, and even wonder whether I will ever be able to believe in him again. Once upon a time, I would have trusted him with my life but the Alfie I have known since I was a child, the man I fell in love with, seems to have disappeared and I'm afraid I'll never find him again.

I think my marriage might be over. The thought is unbearable.

Friday 4th August
Last day before the summer holidays. It should be a happy time, a family time, for planning day trips or visits to the seaside. But Alfie and me are still at loggerheads. He came round last night all shamefaced and apologetic. We had tea and talked in a civilised manner but I am still so angry with him I don't seem to be able to forgive. I cannot forget Johnnie's terrible screams and the demented look on Alfie's face, as if he could have killed the boy if I hadn't walked in at that precise moment.

The only thing that's kept me going these past few days is being at work with the girls and seeing Walter every morning. He lifts my heart with his idiotic jokes and soft-soaping words, naughty things like 'your hair's so shiny today I can see my reflection in it', or, 'I love the way you laugh'.

He is very naughty, hanging around after taking his tea break in Mitchell's canteen as we girls arrive for ours, and secretly slipping me a chocolate bar or a flapjack to have with my coffee. Mr Mitchell keeps telling us we're not supposed to consort with The Poppy Factory boys but Walter and me are not the only ones.

I've tried to warn him off, telling him that I am happily married (ha ha) and there are plenty of single girls to flirt with, but he's so hard to resist, especially when he tells me that those few minutes seeing me each morning makes his day. As he says, we're only walking together, after all, nothing more serious.

Except . . .

Today he said he would miss me during the factory's fortnight break, and would I like to meet him for a cup of tea some time? My head was telling me 'say no, say no, it's not right'. But my mouth had other ideas. 'Yes, that would be lovely,' I heard myself saying, and he pressed a piece of paper into my hand. I threw it down the lavatory but couldn't resist reading it first. It said: *Station tea room, Waterloo. Just ask for me.*

Tuesday 8th August

At last, a letter from Freda arrived here this morning addressed to Alfie and me. She is safe, thank heavens. But otherwise it is not good news.

Paris, 3 July 1922
Dearest Alfie and Rose,
I am such an idiot. Why did I ever think it could work out with Claude?
The first few months were such fun, finding our way around the city, and he seemed to be making plenty of money so we rented this large airy flat in Montmartre (a hilly area to the north of the

centre). He bought beautiful clothes for me and Annie, and found a French nanny to look after her so that we could go out dancing twice a week.

He went off on his business trips as usual, and was usually back within a day or two, so last month, when he didn't reappear for a whole week, I started to worry. Turns out I was right to be concerned, because when he finally returned he could barely look me in the eye and when I pressed him he muttered something about 'things turning out bad again' and that he'd have to move on.

Of course I felt sick with the whole idea of starting again and asked where we would go next, and then it all got horrible. He said he was going to North Africa and that was no place for a woman, and I would have to stay here. I'm sorry to say I screamed and begged, but his mind was completely made up. He left that night, promising to come back and get me when 'things get sorted out'. A whole month has now passed and he's sent no word.

The worst thing is this: I have run out of money. The landlady is threatening to turn us out onto the streets unless I pay her next week, and we barely have enough to eat. In my heart of hearts I do not believe Claude will ever come back again, not after all this time, and I am so anxious about our future. This is no life for little Annie.

I have been so lonely and miss you all so much. Now I am desperate to come home, but I don't even have enough money for the train and ferry fares, and am afraid Ma and Pa will not accept me after the way I have treated them. I am sorry for writing to you like this but I cannot think what else to do. Please forgive me for being such a fool.
Freda

Of course I went straight round to the Barkers' house and showed them the letter. Mrs B burst into tears while Mr B and Alfie shouted a lot about how they were going to kill that b****** if they ever laid eyes on him again. I made tea and after a while everyone quietened down a bit and started to talk about what we could do.

Mrs B sniffled and said we've got to get her home, she didn't care what it takes. Mr B said he had some money put by, ready to pay back Pa for the loan, but I told him I was sure it wouldn't be a problem waiting another month, so he popped out to the butcher's to ask if he could defer the repayment.

He was back within an hour saying it had all been arranged. Pa had told him to take as long as they needed, and he'd also been to the Post Office and sent a telegram to Freda. He gave me the copy: 'TICKET MONEY EXPRESS MAILED C/O YOUR NAME MONTMARTRE MAIN PO STOP COME AT ONCE DO NOT TALK CLAUDE STOP PA.'

After that, Alfie suggested we all go to The Nelson for a celebration, but I cannot bear to watch him get drunk again, so I made an excuse. Things are as frosty as ever between us and I can't see anything improving until he starts to prove that he is seriously looking for work, and keeps away from that ruddy pub.

Friday 11th August
I met Walter for tea today. It's wrong, I know, but I couldn't help it.

What with the factory being closed I've been going crazy stuck in the house by myself and not having the distraction of the girls at work. I am so anxious about Freda; last night I was almost ready to pack my bags and take the train and ferry to Paris myself, to try to find her and make sure she gets out of that man's clutches. Alfie has made no further move to talk to me or even visit his son. I haven't seen hide nor hair of him since Tuesday lunchtime. I wouldn't be surprised if he's even forgotten that it's Johnnie's first birthday tomorrow.

I was feeling so low – and then realised that what I was really missing was my daily dose of laughter with Walter. Don't they say it is 'the best medicine'? Once the idea wormed its way into my head I couldn't seem to get rid of it. He makes me happy, just for a few moments each day, whereas much of the time I've been feeling quite miserable: guilty about Alfie, or about being an inadequate mother for Johnnie, or just simply exhausted from holding down a job, shopping, cooking, cleaning, washing, ironing. I never seem to have time for any fun these days.

I hated lying to Ma, saying I'd seen a notice for a big sale of children's clothing near Waterloo and since Johnnie was growing out of everything so fast this was an opportunity not to be missed, so would she mind having him for a couple of hours?

My heart was hammering in my chest when I arrived at the tea room, and realised that I didn't even know his surname. I was about to make a run for it when a woman behind the counter asked if she could help and I blurted out that I was looking for Walter. She didn't bat an eyelid: it seems he shares a bedsit just opposite the station with one of the chefs there so they sent a young lad over the road to fetch him. He arrived within minutes and greeted me with that cheeky grin and handed me a slightly ragged pink carnation (wherever did he get that, at such short notice?). Then he paid for tea and buttered teacakes for both of us and I carried the tray for him (he can do most things, but not that, with one arm) over to a quiet corner table.

It was really uncomfortable at first; I felt strangely tongue-tied, wondering what on earth I was doing here in this gloomy restaurant with a stranger. His cheery banter seemed to have abandoned him. We chatted about weather and the latest movies people are talking about, which neither of us have seen and, after about quarter or an hour, ran right out of conversation.

In the silence, the words seemed to burst out of my mouth without any warning: 'I shouldn't have come. It's wrong, I'm a married woman with a child.'

All mock-innocent, he asked what was wrong with eating teacakes and I said it wasn't what we were doing, it was *why* we were doing it. The intention.

The smile disappeared off his face then and he reached across the table to take my hand, but I pulled it away. He looked directly into my eyes and said, 'You're right. I can't help it either.'

The pull between us was so strong, like a magnet, almost impossible to resist. I could have leaned across the table and kissed him right there in the restaurant, not caring what anyone thought. But, just in time, I closed my eyes and took a deep breath instead and came to my senses. I really had to go now, I gabbled, it had been lovely meeting him and I would see him again soon when the factory started back ... and then I grabbed my coat and ran for it. What a fool I am – whatever must he think of me? I should never have let things go this far.

Sunday 13th August
Johnnie received a very special present for his first birthday yesterday – his auntie Freda and little cousin Annie came home!

We were in the middle of celebrating – I'd made a cake and invited Ma and Pa and Mr and Mrs B. Alfie came too of course. It felt horrible having to invite my husband to his own son's birthday tea, at his own home.

Mr B brought a beautiful silver spoon he'd found among some bric-a-brac he'd been selling for someone, and had shined it up till it glittered like new. 'Mightn't have been born with one in his mouth, but this is the next best thing,' he mumbled, as I opened the parcel with Johnnie 'helping' on my lap. Dear Mick, he's not good at expressing his thoughts but he has a heart of gold. When I kissed him, his ears flushed bright red.

Ma had knitted some bootees and a hat for winter, and Pa brought two pounds of best sausages so we could have a proper high tea with mashed potato and gravy, which even Johnnie can enjoy.

Alfie had drawn a birthday card with three stick people on the front: a tall skinny mum with a short brown bob, a dad with curly hair and a walking stick, and a little boy holding hands between them. I had to get busy putting the kettle on to stop myself from crying.

I suppose it was his way of saying he wants us back together again. He was very quiet; perhaps afraid of saying something out of turn. But I was glad he came and it felt almost normal, even though we haven't yet talked at all about that day or how we can mend our marriage from here.

Then, just as I was cooking the sausages and Pa had gone out to the pub for a jug of beer, there was a knock on the door and in walked Freda, with

Annie in one arm and a small suitcase in the other. Mrs B shrieked so loudly it set both babies off crying and soon we were all weeping with joy and clutching on to each other in our delight at seeing them safe and well. Elsie from next door had seen Freda coming down the street and she called in, to wish her well.

When the hubbub had died down a bit I went to put the kettle on again to revive the pot. Looking at her from the side, as she sat with Annie on one knee and Johnnie on the other, I could see how the strain of the past six months had told on Freda. For all her elegant clothes – far fancier than anything I'd ever seen her wear at home – she is painfully thin, with cheekbones I never knew she'd had now showing in her face. Annie, with her dark hair and Claude's olive complexion, is a solemn little thing. I suspect she's never had much company before, and was probably overawed by all the people and their chatter.

But they're back safely with us now. They'll both soon be blooming.

It was only when it came time for everyone to go home – Freda and Annie were plainly exhausted from their journey – that things became a bit awkward. Ma and Pa went first, then Alfie went to pick up Freda's suitcase, she looked at him a bit oddly and asked, 'Where are you going?' He flushed and muttered something like, 'I'm bringing your case for you.' She looked at me and then him, with her eyebrows raised, until Mrs B nudged her out of the doorway with a loud whisper of 'don't ask questions, we'll explain later.'

This morning, Freda came round without Annie.

'Please tell what's going on,' she said, outright, almost before we'd sat down. 'Alfie won't say a word, and Ma says it's none of my business. But why the hell is he staying with us?'

Her worried eyes brought home to me the seriousness of the situation, the shocking state we'd got ourselves into. Six months ago it would have been unthinkable that Rose and Alfie, childhood sweethearts, the perfect couple everyone always said were meant for each other, could be on the rocks. And yet here we were, living apart and barely speaking to each other.

'There's so much to explain,' was all I managed before breaking down. Two hours later, after crying in each other's arms, then talking, laughing, making cups of tea and then talking and laughing some more and weeping all over again, I'd told her all about Alfie's drinking, how he'd given up looking for work, the terrible incident with Johnnie that left me feeling that I'd been living with a stranger, and how difficult it was to find it in my heart to forgive him. She'd told me about her extraordinary adventures in Paris, the 'high life' they'd enjoyed until Claude reverted to his old ways and doing his disappearing act again.

'What a pair we are,' I said, putting the kettle on again. I was just starting to think that, now Freda was back, everything was going to work out just fine, when she dropped the bombshell. 'There's just one thing. Who were you with at Waterloo on Friday afternoon?'

It felt as though all the air had been sucked out of my lungs. I've been feeling so guilty about meeting Walter, terrified by the strength of feeling I'd had for him in the tea room. But with the excitement of the birthday and Freda's homecoming, I'd managed to push it to the back of my mind.

'You were at Waterloo on Friday?' I managed to gasp, burning with embarrassment from head to toe.

'No, I wasn't. But Ma was,' she said, looking me straight in the eye. 'She saw you having tea with a good-looking fellow with yellow hair, was what she said. She's worried it might be . . . you know?'

I jumped in a bit too hastily, saying that she could tell her ma that it wasn't anything, that he was just a friend, a lad called Walter, lost an arm in the war, works at the Poppy Factory opposite Mitchell's, and we . . . Then I dried up.

'We . . .?' she prompted.

'He asked me out to tea and I was feeling so low . . .' I ran out of words again.

'It's serious, isn't it?' she said, after a moment.

I shook my head and then changed my mind and nodded. We sat in silence for a long minute and then she said, 'We've got to sort this thing out, between you and Alfie. Otherwise you're going to get off with this yellow-haired chap and that would be a disaster.

Believe me, I know how difficult it is to resist a handsome man, even when you know it'll all end in tears. I'm a walking example of how not to do it. Just stay here and I'm going to talk to my brother.'

I pleaded with her not to tell him about Walter. 'Of course not, silly,' she said. 'Your secret's safe with me. I'll make up some story to reassure Ma. I'm going to tell Alfie what he needs to do to save his marriage.'

Tuesday 15th August
Alfie moved back last night. It's still early days, but I think it's going to work if we are careful with each other.

Freda was good as her word. By her account, she went straight round to the pub on Sunday lunchtime after she left me, and demanded that Alfie should leave now and come for a walk with her. When he refused she announced in a loud voice that if that was the way he wanted it, they could talk about the problem with his wife and child right there, in front of everyone. Well, that got him to his feet quick enough, she told me, and they went out to the park.

When she relayed to him what I'd told her, about the drinking and shaking the baby, he apparently broke down in tears and said he was a failure of a man, disabled and unemployable, not good enough for me and Johnnie, and it was best if the marriage stayed broken so that I could be free to find a proper husband and father instead.

She shouted at him to pull himself together and

start thinking of other people for a change rather than just feeling sorry for himself, and he looked pretty shocked that his little sister could be so fierce, at least that's how she put it.

Then she went on to tell him that his drinking had to stop, *now*: it was becoming too much of a habit, and one he couldn't afford, and if he carried on like this he'd end up in the gutter like a tramp, and didn't their ma and pa have enough to worry about what with business being slow, and her and Annie with no income and nowhere to live?

He got angry at this and said that was her lookout not his, and stood up to go and when she asked him where, he said 'to The Nelson', and she said, 'over my dead body. You're going to see Rose, right now'.

So she virtually dragged him to the flat and then she put Johnnie and Annie together in his pram and said she was going to take them both home for tea and wouldn't be back for several hours. Before she left, she looked at us both sternly and said that by the time she returned she expected us both to have apologised to each other and sorted out our differences.

In the first few moments after she left, both Alfie and me were so astonished that we could find no words to say to each other. Standing there in our parlour, wet from the rain, he looked so pale and dejected, like a dog that's stolen a bone and is afraid of getting beaten, that all I could think of doing was to give him a big hug.

After a little while he wrapped his arms around me, too, and we stood there for several minutes, just breathing and feeling each other's warmth. Then he turned his face to my cheek and kissed it, and I turned my face too and we kissed properly. It was a warm and comfortable feeling, like putting on a familiar glove. It didn't feel sexy, but I'm hopeful that will come back as we learn to forgive each other.

By the time Freda returned with the babies three hours later, we had both apologised for all the thoughtless and hurtful things we'd said and done, Alfie had promised to lay off the booze, and I had promised to be less snippy with him at home. I'd nearly exploded when he asked me to give up my job, but managed to hold my tongue and told him that as soon as he found something that earned him enough for us to rent a two-bedroom flat, I would definitely stop working.

He seemed to accept this but then started to grumble about how was he expected to go out looking for work when he had to look after the baby and do all the household chores too? I had to bite my lip again because Ma has done most of the childcare these past few months, and he's done precious little around the house. But then I had a brainwave and suggested we could ask Freda if she would look after Johnnie while I was out at work, since she had to be at home with Annie anyway and this way she could earn a few shillings to contribute to her keep and he could go on looking for work.

Finally, I reminded him that there was a possibility of work right here on our doorstep, at the Poppy Factory, but this was the final straw.

'I've agreed to everything you've asked,' he said. 'But spare me the bleeding heart sympathy from some ruddy charity, paying tuppence halfpenny to make artificial flowers.'

That made me think of Walter, and his pride in the job which had – his words – 'given his life back', but of course I said nothing. Alfie is still clinging to the belief that he can get the sort of job he might have had as an able-bodied man, even though there are nearly three million unemployed. But perhaps it's a step too far, just now, to insist.

It will take a while to rediscover the trust we once felt for each other, but I am confident that now it will happen. Tomorrow I will go and buy Freda a present – perhaps some new nylons? – as a thank you for making us both see sense, at last. And I will ask her about looking after Johnnie. I pray she agrees.

Monday 21st August

Saw Walter again this morning when I went back to work after the break. It was embarrassing at first, recalling the undignified way I'd rushed out of that tea room, smitten with guilt. But he reassured me, saying he fully understood how I felt and although he thought me the most beautiful girl in the world he didn't want to cause any problems at home and couldn't we try just being friends?

Then he told me a joke, the kind of gallows humour that only an amputee could get away with: *An injured British soldier captured by the Germans has to have one of his legs amputated and asks the camp doctor if the limb can be sent back to his family in England. The doctor thinks it a strange request but agrees. A few days later, they have to amputate his other leg, and agree to the same curious request. Then they have to take off an arm, and finally the other arm. This time, the camp Kommandant refuses. 'Nein!' he says. 'Ve cannot do zis! Ve suspekt you are trying to escape.*

I love the way he is determined to make light of his disability. Perhaps because it is very obvious that he's lost an arm, so he might as well admit it and joke about it. But while Alfie has got a pronounced limp, he can 'conceal' the fact that he's only got one leg, which allows him to deny it to himself.

Still, I can't complain. He has been the most loving and attentive husband since our reconciliation. Freda agreed to look after the babies; in fact she was thrilled by the idea of being able to earn a few shillings, and this was the first day that Alfie has been out job hunting.

He returned limping more than usual and quite grey-faced with tiredness. Most places he approached told him to come back in September after the summer break, but he wasn't rejected out of hand, which has cheered him up a little.

Tuesday 22nd August

Walter told me today that Major Howson is still hiring. When I mentioned it to Alfie he bit my head off. I'm not going to mention it again.

Monday 4th September

Alfie's got a job! In 'sales', no less. I am so proud of him.

Today was his first day and he came home utterly exhausted, falling into bed immediately after tea so I hardly had a chance to ask him how his day went, let alone what 'sales' means. Perhaps tomorrow?

Saturday 9th September

I am still no wiser about what Alfie's job is, but it involves working Saturdays. 'Busiest time for customers', was all he would say.

He's equally cagey about how much he is earning, but it's obviously enough for a pint or two because he went straight to The Nelson on his way home, and has been there ever since.

Saturday 16th September

What was supposed to have been a lovely day turned into a disaster.

Freda's been on at me to go with her to the West End, not to buy anything since neither of us can afford that, but for what she called 'window shopping' and perhaps have a teacake in Lyons. I think she still secretly hankers after the high life.

Alfie's still working on Saturdays but Mrs B agreed to look after Annie and Ma is always willing to have Johnnie for the day, so off we went and I'll have to admit I was pretty excited – I so rarely leave the Old Kent Road now that I'm working full time. I've certainly never been shopping in those big stores before, let alone for clothes. In our house it's always been hand-me downs or home-mades.

Those shops! They're like palaces, with their huge windows, marble pillars and sculptures, and it was all I could do to keep my mouth from hanging open, like some country bumpkin fresh in town. I've never seen so many smartly-dressed and beautiful ladies, cruising along the pavements with their children and, in some cases, their servants, in tow.

I thought window shopping meant we were just going to look at the window displays, but Freda's bold as brass and said there was no point in coming all this way if we weren't going to look around inside. I felt so scruffy and out of place that I pleaded with her to let me go and sit in a café while I waited, but she dragged me into a shop called Selfridges, which was so enormous and so crowded, that I wondered that anyone could ever find anything.

Freda seemed to know her way around, and led me towards the back of the store where she pressed a button beside a pair of double doors. They opened with the tinkle of a bell, and we stepped into a tiny room with ornate gold-framed mirrors on three sides. When the smart man in uniform closed the doors I felt panicky, but Freda just said 'bend your knees' and there was the hum of machinery working and the strangest sensation of leaving my stomach behind. After a moment there was a gentle bump and the man opened the doors again, and I was astonished to find that we stepped out into a completely new place.

I asked where we were, and Freda just whispered, 'We're on the second floor, silly. We just came up in the lift.' Imagine, we had risen up two floors by just standing in that little room. I wanted to know how it worked, but she took my hand and pulled me along between the racks of clothing, saying she needed to find some dresses to try on. I started muttering that we shouldn't do that if we weren't going to buy, but she was not to be deterred. The rest of the afternoon is a bit of a blur. The shop assistants buzzed around Freda like bees tending their queen, and she must have tried on a dozen dresses, each one more beautiful than the last. I could see them forcing smiles as she politely proclaimed in a posh voice that she hadn't found *precisely* what she had in mind, but might come back later.

It was the same in Dickens and Jones, and John Lewis. By now I was wilting, so we started heading for Lyons for a cuppa before catching the bus home. We turned a corner and what I saw stopped me in my tracks. Someone pushed past, knocking me sideways, and I could hear Freda shouting, 'Come on, Rose,' but my legs were paralysed with the shock.

There on the opposite corner, by the entrance to

another large store, was a man with a tray hung from a strap around his neck hawking tobacco, pipes, matches and cigarette papers, with a sign above his head showing the prices and the words: *Help a Disabled Serviceman*. The crowds streamed past him; no-one wanted to buy from such a miserable-looking salesman.

Surely I was mistaken? But no, when I looked again it was definitely him. My strong, proud Alfie, reduced to selling matches on street corners like a pauper? *Why?* When he'd rejected out of hand my suggestion of applying to the Poppy Factory?

I stepped out into the traffic in a daze, hardly hearing the car horns or Freda's shouts. How I reached the other side unscathed I'll never understand; all I knew was that I had to reach Alfie and drag him away. When he caught sight of me, his face turned even greyer. As I approached he hissed, 'What are *you* doing here?' I grabbed his arm and said he didn't need to do this, we could find another way, but he pulled it away and told me to let him be.

'I can't leave you here, like this,' I said again, but he said that was what I wanted, wasn't it, for him to get a job? 'So now I've got one.'

'But not *this*, Alfie,' I tried to explain, but he snapped at me to go away and stop drawing attention. 'I've got to finish the shift and return the goods or I'll be in for it. Go home. We'll talk later.'

On the bus Freda tried to pump me for information. When I told her I hadn't even known he was doing it, she said she expected he 'has his reasons'. But I have simply no idea why he would take up such a demeaning job when there's perfectly respectable work at the factory. He refuses to accept charity, but he's prepared to stand on a street corner selling matches. It doesn't make any sense.

(Later) It's now eleven o'clock and, as I feared, he hasn't returned home and he's not in The Nelson. I'm too embarrassed to check whether he has returned to his parents' house and I'm sure Freda would have popped round to reassure me, if he had. I must try to rest, even though I won't be able to sleep without knowing that he's safe.

Sunday 17th September
It's been a very long day and I am exhausted from a short, restless night and all the talking we've been doing.

Alfie returned early this morning, soaking wet and shivery, having spent the night on a park bench. When I asked him why he didn't come home, for goodness' sake, I'd been up most of the night waiting for him and worrying, he just said he was too exhausted and confused about everything to face getting a grilling from me.

Well, of course that made me feel thoroughly guilty, as if it was all my fault he'd taken that demeaning job, and had to sleep rough on top of it all, so I burst into tears and that set Johnnie off too,

332

so we were all in a right mess. I put the kettle on and we drank tea for hours, trying to talk and make sense of everything. Eventually I got him to understand that I'd rather live in our cramped little flat than watch him humiliate himself each day, and made him promise not to go back to it tomorrow. Soon after this, he started to look really peaky and I sent him off to bed with two hot-water bottles, which is where he is now, still sleeping it off, poor boy.

Freda called around after lunch to make sure he was safe, and I had to admit that I still didn't understand what was going on in her brother's head, what he's thinking and why he does what he does. We agreed that love them though we might, the minds of men are a mystery.

Monday 18th September
We seem to struggle from crisis to crisis. Today it got worse, if that's possible.

I arrived home from work to find Alfie sitting in our kitchen with a miserable face on him and when I asked him, as cheerily as possible, if he'd like a cup of tea, he snapped no thank you, not until I'd cleared a few things up with him.

'Okay, so now you can tell me,' he said in a menacing kind of whisper. 'Just who *is* that creep with the yellow hair you seem so pally with?'

Well, that nearly floored me. It had to be Walter he was referring to, who else could it be? My first thought was that Mrs B must have told him about seeing us together at Waterloo. How else could he know about Walter, and where could he possibly have seen us together?

I played for time by muttering something about not knowing what he meant but then he said he'd seen us together on our way to work this morning.

I was flabbergasted. He'd been spying on me?

'I was not spying,' he said, looking me straight in the eye. 'I just wanted to take a look at this flipping Poppy Factory you keep rabbiting on about, so I followed you.'

I said I'd have told him in an instant if he'd only asked. For a moment I felt pleased that at last he was showing a flicker of interest, then quickly realised that seeing me with Walter had surely put an end to any spirit of enquiry he might have felt.

'Ah, then I wouldn't have seen you with lover boy, would I?' There was a vicious edge to his voice I'd never heard before.

'For Christ's sake, he's *not* my lover boy,' I said, 'he's just a friend who makes me laugh. Nothing more than that.'

'Oh yeah, I saw the way you looked at him, the way you touched his arm as you parted,' he said, even more bitterly. It was true, Walter and me are so comfortable with each other these days that those little gestures seem perfectly natural, but I could imagine what Alfie was thinking.

I'm not sure why, but in that instant something flipped in my head and I decided that instead of trying to conceal it I would clear the air by telling Alfie everything: how miserable I'd been, how Walter and I happened to meet one day because our paths crossed on the way to work, and how he made me laugh. How, yes, he was quite flirty with me, and I'd found it flattering at a time when I was at a very low ebb. I went even further, and told him how I'd met Walter for tea at Waterloo and realised just in time that I was being a silly idiot. How I'd been so pleased to have Alfie back in my life, and how I now saw Walter as just a friend.

'But what I most admire about him,' I heard myself saying, thinking all the while that this bold talk must surely be going too far, 'is how he treats his disability. He doesn't try to conceal it, pretend it's not there, or feel sorry for himself, he's just making the best of it. He was out of work for four years and now he's pleased as punch to have a job which pays a proper wage.'

Alfie's face was a picture of disbelief. How did I have the nerve to carry on? Johnnie, who'd been playing happily at our feet, sensed the atmosphere and began to whine for attention.

'He says he won't be making poppies forever but he loves being able to earn for himself, while doing something worthwhile which will help others. The Major and the other staff are caring, but there's not a whiff of what you call "bleeding-heart charity" in the place, they're just getting on with the job in the best way they can. But you think you're so above all that, don't you, that you're prepared to sell matches on the street instead?'

As I spoke, Alfie's face had become steadily more and more flushed and by now he was puce with rage. He pushed himself up and grabbed his walking stick, and I feared for a moment that he might hit me, but I stood my ground and he stumbled past me, heading for the door and slamming it behind him.

That's it, I've definitely gone too far now, I said to myself, holding Johnnie tight to still his distress but feeling strangely calm and proud of myself for having been so honest, at last. If Alfie didn't like hearing harsh truths, then too bad, he was not the man I thought I'd married.

Saturday 23rd September

What a week it's been! Looking back at my previous entry I can now see that this was the tipping point.

To keep my thoughts in order, I'll have to tell it as it happened.

Alfie did not return home on Monday night and when I dropped Johnnie around to the Barkers' house the following morning on my way to work Freda answered the door.

'Yes, he slept here again,' she said, shaking her head at me in a despairing kind of way. 'For God's sake, I thought you two had sorted out your differences?'

'I told him a few home truths, Freda,' I replied, relieved to hear he was safe. 'But if he can't take it, then that's his problem. Can't stop now, though. See you later.'

On the way to work Walter was his usual sweet, charming self and when I told him things were bad at home he promised to buy me a chocolate flake in the canteen to cheer me up. Too bad he never got the chance.

It was nearly eleven o'clock, us girls were getting ready for our break, and we could hear the scraping of chairs signalling that the Poppy Factory lads were finishing off theirs ready to go back over the road, when there was the most almighty rumpus outside in the corridor, with men shouting and doors crashing. Just then the klaxon went off for our break and we all downed tools and rushed outside to find out what was happening, squashing each other through the doorway and out into the street in our haste to find out what was happening.

I could see over the heads of the girls in front that two of the Poppy Factory men were wrestling with a third man – they'd pushed his face down towards the ground and pinned his arms behind his back.

Walter was standing to one side, his face pale as death, being supported by a mate. I would have run to him if my way hadn't been blocked by the girls in front. Then I noticed the red weal on his cheekbone. Had he been punched? Whatever had happened?

The man they were restraining lifted his head for a second, just long enough for me to see his face. He was hollering things like 'Let me at him, I'll show the f******** creep.' And worse still, 'Think you can have my wife, do you? Well you'll have to f******* fight me for her.' Then the horrible truth dawned. Mary whispered in my ear, 'Isn't that your Alfie?' and I knew she was right. By God, I wished at that moment that the ground would swallow me up, or that I could be anywhere else but here.

Someone shouted, 'Call the coppers' and another one said, 'No, call the Major' and at that point Mr Mitchell pushed his way through the gaggle of us girls, booming, 'Make way, make way', and 'let that man go, at once.' Then he took Alfie firmly by the arm and dragged him towards the entrance to the Poppy Factory.

'You're coming with me, young man,' he said. 'No-one picks a fight outside my premises, especially not with a disabled soldier. You and I are going to take a little visit to the Major, so you can explain to us both what the hell's going on.'

In spite of my embarrassment, instinct took over. He might have been impossible of late, but he was still my husband, we protect our own. I rushed forward, ignoring the look of horror on Alfie's face, and shouted that I could explain everything. Alfie was my husband. It wasn't his fault. I finished, rather lamely, that he was a disabled soldier, too, as if that might excuse his shocking behaviour.

Mr Mitchell said calmly that I'd better go with them so I could tell the Major my side of the story behind this sorry state of affairs. It was only as we were climbing the stairs to the Major's office that the seriousness of our situation began to dawn on me.

Alfie could be arrested for assaulting another man and I could lose my job for standing up for him.

Major Howson has quite the kindest eyes of any man I've ever met, although when we walked into that neat, sparsely furnished office I thought him utterly terrifying. He stood as we entered, towering over us (he must be at least six foot) with that officer's ramrod bearing and a strong, direct gaze that seems to miss nothing. I learned later that he earned the Military Cross for battling on at Passchendaele in spite of being wounded, which comes as no surprise. He seems like just that kind of man.

He invited Mr Mitchell to come in, saying what a pleasure it was to see him, and asked to be introduced.

Mr Mitchell explained that Alfie had just assaulted one of his men outside. And this was Alfie's wife, Mrs Barker. The Major's bushy moustache twitched a bit, then he asked who the other man was, and whether he was hurt.

'Bruised cheek. That's all I think,' Mr Mitchell said, then looked at Alfie. 'What's the name of the man you attacked?'

Alfie looked at me. 'It's Walter,' I said.

'Shall we get him in, too?' said the Major. 'Would you mind, Mitchell?'

As Mr Mitchell clattered down the stairs again, the Major pulled up chairs for us. I caught him watching as Alfie sat down in his usual slightly ungainly way, kicking the artificial leg with his other foot to allow him to sit, and then pulling the lower part of it inwards with his hand, forcing the knee into a bend. He asked, quite simply, was it a war wound, and Alfie explained how he'd been caught by a shell and they'd been unable to save the leg. Then the Major asked whether he'd managed to find work and Alfie shook his head and said he was looking.

At this point Mr Mitchell arrived with Walter, whose bruise seemed to have doubled in size in the few minutes since we'd left him in the street. The Major pulled up two more chairs, invited them to sit, pulled out a packet of Turkish cigarettes from his desk drawer and offered them around. The room filled with smoke as all the men lit up, and the Major threw open the window before sitting down again.

First of all, he asked Walter if he was badly hurt, and Walter touched his face and winced a bit but said he thought it was just a bruise, no real harm done. Mr Mitchell said he should go over to the collar factory kitchen and ask for some ice to put onto it just as soon as we were finished here.

The Major then turned to Alfie and asked him why he took it into his head to assault one of his workers, and Alfie glared at Walter and said he bloody deserved it.

'And *why* did he deserve it, if you don't mind my asking?'

'He's been trying to lead my wife astray.' The words

were out, now. No putting them back in the box like the poppy in Walter's toy.

'Is this true, Walter?'

Walter looked towards me, as if to apologise for what he was about to say.

'No, sir,' he said firmly. 'We're just friends; we talk as we walk into work. She's a very attractive woman, of course, and if she was single I'd've acted very differently. But from the start she made it clear that she's married, and I'd never touch another man's wife.'

Alfie glowered and said he had invited me out to tea, and he couldn't pretend otherwise because I'd already admitted it.

'Yes I did. She needed cheering up, sir. From what I gather, Mr Barker here couldn't find work and things were a bit difficult at home.'

The Major turned to me and asked if I had anything to say? I shook my head at first and then realised I needed to back Walter up. 'It's just as he says: we are friends, nothing more. He makes me laugh, and heaven knows I've needed it in the past few months. My husband is a proud man, sir, and he doesn't like to admit it, but he's a hard worker and being unemployed is really getting him down. It's affecting our marriage and I don't like that one little bit.'

'Is this correct, Mr Barker?'

Alfie looked down at his shoes and, when he looked up, his eyes were swimming. I wanted to hug him and tell him that everything would be okay. He admitted that I was right; everything had been getting on top of him lately, and seeing me with Walter had just capped it. He'd lost his rag and was now very ashamed. He pushed himself up out of the chair, limped over to Walter and held out his hand. 'I have treated you wrongly. No excuses. I am sorry.'

Walter stood up too and said, 'No harm done, Mr Barker, apology accepted.' And they shook hands.

The Major stood up, beaming. 'Good lads. Walter, I think it's time for you to get back to work. Mr Mitchell, I think you'll agree that this concludes the matter satisfactorily?' Mr M nodded. 'In that case, you'll forgive me if I keep Mrs Barker here for a few more minutes? I'd like to have a word with her and her husband in private.'

When the others had gone, he sat us both down again and then leaned around the door of his room to ask his secretary for a pot of tea for three. Then he handed Alfie another of his curious cigarettes and, as they lit up, he asked if he was still out of work. My heart leapt. Was he going to offer Alfie a job here at the factory?

But it wasn't quite so easy. He explained that because places at the factory were limited, the Disabled Society had certain priorities for who they would employ. There were lots of questions about Alfie's disability, what pension he received, what jobs had he applied for and what sort of work he'd done before the war. And finally, he said, it depended on what kind of family responsibilities you have. Alfie said we had a baby son and the Major turned to me and said he gathered that I had a job at Mitchell's. I nodded, wondering why that should be relevant. But then he explained that was a problem, because we were not what the Society describes as 'in greatest need' because, as well as Alfie's pension, there was a second income coming into the family.

The room fell silent except for the clonkety-clonk of the machines downstairs, cutting out the red fabric for the poppies; machines that Alfie could be operating, earning himself a proper wage, if it wasn't for me and my beloved job.

And then, in a flash, I realised: in all the mayhem of the morning it had completely slipped my mind. I hadn't mentioned anything to Alfie yet, but the day before yesterday my monthlies failed to arrive. I'd put it down to stress and worry, but this morning my breasts had felt ever so slightly tingly, like they did when Johnnie was first on the way.

'Not for very long, sir,' I piped up. 'Mr Mitchell won't employ women if they're expecting.'

Alfie's mouth fell open with astonishment and then split into the widest, happiest smile I've seen on his face for many a long month and the Major put out his hand to shake mine and then Alfie's in turn.

'What splendid news. Many congratulations to both of you,' he said. 'This changes everything, of course. Mr Barker, would you like to have a tour of the factory to see whether you think a job here would suit you?' And my lovely husband, still smiling broadly, said he definitely would, thank you, sir. During their tour, he went over to Walter and asked him whether he would accept him as a fellow worker, should he be offered a job there. Walter, bless his soul, said he'd be happy to let bygones be bygones, and he'd be welcome there.

To cut a long story short, the Major offered Alfie a job and he starts next week. It's early days, but I am now starting to hope that this will be the start of a brand new chapter in our lives.

Saturday 11th November
It's nearly two months since my last entry and the only excuse is that we have been so busy. The baby is due on my own birthday in May next year. Freda agreed to go on looking after Johnnie and I shall carry on working until Mr Mitchell tells me I can't stay. With the money we're both earning we have been able to afford a flat with two bedrooms – such luxury – in the next door street. Oh, and Bessie had a brood of beautiful puppies and we've taken one as our own.

Alfie is a new man. He's not going to make poppies for ever, he says. Essentially it's quite repetitive work, but he really enjoys the company of the other lads and he seems so much happier in himself. After all he's been through it was bound to take him a while to recover, but it would have been much easier for all of us had he not been so proud about accepting help. Not 'bleeding heart do-gooder's charity', but genuine help from the likes of Major Howson.

A couple of weeks ago he told me he'd thought of a way to make one of the machines more efficient. When I suggested he tell the Major, he pooh-poohed the idea, saying the man had better things to do. But yesterday I could hear him whistling down the street on his way home from work and he arrived even more cheerful than usual. Apparently he'd mentioned his idea to a mate, who told the Major, who came down from his office especially to ask Alfie to explain it. He listened really carefully and nodded a great deal and sketched some drawings, saying it was an excellent idea and would Alfie like to help him make it? Well of course he jumped at the idea and later he had a go at what he calls 'machine tooling'.

So now he says he wants to become an engineer like the Major. I didn't mention that you probably need better writing and arithmetic for that sort of thing but I can tell it's got him thinking, and who knows what might come of it?

Most exciting of all, Freda is dating again. It happened when she visited the collar factory to see whether there were any jobs for her – there weren't, but there will be once my belly starts to show. As it was the end of the day I walked home with her, and the Poppy Factory lads were clocking off too. Walter asked for an introduction and that was the start of it all.

It could have been awkward with Alfie, but the

two of them have already made up their differences – they were pretty much forced to, working side by side on the benches. I am so pleased for Freda because, although Walter is a flirt, underneath he is a genuine kind of man and to see him playing so affectionately with little Annie you'd think he was her real father.

So I've barely had time to think, let alone write my diary and, as I'm coming to the end of this set of notebooks, I'm going to give it a break for a while. But I couldn't let 11th November go by without a final entry. We didn't go to the Cenotaph this year, but as I pinned on my poppy I reflected on what a strange four years it's been since that very first Armistice Day.

These poppies they make – and they sell in their tens of thousands now – are not just a symbol of loss and sadness, I've come to understand. They are also a reminder of how important it is for the rest of us to go on living the best and fullest lives possible, in honour of those who didn't survive.

Chapter Seven

For perhaps the first time in her life, Jess held nothing back from her mother.

With Milly their constant companion, they took bracing walks along the beach and long sojourns sheltering from the wind behind the sand dunes and she told her everything: about the nightmares, the sleeplessness, the flashbacks and the uncontrolled drinking; her experience with the ambulance services; her hatred of the timewasters and despair at the plight of the old people she'd encountered; how she lost her temper with the counsellor and how she'd tried to pull herself together but had drunk too much and made a fool of herself at the wedding, embarrassing Nate at his big moment; how he had told her to leave.

'I thought he was the one for life, Mum, but now I think it's all over,' she said. 'I just can't imagine life without him. It's unbearable.' The words resonated in her head. 'My God, that's what Rose wrote in her diary.'

'What was that?'

'There's a point where Rose says she thinks her marriage to Alfie might be over and she can't bear the thought.'

'Every couple has bad times, and most of them get through it just fine,' her mother said, putting an arm around her. 'Rose and Alfie survived, didn't they?'

'What happened to them?'

'They spent the rest of their lives together, thank heavens, or none of us would be here. They had your Grandfather Johnnie and his sister, my aunt Alice, and lived into their seventies, as far as I can remember.'

'Alice? The one who lost her lover in the trenches and never married?'

'That's the one. Became a professional pianist and drove intrepidly around London in a Morris Minor, well into her nineties. When we get home I'll show you the photos I found among Granny's things.'

Jess opened the small, dog-eared album with the greatest care: sheets of black paper were held between brown cardboard covers tied together with cord that was now frayed and in danger of unravelling completely. The ancient photo corners had long since lost their stick, and the tiny black and white prints were now jumbled loosely between the pages.

She picked up one of the larger photographs, in sepia with serrated white borders and the name of the photographer embossed in gold script at the bottom, turned it over and read the words handwritten on the back: *Rose and Alfie Barker, married Boxing Day 1917.*

His sweet face had a faraway gaze and he looked no older than a schoolboy despite the army uniform and fierce military haircut with a parting like a white scar slitting his scalp from front to back. Rose stood as tall as her new husband, slim and wiry, in an unflattering dress and a hat that didn't seem to match, her face fixed for the camera with a grin that had almost become a grimace. Peering more closely, Jess imagined she could recognise something of herself: the determined jaw, the eyes close-set either side of a straight nose, the widow's peak on a high forehead.

Another photo showed the families formally posed: the newly-weds with their parents, and a young woman of Rose's age. 'That's Alfie's sister I think,' Susan said, peering over Jess's shoulder. Freda was shorter than her brother, slight and curvy with fashionably bobbed hair and a flirty grin. They must have looked an ill-assorted pair, Jess thought, the tall, serious-faced Rose towering over her bubbly friend.

The only person without a smile was a woman standing beside the bride, her face strained and wan. 'Is that Rose's mother?'

'Betty Appleby, your great-great grandmother. Both her sons died in the trenches.'

Jess remembered how she'd cried over James; how painful it still felt to think of him even now, six years later. She couldn't even start to imagine how much worse it would feel to lose your own child, let alone two of them.

'And this is your grandfather Johnnie, aged about twenty.' Susan handed her an official-looking photograph – larger than the rest – of a fresh-faced young man with a huge grin, wearing an air force uniform with the beret set on his head at a rakish angle. 'He was a bomber pilot in the Second World War. Got shot down and spent half the war in prison camp.'

'I'm sorry I never really knew him, Mum. Did he ever talk about it, at all?'

Susan shook her head. 'Never. He just wanted to forget, he said.'

They turned a few more pages and found photographs of his wedding to Jess's Granny Mary, on 11th April 1946. This was clearly a 'proper do' in a church, and even the small, grainy monochrome prints seemed to capture the joy of the day: everyone dressed to the nines, determined to have a great time despite postwar austerity. The sun was shining and, in the background were apple trees heavy with spring blossom.

The groom Johnnie, a tall, straight backed young man, seemed to dwarf his parents: Alfie in a smart suit, older now of course and going grey but still with a full head of curly hair, and Rose, resplendent in a smartly tailored calf-length skirt and blouse, her face shadowed by a wide-brimmed lacy hat. Her expression was hard to make out, but Jess felt sure she would have been grinning with fierce pride.

'Was Alfie still working at the Poppy Factory by then?' she asked.

Susan shook her head. 'He only stayed there a couple of years, as far as I know. At some point he managed to get himself a job in a garage and they trained him up as a motor mechanic.'

'That makes sense. Rose wrote about how much he loved driving the motor van for his father.'

'They eventually set up their own company, somewhere on the Old Kent Road I think, and they certainly prospered, although everyone used to say that Rose was the one with the business brain. I remember he always smelled of engine oil, even as an old man.'

The bridesmaids – two hatless young women in matching floral dresses – stood arm in arm beside the bride and groom, throwing their heads back with laughter. 'That's auntie Alice, Johnnie's younger sister,' Susan said, pointing to the fairer one of the two. 'She looks so like her pa, don't you think?' The other girl was tall and slim with straight dark hair blowing across her face. 'Not sure about this one.'

'Could that be Annie, Freda's daughter?' Jess asked. 'Freda was Alfie's sister, and Rose's best friend.'

Susan peered at the print. 'She must have died before I was born, or at least before I was old enough to know her.'

'Did you know who Freda married? Rose wrote about her dating Walter, the guy Rose wrote about, who also worked at the Poppy Factory? He lost an arm in the war.'

Susan shook her head. 'I never heard tell of that, sorry.'

They flicked through the rest of the wedding snaps until Jess's eye was caught by a group who seemed to be sharing a joke. 'Oh look, could this be him?' She pointed to a man with tight wiry hair and an empty sleeve. To his side, looking up at him with a fond smile, was a small, slightly dumpy grey-haired woman. 'And perhaps this is Freda?' She scanned the group more carefully. Beside Freda was a young man, in his late teens or early twenties, with pale curly hair. Did Freda and Walter have a son together, perhaps?

Jess turned back to the photographs, studying the faces, eager to learn more about the people she'd grown to know through the diaries. What a resilient bunch, she thought to herself. They had endured so much, struggled with unemployment and poverty, lost family members and friends and suffered terrible setbacks yet here they all were, having a great time on this sunny day, just a year after the ending of a second terrible war. How much they must have longed for a few years of peace. Her own losses and difficulties seemed so slight in comparison, yet why did she find it so difficult to be optimistic about her own future?

Under her mother's watchful eye Jess gave up drinking, but the nightmares returned with a vengeance. After a third night of waking to her daughter's anguished screams, of holding her, stroking her forehead and trying to soothe her, Susan begged Jess to make an appointment with the local surgery.

The GP was an elderly, avuncular man in a three-piece suit, with thinning grey hair and a spotted bow tie. Jess's heart sank – someone so old-school was hardly likely to understand what she'd been through. When she explained, in as casual a manner as possible, that she was only after a repeat prescription for the tranquillisers she'd been taking before, he turned from the computer screen and leaned forward in his chair.

'It would be helpful to know why you needed them in the first place,' he said, gently. 'Take your time.'

She sighed, reluctant to recount the dreary story all over again, dreading the inevitable look of puzzled sympathy that would cross his face. She felt like a wimp; while her friends were trying to rebuild their lives without limbs she was sitting here trying to explain why she wanted medication for a few bad dreams.

Then, for some unknown reason, Rose's words about Walter drifted into her mind: 'He doesn't try to conceal it, pretend it's not there, or feel sorry for himself, he's just making the best of it'.

With a jolt, she understood. For too long she'd made light of her problems, pretending to herself that they weren't really there, that they were a kind of punishment to be endured, that she was strong enough to cope, that she could sort herself out. Deep down, she hadn't been entirely certain that she wanted to be 'cured' and even, in a warped kind of way, had come to consider that the nightmares and flashbacks were the price she must pay; her penance for living when James and so many others had died. She seemed to have lost sight of that long-ago promise to herself: that she would justify the loss of his life by living her own in a way that would make him proud.

So why could she not now acknowledge that she needed help to 'make the best of it'?

The doctor's kindly face was still waiting. She took a deep breath, and began.

Jess left the surgery with a prescription given for a single month on the understanding that she would agree to being referred to a psychiatrist. 'For a proper diagnosis, so that we can make sure you're on the right medication. I honestly think it will be worth it in the long run,' he said.

The appointment came through faster than she'd expected, and now here she was, reluctantly, at a hospital she had never visited before, in an unfamiliar town, sitting on an uncomfortable bright orange chair with a polystyrene cup of over-stewed tea from the 'Friends' café. Around her were a dozen other sad-eyed people of all ages and types, none of them displaying any obvious symptoms of insanity.

The psychiatrist, a tiny, elegant woman in a bright green sari, invited Jess to sit down and went straight to the point: 'Your GP seems to think you might be suffering from post-traumatic stress after your experiences in Afghanistan, Miss Merton. Would you like to tell me more?'

The story came out more easily this time, almost as though she were talking about someone else's experiences. It didn't upset her or make her angry any more, as she described briefly how when they were out on tour she seemed to cope fine, even when close mates had died, even after the attack on the compound and the IED explosion, even after coming under fire in the poppy field.

She talked of how she missed the team spirit and the closeness of the unit, her pride in the job and the fact that she'd helped to save several people's lives. And then she recounted how, when she had got back to the UK, the flashbacks and nightmares and the anger had started, the way she seemed to lash out at the people she loved, how tranquillisers had made her feel brain-dead, how alcohol had seemed to help, for a while, how she'd resigned from her job after the accident on the pavement because she felt she could no longer trust herself, and how the counselling had just made her even more angry.

The doctor listened in silence, her deep brown eyes watchful and compassionate, taking notes, nodding from time to time and prompting gently when Jess faltered: 'tell me a bit about yourself before you joined the Army?', 'how did that make you feel?', or 'how might you have reacted to that sort of thing, before going on tour?'

When Jess finished, she sat back in her chair and said: 'I think there is no doubt that you are suffering from symptoms of post-traumatic stress, Miss Merton. I would describe it as mild to moderate, and certainly nothing that cannot be sorted out, given time. I don't think that the tranquillisers you've been using are quite right for this condition, so I'll prescribe a different kind of anti-anxiety medication to take for at least three months, and would like to see you again after that. And I would urge you to try counselling again, a different approach this time. I will refer you to a specialist in Cognitive Behavioural Therapy, or CBT, who has specific experience of working with veterans.'

Jess nodded. There was something about this quietly spoken woman that inspired confidence. 'If you really think it will help,' she said.

'I do,' the doctor replied. 'But there's one other thing. You said you had resigned from your job? I would urge you to reconsider this. Is there any prospect of returning to work? Having a meaningful occupation can be a critical factor for recovery.'

'Being a medic, or a paramedic, is the only thing I've ever wanted to do, the only job I'm trained for,' Jess said. 'But I'm really not ready to go back to that, not right now.'

'Do you have anything else in mind?'

'Not really.'

'It's worth giving it some thought, you know, and there are organisations that can help.'

While the prescription was printing, the doctor picked up her pen, made a few short notes on a slip of paper and handed it to Jess. She read:

- *PTSD and CBT: Combat Stress*
- *Employability/jobs: British Legion Civvy Street, also The Poppy Factory*

'The Poppy Factory? That's where my great-grandfather ended up after the First World War,' she said, incredulous. 'You're not seriously suggesting I should go and make poppies?'

'Of course not,' the doctor said, smiling. 'They help disabled veterans back into work of all kinds these days. "Employability", they call it.'

'But I'm not disabled.'

'PTSD counts,' she replied, simply. 'Anyway, it is up to you to decide what kind of help you need. It's just a suggestion.'

Later that evening, after everyone else had gone to bed, Jess braved her parents' painfully slow broad-band connection to send some emails, and found herself checking out the organisations the psychiatrist had mentioned.

The *Combat Stress* site provided a clear definition of PTSD and, after reading the case studies, Jess reckoned she'd got off quite lightly. CBT seemed to have been helpful for many people, and the process seemed straightforward enough: in addition to sessions with a therapist, you would be given exercises to do for yourself, which sounded practical and sensible. She remembered how shamefully she had treated Alison in that colourless room, how quickly she lost her temper, how rude she had been, and the look on the poor woman's face as she stomped out. It's time to grow up, she said to herself. She would give counselling another go, when the appointment came through, and this time she would stay with it, to the end.

Civvy Street listed plenty of vacancies but reading the descriptions only served to clarify her thoughts about the kind of job she really did *not* want: there were lots of admin and sales positions but she'd surely go crazy stuck in an office, and she'd make a lousy salesperson. She searched the database for 'work with animals' but it came up with no results.

She looked at the slip of paper again but something stopped her from looking up the third organisation named: The Poppy Factory. Remembering the picture Rose had painted, of men with missing limbs working at machinery to produce the red poppies for Remembrance Day, it still felt wrong, not appropriate somehow. I'm not really 'disabled', she thought to herself, I haven't lost a limb like Alfie, or Scotty or Alex. It's only in my head.

She closed the laptop and tried to sleep, but her brain wouldn't switch off: the events of the day and the words of the psychiatrist still jangling in her head: *Having a meaningful occupation can be a critical factor for recovery.* Am I crazy, giving up the career I've always planned for myself, she thought? And anyway, what kind of job could I do now that's not too stressful, yet isn't going to bore me rigid?

Her thoughts turned again to Rose's diaries. It was almost a hundred years ago, but there seemed to be so many parallels. Besides losing a leg, her great-grandfather had also displayed symptoms of what Jess now knew was PTSD: the nightmares, the fear of raw flesh, the outbursts of anger with those closest to him, and the drinking. Rose had learned from bitter experience how Alfie's unemployment made him depressed and led him to drink. Not for them, in those days, the free healthcare and support of psychiatrists, counsellors, tranquillisers or a choice of organisations dedicated to helping veterans, all available at the touch of a button.

All Alfie got was a wooden leg, and he was too proud to ask for any further help. 'Spare me the bleeding heart sympathy from some ruddy charity paying tuppence-halfpenny to make artificial flowers.' Jess understood only too clearly how he felt.

Perhaps pride was a family trait, inherited down the generations? It had taken her months to accept that she needed help, and even then she'd quit the tranquillisers and walked out of the counselling sessions. Until now she had been too embarrassed to admit her frailties except to closest friends and family and, even now, too proud to admit that, in some senses, she too was disabled. But, in the end, it was The Poppy Factory that put Alfie on the road to recovery, helped him into an entirely new career as a car mechanic. Why was she so resistant to the idea?

She sat up in bed and opened the laptop again.

The website came up quickly, poppy red, cheerful and uncomplicated. She read: *For nearly 90 years The Poppy Factory in Richmond, Surrey has been making poppies, crosses and wreaths for the Royal Family and the Royal British Legion's annual Remembrance Day appeal. As well as providing work for disabled veterans at its HQ in Richmond, The Poppy Factory uses its unique expertise to help its clients find work with many commercial organisations all over the UK. The Poppy Factory has a vision that "no disabled veteran who wants to work shall be out of work".*

It sounded practical and helpful. Why not give it a try? There was a single-page registration form, which she completed in a matter of minutes. All she now needed to supply was proof of her service record and her medical condition, but a caseworker would help sort that out. She pressed the 'submit form' button quickly, before she could change her mind, lay back on the pillow, closed her eyes and took a deep breath.

She'd made the first step.

The next day, she felt depressed all over again. Post-traumatic stress disorder. You heard of other people suffering from it but she'd never thought it would affect her. She texted Vorny: It's PTSD. Official diagnosis. How grim is that? x

Her phone rang almost immediately. 'It's just a name, Jess, not the end of the world,' Vorny said. 'It affects lots of people, so don't get too hung up on it. At least getting a proper diagnosis means you'll get the right treatment to get you back to work.'

'They've given me pills and I've decided to try counselling again – CBT is what they suggest.'

'Good plan. Look, we haven't seen you for weeks. Why don't you come and stay a couple of nights so we can talk properly? Your room's still free – we might get moved in the New Year and it seems hardly worth letting it again. What about next weekend?'

'Sounds good to me. My diary is completely empty.'

'Just let me check I'm off duty.' There was a pause at the end of the line, and then, 'Oh hang on. It's Remembrance Sunday.'

Remembrance Sunday. She'd almost forgotten, even though she hadn't missed the event for ten years, not since James died. 'I'll be there,' Jess said.

Later that day she had a call from a woman called Kate who described herself as an employability consultant for The Poppy Factory.

'That was quick,' Jess said, surprised.

'We know it can sometimes take a lot of courage to contact us,' Kate said, 'so we like to get back promptly, to reassure you that we'll do all we can to help.' She sounded efficient but also human and friendly, someone Jess felt she could trust.

'So,' Kate was saying. 'I'm sure we can help, but we just need to take a few more details from you so we can get the necessary documents sorted out, your service record, medical reports and so on. You said that you had a diagnosis of PTSD – is that right?'

'That's what the psychiatrist says, but I'm not sure it's really bad enough to. . .' Jess tailed off.

'There's really no need to be embarrassed or apologetic,' Kate said. 'It's more common than you'd ever know. And believe me, it's people like you that we are here for. Once we've got the paperwork sorted I'll arrange to visit you in person, so we can get to know each other better and talk it through from there. Is that okay?'

'Sounds great,' Jess said. 'Thank you.'

'Just out of curiosity,' Kate said. 'Can you tell me where you heard about our employability work?'

'It was the psychiatrist who told me – she said she'd read an article about it somewhere.'

'That's good, we want people to know we are not just about making poppies, these days.'

'And I learned how the factory got started, and about Major Howson, from my great-grandmother. Her husband, my great-grandfather, was one of the very first workers, at the old collar factory premises off the Old Kent Road, just after the First World War.'

'You knew your great-grandmother? How wonderful.'

'Oh no. Sorry, I should have said. She wrote about

this in her diaries from the end of the war when her husband came back injured, and how he eventually got a job at the factory. It's quite a story.'

'That's fascinating. We've got a volunteer here who's trying to write a book about our history in preparation for our centenary in a few years' time. He'd be thrilled to hear about this; we hardly have any case studies from those early days. Perhaps you can tell me a bit more when we meet.'

'I'd be happy to,' Jess said.

After Kate rang off, Jess felt a surge of optimism. The Poppy Factory had put Alfie back on his feet, and there was no reason to believe they would not be able to do the same for her.

Remembrance Day dawned cool and bright. After an early morning panic of pressing uniforms, polishing badges and buffing boots, Vorny left for her shift and Hatts went to catch the train to London, where she was going to visit Alex in hospital.

Jess ate a leisurely breakfast before heading into the town centre. There was usually a good attendance in this garrison town, and the crowds were already three deep along the pavements of the wide high street. She made her way to the war memorial in a small close at the end of the street, and climbed onto a wall. From there she could glimpse Vorny, standing to attention, with the rest of the regiment. It felt odd being here among the spectators, wearing just jeans and a scruffy jacket when this time last year she'd been standing to attention beside them, scrubbed and polished.

In the distance she could hear the band leading a brisk march to a tune she recognised – *The Purple Pageant?* – and before long the street was filled with bandsmen and women, followed by standard bearers and veterans, some of them in motorised buggies and wheelchairs. There was even a small group of 'Town Guards' in civil war costume, wearing shiny helmets and carrying pikes. Finally came the great and good, the Mayor and councillors in their civic robes and silly hats. Everyone just about managed to squeeze into position before the music stopped. The standards lowered, a single gunshot was fired, and a solitary bugler began to sound the poignant notes of *The Last Post*, reverberating off the walls of nearby buildings.

Two minutes feels like a very long time in a crowd. Of course it wasn't entirely silent: people coughed, babies cried, small children asked questions and were shushed by their parents, and a blackbird – or was it a robin – sang loudly in the park behind them, astonished to hear its own voice with the usual traffic stilled.

Jess closed her eyes, thinking of James, Jock, Baz and Millsie, and all those others who she didn't know, those many thousands of dead and maimed in wars through the years, the causes of which, for the most part, people struggled to understand. At hundreds of similar ceremonies all across Britain, not to mention in Basra and Bastion, Canada, New Zealand, and other countries all over the world: millions of people coming together for this single purpose, thinking about the ones they had loved. The thought was almost overwhelmingly moving.

She opened her eyes again. It might be a sombre scene but it was beautiful, too, in its way. The bird was still singing, its long liquid notes more poignant than any words. A low wintry sun beamed between the buildings, glinting off the brass instruments of the band and illuminating the pale, grave faces of the soldiers standing to attention on the far side of the close.

A second gunshot sounded the end of the silence, people cleared their throats, the band's conductor raised white-gloved hands and the musicians lifted their instruments to play the *Reveille*, followed by the slow, heart-wrenching chords of Elgar's *Nimrod*.

This was the moment Jess had been dreading, as the first of the dignitaries stepped forward to lay their wreaths. She took a deep breath. Last year it had prompted painful memories of being under fire in the poppy field and the moment when that single red flower was vaporised by a bullet, leaving just the green stem trembling in front of her eyes. This time, although the memories were still clear as ever, they did not make her head swim and her stomach stayed calm.

I survived, that's the most important thing, she thought. Then the realisation hit her: escaping from that moment in the poppy field had felt like being given a second chance at life, but recently she had spent so much time fretting about the past that she'd almost forgotten how to enjoy the present and, even more important, to make the most of her future.

The band started to play another march, turning to lead the parade back up the high street to take the salute, and the crowds dispersed. She climbed down from her wall and walked over to the war memorial to look at the wreaths, remembering how Rose and her mother had queued to place their little bunch of flowers at the foot of the new Cenotaph, all those years ago.

Vorny and Jess spent most of the afternoon drinking coffee and talking: about Jess's visit to the psychiatrist, her determination to make the counselling work this time, and how friendly and helpful the woman from The Poppy Factory had been. They gossiped about what was happening in the regiment, who had been promoted, or demoted, and who was currently dating whom. Vorny was facing the decision whether to quit the Army or sign up for a second tour in Afghanistan.

In the early evening, Hatts arrived back, her face glowing. 'He's so much better,' she said. 'He was out of bed in a wheelchair and doing daily sessions in the gym. They're already talking about fitting him for new legs.'

'That's incredible. So soon.'

'His sense of humour's back too, it was almost like old times. Guess what?'

'You had wild sex in his wheelchair?'

Hatts blushed. 'Not quite. He told me I shouldn't wait for him because why would I want a man with no legs, and I told him to stop being so stupid and kissed him, right there in front of everyone, and they cheered.'

'Ahhhh,' Jess and Vorny chorused.

'Then, before I left, he told me he loved me.'

'Aaaaahhhh.' Louder and longer this time, with a group hug. Hatts produced a bottle of sparkling wine from her backpack. 'I bought this at the station, to celebrate. It'll be a bit warm but shall we open it anyway?'

'Just a tiny one, please,' Jess said. 'I've been dry for nearly a month.'

'Here's to a sober Jess,' Vorny said, raising her glass. Their second toast was to Alex's speedy recovery and a third to all their lost or injured friends.

Hatts broke the sombre silence that followed: 'I nearly forgot to tell you, Jess. Guess who I saw on the station?'

'Who?'

'Your Nate.'

Jess took a too-large swig from her glass. 'Not *my* Nate any more, remember? Was he with anyone? Someone tall and beautiful, name of Nerissa, I suppose?'

'Nope, all on his own. He said he'd been at some sports fixture with the school and managed to avoid coming back on the coach with the little devils, so he could go straight home.'

'You *talked* to him?'

'It was mad. I was hanging around, people-watching while waiting for my platform to be announced and I'd just been ogling this tall and really fit guy across the concourse when I realised he was walking over and smiling, straight at me. It took me a second or two to realise who it was. Honestly, he was lovely, really friendly, asking after you, Jess, how were you getting on, were you back at work, had you been getting any help, that sort of thing.'

Jess sat down with a bump, light headed. 'Well, he hasn't bothered to ask me.'

'Haven't you heard from him at all?' Vorny asked.

'He texted the night after I got back from the wedding. But I didn't bother texting back.'

'You *what*?' they said, in unison. 'You bored us silly talking about him being the love of your life,' Vorny nearly shouted. 'And you didn't even *bother* texting him back?'

'What's the point? He dumped me, remember? Told me it was over,' Jess said. 'Besides, there was that woman, Nerissa. His long lost "friend" who simpered all over him at the wedding. What else was I supposed to do?'

'You'll have to do better than that if you really want him,' Hatts said.

'But what if he's going out with Nerissa? What if he tells me to get lost again?'

'Trust me, today he did not sound like the sort of man who is going to tell you to get lost. He seemed genuinely concerned.'

368

'The worst thing that can happen is your pride will get a bit dented if he doesn't want to go out with you anymore,' Vorny said. 'But isn't he worth fighting for, the love of your life?'

On the train back to Suffolk, Jess found herself resenting the familiar views of small towns, flint churches and wide estuaries. Charming though they were, they signalled her return to a life she should have left behind, with every mile taking her further from the friends she loved and . . . from Nate.

At one station she saw a black couple with their two small children, laughing together as they waited on the platform. He was tall and long-limbed with short dreads, like Nate used to have, and she felt the recognition like a sharp pain in her chest remembering how they, too, used to laugh together, oblivious of the rest of the world around them.

Why did she feel so reluctant to at least try fighting for him? Was it just the fear of being rejected again? Of finding out, once and for all, that there was no hope for their relationship or, worse, learning that he and Nerissa really were going out together?

He must have known that Hatts would relay the conversation back so if he didn't care, why would he even have bothered to approach her? It would have been much easier for him simply to walk in the other direction if he had something to hide. And he'd even taken the trouble to ask whether she was getting any help. Surely this meant that she must still mean something to him – however small. Was this not a chink of possibility that she ought not to ignore?

Tomorrow, she had a date to meet Kate, the Poppy Factory employability consultant. She was almost looking forward to it – she had sounded so positive and encouraging on the telephone. 'There's a world of opportunity out there for people with your kind of training,' Kate had said. 'It's just a matter of finding what suits you best, and helping you get there.'

Perhaps I really am on the threshold of a fresh chapter in my life, Jess thought, a new career working with animals, perhaps, or even – she was now daring to imagine – a way of recovering her confidence so that she could one day return to being a paramedic.

Only one thing was missing: Nate. She'd been so courageous in other ways – she had the medals to prove it – so why was she so frightened of being rebuffed by him? It was just that stupid pride again, the legacy from her great-grandfather Alfie, the pride that she'd already overcome to get herself properly diagnosed and on the road to recovery. Surely she could steel herself to face this last battle, the one that really mattered to her?

What was it Rose had written? Something about '. . . how important it is for the rest of us to go on living the best and fullest lives possible, for those who didn't survive.'

The best and fullest life possible? She couldn't imagine it without Nate.

She took out her phone and, with a thumping heart, began slowly to type the words, deliberately, letter by letter, ignoring the predictive text. **Hatts says she saw you at the weekend. How's things?** It sounds so pathetic, she thought, like a dumped girlfriend trying to wheedle her way into his life again. That's what I am, after all. She deleted it and put the phone away, sitting back in her seat to watch the fields and farms going by.

The train passed a village cricket match, small figures in white dotted around a wide green field. It reminded her of the day, early in their relationship, that Nate had invited her to watch him play. She had no idea how the game worked and had spent most of the time lolling around on a picnic rug making a daisy chain. When he'd returned triumphant, having clocked up forty runs, she'd hung it round his neck like a garland and he had kissed her, full on the mouth, disregarding the amused stares of his team mates. The memory made her flush with desire, even now.

She took out her phone again and typed, faster this time. **Hi Nate, how's things? I'm really on the mend now. Lots to tell. Fancy a catch-up some time, no pressure? X.**

Nerissa or no Nerissa, if it was over, it was over. At least she would know. But if not, if there was an outside chance, what was she waiting for?

Quickly, she pressed 'send', before she could change her mind.

Book Club Q&A

Q1: What was your inspiration for writing The Poppy Factory?

The anniversary of the First World War was on the horizon when my editor at Harper Collins asked me whether I would consider basing a novel on the subject. At first I hesitated, daunted by the remarkable canon of literature, novels and poetry about the war by some of the world's best writers. But then I realised that relatively little had been written about the war from a woman's perspective, so that offered a new challenge. I decided not to write a 'trenches' novel, but instead try to reflect the impact of that terrible, bloody war on people at home: the wives, mothers and the returning soldiers themselves.

The second inspiration was The Poppy Factory itself, founded in 1922 by a remarkable man called Major George Howson MC, an engineer and veteran of the Western Front, who was determined to employ his skills to help disabled ex-Service men and women. With a grant of just £2,000 given by British Legion, he set up shop in former collar factory in the Old Kent Road. Within a few months the factory was providing work and an income for fifty disabled veterans and has helped many thousands since. The organisation is still going strong today, producing millions of poppies, wreaths and crosses at their base in Richmond, Surrey.

Q2: Why did you choose to write Rose's story in diary form? Did it present any difficulties?

I don't remember consciously opting for a diary format but her voice just seemed to arrive and start telling the story in the first person. I quickly realised that by making it into a journal, written day by day, would give the story a strong feeling of immediacy. It also gives the writer the freedom to write in both present and past tenses. The emotions Rose expresses are absolutely in the moment, unaffected by any foresight of events to come.

Writing as a diary is great fun. You can reflect historical events alongside the very personal story of your character, and you can even look up what the weather was like on that day! But it is also tricky, because diarists don't normally use any direct speech or dialogue, and a book entirely written without dialogue can be quite dull to for a reader. However, once you have established your diarist's voice in the reader's mind I think you can get away with a level of 'artistic licence'. I hope you think so too!

Q3: Why did you choose to parallel the First World War story with a contemporary storyline?

When I visited The Poppy Factory I learned that although producing poppies is still at their core, they have recently developed a new line of work, helping disabled veterans to find employment with companies throughout the UK. Servicemen these days are often highly trained specialists and need to use these skills when they return to civilian life, and also want to live and work in their own communities.

The Poppy Factory provides disabled veterans advice, support, practical tools such as CV writing and interview techniques, and works with employers to meet the needs of an individual's disability. This is such important work I wanted to reflect it in my novel.

Q4: Why is your contemporary character, Jess, an Afghanistan veteran?

Not surprisingly, my WW1 character Alfie is a man so I wanted to reflect the fact that these days many returning soldiers, sometimes disabled, are also women.

In Afghanistan, the only role in which women have been deployed right to the front line was in the role of medics – first aiders highly trained to carry out the first tasks needed to save an individual's life in the immediate aftermath of an attack, so that they can be transported for specialist medical help back at the base. These medics work in the most difficult and dangerous of situations, often putting their own lives at risk.

Through contacts at the garrison in my home town of Colchester, I was introduced to two young women medics who had seen active service in Afghanistan. I have never met such extraordinary courageous, self-less and modest individuals in my life, and I felt compelled to tell their stories, combined into the character of Jess.

Q5: And why did you choose to feature Post Traumatic Stress Syndrome?

In the First World War they called it 'shell shock' and sometimes expected soldiers to 'snap out of it'. These days it has, belatedly, been recognised as a genuine mental illness and disability, and a range of services are available to support sufferers. PTSD can destroy lives and families, can lead people into alcoholism, crime and even suicide. But the syndrome is so complex and varied, and often emerges only years later, so sufferers may find it hard to get the right level of support that they need. An additional problem is that some veterans find the notion of admitting to a mental illness difficult or shameful, and may refuse to acknowledge any weakness or seek help until their lives are already falling apart.

Q6: Why was the poppy chosen as a symbol of remembrance?

It was all started by two women!

In 1918 an American teacher, Moina Bell Michael, found herself so moved by a poem called 'In Flanders Fields' by a Canadian Colonel, John McRae, that she immediately went out and bought poppies with money collected from her colleagues and sold them to raise funds for US ex-Servicemen.

Then, in 1921, a Frenchwoman called Anna Guerin took up the idea and set up a small factory in France to make poppies to raise funds for the rehabilitation of villages in the northern part of the country that had been devastated by the war. She persuaded Earl Haig to adopt the poppy for the British Legion and sent French women to London to sell them.

In 1922 Earl Haig accepted Major Howson's offer to supply poppies and today the poppy is one of the most powerful and iconic symbols in the western world – a corporate brand which any powerful international corporation would be proud of.

If you would like to find out more about how I came to write The Poppy Factory, or about my other novels including the one I am currently writing, please visit www.liztrenow.com. You can also follow me on Twitter @liztrenow.

The Story of The Poppy Factory

As in this novel, the real life Poppy Factory, with its roots in remembering the fallen and helping the wounded of the First World War, has evolved into a modern organisation that helps disabled ex-Service men and women to find employment and rebuild their lives.

After the horrors of the First World War, which left millions of soldiers dead and many more disabled and unable to work, there was a powerful urge both to remember those who had lost their lives and to help the injured and sick.

In 1918 poppies were first suggested as a symbol of remembrance. Inspired by the poem *In Flanders Fields*, written in 1915 by Lieutenant Colonel John McCrae, American teacher Moina Bell Michael bought poppies with money collected from her colleagues and sold them to raise funds for US ex-Service men.

Her idea caught on. In 1921, Madame Anna Guérin made and sold millions of poppies throughout the

US to raise money for the rehabilitation of areas in France devastated by the war. She persuaded Earl Haig to adopt the poppy for the Royal British Legion and sent French women to London to sell them. The first poppy appeal in 1921 raised £106,000 (nearly £30 million in today's terms) and all the poppies were supplied from France.

Then in 1922 Major George Howson MC, an engineer who had served on the Western Front and been awarded the Military Cross for his actions at the Battle of Passchendaele, set up The Poppy Factory – then called the Disabled Society – to help disabled ex-Service men. Howson, who himself had gas-damaged lungs and had sustained a shrapnel wound to his arm in the Great War, had written a book on how to cope with lost limbs, but when he saw for himself how brave men who had been disabled serving their country were struggling to find employment, he realised that what disabled ex-Service men really needed was work.

Major Howson suggested to the Royal British Legion – then in its infancy – that the Disabled Society should make poppies to be sold to the public. With a grant of £2,000 from the Unity Relief Fund, Howson set up a poppy-manufacturing workshop in a small collar factory off the Old Kent Road in London, with just five ex-Service men; it was here that the first British poppies were made. Importantly, the artificial flowers were designed so that they could be assembled by someone who had lost the use of a hand.

Howson was not confident that the endeavour would succeed. In a letter to his parents, he said,

'I have been given a cheque for £2,000 to make poppies with. It is a large responsibility and will be very difficult. If the experiment is successful it will be the start of an industry to employ 150 men. I do not think it can be a great success, but it is worth trying. I consider the attempt ought to be made if only to give the disabled their chance.'

The experiment was indeed successful. Within a few months the factory was providing work and an income for 50 disabled veterans and made one million poppies in the first two months. Soon there was a waiting list for prospective employees, and in 1924 the factory received a visit from the Prince of Wales (later King Edward VIII).

As demand grew, the premises became too small and in 1925 the Factory moved to its current site in Richmond, Surrey –a disused brewery in Petersham Road. In the same year the charity changed its name to The Royal British Legion Poppy Factory.

By the mid-1930s The Poppy Factory had grown further and now employed 350 disabled ex-Service personnel. A new factory was built, together with flats for employees, and the factory went on to contribute to the war effort for the Second World War.

Today the site at Richmond employs around 35 people on site, with a further 20 working from home, making millions of poppies and many tens of thousands of remembrance crosses and poppy wreaths, including those laid by Her Majesty the Queen, other members of the Royal Family and politicians at the Cenotaph on Remembrance Sunday.

Each year The Poppy Factory also plans and hosts the annual Field of Remembrance at Westminster Abbey, another tradition that owes its existence to Major Howson. In 1928 he gathered together a group of disabled ex-Service men from The Poppy Factory around a battlefield cross, familiar to anyone who had served in Flanders and on the Western Front, and invited passers-by to plant a poppy nearby.

Nowadays over 350 plots of regimental and other associations are laid out between Westminster Abbey and St Margaret's Church in London for 10 days around Remembrance Sunday. Remembrance crosses are provided so that ex-Service men and women, as well as members of the public, can plant a cross in memory of fallen comrades and loved ones.

The manufacture of poppies, wreaths and crosses is just part of the work that The Poppy Factory does. Over recent years it has evolved into a specialist employability charity for veterans with physical and mental disabilities. Through its programme, "Getting You Back to Work", it helps them to find work with civilian companies throughout the UK.

Ex-Service men and women have an enormous number of transferable work skills to offer employers.

As Poppy Factory Employability Manager Elisabeth Skeet explains, 'In addition to specific skills they are organised, hardworking and very loyal. They are good planners, great team players and many have leadership experience.'

So why do they need the help of The Poppy Factory? Well, the transition to civilian life can be tough. Most have never worked in the civilian world and are unfamiliar with employment and recruitment procedures. What's more, without the structure and camaraderie of the Forces, many veterans struggle to cope with their new life, and the added stress of dealing with their disabilities can lead them to lose confidence.

Alongside physical disabilities, clients come to The Poppy Factory suffering from a range of challenges, each presenting its own obstacles to finding employment. Whatever their history, The Poppy Factory aims to get them all back on their feet and into work.

Steve's story is not uncommon. Having served as a leading radio operator in the Royal Navy for 10 years, he then spent 15 years on the road, selling locks and hardware. When he came to The Poppy Factory he was recovering from alcohol addiction.

Although Steve had a number of barriers that made it difficult to find work, with time and support from The Poppy Factory he secured a role working at a community farm and is planning to undertake a foundation degree. 'I might have got into a rut,' he says, 'but The Poppy Factory gave me the incentive to get off the settee, sort myself out and look to the future. Without The Poppy Factory I wouldn't be where I am now.'

Each client who comes to The Poppy Factory is thoroughly and individually assessed to understand his or her readiness for work. Depending on their situation, they may be offered support to help them define their future direction, to understand the options open to them and to gain the practical skills they need to achieve their goals.

Crucially, they are assigned an Employability Consultant who works directly and intensively with them, helping them to develop practical skills such as CV-writing and interview techniques and suggesting suitable positions. They may also work with a volunteer mentor who provides additional support.

The relationship with the Employability Consultant is the key to the success of The Poppy Factory. Having one-to-one contact with someone who understands the obstacles the client is facing can make a huge difference to their confidence levels and their ability to handle the challenges of re-entering the workplace. They are also able to teach them essential skills necessary for applying for civilian jobs.

The Poppy Factory has so far supported more than 350 disabled veterans into employment, of whom 75% have stayed in work after the first 12 months.

In 2012-13 it supported a record total of 239 disabled veteran clients.

The support provided by The Poppy Factory doesn't just help the veterans themselves; it can be a lifeline to families who have buckled under the strain of supporting their loved one. Shelley's partner, Paul, served with the Royal Signals for 13 years, but it was some years after leaving the army that problems came to light. Shelley explains.

'About eight years ago Paul started withdrawing into himself and drinking too much. I eventually got him to the doctor and he was diagnosed with Post Traumatic Stress Disorder. The GP made a referral but there was a long waiting list. We needed help right away.

'The Poppy Factory supported Paul as he looked for work and helped him with interviews. Kirsty Morgan, Paul's mentor, has been absolutely wonderful. Paul could ring her and talk to her. It was a lifeline for me – having someone he could talk to apart from me took the pressure off. Without them I don't know how I'd have coped.'

We may live in relatively peaceful times compared with the First World War, but The Poppy Factory is needed as much as ever, supporting disabled ex-Service men and women who have served in conflicts from Northern Ireland to Bosnia, the Gulf, Iraq and Afghanistan. The Poppy Factory is proud to be still carrying on the mission of Major Howson more than 90 years after its foundation.

To learn more about the work of The Poppy Factory, to arrange a visit to the Factory or to support its work, please visit its website, join the Facebook group or contact it directly.

10p per sale of The Poppy Factory, a novel by Liz Trenow will be donated to The Poppy Factory. For more information please visit www.poppyfactory.org

The Poppy Factory, registered charity no. 225348

Facebook page: www.facebook.com/ThePoppyFactory

The Poppy Factory
20 Petersham Road
Richmond Upon Thames
Surrey
TW10 6UR

Email: admin@poppyfactory.org

telephone: 00 44 (0) 20 8940 3305

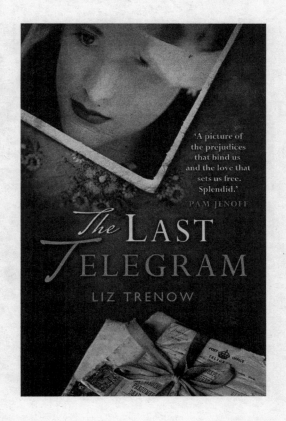

'A picture of
the prejudices
that bind us
and the love that
sets us free.
Splendid.'
PAM JENOFF

The LAST
TELEGRAM

LIZ TRENOW

The war changed everything for Lily Verner . . .

She kept her secret for a lifetime . . .